YOUR LAST LIE

An absolutely gripping crime mystery

GRETTA MULROONEY

Published 2019 by Joffe Books, London.

www.joffebooks.com

This book is a work of fiction. Names, characters, businesses, organizations, places and events are either the product of the author's imagination or are used fictitiously. Any resemblance to actual persons, living or dead, events or locales is entirely coincidental. The spelling is British English.

ISBN 978-1-78931-075-7

For Helen, Su and Kate.

Prologue

It was midsummer. A quiet, warm evening with scents of lavender, roses and honeysuckle perfuming the air. Windows open, music drifting, people chatting lazily, the sun sliding down the sky. Perfect weather for a bit of al fresco romance.

He was on a promise. She was slim, in her twenties. Older than his preferred type but she seemed much younger with her shy, hesitant smile. She had brown, shoulder length hair and soft, kind eyes. She was no beauty but attractive enough. Not too much make up, just some mascara and lipstick. Enough to show she'd made an effort. A bit demure, which was fine with him. Made a change from pushy, opinionated women with their cleavages and belly buttons on show. Made a change too from Sam all those years ago. Sam with her expensive boob implants that he'd paid for before she told him he needed to see a shrink, packed her cases and ransacked his savings. She'd certainly taken him for a ride. And this girl had such a pretty name: Collette.

She'd come into the bar, sat on one of the high stools and ordered a wine spritzer. Nice simple navy skirt, white lacy blouse and patent shoes. Not putting all the goods in the shop window; leaving a bloke something to imagine. They'd got chatting. He'd told her about his career to date and his plans for the future. He could see she was impressed. A young woman like her appreciated a touch of maturity in a man — bit of life experience. When he talked to his wife, Ashleigh, about his job, she half listened; sometimes she yawned, trying to hide it behind her hand or worse still, rolled her eyes in boredom. Collette had nodded attentively, her gaze lingering on his. She'd asked intelligent questions as she sipped her drink. She hadn't said much about herself, just that she worked in a bank, dealing with mortgage enquiries. It wasn't exactly exciting but it suited her. He'd liked that. She seemed contented with her life. Not like the women he'd ended up marrying, always nagging and wanting cosmetic surgery, a bigger house, exotic holidays, spa breaks or a new kitchen. Talk about breaking the bank.

With Ashleigh, it was the fortune she spent on massages, health supplements, facials, exercise classes and her cranky bloody diets — no carbs one week, no protein the next or day after day of cabbage soup. It was hard to get a square meal at home. The previous winter, she'd spent a week at a spa in Surrey, where they charged her a small fortune to wake her at six thirty in the morning for long walks, hours sweating in the gym and bowls of steamed vegetables with quinoa a couple of times a day. Why not just stay at home, run around a lot and starve yourself? As for Yvette . . . no, best not to think about that rotten bitch tonight. Tonight was for enjoyment.

He'd been very gentle and well mannered, kissing Collette on the cheek as she left the bar. Softly, softly, catchee monkey. She'd agreed that it would be nice to meet again and, given the lovely weather, a picnic by the river would be just the thing. When he said how much he liked it, she'd agreed to wear the lacy blouse as well. They'd arranged a date and time and he'd watched her walk away, satisfied that he'd still got it. It had been a while since he'd had a new interest and he deserved a treat. A man could only behave for so long. And he hadn't even had to go looking. Minimum effort, maximum benefit. Just how he liked it.

Using the magnifying mirror, he shaved extra close and plucked a few errant hairs from his eyebrows. He could hear Havana in her room, chatting away to some friend on her phone in that incomprehensible adolescent slang she used. He'd lied to Ashleigh. Through the frosty chill in the air between them, he'd said that he had to go to an evening meeting about a fly-out. Well, it *was* a meeting — that wasn't a fib; just not the kind she'd approve of. He didn't really need to lie any more. The way things were between them, she was lucky that he told her anything about what he was doing, but old habits died hard. Ashleigh had thought she had him boxed and coxed these days, thought she'd played it clever. But no way was he going to be under the thumb, especially after what he'd found out about *her*. She'd gone quiet and sullen since he'd told her he knew. There'd been a blazing row, but she could see he had the edge for now. Knowledge was power, as the saying went, and the balance of power between them had tilted in his favour. About time, too. When he'd mentioned the meeting, she'd looked sulky and said nothing, just shrugged and carried on reading one of her style magazines.

He wouldn't be surprised if Jude, her bloody cow of a best friend came round tonight, despite him telling her to get lost. She'd be through the back door as soon as she knew he'd gone out. There might as well be a tunnel between her place and theirs. She was there in the living room most evenings, swigging his booze, swapping beauty tips with Ashleigh and more than likely slagging him off. The two of them were joined at the hip and when Jude was there, Ashleigh barely noticed him. No wonder he looked elsewhere. No thrills to be had at home.

He patted on some skin balm. It was creamy and smelled of lemon and thyme. Masculine but not too sharp. He was satisfied with the image in the mirror. Wearing pretty well, no paunch and just a few crow's feet.

In the bedroom, he grimaced at Ashleigh's latest addition: a four-poster queen-size bed with a canopy of gauzy voile curtains threaded with poppies. The curtains made him feel hemmed in and sometimes when he woke in the night, they reminded him of mosquito nets. He tripped over the trailing end of one of the curtains as he made for his wardrobe and thought it was fitting that it was trying to snare him — just like his wives. He dressed in black jeans and a cream cotton shirt, which he wore loose over the jeans, as the young blokes did. He thought about Collette's blouse and the coy girlishness of the lace, especially where it ruffled at her neck. There was something so attractive about a covered up woman. All that promise beneath, waiting to be unbuttoned.

His phone rang as he was enjoying a little fantasy about teasing open her blouse and he tensed as he saw the caller's name and anticipated the familiar grumbles.

'How did your meeting go today? Productive?'

He swallowed and kept his voice quiet and steady, making the lies glide more easily. 'Early days. Looking promising but can't rush things.'

'Can't rush? Listen, I've waited long enough and my patience is running out. I've told you, you need to pay up. I'm having to watch my back.'

'Look, I'm doing what I can. I need more time to work the old charm and persuasion. You've got the wrong end of the stick about all this.'

'You don't have more time. Neither do I. I know you — I know you're lying. You've had your chances.'

'Come on! Like I've said, I'll manage something. Even if it means I'm out of pocket myself — and I bloody well will be.'

'Yeah, well, it was all your idea so you can soak up the crap. I wish I'd never listened to you.'

'Look, I just need to—'

'You heard! I'll give you another two weeks and that's it. I don't care how or where you get the money — that's your problem.'

The caller vanished. It was the second threat he'd received that day. He took a deep breath, smoothed his hair and checked his reflection in the mirror. People thought they could corner and coerce him. It was a worry; he had to admit that to himself. And there was that bloody creep Cairns, complaining and causing trouble. But he'd sort it all somehow. He could probably spin out the money stuff a bit longer. He'd pack up his troubles for tonight and think about it all in the morning.

Downstairs, he picked up his car keys, poked his head around the living room door and announced he was off. Ashleigh waved a hand, focused on a home makeover programme on TV. He knew what that meant. It would hurt his wallet. She'd want to redecorate/get new furniture/have a log burner installed/order a gazebo for the garden.

He left the house with a spring in his step. The air was balmy. Forty-seven and on a promise. He'd bought white wine, posh vegetable crisps and pretzels earlier and stowed them in the car. The wine was in a cooler. Give the lady a deliciously chilled drink before things warmed up. Maybe Collette would like a stroll by the water and a sit down on the warm grass. Then later they could visit the airfield. It had little nooks and corners tucked away. They were shady and welcoming. He'd got to know them well over the years. There was a thrill to misbehaving where he now worked. When you were taking a gamble and breaking some rules, you knew you were alive.

He pulled the front door closed behind him and pointed the car keys at the Mondeo in the drive.

He opened the car door with a smile of anticipation, turned off his phone and started the engine.

He had six hours to live.

Chapter 1

Oliver Sheridan ran at Tyrone Swift in the street and spat in his face. Swift felt the hot glob of mucus trickle down his cheek. Some splattered onto the arm of his jacket. Sheridan was yelling and jabbing a finger at him. There were flecks of foamy spittle on his lips.

'You think this is finished? You can think again! I could see they were all your pals in there. All pals together. Very cosy. I don't care what that stuck up judge said. That wasn't justice! You're a thief. You stole from my dad and you're stealing from me.'

Swift wiped his sleeve against his face and stepped forwards abruptly. Sheridan moved back. Swift had gauged that he would. Beneath the bluster, Sheridan was a coward.

'You come near me again,' Swift said quietly, 'and I swear I'll hurt you. I've had you up to the eyeballs. You're not dealing with a frail old man now, Oliver. I don't live in fear of you. Not like your dad did. You might remember that I almost broke your arm once when you'd been abusing him.'

He looked down into the broad, sweaty face. Sheridan was a sculptor of mediocre talents who funded himself by cadging money wherever he could. He had combed his hair for the court case but it was lank and greasy. The tired navy suit he was wearing radiated a faint air of mildew and the trousers were too long, skimming the pavement. He had a nasty shaving cut on his chin. Cedric, his father, had always looked effortlessly elegant and spruce, even in the bright colours he liked.

'Are you threatening me?' Sheridan turned to a woman with a pushchair at the nearby bus stop. 'Did you hear him threaten me?' he yelled.

The woman glanced down nervously at her child. 'I saw you spit at that man,' she said. A bus approached with the hiss of brakes. She got bolder as the doors gasped open and she prepared to board. 'That's disgusting, spitting like that and in front of a child! You can spread all kinds of germs.'

'You heard the lady,' Swift said. 'Go home and grow up, Oliver. Maybe you can spend your inheritance on some classes in manners. Try googling social etiquette.'

Before Sheridan could respond, Swift hopped on to the bus as the doors were closing, nodded to the woman who was parking her pushchair and headed upstairs. He ripped off his necktie, stuffed it in his pocket and opened his shirt collar. Well, that was over at last. At least, he hoped it was: with Oliver Sheridan, you never could tell.

Nora phoned as the bus got stuck in a traffic jam near Holborn. It was good to hear her light voice. Her Dublin accent was still strong, despite having lived in London for some time.

'How did it go?'

'In my favour. But it was nasty. The judge advised Oliver to calm down and accept the outcome.'

'Great! Did he behave at the court hearing?'

'Of course not. He got excitable. Interrupted the judge and his solicitor a couple of times and got a warning at one point.'

'He's so full of crap. Was he still claiming that you influenced his dad?'

Swift sighed and scratched his head, his fingers tangling in his unruly curls. He'd tried to flatten them for the court with a product Nora had bought him. *Get a Grip Curl Tamer* came with the promise that a walnut-sized amount would *keep your curls obedient all day*. Other than making him sneeze, it had failed to get a grip — but then his hair had always resisted efforts to mould it. Some people said that his hair was like him: stubborn.

'Yes, that lovely phrase . . . *undue influence*. Oliver trotted out the usual stuff in court . . . that I prevented him from seeing his father, blocked phone calls and I put pressure on Cedric to give me his car. He claimed that, because I was Cedric's landlord and living on the premises, I was controlling towards him. He said that I influenced Cedric into changing his previous will, which named him as the main beneficiary. I explained that I never saw that will and that Cedric had destroyed his copy and the one held at the solicitor's.'

Cedric Sheridan, Swift's dear friend and tenant, had collapsed with a heart attack just over a year before after a blazing row with his son. Cedric had rallied for a while but died later in hospital. The complexities caused by his will had been troubling Swift for months. He was Cedric's executor and after his friend's death he had found the new will, written on a form bought from a chain of stationers. Two of Cedric's friends at the Silver Mermaid, his local pub, had witnessed the updated will. Cedric had left twenty thousand pounds to his son Oliver, a hundred and fifty thousand each to Swift and Milo, one of his oldest friends, ten thousand to Yana Ayo, a refugee he had helped and ten thousand to Oxfam. Oliver had been enraged by the will and challenged it, refusing mediation and insisting on his day in court. The hearing had been delayed several times, finally taking place on this late October day. It had hung over Swift's head like a dark cloud for most of the year. It was petty, exhausting and a nasty epilogue to his friend's life.

Nora clicked her tongue. 'A pity Cedric didn't update his will through the same solicitor. Then there'd have been a clear paper trail that would have been much harder for Oliver to challenge.'

'Well, he reckoned his old solicitors charged too much. I presume he opted to save himself money once he got sufficiently fed up with Oliver's carry-on to make the change. Anyway, I gave the court the long history of Oliver's abusive behaviour — how his dad was often frightened of him and that he stole Cedric's credit card. That last bit was tricky because Cedric never reported it. Milo gave a statement as well, saying he knew that Cedric was anxious about Oliver's visits. Cedric's doctor confirmed that he had no mental impairment. It was all messy and unpleasant. Plenty of mudslinging.'

'At least in the end the judge saw through Oliver's bullshit.'

'True. You could see her looking him up and down when he started ranting about unfairness. Luckily for me, he showed his true colours, despite the fact that he'd attempted to smarten up and look less like the struggling artist from the garret. The judge decided that there was no evidence that Cedric lacked mental capacity when he updated his will or that he was influenced in any way. She said that Oliver's twenty thousand pounds satisfied the terms about making reasonable financial provision under the 1975 Inheritance Act. So, after months of wrangling and solicitors' letters, he left court with no more than he went in with. Presumably a lot less after he's paid his legal bills.'

'At least it's all over.'

'Hmm . . . you think? He's just spat in my face in the street and threatened me.'

'What a bastard!'

'Sums him up. And I'm wearing my suit and now I'll have to clean his slime off the jacket.'

'Insult to injury. Mind you, it's a bit like being threatened by an annoying fly.'

'Hmm . . . I know Oliver. I wouldn't underestimate him. He'll be brooding and feeling angry and cheated. He has the emotional maturity of a teenager and he can be a slow burner. I'll have to watch my back.'

'You have a very fine back. I like stroking it. Got to leave you with that thought — imminent arrest to deal with. See you later.'

Swift watched the traffic inching through a maze of roadworks and temporary traffic lights. He wondered what Oliver's father would have made of today's drama. His son's behaviour wouldn't have surprised him, even if he had always made excuses for him. Cedric had endured a deeply troubled relationship with Oliver, who had visited his father intermittently, usually to demand money. He had often abused Cedric verbally, and on some occasions had hurt him physically. It was hard to think that Cedric could rest in peace while the wrangling continued.

The bus finally broke free of the traffic queue as the last set of lights turned to green and charged along the road. Swift put thoughts of Cedric and Oliver aside.

He had to see a man about a murder.

* * *

The sports centre was called Health Crunch and occupied a big corner plot in Blackheath, opposite the eastern edge of the heath itself. He introduced himself at the desk, showing his ID.

'Tyrone Swift. I have an appointment to see Niall Roscoe.'

A cheery woman in white shirt and grey trousers tapped a keyboard. 'Oh yes. He said he was expecting you and to let you know he'll be about twenty minutes late.

Take a seat in the café area. He'll be here as soon as he can.'

In the café, Swift sat on a moulded orange plastic chair at a table by the counter. It was almost 2 p.m. and the last of the lunchtime fitness fanatics were leaving to return to work, hair still damp and clothes crumpled from lockers. A charge of aromas mingled in the air: changing room fustiness, chlorine and toasted cheese, overlaid with musky and floral deodorants and scents. His nose tingled but for once he didn't sneeze. He studied the posters on the wall beside him, advertising classes in Senior Water Workout, Aqua Splash, Tone and Burn, Body Balance, Yoga for Mind and Body and Group Cycle. He preferred solitary exercise in the open air, rowing his boat on the Thames. Thinking time. Breathing in other people's sweat and deodorant had never appealed.

He was about to return to reception and ask how much longer he'd have to wait when a man approached, panting. He was late forties, slightly pigeon toed, in a white T-shirt, grey Bermuda shorts and white trainers. He was beefy but fit and his top half looked muscle bound, not matching his slender legs. His handshake was damp, his accent broad cockney.

'Hi, I'm Niall Roscoe. So sorry to keep you waiting. Mind if we talk here, as it's quiet for now? I can grab a bite to eat. We had a problem with the pool pump and I've not had time for lunch.'

'Fine with me.'

'Can I get you anything?'

'Just a coffee, thanks.'

Swift waited while Roscoe bantered with the woman behind the counter.

'Give us an extra dollop of them beans, Treacle. Thanks, you're a true darling.'

He had an ID card around his neck that swayed whenever he moved. He brought a tray to the table with

Swift's coffee and a baked potato with grated cheese and baked beans and a glass of water for himself.

'Need the carbs after a long morning,' he said.

Swift nodded politely and watched as he cut the huge potato. He had hairy forearms and large hands.

'In your email,' Swift said, 'you said you'd looked at my website and that you wanted to talk to me about your brother.'

Roscoe ate fast, shovelling food in. He chewed, took a drink of water and nodded. 'So, you popped up when I was googling *private investigators*. Your background looked reassuring — the Met and Interpol. I didn't want some bloke who's been a security guard or a prison warder or just fancies himself as a detective. I've always thought your game is probably a bit like alternative medicine. Lots of unqualified people advertising and making money from gullible punters.'

'I'm sure there's some of that. I have a solid CV and track record.' Swift sipped his coffee. It was weak and tasted faintly of chemicals.

'Yeah, I saw that. Some impressive endorsements on your website.' Roscoe heaped beans on to his fork. He had full, moist lips and his jaw clicked as he ate. 'That's why I contacted you. Might as well have the best if we're going down this road.'

'And what road would that be?'

Roscoe lifted a chunk of potato. Strands of melted cheese hung from it like elastic. He wound them around his fork as if they were spaghetti. 'Heard of Greg Roscoe?' he asked.

'I don't think so. He was your brother?'

Roscoe nodded. 'That's right. He was murdered.'

'I'm sorry. When and how did your brother die?'

'It was summer last year. He was found in the cockpit of a small plane at Cornford airfield in Hertfordshire. Stabbed in the chest and neck. He was a mass of wounds.' Roscoe poured his drink. 'There was other stuff done to

Greg as well. If you don't mind, I'll let the police tell you. I'm not squeamish but I don't like to talk about it.'

'Okay. Why was he at an airfield?'

'He worked there, taught people to fly. Actually, he was the CFI.'

'What's that?'

'Chief Flying Instructor.'

'I take it that no one was charged with the murder?'

'That's right. The police questioned a guy . . . Paul Cairns. He was in the papers and on telly a while back. Weedy looking bloke with bad skin. He'd been mouthing off to people after he heard Greg was dead, saying it was good news. So they got him to the police station but then Cairns ended up in a diabetic coma in an interview room and sued — successfully. And he didn't do it.' Roscoe scooped up the last of his meal and sat back with his water. 'So, if Cairns didn't do it, there's someone out there who killed my bro and the police haven't got a clue.'

'What was the evidence that Cairns didn't do it?'

'He claimed that he'd been plane spotting at Heathrow the night Greg died. Turned out the police hadn't checked his camera. There were photos on it that proved he had been at the airport.'

Swift gave up on the coffee. 'The police had no other suspects?'

'That's what they told us. I don't like it, that Greg's dead and no one's answered for it. My mum and me are the only ones who give a toss, as far as I can see. She was gutted when no one was arrested. She said it was as if Greg had just been forgotten, like. Don't get me wrong . . . neither of us would want an innocent person to be banged up. But I don't think someone should get away with murder, do you?'

'Clearly, no. That's partly why I do what I do.'

'Yeah. Sorry. Teaching my grandma to suck eggs.'

'Did your brother have a partner or family?'

Roscoe gave a dry laugh. 'There's Greg's widow, Ashleigh. I wouldn't say she missed him much. She remarried not long after he died. She's Ashleigh Grafton now. I don't blame her. He was a rotten husband. And he had a daughter from that marriage — she's called Havana. What a moniker to give the poor kid! She's fourteen now. She was like that with her dad.' He held up two fingers nestled together. 'She went into a terrible slump after Greg's death. Developed anorexia. She was still horribly thin last time I saw her. Broke my heart to see her looking like that.'

Swift shifted on the uncomfortable chair. 'It can't have been easy for Havana that her mother remarried so soon.' When he was fifteen his father had married again soon after his mother died of cancer, providing him with Joyce, a stepmother he didn't want or need. He'd felt a bitter loss and fury that still lingered deep somewhere.

'Yeah, I know. I can't blame Ashleigh for wanting a bit of company, especially as Greg led her a merry dance. But if I'm honest, I thought she could've held off for a while and given Havana time to grieve. But, you know . . . I didn't say anything. Not my place. And Ashleigh would've cut me dead if I tried. She doesn't have much time for me.'

'Why's that?'

Roscoe folded his arms and rocked a little on his chair. 'I sound a bit common for her liking and I do an ordinary kind of job. My house is ex-council and my wife's a general gopher here. Get my drift?'

'Yes, that Ashleigh's a snob. What does she do?'

'She used to call herself an optometric technician, although I think she might have given up work now. The new husband seems comfortably off and he sold his flat so I suppose they've had the proceeds from that. Ashleigh was busy doing things to the house last time I was there. By the way, that grand sounding job title is like the rubbish bins being emptied by refuse collection specialists. She worked part time, in glorified sales. She was an assistant in a high street optician's, clicking buttons on a machine to check eye fields and pressures. Y'know, measuring the space between eyes with a special ruler and stuff. Then she schmoozed the customer, distracted them from the cheap frames they were thinking about and persuaded them those new designer ones really suited them, just right for their face shape. Kerrching! She rang up the cash till.' He chuckled. 'Don't tell her I said that. Want another drink?'

'No thanks.'

'Don't blame ya. It's disgusting. I'd change the supplier, but we're locked in to the contract for another year.' He turned to the woman at the counter. 'Be a darling, Treacle . . . fetch us a diet Coke and put it on my tab.'

'You're a nuisance, you are,' she said, fondly. 'I'm trying to clear up.'

'Yeah, but you love me.'

'Says you.' She brought him a can and a glass, giving him a playful tap on the arm.

Swift had to ask. 'Treacle? What does it mean?'

Roscoe grinned. 'Cockney rhyming slang. Treacle as in treacle tart as in sweetheart.'

'Ah, got it. What did you mean by saying your brother was a rotten husband?'

Roscoe cracked his fingers together. 'Look, Greg was no saint. Didn't always like him all that much myself. Certainly didn't approve of him but . . . y'know . . . family's family and he was my only sibling. My little bro. Our dad died when we were young. He had an accident on a building site and he didn't last the year. He said he was leaving me in charge, looking after Mum and Greg.'

'Quite a responsibility.'

'Yeah, I know. I keep my word and I promised Dad. He knew Greg was a tearaway from the start and that Mum wouldn't discipline him. We were chalk and cheese, the two of us. I've been in this business since I left school, worked my way up from the front desk to management. I married when I was twenty-three and I think the world of my wife. I'm a steady plodder and I know it. I'm the tortoise. Greg was the hare, if you like. He was always the brains. Always had that glint in his eye. He knew from when he was little that he wanted to fly. He even had a tiny captain's uniform for his fourth Christmas. Flying training isn't cheap but we scraped the money together for him. Mum did two jobs and saved hard. Greg did well. He was a qualified airline captain at twenty-two. Then he was in and out of different airlines. Changed jobs like he changed clothes. Travelled all over the globe. He always thought the grass was greener somewhere else.'

'You didn't resent the money spent on him? I think I might have.'

Roscoe took a swig of his drink and wiped the back of his hand across his mouth. He gave a little belch. 'I'll level with you. I did sometimes, back in the day. But not so much in recent years. Greg was really bright in a way I was never going to be. But d'you know . . . his glitzy career and his money didn't seem to make him happy. So, out of the two of us, I reckoned I came off best in the end. That's what Jeanie, my wife's always said.'

And Roscoe was still alive and Greg was dead, so that was certainly the case now. 'I assume that if Greg was a rotten husband, you mean he had affairs?'

'And some! He was divorced twice during his twenties before he married Ashleigh. He had a son, Axel, from his second marriage. I got the impression he'd lost touch with him. He never spoke about him.'

'How old would he be?'

'Early twenties. Yeah, Greg always had an eye for the ladies and he played away a lot. He gambled, too. Poker mainly. Lost quite a bit of money along the way as well as making it. He'd say that long haul flying was boring. The computer did most of it so he had to find ways to pass the time. And of course there'd be casinos in places he flew to and stayed over.'

Swift's heart sank. Greg Roscoe's global and varied career history didn't sound promising. If someone had murdered him because of bad feeling over an affair, a gambling dispute or debt, he or she could be anywhere in the UK or abroad. 'Did Greg fall out with people?'

'Generally? No idea. He could be tactless. He was very sure of himself. He'd had run-ins with Paul Cairns, which is why the police focused on him as their suspect. Cairns is a geeky kinda bloke. He was always hanging out at the airfield. A bit of a nuisance from what I gathered. He wanted to get a flying licence, but Greg had told him he was wasting his time and money. So he was supposed to have stabbed him for revenge.' Roscoe fingered the keys at his belt. 'Look, I didn't see Greg often. A couple of times a year — sometimes not even that. I can't tell you much about how he was or what he was doing before he died. We were never close and we didn't have a lot in common. So, I didn't know much about his life, except for the main items. But it tears me up, thinking that he died like that and that whoever did it is laughing. Havana's life has been blighted and my mum's never going to get over what happened. She's always crying about Greg. She's had poor health ever since he died and I'm sure it's a reaction to the shock.' He ran his hand across his forehead. 'She often says she wants to die, so she can be with him.'

'I'm sorry. That must be hard to cope with. Murder does terrible damage to families. Where does your mother live?'

'She lives with me and Jeanie now, here in Blackheath. She was in a flat in Lewisham, where Greg and me grew up. The stairs got too much for her and drug pushers were hanging out in the block. They move in, don't they . . . make it their territory. She was frightened and I didn't want her living there anymore. Greg was very keen on her moving in with us. Well he would be, wouldn't he? Meant he didn't have to worry about her.'

'Was Greg close to your mum?'

'He was fond of her but he didn't see much of her. He rang her every couple of weeks and you'd think the president of the USA was on the blower. He'd send her flowers now and again or turn up out of the blue and take her out for lunch somewhere swanky. It was Mum's constant gripe that she didn't see enough of him but she'd never have a word said against him. She'd always make excuses for him, saying his flying career was a huge responsibility.' He shrugged. 'I was used to Greg being Mum's favourite. His pilot status always outshone anything I achieved. She took me for granted, knew that boring old Niall could always be relied on.'

'That's just as well, I suppose. Your mum would certainly have needed you after your brother's death.'

'Yeah, I know. But it used to grate when he was alive. I'm the one who had an extension built for her on my house and who takes her to her hospital appointments but Greg was always her golden boy, the man with the captain's stripes. He took her for a trip to Deauville in a small plane one day and she went on about it for months. She came with us to Madeira for a fortnight but all she did was complain about the food in the hotel. She'd brag about "my son the pilot" and his brilliant career to anyone who'd listen. He'd had his photo taken with Jane Fonda once in first class when he flew long haul and Mum had it blown up and framed. Sorry, I'm sounding a bit sarky about him now and I shouldn't.'

'Why was he flying small planes in Hertfordshire rather than still working with a big airline and globetrotting with celebrities?'

'That was down to Ashleigh. She got tired of suspecting there was a girl in every airport or on every plane. She wanted him where she could see him so she gave him an ultimatum. I imagine he caved in because he couldn't afford another expensive divorce and he was mad about Havana — wouldn't have wanted her out of his life, especially after losing Axel. Mind you, it wouldn't have stopped him roving, but at least Ashleigh found it easier to check up on him and he couldn't stay away overnight so that cramped his style. Of course, Mum took against Ashleigh when she heard that, said that she was being mean and undermining his career. She never had much time for Ashleigh anyway.'

'Oh, why's that?'

Roscoe shifted, embarrassed. 'Ashleigh's grandmother was from Singapore. Mum can be a tad prejudiced that way. So . . . they had hard words on the phone. Nasty, it was. Mum didn't get to see much of Havana after that because Ashleigh kept her at arm's length. So then, Mum would go on about how she was deprived of both her grandchildren. Trouble with Mum is she doesn't think about consequences. I took her to see Havana a while back but we weren't welcome. You could have made ice in the living room — the atmosphere was that chilly. Ashleigh's still frosty towards us, especially as Mum voiced her opinion about the remarriage despite me asking her not to. We haven't been there now for a long time and I shouldn't think we'll be invited.'

Swift watched Roscoe rubbing his temples. He seemed to have the thankless role of family troubleshooter. Perhaps he was one of those people who liked to take on emotional burdens.

Roscoe shook his head. 'I don't want to sound hard about Greg. I do miss him, in a strange way. He's not around to bug me. I loved him because he was family and I'd have done anything to help him if he'd needed. But I thought the way he carried on with women was . . . well, sort of crude. You'd think he'd have mended his ways after two divorces. What's a marriage about if there's no loyalty and trust? I never understood why he behaved like that.

My dad was devoted to my mum and I am to my Jeanie. That's how families should be.'

Swift reflected that considerably less work would come his way if people stayed devoted and families intact. 'I appreciate that you did love him. That's why you want the truth about his death. Is your mother on board with you consulting me?'

'Absolutely. She's paying your fee and she'll want to see you. She had a win on the Premium Bonds last month and that gave her the idea. She can bore you with Greg's achievements and show you one of his uniforms that she keeps in her wardrobe. Ashleigh and people he worked with could tell you a lot more about his life in Cornford than me. What do you think? Will you take the job?'

'Yes, I'll take a look. Did Greg live in Cornford?'

'Yeah, that's where he settled in his late teens when he was doing pilot training. He used to hang out and socialise at the airfield then. He bought a house there when he qualified and lived there till he died. That was his base, the one stable thing in his life.'

'He managed to keep the house despite the divorces?'

'Yeah. He paid the wives off. He earned big but his mistakes cost him big too.'

'And what about Ashleigh and Havana? Do they know you're asking me to investigate?'

'Not yet. I thought I'd wait and see what you said. I'll email Ashleigh tonight. She might well be chippy about it.'

'I'm sure the police will have asked this question . . . but who benefited from your brother's death?'

Niall Roscoe raised his eyebrows. 'As far as I know, he left everything to Ashleigh. Don't ask me what she got, though. I wouldn't ask and she wouldn't volunteer.'

'Do you have a police contact?'

'Yeah, a DI Fitz Blackmore. I can give you his number. He was a bit swaggery and opinionated for my liking but he was very careful and kind with mum. I appreciated that. He explained that Greg's case hadn't been closed. I think that helped her a bit even though I knew it meant it's just lying in limbo. So I suppose I'm hoping you can find out something the police won't have time for now.'

'I'll see what I can do. I'll start with DI Blackmore and take it from there.'

'That's great. Ah, here's my Jeanie. She's just finished her shift. Half three on the dot every day. I could set my watch by her. I'll introduce you.'

Roscoe stood, beaming at a tall, heavy boned woman dressed in a dark green pleated skirt and blouse that reminded Swift of a school uniform. 'Jeanie, this is Mr Swift.'

'Pleased to meet you, I'm sure,' she said, extending a hand.

She had a dated, slightly faded look that went with the old-fashioned greeting and she looked older than Niall.

'Your husband's been telling me about Greg.'

'Well, there's plenty to tell. Greg the golden boy.'

'Your tone tells me you didn't like him much.'

She spoke levelly, looking straight at him. 'I thought he was a chancer and a taker. Always causing his mother worry with his divorces and relying on Niall to mop up the spilt milk.'

Roscoe patted her on the back. 'Now, Jeanie, that's all in the past.'

'Is it? Your mum's still spending her money on him, even now — paying for an investigation. She's been saving from her pension and her benefits and now she's squandering her bit of good luck. I've told her she's daft but she won't listen. Still . . . I suppose if it brings her some comfort . . . '

She looked at her husband and Swift saw the gentle pulse of warmth between them.

Roscoe glanced at the clock. 'Listen, I'd better get back to work. I'll email you the details you need, Mr Swift.'

'Can I have DI Blackmore's number now?'

'I can give you that,' Jeanie said.

Roscoe pecked her cheek. 'Great. Got to go. Oh, Mr Swift . . . when you talk to Mum, don't go into any details about how Greg died. All she knows is that he was stabbed. She didn't attend the inquest and I wouldn't want her to get even more upset. See you later, Jeanie.'

'I know you! Don't be late!' she called after him. 'Shepherd's pie for dinner!'

Roscoe waved a hand over his shoulder and disappeared. His wife gave an indulgent laugh.

'He's often late home, seeing to problems, making sure he doesn't leave anything unfinished. He's too conscientious, I suppose — but I wouldn't want him any other way.'

Her short hair was badly cut in uneven layers and sat low on her brow. She wore no makeup or jewellery. Her eyes were her best feature, large and kindly. Swift liked her direct gaze and smiled at her.

'Your husband and his brother weren't much alike, from what I've heard.'

'No. Niall got the good qualities, as far as I'm concerned. Greg just took from people all the time. The big *I Am*.'

'Do you know if he had any enemies?'

'I've no idea. I had as little to do with him as possible. There must have been a number of husbands who had it in for him at one time or another after he'd made a move on their wives.' She assumed an upright stance, chest stuck out, and mimicked a deep, warm voice. *'Hi, I'm Captain Roscoe. You'd definitely be in first class if I was your pilot.'*

Swift laughed. 'Did he really use corny lines like that?'

'I heard him say that to one of the guests at his third wedding. His own wedding with the bride pregnant and he had his eye on someone. I remember looking at Ashleigh and feeling sorry for her. She's a shallow, vain woman but I wouldn't have wished Greg on her.' Jeanie tapped her mouth with a hand, as if admonishing herself. 'Look, Greg might not have been my favourite person but his murder brought awful misery to his poor daughter and his mum. Their lives have been horribly damaged. Maybe they'd get some relief from the pain they've suffered if the person who killed Greg was caught.' She took her phone out and scrolled down. 'Here's DI Blackmore's number. I must go, I have to take Pat — Niall's mum — to the supermarket.'

'I'll come and visit her soon.'

'I'll let her know. Be prepared for a long sitting with all the highlights of golden boy's life. You know she and Ashleigh have a standoff?'

'Niall mentioned it.'

'It doesn't help that Pat usually calls Ashleigh *Yvette*. That was Greg's second wife. I can never tell if she does it deliberately. So, you know . . . no love lost. Pat never had a good word for any of Greg's wives and fell out with them all.'

'Yvette is Axel's mother?'

'That's right, he's Greg's other child. The one who's gone off the radar. I think Yvette stopped Greg seeing him.'

'Where does Yvette live?'

'I'm not sure. Pat might have an idea. Now and again she tries to get in touch with Axel but he doesn't respond.'

'Because his mother would disapprove?'

'I suppose.' She pressed her lips together.

He thought she knew more but didn't want to say. It could wait.

Chapter 2

Swift had a walk on the heath after he left the centre. Winter was advancing and the day was cold, the grass squelchy from morning rain. He knew the urban myth that the Blackheath area got its name from being a medieval burial ground for people who had died of the plague. The less dramatic truth was that it was named for the dark local soil. He skirted a couple of teenagers on skateboards, stopped to watch a man flying a wheeling, snapping kite and perched on the arm of a bench near a funfair. A carousel boomed out a Strauss waltz as he googled *Greg Roscoe* and found a number of hits. He skimmed through some reports of the murder and then focused on Roscoe the pilot. The top item was on a website for pilots called *Come Fly*. It was a general chat and information forum. It hadn't been updated to reflect Roscoe's death and had a cheery self-penned profile under the name: *Speedbird 44*.

Hi Everyone.
My name's Greg Roscoe, aka Speedbird 44. That's the age I was when I left the big air players.

I decided I wanted to be a pilot when I was four. Little guy, big ambition!

I've flown for half a dozen major airlines, long and short haul as well as flying business jets for a couple of years. My favourite routes? Rio — as it's a real party zone when you're there. Then Cairo, where I usually fitted in a two-day cruise on the Nile. And Sao Paulo — I used to get six days off in a five star hotel before flying back. Not forgetting Buenos Aires where I learned to tango and loved going to milongas.

Now I'm CFI at Cornford airfield, in Hertfordshire. 'Why have you given up the high life?' I hear you ask. Well, the missus insisted I stay closer to home and hey, I have to keep her happy, otherwise she reminds me of the woman in that poem by Rabbie Burns:

Whaur sits our sullen sulky dame,
Gathering her brows like gathering storm,
Nursing her wrath to keep it warm.

Teaching isn't as exciting, but it's rewarding and it's good to pass my skills and experience on. I'm not quite as young as I was and I don't miss the constant switching of time zones and messing up my body clock. And it's good to get regular sleep!

So, if you know anyone who wants a private pilot's licence or just a fun trip skywards . . . I'm their man.

See you up in the deep blue!

The accompanying photo showed Roscoe in the wide cockpit of a jet, presumably in his glory days. In front of him was a complex control panel illuminated with red and blue lights. He was holding a thumb up for the camera and his other hand tipped his cap in salute. He was wearing aviator sunglasses, a captain's uniform and a wide, cheesy grin. Swift reckoned that Roscoe was a man who hankered after his previous exciting career but was trying to persuade himself that he liked his life as an instructor. There wouldn't be as much opportunity to tango in Hertfordshire. He wondered if Ashleigh Roscoe had ever read her husband's unflattering comments.

The Cornford airfield website had a piece about Roscoe's tragic death, with tributes and praise for his skills, dedication and the number of students who had passed their exams because of him, etc. etc. Their photo showed him head and shoulders, standing by the wing of a small plane parked beside a hangar — a less glamorous photo for a less glamorous job. He had pronounced brows, a slim nose, triangular jaw and thinning fair hair combed straight back from his forehead. Not a handsome man but it was an interesting face and the angled eyes looked secretive.

When Swift googled Paul Cairns, he found multiple stories about his successful case against the police and scrutinised one in the Cornford Mail. A Camilla Finley in her opinion column, *Finley's Finds*, had written it up.

Local Man Wins Negligence Case Against Cops

Cornford man Paul Robert Cairns, 32, was 250k richer yesterday. He sued the police after suffering a diabetic coma at Cornford police station. Mr Cairns was being questioned about the horrific murder of pilot Greg Roscoe at Cornford airfield. Mr Cairns had timed and dated photos from Heathrow airport on his camera. These undermined police suspicions that he had concocted a false alibi for the night of the murder.

Judges were scathing in their comments about the police investigation and the way the police tried to 'browbeat' Paul Cairns. Judges also said that the police failed to conduct a thorough scrutiny of Mr Cairns' movements. They stated that the police should have done their job properly and checked Mr Cairns' camera. Had they done so, Mr Cairns 'probably wouldn't have been subjected to the stress that contributed to him becoming hypoglycaemic while in their care.'

They said that the police knew that Mr Cairns was diabetic but failed to carry out appropriate checks on him. He found them intimidating and couldn't speak up for himself. Mr Cairns then had a heart attack while in a coma in hospital. He has been unwell since with multiple health issues, including stress and depression.

The savage murder of Greg Roscoe has shocked Cornford. Nobody else has been arrested for the crime.

When Paul spoke to me he said: "I've been through a terrible ordeal. I'm an innocent man who was treated appallingly. I've thought about suicide a lot. My nerves are shot to pieces. My mum died while I was recovering in hospital. Two years of my life have been wasted because of police failure. I'm very angry about what's been done to me. I've been diagnosed with Post Traumatic Stress Disorder and I'm going to need counselling. No amount of compensation can ever make up for what's happened to me but I still dream of getting my private pilot's licence one day."

I contacted Mr Roscoe's widow, who has since remarried. She refused to comment.

I will be working with Paul Cairns on a book to tell his full story. It's called One Man's Voice and will be published next spring. Paul's voice was silenced for a while by police who could not be bothered to do their job properly and failed in their duty of care. I aim to make sure that he is heard at last.

The bullies of this world need to know there are people who will stand up to them!

The photo with the article was of Paul Cairns on the steps of the court. He was small, slightly built and balding and looked as if he could do with a square meal. Often in such cases, there would be mention of family, supporters and friends who had campaigned on behalf of the person. Only two women flanked Cairns. The caption said that one was his lawyer, the other the reporter, Camilla Finley. Swift wondered if the police had focused on him because he was that obvious and tempting suspect: the eccentric loner.

The wind had veered east and Swift shivered, zipping up his leather jacket. He could smell the delicious, spicy aroma of mulled cider and warmed himself with a cup and a slice of sticky gingerbread at the nearby stall.

Back at home, he wandered out into the garden, where Cedric's ashes were buried beneath a tea rose. He hunkered down, smoothing a hand over the cold earth.

'To be honest, Cedric,' he murmured, 'I wish you'd never left me any money. I know you did it with a warm heart but it's hard, coping with Oliver's cussedness. Anyway, I just wanted you to know we won today. But I have a feeling it might only be round one. Sleep well, old friend.'

* * *

The River Rother was still and sun dappled. Not the most fascinating stretch of water, but easy to navigate and safe to travel with two toddlers. The November day was clear and mild. A couple of oak trees still held on to most of their leaves. Dainty clumps of Red Campion were flowering high on the bank above creamy fronds of Yarrow. Jackdaws chattered overhead and Swift could hear the distinctive song of a chiffchaff. As he pulled, the oars sliced smoothly through the clear water. He took deep breaths of the sweet air. He loved London but it was good to have a break from the noise and pollution.

Branna, his daughter, was staring up at the sky. He said her name loudly to catch her attention. 'Look over there. Two swans,' Swift said to her and Louis. Branna looked and laughed, then held out her thumb and forefinger, making the sign for *swan*. Louis gazed, nodding thoughtfully, his chin cupped in his hand.

Swift smiled at his cousin Mary, Louis' mother. 'I always feel as if Louis is humouring me. He knows that this is how adults go on and you have to keep them happy.'

Mary sat between the two children, an arm around each. 'He's a careful, measured boy. He likes to take his time and contemplate a situation.'

'Maybe he'll be a philosopher.' He nodded to the children. 'Keep still now, the water gets a bit deeper here.'

Louis looked at him steadily as if to say, *I know*. Branna adopted her mock serious expression, nodding. Her bright yellow and red flotation suit matched the colours of her hearing aids. She looked down intently at the water. Sometimes she was frowning and studious, then she would turn into a comedian. Her laugh was loud and startling, partly because of her deafness. She was much more boisterous than Louis. Swift was glad that she had an outgoing personality. She'd need it to make her way in a hearing world. Swift rowed on, facing the low sun, feeling its soft glow. A quick breeze stirred his hair and stroked the back of his neck.

'Pizza for dinner?' he asked the children.

Louis looked up at his mother, who said that sounded terrific. Branna stamped her feet, chanting *pizza* and working her chubby fingers. Then she held her arms out, pretending to row, puffing her cheeks.

'That's it. When you're older, you can have your own oars. Louis, too, if he'd like. Then you'll have rock hard muscles in your arms and calluses on your hands like me, and you'll have to buy industrial strength moisturiser. Watch and learn! And there's a heron up ahead, you'll see it in a minute.'

Swift watched Branna as she spotted the heron, wriggling with pleasure. He slowed the boat, angling it sideways, glad that the fatigue he sometimes experienced had left him for now. He'd caught cryptosporidium, a waterborne parasitic infection during his last major case. Although the parasite was long gone, he sometimes had nausea, aching joints and tiredness. It would pass eventually, the doctors had said, telling him to eat sensibly, exercise as usual and rest when he felt tired. Sound advice, but not always easy to follow.

He was pleased that he and Branna had a few peaceful days with Mary and Louis. Mary had been busy at work, away at conferences and he hadn't seen her for several months. They'd booked a two-bedroom cottage on the outskirts of Rye where they'd messed around, rowing on the river, walking by the ancient harbour and spotting wildlife. Branna had learned the signs for fox, curlew and hare.

At night, he and Mary made simple meals with chicken, fish and salads. After the children were in bed, they opened a bottle of wine and cloaked themselves in the soft woollen blankets considerately left by the owner. They sat out on the balcony overlooking the harbour, watching the lights and chatting. The evenings were clear and chilly with a salty breeze. It was good to have some time with Mary. They had been close since childhood and she was a reliable, constant presence in his life. Since she got married to Simone, it was more difficult to see her on her own. Simone was one of those people who believed a couple should do everything together and was quick to perceive slight if she felt left out. He assumed that Mary must have had to be persuasive to get this time away.

The previous night, she had talked about her job as an Assistant Commissioner in the Met, saying that she was wearying of bureaucracy and thinking about going into police training.

'It would be a drop in salary, but Simone earns well so that's not such a problem. Although she's not so keen on the idea. She likes my professional status. Anyway, I'm going to put some feelers out.'

He'd stretched his long legs on the balcony railing, sipping his Shiraz. 'You'd have loads of skills and experience to bring to training.'

'Hmm. Well, we'll see. How about you, got any work lined up?'

'A murder case. I talked to a guy called Niall Roscoe last week. His brother was stabbed a while back and no one was charged.'

'A nice little murder's always good in your line of business.'

'You're right and I've had mundane stuff to deal with this year. Steady, but nothing too interesting.'

'Just as well after being drugged, half drowned and infected with a parasite during that Woodville case.'

'Don't forget the dog bite,' he teased.

'I haven't. Don't *you* forget I saw you lying in that hospital bed, looking whiter than the sheets. I was worried sick.' She gave him a gentle punch in the arm. 'You still look a bit gaunt and pale. You've got more cheekbones than you used to have.'

'You should see me on a bad day. You know, I think I almost preferred the dog bite to Oliver Sheridan yapping and nipping at my heels. I thought of sending him the cleaning bill for my jacket but no point in provoking him.'

'You haven't heard from him since?'

'No. But I will. I will.'

'Poor Cedric. It must have been be hard to look at his only child and realise he was the spawn of the devil.' Mary formed a pair of horns with her fingers, making him laugh. 'So, what are you going to do with your inheritance, now that Cedric's wishes can be acted on?'

'I want to put it in a savings bond for Branna. But my solicitor's advised waiting a while in case Oliver lodges an appeal.'

'Good plan on both counts.' Mary drank some wine, murmuring with pleasure. 'I notice you haven't mentioned Nora so far,' she said. 'How's that going?'

'Good question. We have great times but I can't help thinking that she's often suspicious of me, waiting to catch me out. It's not a good feeling and I resent it. We both get prickly. So . . . I just don't know where we're heading.'

Mary sighed. 'She's suspicious because of Bella Reynolds?'

'Yes. I can't apologise because I slept with Bella years ago when we were at university. Nora knew I'd only met up with Bella again by coincidence, because of the Woodville investigation but she got so fired up when she saw us together . . .' He glanced at Mary, cleared his throat. Confession time. 'Actually, I slept with Bella a couple of times late last year as well.'

Mary twisted in her chair, staring at him, her blanket slipping. 'Ty, no! What were you thinking?'

'Don't guilt trip me. It was just after I came out of hospital. I thought that Nora had condemned me already for having an affair, based on suspicion and gossip. She'd ended it with me, as far as I could tell. So . . . I was knackered, Bella was friendly and good company and Nora had told me to get lost. I wasn't cheating on her because I thought we were over.'

'Does Nora know?'

'No. I thought it best to stay quiet. It wasn't anything serious with Bella.'

He had been seeing Nora Morrow for a while when things soured. She had been furious with him when he offered accommodation to Ruth, his ex and Branna's mother. He had abandoned that idea but then Nora became convinced that he was cheating on her with Bella. There had been some nasty scenes. After weeks of silence, Nora had contacted him in the run up to last New Year, tipsy with wine and goodwill after a party. She was a DI in a serious crimes squad in the Met and had been buzzing after a long, fraught case and a successful conviction. She'd asked if they could try and mend things and he'd been more than willing to meet her half way. He'd missed her keen wit, her sharp intellect and the feel of her head in the crook of his neck. They'd had a delightful weekend in Copenhagen in January and their fracture seemed to have healed. He knew that if he told her about Bella, she'd probably see red and slam the door again. Her temper was fierce and short-lived but he didn't want to tempt fate.

'I hope you two can work things out. I think you're good together.'

'I hope so, too. But there are obstacles.'

He listed them in his head: Nora's quick temper and jealousy, her unreasonable assumption that he'd been cheating on her and, most difficult of all, her lack of engagement with Branna. Nora was upfront about not wanting children and not being that keen on their company. She was kind enough to Branna as long as their meetings were reasonably brief but grew bored after a while. But it was her suspicion that had soured their relationship. He wasn't sure he could handle someone possessive and prone to jealous outbursts. He exhaled, half sigh, half laugh as he thought of Nora and Bella.

'What's funny?' Mary asked, topping up their glasses.

'My life and its ridiculous, contradictory tensions. There's Nora, who doesn't much like kids and Bella, who hears her biological clock ticking and is desperate to find a man to procreate with. I'm somewhere in the middle.'

'You like Bella though?'

'Very much. But I don't see her now. I explained that I was back with Nora. It's just as well because I don't want any more children and I'm not sure I want full time domesticity. Bella craves and needs both. I didn't want to waste her time.'

'So you've let another woman down.'

'Ouch, that's below the belt. It wasn't serious with Bella.'

'Did she know that? I bet she was harbouring hopes, as you say.'

'Give me a break. I can't be responsible for other people's dreams and fantasies and I didn't make any commitments to her.' He'd wished then that he hadn't mentioned Bella and changed the subject, talking about the river trip he proposed for the following day.

They didn't stay up late, as both children woke just after 6 a.m. He lay reading in bed while Branna slept in the bunk bed below him, her downy cheeks flushed pink, her arms thrown above her head. He'd wondered if she would miss her mother, Ruth, or her friends at nursery but she had been fine. She and Louis accepted each other's company, with few arguments. It helped that he had such a placid nature. And Branna loved being on the water, which was a bonus.

Now he tucked the boat nearer to the bank as another rower went past, heading upstream. Mary's phone buzzed and she took it from her pocket, scanning the screen.

'It's a message from mummy Simone,' she told Louis. 'She says she's missed us but she's been very busy at work.'

Louis put his thumb in his mouth and sucked. Swift had assumed it would be Simone. She had emailed, texted or phoned half a dozen times a day to check their welfare. Swift secretly thought that Louis was so docile because Simone treated him as if he was made of porcelain. He was always dressed beautifully and immaculately in traditional outfits like a Prince George clone. Swift thought that Simone must source his clothing from the same outfitters as the royals. Louis seemed to shine and sparkle; unlike Branna, you rarely saw him with food around his mouth or mud on his knees. Simone had kitted him out for this brief holiday with expensive Scandinavian outdoor wear more suited to a voyage on the Atlantic than a sedate trip in rural England. He'd brought several state of the art neoprene wet suits and jackets, thermal hats and gloves suitable for gale force winds, three lifejackets and two buoyancy aids. Simone usually allowed him only organic foods and no sugar or ready-made meals so takeaway pizza for dinner would definitely be pushing the boundaries.

'Back to the real world tomorrow,' Swift told them. 'Back to nursery for you two mischiefs and work for Mary and me.'

Branna patted her cheeks with her hands, and then yelled, making the sign for *woman* as she spotted a walker on the riverbank. The woman turned and waved and Branna waved back. Mary lifted Louis' arm and told him to wave to the lady. Swift raised a hand in salute. His upper arm ached, the skin pulling. He had a semicircle of dark pink scar tissue there, courtesy of the serious dog bite the previous year. A woman who had committed murder and didn't like being cornered had set her Alsatian on him. These days, when he rowed, either that scar ached or the sickle shaped one on his thigh, earned while he'd investigated sex traffickers for Interpol. Branna was fascinated by the scars and would ask to see them, much to her mother Ruth's disapproval. His ex-partner saw his scars not so much as badges of honour as gruesome emblems of his hazardous choice of occupation.

The walker picked a sprig of gorse, stuck it in her buttonhole and sauntered on. Swift spent his days dealing with violence, crimes, lies, deceit and greed. It was good to be reminded of the simple, innocent pleasures of most people's lives.

* * *

Swift drove to Cornford in his burnt orange Mini Cooper convertible. Cedric had given it to him a while back, saying he no longer needed it. It had been one of Oliver Sheridan's gripes, yet another example of his father favouring the rapacious landlord over his more deserving son. The car was nippy and easy to handle in the light traffic. He covered the miles from Hammersmith inside an hour.

Cornford was a pretty, spacious market town about fifteen miles north of London, commuter land for people working in the capital but priced out of the city. The River Lea skirted it to the east, with the remains of an ancient priory by its banks. The police station was near the town centre, housed in a small and functional Edwardian building in yellow brick with wide, panelled front doors. Inside, it had been modernised with a bright reception area, grey padded chairs, a water dispenser and a mission statement that Swift read as he waited for DI Blackmore.

We're here for VICTIMS

We're here for JUSTICE

We're here for COMMUNITIES

We're here to protect INDIVIDUALS and PROPERTY and prevent HARM

We're here for YOU, WHEN it matters, WHERE it matters

'What do you think, mate? We paid a consultant quite a bit to come up with it after we got slaughtered over Paul Cairns.'

Swift turned to the man at his elbow and saw skin the colour of rich sherry, melancholy eyes and a cynical grin. 'It states the obvious. I always suspect things written in capitals.'

'Yep, it's bollocks. But nice shiny bollocks to go with our nice shiny accommodation. Fitz Blackmore. You're Tyrone Swift?'

'That's me.'

They shook hands. Blackmore had an iron grip. He was almost as tall as Swift and lithe, with a narrow face.

'We can talk in my office. I share it, but my sergeant's out this morning. This way.'

He moved fast, using a code on the security doors and taking stairs two at a time. He led the way through two more sets of doors to a tiny room with a view of the car park.

'Want an illegal coffee?' he asked. 'I keep a kettle under the desk. It contravenes health and safety but it saves me from having to waste time chatting in the kitchen. That's where the moaners, whiners and slackers tend to congregate. And the women who talk in low voices about their wombs and hormones. I know more about sodding endometriosis from trying to get to the fridge than

I ever thought possible.' He threw Swift a challenging look, as if testing his reaction to these non-PC views.

'I believe it's a painful condition,' Swift said, batting the challenge back.

'Yeah, but I don't want to hear about it over my mid-morning snack. Ruins the digestion. Blokes don't congregate around the kettle to talk about their testosterone or their prostates, do they?' He fluttered his eyelashes, which were thick, long and sooty. The kind that some women would envy and spend time and money achieving.

'Maybe they do it in other ways. Non-verbally. You know, in the squash court etc. And maybe it would be better if men did talk about those things.'

'Oh, very right on. I can see I'm getting nowhere with you. I suppose you're a goody-goody feminist metro male. Yeah, mate, I can see the London feministas have got you brain washed.'

Swift wasn't sure how much Blackmore meant any of the provocation. The in-your-face style could be a well-honed tactic. 'Were you making me a coffee?'

Blackmore grinned. 'Well deflected. Sure. I don't run to milk.'

'Black's fine.'

Blackmore flicked a switch with his foot and a tell-tale wisp of steam appeared above his desk top. He took two mugs from a drawer, tipped coffee in from a jar and bent down to pour the water.

'So,' he said. 'Tyrone — that's a bit Hollywood, isn't it? Don't I remember a Tyrone playing Zorro? Small guy with a sword and attitude.'

'You mean Tyrone Power. My Irish mother named me. But not for the actor. I had an ancestor called Tyrone who went to Australia in the late nineteenth century and was never heard of again.'

'Aha. Well, I can't be calling you Tyrone. It doesn't seem to slide off the tongue.'

'Most people call me Ty.'

'Hmm . . . nah, let's see . . . Mind if I call you Ron?'

Swift did, but he thought saying so probably wouldn't get him anywhere. 'Call me whatever you like if it means you're going to give me useful information.'

Blackmore stirred the coffee vigorously. 'Good answer.'

If Blackmore was the type who made every conversation a test, this meeting was going to be hard going. Swift had noted the ridged calluses on his skin when they shook hands and watched the well-developed biceps moving under his shirt. He reckoned a bit of man chat might move things forward.

'Are you a rower?'

'I do row. Mainly canoeing. Well spotted.'

'Takes one to know one. I row as often as I can.'

'On the Thames?'

'Right. I live near the river in Hammersmith. I keep my boat at my club, Tamesas. Do you canoe on the Lea?'

'Yep. We have a marina here in town and good river access. I often do a trip down to Broxbourne and back. Takes a couple of hours. Keeps me fit and clears my head of this place for a while.' He pushed a coffee across the desk and leaned back languidly in his chair, legs stretched wide. Swift could hear Nora's voice in his head, complaining about manspreading. Blackmore had an attractive, wry smile but his eyes were like glass splinters. 'Enough of the niceties. You want to know about Greg Roscoe.'

'His brother contacted me. Their mother wants me to look into his murder. Anything you can share would be a plus. I've read about what happened to Paul Cairns and the compensation.'

Blackmore nodded. 'Paul Cairns. Not our finest hour. We certainly got our fingers burned.'

'Any doubt in your mind about him?'

Blackmore picked up a dice-shaped stress ball and squeezed it in his right hand. 'He's a pathetic creep of a man but it seems we got it wrong. I was a sergeant at the time so I have to hold my hands up for some blame. Having said that, Cairns was his own worst enemy. He was always hanging about at Cornford airfield. They often had to chuck him out late at night when they were locking up. He was a wannabe pilot but couldn't make the grade. He'd failed exams, even when he repeated them. Roscoe had taught him and told him that he'd probably never get a licence. Cairns had demanded a different instructor. He'd made threats against Roscoe and badmouthed him at the airfield and around town, saying he was discriminating against him because he was dyslexic as well as diabetic. He'd sent a letter of complaint to the Civil Aviation Authority. He called Roscoe incompetent and prejudiced and was demanding an investigation. That could have been nasty for Roscoe, although by all accounts, he laughed it off. There was a photomontage of the staff in the airfield foyer with information about them. The week before Roscoe died, Cairns had dragged a key across his photo and damaged it. The airfield management had just threatened to ban him from the site because of his behaviour and his verbal aggression.' Blackmore rose and paced up and down behind his desk, stretching and then stopping to look out of the window for a moment. He knocked against it with his knuckles as if he'd like to escape. He had a fizzing energy that seemed to use up more than his fair share of oxygen.

Swift's large mug was white and bore the logo: THIS IS WHAT AN AMAZING POLICE OFFICER LOOKS LIKE. He blew on his coffee before taking a sip. 'I can see why you took a good look at Cairns. What kinds of threats had he made?'

'General stuff about Roscoe getting his comeuppance, how he'd never fly again, better watch his back. Pathetic, but nasty. So we thought we should talk to him.'

'What about his alibi?'

Blackmore was still walking up and down, wearing a path in the thin office carpet. He spun his chair so that it rocked on its base and flung himself back into it. 'He claimed he'd been plane spotting at Heathrow the night Roscoe was murdered. He did go to airports regularly — Gatwick, Luton and Heathrow — sometimes Stansted. A real anorak guy. He lived alone, so no one could vouch for him and we couldn't spot him on airport CCTV. He'd left his mobile phone at home so that was no help. We had several witnesses from the airfield who testified that Cairns had threatened to harm Roscoe. The landlady at his local said he'd been in a rage the day before Roscoe died because he'd had a letter from the airfield, confirming that he'd be excluded if he didn't mend his ways and he blamed Roscoe. Said Roscoe wouldn't see his next birthday. He was convinced that he was marking him down and blocking his way to being a pilot.'

'So what proved his innocence?' He wanted to hear if Blackmore would try to put spin on it and was gratified to get a surly but straightforward response.

'Turned out he had photos on his digital camera that he'd taken at Heathrow with date and timings that put him there when Roscoe died. We cocked up. Didn't check it soon enough. But even so . . .'

'Even so?'

'If he'd been in cahoots with someone, they could have taken his camera to Heathrow to place him there.'

'You don't sound sold on that possibility.'

'No, well, Cairns is a Billy Nomates, always has been. There was no evidence that anyone would have planned it with him.'

'So I guess there were no forensics placing him at the crime scene.'

'There was DNA. Trouble was, the plane Roscoe was killed in was teeming with prints and DNA. It hadn't been cleaned for a month and there'd been a dozen students taking lessons in it so it was chock full of the stuff. We found Cairns' in a thumbprint and a tiny smear of mucus. But he'd been in the plane having a lesson a couple of weeks before Roscoe died so that was accounted for. His threatening behaviour and witness statements made us focus on him.' He moved the stress ball to his other hand.

'It can't be easy discussing this, given the outcome. I read that Cairns went into a diabetic coma here in the station.'

Blackmore shrugged. 'We're human. We can't always live up to our shiny mission statement. It was frantic here the night Cairns got ill. There'd been a major pile up on the ring road and the duty sergeant took his eye off the ball. We'd gone to bring Cairns in for questioning that afternoon and he'd run when he saw us coming. So there was a chase and he got pretty stressed. We checked he'd had his insulin and he seemed fine. But . . . he was left alone for ten minutes and next thing, he was unconscious.'

Swift nodded. 'Could have been worse. He could have died.'

'Yeah. We messed up badly, though. Can't deny it.' He stuck his chin out. 'I expect you've messed up.'

'When I was in the Met or as a private investigator?'

'Both. Either.'

'Not in the Met, as far as I know. I've made mistakes as an investigator. Last year a young man was murdered and his body dumped in a wardrobe on the top floor of my house. I'd agreed to let him help me with a case but he was out of his depth and he stirred murky waters. I shouldn't have encouraged him.'

Blackmore put his hands behind his head and spun in his chair. 'We could both wear hair shirts but I don't think that would help your dead man or Roscoe.'

'True enough. What can you tell me about the crime scene?'

'I was there, as it happens. One of the maintenance staff found Roscoe at six thirty in the morning. It was one of those still, hazy summer mornings. I remember seeing loads of baby rabbits bouncing around by the hedge as I drove into the airfield. Is there a name for a baby rabbit?'

Swift smiled. 'They're called kits, short for kitten.'

'I've never heard that. Anyway, Greg Roscoe . . . He was in a small plane in a hangar, sprawled back on the pilot's seat in the cockpit of a Piper Cherokee. His neck and chest were drenched in blood, lacerated by deep, long gashes. He'd been stabbed half a dozen times. Whoever did it was in the passenger seat beside him. There were no defence wounds on his hands so he was taken by surprise. He'd had a fair amount to drink, too, so he wouldn't have been at his sharpest. We never found the weapon. I can tell you, the combined smell of blood and aviation fuel is one I won't forget for a long time.' Blackmore opened a desk drawer. 'I've taken two photos from the file to show you.'

The first photo was of a greetings card, attached to the opened zip of Roscoe's jeans with a huge safety pin. It featured a spray of white lilies against a pale pink background. The second was of the inside of the card. The greeting had been struck through and replaced with capital letters cut from a newspaper.

~~Live~~
~~Laugh~~
~~Love~~
DIE
SIGH
CRY
SO MANY TEARS

'The *Live, Laugh Love* bit is a rip off from an American poet called Bessie Stanley,' Blackmore said. 'You find it on fridge magnets and the like, apparently.'

'I wouldn't have had you down as a poetry type.'

'I'm not. A female colleague told me. Some claptrap about you're successful if you live your life well etc. etc. If we're indulging in stereotypes, we might say it's a girly kind of card.'

'Or that's what the police were supposed to think.'

'Hmm. The card's mass-produced and can be bought in at least three shops in Cornford and widely elsewhere. There was no DNA on it. The letters were cut from the *Daily Mail* and glued in. The safety pin was interesting. It had been jabbed right through Roscoe's penis. It was done after he died. Makes me flinch now, thinking about it, even though he can't have felt it.'

'So making a statement of some kind.'

'Yep. Or to humiliate him, even in death. There was something else . . . Tap water mixed with table salt had been poured over his eyes and face. About a glassful. Again, after death.'

'As if he'd been crying?'

'Presumably.' Blackmore cracked his knuckles loudly, and then tapped a tattoo on the desk with them. 'It so happens that Cairns's mum owned one of the stationers where that card was on sale.'

'It would be a bit of an obvious lead to him, using a card from a family-owned shop.'

'True. But killers can be stupid. So, you know, that's why we fancied him for it — plus all the threats he'd been making. I have to admit, the card always bothered me. It didn't seem to fit with the kind of anger Cairns had been expressing. The stab wounds, yes, but not the card. But he did read the *Daily Mail*.'

'As do many. You obviously didn't find any copies of the paper in his home with the letters cut out.'

Blackmore grinned. 'No such luck.'

'What about a partner? Did Cairns have one?'

'Nope. I can't imagine any woman going near him. I don't think he's gay, just sort of . . . neutral.'

'Can I take copies of these photos on my phone?'

Blackmore gazed at him for a moment, cleared his throat and wiggled a finger in one ear. 'I reckon I've gone a bit deaf and I just need to go to the loo and check a statement's being taken.'

He shot out of his chair, leaving it rocking, and left the room.

Chapter 3

He waited until the door had banged shut. Blackmore seemed to be the genuine article, despite his posturing. Swift took copies of the photos and laid the originals back on the desk. Someone had carried out a frenzied attack and then taken time to damage Roscoe's genitals. The murder had been planned, with the card selected and prepared, water and salt mixed. The killer had wanted to communicate a message. Contempt seemed to be the main component.

Blackmore came back, smelling of pine soap and finished his coffee in one long swallow. 'Anything else I can tell you?'

'Time of the attack?'

'Hard to call because of the heat. Sometime between midnight, when the last flight had come in and the hangar was locked, and 4 a.m. Whatever Roscoe was doing at the airfield, he didn't enter by the main gates, where there are cameras. When you go there, you'll see that there are fields surrounding the place and it would be easy enough to get over the perimeter fence or even through a hedge. We had stern words with them about their security as a result of that investigation. Roscoe's car was parked in a lane that runs at the northern tip of the airfield.'

'You had no other suspects?'

'No one who stacked up. Of course, by the time we'd finished messing around with Cairns we'd lost ground and time. Roscoe told his wife that he was going to a meeting at the flying club that evening, but that was a lie and no one saw him after he left home in his car around sevenish. He'd turned his phone off, which suggests he was up to something his wife wouldn't approve of, so the last signal tracked him to home. We picked him up on a traffic camera on the ring road at 7:20 but that was it. The main prints and DNA in his car were his, his wife's and his daughter's. A few other samples of dead skin on the front passenger seat indicated a woman's DNA but we could find no match with his family or on databases. Our Greg was known to be a bit of a player, so it wouldn't have been surprising if he'd had a female friend in the car at some point. No one knew of anyone he'd been seeing around the time he died. His wife had put him on a short leash and it seemed to have worked in restricting his activities.'

'Did you find any girlfriends?'

Blackmore woke up his computer and looked at the screen. 'There was a Holly Armstrong. She was another instructor at the airfield. She told us she'd played around with Roscoe a couple of times but then the owner of the flying club found out and warned them both off. The "don't screw the crew" lecture. She said she was home alone that night, so no one could vouch for her. But there was no DNA match to her. She used another plane to teach in.'

'Roscoe's sister-in-law told me he pursued other women.'

'That's what we understood. His wife, Ashleigh, was upfront about it. Didn't mince her words. In fact, I felt uncomfortable about some of the stuff she said in her daughter's hearing when we went to the house. The kid was only twelve at the time and I don't think she should have been exposed to that. Can't recall her name. Something weird to do with Cuba.'

'Havana.'

'That's it. Strange name to saddle a kid with. Mind you, I came across a boy called Berlin a few months back.'

'What kind of stuff was Ashleigh saying?'

'That Roscoe couldn't keep it in his pants, that he was on heat whenever he saw an attractive woman, that he liked them young . . . I think "fresh young meat" was a phrase she used. I can't stand blokes like that. I mean, I take my chances where I can like most men but I prefer my women to be free of teeth braces.' He rolled his shoulders and scratched an armpit. 'Tell you what I reckon happened to him . . . Roscoe had flown all over the world and we heard he liked to gamble and screw in equal measures. Maybe someone caught up with him because of one or the other or both. But given the number of people he could have pissed off, that leaves a very big pool to fish in for suspects. My guvnor took that line too.'

'That thought had occurred to me. Was Roscoe liked at the flying club?'

Blackmore waved a hand from side to side. 'By some. Others not so much. Bit of a know-it-all and boasted quite a lot about his glory days in long haul. He saw himself as a good catch for a smallish club. But there was general agreement that he was a skilled instructor and the school got some kudos from having him on board.'

'I'd guess you're not actively investigating the case now, especially given the possible parameters you talked about.'

'That's right. I keep a watching brief — you know how it is . . . there's too much else to do so to use a term Roscoe would have understood, he's in a holding pattern.' Blackmore laughed at his own wit. 'I reckon he'll be circling indefinitely. I felt sorry for Roscoe's poor old mum. She's hard work and makes no bones about who was her favourite son but she's had a tough life. She worked her fingers to the bone to pay for Roscoe's flying lessons and she worshipped the guy.'

'You've been very helpful, thanks.' Swift rose, hitching up his jeans. 'I won't take up any more of your time for now.'

'Been on a diet? You don't look like you need to,' Blackmore observed.

'I contracted cryptosporidium from the Regent's canal last year. I'm fine, but I lost weight and my appetite is still come and go.'

'I've heard about it. They say it can take ages to get back to full fitness.'

'So I'm finding. It gets frustrating but I just have to wait it out.'

Blackmore locked his computer and pushed his chair back. 'What happened? Capsize?'

'No. I'd found some people who'd committed murders and didn't like being tracked down. They drugged me and tried to drown me. That's when the parasite found a home. Occupational hazard.'

'The joys of mixing it with criminals.' Blackmore grinned. 'You married? Got someone to look after you at home, cool your brow and give you your medicine?'

'I'm not married. Almost. Once. You?'

Blackmore shook his head. 'No chance, mate. I like my freedom. I watch other coppers worrying about getting back to the wife and kids and breaking out in a sweat. Not for me.' He stood and shoved his hands in his pockets, feet planted apart. 'I won't charge you for picking my brain. Any man who rows a boat has to be okay. Come on, I'll take you back down.'

In the station foyer, Swift shook hands with him, ready this time for the bruising grip. 'Do you think a woman could have killed Roscoe?'

'I don't see why not. It's not hard to stab a man in a confined space, especially with the element of surprise. I don't want to rain on your parade, Ron, but I honestly don't think you're going to find who did it.'

He said it provocatively — a challenge. Swift understood it was Blackmore's way of saving face.

'Maybe I'll get a lucky break,' he said. 'The one you didn't.'

Blackmore scowled and turned away, muttering under his breath and left the door swinging after him.

* * *

Holly Armstrong was now the CFI at the flying school. When Swift rang her she said that her last lesson finished at 4 p.m. and she'd see him in the bar then. The white metal gates at the airfield were open, with a tarmacked driveway leading to a handsome 1930s building. It was built of white concrete with narrow green tinted windows set into darker green metal frames. A central tower was flanked by two low, wide sections with decorative wrought iron fencing running along the front. Swift parked outside the central door. Above it was a huge pair of bronze wings, sitting on top of the sign:

Cornford Airfield - We Fly High

Swift was early. It was an intensely cold day with a clear, bright blue sky. He walked to the left of the building in an icy wind and saw a line of hangars and a runway just beyond them. In the distance, a single-engined plane came in to land, skimming the dense purple beech hedge that lined the airfield perimeter. As it touched down, it was buffeted by the breeze and bounced along the narrow runway towards the furthest hangar. With its bright orange and green fuselage, it looked like a toy and too flimsy to carry passengers. Swift's stomach fluttered as he watched it. It reminded him of one of the glued models that some of his school friends used to stick together and hang from their bedroom ceilings where they dangled, gathering dust. Maybe some of those boys were now like Paul Cairns, hanging around airfields and plane spotting.

In the foyer, he found glossy parquet flooring and a curved reception desk in polished walnut. Several huge TV screens showed planes taking off and landing and another had a map of Europe with weather and meteorological conditions. It was a jigsaw of pale blues, purple and yellow. Westerly winds were bringing swathes of rain across France to the UK later on. A local radio station played softly in the background with the Beach Boys singing about the delights of California girls. Although a sign said *No Smoking*, Swift was sure he could smell the rich whiff of cigar. A young man at the desk asked him to sign in and pointed the way to the bar, which was called the Check-In.

The music followed him through to a large room with wide windows and a heated veranda looking out to the airfield. Several older men were out there, muffled up with scarves, sipping pints and smoking. A couple of them puffed at fat cigars. The front of the bar was decorated with signage from world airlines. Swift ordered a coffee from a woman arranging slices of cake on a stand. She was wearing a cabin crew outfit: a pale blue skirt, ruffled shirt and jacket and a jaunty blue hat with a red trim.

'Is that an actual airline uniform?' he asked her.

'No way. I got it from a fancy dress website. A new franchise took over last year. Shook this place up. It needed it. We decided to dress the part. I haven't seen you here before. Are you having a lesson?'

'No, I'm here to meet Holly Armstrong.'

'Good old Holly. She started some of the changes round here and not before time. The old guard don't much like it.' She rolled her eyes and gestured to the men sitting on the veranda. 'I've been here for ages but I love the new look.'

'Did you know Greg Roscoe?'

'Course. He was a laugh, was Greg. He used to sit there yarning to me about the parties they'd have in hotels when he flew long haul. Most of them seemed to involve crew taking their clothes off and drinking the bar dry. I don't know how they were ever sober enough to fly.' She smiled, shaking her head. 'He'd tell me about the pilots called "door knockers". The ones who always tried their luck with the flight attendants, tapping on their doors.'

'Do you think he was a door knocker?'

She gave Swift an eloquent look. 'Takes one to know one, as they say. He was one of those men who always glances at a woman's chest when he meets her. Awful though, what happened to him. This place felt weird for months afterwards.'

'I hear the police didn't arrest anyone.'

'No. Well, they got their knickers in a twist about that Paul Cairns. I could have told them he hadn't done it. He's all wind and hiss. He wouldn't have the nerve to stick a knife in someone. I've never understood it. Greg was a sociable chap, always up for a chat.'

Swift gestured around. 'This is a much bigger place than I expected.'

'It used to be a bit run down and dusty looking. The guy who owns it now started expanding the business a while back. There are four runways, a new viewing area and a couple of conference rooms. Want a bite to eat with that coffee? Have a look at the menu — it's all good.'

The menu was printed on a picture of a Jumbo Jet. It was headed, *Your Ticket to a Tasty Treat.* Starters were listed under *Pre-Flight,* mains under *In-Flight* and desserts under *Post-Flight.* There was a *Captain's All Day Brunch*, a *Head Steward's Soup of the Day* and a *Purser's Platter*.

It was the kind of set up that aroused his suspicions of microwaved ready meals. 'I'm not that hungry, to be honest. What's the Purser's Platter?'

'A smoked salmon omelette with Greek salad. If you don't fancy a meal, the orange and lemon cake's delicious. Try a slice. You know you want to. You look as if you could do with feeding up and I bet you've got a sweet tooth.'

'What makes you think that?'

'Tall, slim men always do. They burn the sugar off,' she said knowingly.

He laughed. 'Go on, then. Coffee and cake.'

It was a pleasant surprise. The coffee was robust, the cake moist and tangy. He was licking his fingers as a nimble woman in navy blue trousers, white shirt and navy tie came in through the veranda, nodding to the group of men. One of them gave her a mock salute, which she returned. She saw Swift and walked briskly across the room, calling a greeting to the woman at the bar and asking for a pot of strong tea.

'I see you're catered for,' she told Swift as she sat opposite him.

'I can recommend the cake.'

'Better not. I've got a work medical next week and I have to be okay on the scales.' She removed her clip on tie and rolled her shirtsleeves up. Her arms were sturdy and freckled. She wore a large, complicated looking watch on her left wrist. Her fine, pale hair was pulled back from her high forehead in a clasp. She looked in her mid-thirties. 'So, what can I help you with?'

He explained about Greg Roscoe's family. 'I've spoken to the police. You're my next port of call as you worked with Greg.'

She nodded, poured tea and added a splash of milk. 'It plunged us all into confusion here when Paul Cairns had an alibi. He seemed such a likely suspect, the way he'd been behaving. Then it was all thrown up in the air and we were back to square one. Cairns still visits here and drinks in the bar. He talks to anyone who'll listen about how he was mistreated and his compensation. He was buying drinks all round the evening after his court win. I'd rather he didn't come here, but we can't stop him and we don't want to antagonise him. At least he doesn't want to learn to fly these days.'

'I didn't think you could be a pilot if you were diabetic.'

'You've been able to get a private licence for a while. That was extended to commercial flying in 2012. You have to be able to demonstrate good overall management of your condition and of course commercial pilots are monitored through regular medicals. That's how some of them find out they have diabetes. Cairns always seemed to have his under control when he was learning here.'

'And he behaves himself generally now?'

'Yes, so we've no reason to exclude him. He bores on like he always did about airline crashes. He's full of conspiracy theories. He spends hours watching programmes about air accidents. He knows everything there is to know about flight MH370 and has his own ideas about what happened.'

'Was that the Malaysian aircraft that went missing?'

'That's the one. It's never been traced. If I see that Cairns is in here I often give the bar a miss.' She shook her head. 'Greg's family have never had . . . that awful expression . . . *closure*.'

'Yes, and whoever attacked your colleague is still free.'

'Hmm. And that.'

'Did you have any suspicions about anyone else at the time?'

'No. I mean, the way he was stabbed . . . seemed like some lunatic.'

'And Paul Cairns fitted the bill?'

Her cheeks were pink flushed, as if she had caught the sun. 'We thought so. We'd had so much trouble with him and he was furious with Greg. You get blokes like Cairns hanging out here. A lot of people find flying a bit exotic and fascinating so we do attract wannabees. It's open, friendly and clubbable here and people chat. I used to feel sorry for Cairns because he was one of those sad people who never quite fit in and are desperate to. He was always that bit too friendly, his laugh a bit forced. And he wanted to be good at something he had no talent for. Taking flying lessons isn't a cheap hobby but his grandfather had left him some money so he had the resources to pay.'

Swift thought she was astute and wouldn't miss much. She'd be a good liar, too. 'And Greg Roscoe had told him he wasn't up to flying.'

'That's correct, and Greg was right to do that. I'd seen some of Cairns's landings and his paperwork. He just didn't have the concentration or ability. I'd have told him the same if I'd been teaching him. We like to be straight with people because lessons are expensive and this school is popular and has a good reputation. We're not here to rip people off.' She moved her teaspoon on the saucer.

'Do I detect a hesitant *but* in there?'

'Well, in a way. I thought Greg could have handled Cairns better.' She nodded and looked up at him. Her pale eyes were narrow and crinkled. 'You see, Cairns idolised Greg to start with. He thought he'd hit the jackpot, having lessons with the CFI. He was really excited about going up with Greg. So when Greg started criticising and failing him, he was seriously cut up. Like his bubble had burst. Greg was a bit impatient and full-on with him. Cairns is bumptious but sort of fragile. Yeah, that's it . . . a fragile ego. I heard him rowing with Greg in the office and Greg was telling him he'd contact other flying schools and warn them not to touch Cairns. That was over the top. Cairns had a right to approach other schools if he wanted. I reckoned that maybe that was the tipping point for Cairns because he lived and breathed planes and flying. I thought that was why he'd contacted the Civil Aviation Authority to complain about Greg.'

'I've heard about that. It could have been serious for Greg, presumably?'

'Definitely. Especially once Cairns talked about being dyslexic and discrimination. The truth is, we knew about his diabetes but he didn't tell us about his dyslexia until Greg started failing him and he hadn't declared it on his application form. Then suddenly he was going on about needing information presented differently and having more time for exams.'

'Did you talk to Greg about the way he handled Cairns?'

'I tried to but he wasn't receptive. He didn't like being questioned as the CFI. His word was law. He said that Cairns was a nuisance, hanging about the place and lowering the tone.' She looked at him with steady concentration, her face expressionless.

A middle-aged man and woman carrying leather satchels came into the bar and called loud greetings to Holly as they ordered drinks. She nodded hello back.

'Just in from Amsterdam,' the woman said. 'Lovely but a bit bumpy over the channel.'

'There's weather coming through,' Holly confirmed and raised a thumb when the woman said they'd see her at the meeting in the morning.

'Got to keep them sweet,' Holly murmured. 'They're buying into part ownership of an expensive jet. Baby boomers and their cash!'

Swift waited until the couple had moved away. 'I've heard that you and Greg Roscoe were more than just colleagues.'

She blushed. 'I suppose the police told you that.'

'Yes. But that you thought better of it.'

She crossed her legs, nursing her tea between her hands. 'It shouldn't have happened. He was married and the CFI, and I was the senior instructor. The truth of it is I didn't even fancy him that much. He was an attractive enough man with great skills and drive but not really my type.' She sipped her drink, staring into the cup.

He could see that she was deciding how much to tell him so he kept quiet, wondering why Roscoe had fallen for her. She was pleasant in an understated way but there was no spark to her. Maybe she had simply been available. He looked out at the group on the veranda who were now dealing cards, their heads close together. They reminded him of Cedric, who used to sit playing dominoes with his cronies in the pub. He thought of his friend's ashes buried in the back garden as he had requested and felt a sharp stab of grief. He had known Cedric for most of his life. They'd shared an easy companionship and in many ways had fulfilled a father-son role for each other. Swift still expected to see Cedric on the stairs, smell the aroma of one of his casseroles when he opened the hall door or hear him playing jazz in the late hours of the night.

Holly pulled her chair in nearer to him, speaking softly. 'We only saw each other half a dozen times. The first was after my birthday party in the bar here and I was pissed as a newt. Too drunk to drive. Greg drove me home and next thing I knew, we were grappling on the sofa. To be honest, I didn't remember a lot about it afterwards. Anyway, he suggested a picnic by the river a couple of days later. Well, he brought a bottle of cheap wine and some nuts. Last of the big spenders. I'd been on my own for a while and there was no one else asking. I knew I shouldn't because he was married and there was the work complication but he could be very charming . . . '

'And you were lonely.'

'Yeah. Lonely and fed up of just going home to the cat.' She gave an embarrassed shrug. 'Greg came to my flat on a couple of evenings. Otherwise, we met up by the river and there were a few times in the bushes at the edge of the airfield. All a bit hurried and functional. I got the impression that the airfield grounds were a favoured spot for Greg and he'd taken other ladies there. I wasn't exactly being wined and dined, was I?'

'No. Greg sounds like an opportunist.'

'I suppose. Anyway, he'd stood me up a couple of times when we were supposed to meet. Sometimes he'd be like a little boy, giggling because he'd lied to his wife again and got away with it but then he'd get anxious, worried that he'd been painted by her.'

'Painted?'

'Sorry, that's pilot slang for scanned by radar. I was having serious doubts and then Silvio, the owner, called us in and tore us off a strip. One of the maintenance guys had spotted us. We had to apologise and promise to behave. I was relieved more than anything because I'd wanted to tell Greg it had to stop. But it's difficult, turning your boss down.'

'And Greg was okay towards you afterwards?'

'He behaved as if nothing had happened. No awkwardness, nothing. I reckoned that he'd screwed so many women I was just a brief addition, so I decided to behave the same way.'

'How long was that before he died?'

'A year. Almost. Yeah, the previous autumn. It was a warm September, hence the al fresco hanky-panky.'

The humour seemed forced and he thought it still bothered her. Maybe she'd been keener on Roscoe than she was admitting. 'Did you know of any other women Greg was seeing?'

'Best to ask his widow. I reckon that Greg usually had another interest on the side. It was a way of life with him. I didn't know of any women in particular, but there were evenings when he came out of the gents' loos smelling of aftershave and wearing a clean shirt. I doubt he was doing that to go home. He had an easy charm with women. He'd compliment them on their hair, notice a new skirt, scent or piece of jewellery. The kinds of details lots of men miss. He always flirted with good-looking female students. We don't get that many women but when we do, they're usually fairly young. That certainly appealed to Greg.'

'So you became CFI after Greg died?'

'His death obviously left a vacancy. I decided to apply. There were a couple of other candidates but I suppose they decided better the devil you know . . . '

She had a calm, controlled exterior. Not a woman to underestimate, he thought and wondered if the flashy Roscoe had. He supposed she could have used a knife on him to create the vacancy she'd stepped into. 'Would you say Greg was popular here?'

She pressed her lips together. 'Mostly. A lot of students liked him and requested him. He had high standards — which was good, but sometimes it made him impatient with people. He could be abrasive if any of the ground staff didn't come up to scratch or if someone filed a poor flight plan.' She rubbed her eyes and stretched. 'I've been cooped up and staring at the sun a lot today.' She patted her cheeks. 'And I forgot my sunscreen.'

Swift smiled. 'You have caught some rays. You enjoy being CFI?'

'It's grown on me. It's a very male environment but I'm always up for a challenge. There are blokes here who needed to realise it's the twenty-first century. Some of the members didn't take to having a woman in charge, especially as I wanted to implement changes, lighten the place, make it more accessible and friendly. Luckily Silvio, the guy who bought the outfit, is like minded.' She nodded at the bar. 'This bar used to be called The Spitfire and served ham and eggs or sausages with greasy chips. It was very dark, like a room in an old-fashioned gentleman's club. Lots of black leather and wood panelling. The soundtrack was favourites from World War 2 and martial music. I worked with Silvio to modernise in here and in the foyer. It's been good for business. Now we get families and younger people visiting — just to have lunch or to view or have what we call "look see" flights. Half an hour up in the air and your pilot points out major landmarks. Quite a few people come from London.' She smiled. 'I don't suppose Greg would have liked the changes. He talked the talk when it came to women being equal but I reckoned that was skin deep. I'm not sure he'd have liked me becoming CFI.'

'He was a misogynist?'

'I think so, although he tried to conceal it. I've read that men who have lots of affairs usually are. They don't really like women, do they?'

'I'd say you've got a point. Although maybe they're fascinated by them or enjoy having power over them.'

'I worked that out about Greg. Despite the charm and the flirting, he didn't value women much. Mind you, I can't complain. Nobody made me screw him.'

There was a shout of laughter from the card players and two of them had a mock fight. Holly shook her head and said they were like a bunch of kids.

Swift watched as the cards were shuffled and another hand dealt. 'Greg was power playing with you though, surely. And abusing his authority.'

'I guess. He'd always worked in an industry where most of the women were in junior positions . . . cabin crew or support staff. He used to like telling people about his flights to the Far East, when the female flight attendants brought him peeled and sugared oranges and I suspect other treats once they'd landed. He'd give the impression he had his pick of the flying harem. The Sultan of the Skies.'

Swift laughed. 'That's a good description.'

'I'm not that quick witted. I pinched it from someone else who worked here. I must have heard Greg tell that story a hundred times.'

'Had he fallen out with anyone else apart from Cairns?'

She rubbed her chin. 'There was some trouble here with a colleague a while before he died. There was a lot of bad feeling but I don't know all the details and I don't think it's my place to talk about it. I like my job and I don't want to overstep the mark.'

'Who could tell me?'

'I think it would have to be Silvio Horvat. Yes, you'd best contact him. He's away in Croatia at the moment but I can give you his email.'

'Is he a pilot?'

'Flies his own small jet. He has a home in Split and he travels back and forth.'

'Greg died in one of the planes. Any idea why he would have been in a hangar in the early hours of the morning?'

She raised an eyebrow. 'All the instructors have keys to the hangars. I assume he might have gone there to meet a lady friend. Although there's not much room in a Piper for terrestrial acrobatics.'

'Could I see the hangar where Greg died?'

'I don't see why not.' She glanced at her watch. 'I'll show you — then I have to go and mark some exam papers. We can go out via the veranda.'

She led him to one of the metal frame hangars with a dome-shaped roof that he'd seen earlier. There was no one else around. Inside were five small planes. On a wall just by the door were two wooden shelves. The top one held a carved wooden image of the Buddha. A tiny brass bell, a bowl of water, two red candles, flower petals, slices of apple and incense cones had been placed on the lower shelf.

'That's Niran's shrine,' Holly said, as she saw Swift examining it. 'He's one of our engineers. He likes to meditate twice a day.' She pointed to the second plane on the left of the hangar. It was red and blue with red stripes on the tail. 'That's the plane Greg died in. We took it out of service for a while but it's been back in use since. Greg liked it and flew many hours in it. It's the one he taught Cairns in. You can look in it if you want.'

Swift climbed up and glanced inside. It was a warm, snug space with a couple of headsets lying on the dashboard. It would be hard to get away from someone who suddenly lashed out at you, even if you had the presence of mind. He jumped back down. Holly was standing at the hangar door, arms folded, staring across the airfield.

'Do you know the details of how Greg died — apart from the stabbing?' he asked her.

She didn't turn towards him, just nodded. 'You mean the card, the safety pin and salt water. Yep. I attended the inquest with Silvio. He thought we should. Horrible. None of it made any sense.'

'Any idea why someone would have wanted him to cry, as in "so many tears"?'

'Regret? Remorse? Sadness? That's what I'd typically mean if I said that.' She rubbed her arms. 'I'd better get marking or I'll have students complaining about *me*.'

Swift returned to the bar, ordered a beer and sat making notes. Roscoe had been a show off. Maybe on the night he'd died, he'd taken someone to the plane to boast about his flying skills. If his companion had been a woman, perhaps he'd planned to have sex with her after dazzling her with his Sultan of the Skies stories. He might have intended to escort her to the same bushes where he'd romanced Holly. He'd missed his opportunity according to what Fitz Blackmore had said about lack of sexual activity.

Swift emailed Silvio Horvat, then wandered on to the veranda and watched a couple of planes taking off and landing. The group of old men had abandoned their cards and chatted on, talking animatedly of altitudes, wind speeds and engine troubles, their cigars glowing red in the falling dusk.

Chapter 4

Chand Malla, a friend of Nora's from the Met, was moving in to the top floor flat where Cedric used to live. Swift had had the flat redecorated after his friend died, thinking that Ruth and Branna might move in. But then that plan had caused a major rift with Nora and when a young man had been murdered up there, Ruth had understandably vetoed the idea.

Chand was a detective sergeant who worked with covert operations in specialist crime. He was keen to leave his parents' home in Hounslow. He loved his family but he needed space, independence and to stop his mother worrying about him and waiting up through the night until he came home.

'I love my mum, but she wants to debrief me and feed me dal and samosas at four in the morning when all I want to do is get my head down,' he'd told Swift when he came to look at the rooms. 'I can't take the fussing any more. I'm thirty. Time to make a stand.'

Swift had nodded understandingly although he wouldn't have minded having his own mother still around. She hadn't been a fusser. He was like her by nature:

observant, reflective, dispassionate — perhaps a little too dispassionate. Sometimes he felt a stab of jealousy when friends took their mothers for granted. Chand knew about the murder and was unfazed by it. He'd loved the flat and the below-the-market 'mates rates' that Swift was charging for it. It suited Swift to have someone living there, and a person who came with a solid reputation.

Nora and Swift had helped Chand when he arrived with his meagre collection of boxes in the back of his car on a Saturday morning. Swift moved more slowly than usual. It was one of the days when he'd woken up with aching joints and a sense of fatigue.

'You travel light,' he said.

Chand shook his head. 'This is just a small amount of my stuff. My mother's behaving as if I've emigrated to New Zealand. There have been tears and handwringing, so I'm going to smuggle things out bit by bit. My sister will bring some more while mum's at prayers.'

'Your very own covert operation,' Nora said, dusting her hands.

'Exactly. So I should be skilled at it. Except my mum is like Hounslow's branch of MI5 and MI6 combined.' He ruffled his sleek blue-black hair, which grew to a widow's peak at the centre of his forehead. He was a pleasant looking man with regular features and a mild, unassuming manner, the kind of man who wouldn't stand out in a crowd, which may have drawn him to his specialism.

They left him to unpack and went down to Swift's flat where he made fish finger sandwiches for lunch in his galley kitchen. They were one of Nora's favourites, which she decorated with liberal quantities of Dijon mustard and tomato ketchup. The day was mild and bright, so they took their food out to the little garden and sat on the canvas swing seat. Nora shucked her shoes off and wriggled her toes through her thick, stripy socks.

'Isn't it amazing, being able to sit out in November?' she said. 'Fierce confusing weather, though. Freezing yesterday and now this.'

'Your plate looks like a Jackson Pollock painting,' Swift said, glancing at the swirls of yellow, red and khaki.

'Disgusting, isn't it?' She tucked in happily. She rarely cooked and preferred simple dishes with strong flavours. Her own kitchen was full of empty containers from the local Indian take away. She was wearing her off duty uniform of jeans, jumper and a body warmer. Her short hair was tousled and she yawned between mouthfuls. 'It's been a crap week with shed loads of hassle and not much sleep. I've spent hours investigating in a fierce-cold, shitty squat full of filth and used needles. It's good not to be at work and to be out in the air with you.'

He blew her a kiss. 'Fancy a row when we've eaten?'

'Great. Where shall we go?'

'I'll check the tides. I reckon we could go to Barnes and look at the wetland centre.'

'Sounds good. What's your new case about?'

He explained about Greg Roscoe's murder and the release of Paul Cairns.

'I remember Cairns,' she said. 'Embarrassing, that schoolboy error with the camera. A pin through Roscoe's penis? That's an interesting one. What with that and the card, I reckon it's a woman you're looking for. The murder seems to carry a meaning. I've always thought that if I ever committed a planned murder, I'd leave a signature. I can understand the satisfaction of that type of communication.'

Swift rocked the seat gently. 'Remind me not to get on the wrong side of you. I'll keep an open mind about the killer's gender but I agree about a message or meaning. I don't know much about Roscoe yet except that he was a womaniser with a healthy ego and a gambling habit.'

'Sounds like there might be rich pickings.'

His phone pinged with a text. 'It's Ruth,' he said, scanning it. 'We have an appointment at the audiology clinic in two weeks, to start discussing cochlear implants for Branna.'

'Would that mean surgery?'

'Yes. It's a complex situation. That's why we need to look at the pros and cons, start the process of looking into them. They'd implant receivers under the skin behind her ears. They work with external parts like hearing aids and they digitise sound, provide a sensation of hearing. It's a difficult decision because hearing aids and signing are helping her and the implants might not work that well. If they do, they make her part of the hearing world and that's a massive thing for her. Surgeons advise against implants after the age of four, which is why we have to think it all through in good time. It's going to be a case of now or never.'

'But if Branna had them, would they make a big difference?'

'They could but they're not a "cure" and they might upset or confuse her.'

It was an issue that kept him awake at night. He and Ruth had been reading extensively on the controversial subject. He felt pushed and pulled in different directions. One the one hand, implants might boost Branna's hearing and confidence and open up her options to make decisions about speaking or signing. On the other, she could lose any remaining hearing if they didn't work well. They would have a major impact on her life and change her. In the end, he'd agreed with Ruth that all they could do was examine the possibility from all angles. They couldn't offer Branna a choice about it because of the age limit for having implants. They had to make the decision for her. It was a huge responsibility and at times seemed almost impossible. If the implants didn't work, they'd have put Branna through surgery for nothing.

'It's a hard one,' Nora said, squeezing his hand. 'I'm glad I don't have to make that kind of decision. You have to be as tough as old boots to be a parent. It's one of the reasons I don't want kids. I know I'm not brave enough. Talk away about it if you want to.'

'Thanks, but I won't just now. I'll tell you more when we've been to the clinic. That would help me to sort out all the angles.'

Chand opened the window upstairs and waved down to them, calling out that the peace and quiet was 'seventh heaven'.

'Does he know about the trumpet player next door?' Nora asked.

'His name's Andy Fanning. I did mention him, although the soundproofing means any noise is pretty subdued now.' Fanning had had a soundproofed loft conversion the previous year, to provide him with a practice space. Now and again, the muted tones of his playing drifted through. Swift liked it and enjoyed identifying tunes. 'It'll be reassuring to have Chand upstairs,' he said. 'The house has felt odd on my own and it seems wrong to have accommodation standing empty.'

'He's a lovely guy. What you see is what you get with Chand.'

'Apart from when he's operating undercover.'

'Of course. You'll have to behave yourself, you know, with him upstairs. I might have inveigled him in here on purpose to keep an eye on you and report back to me.' She pointed at him, and then tapped the side of her nose.

'What's that supposed to mean?'

She laughed and coughed on a crust of bread, patting her chest. 'Oh, you know, making sure you're not recycling old girlfriends behind my back.'

He swallowed his last chunk of fish. He thought they'd managed to put that behind them and was annoyed that she was raising it again. 'You never know when to leave things be, do you?' He spoke mildly enough but she picked up his irritation.

'And what's *that* supposed to mean?'

He could read the danger signs but he didn't care. He was tired and achy and he was fed up with her snide remarks. Just when things were going well, she had to throw in a spoiler. It usually happened when she was exhausted but still edgy and fired up from her work. He understood that tension but didn't want to be the butt of it. 'It means I don't find you amusing. Seems to me like you always need to have the upper hand, or think you have. You can never let the past stay in the past.'

She put her plate on the ground. 'Stop being so fiercely sensitive. It was just a joke, Ty.'

'I don't think it's funny. And you know what they say, there's no such thing as a joke. I think yours conceals hostility.'

She threw her hands up. 'Oh God, now you're getting all Freudian on me! I was having a laugh.'

'Yeah, if you say so.'

She folded her arms. 'Is my joke a problem because there's some truth in it? Freud said that about jokes too, didn't he? Should I look under the bed? Would I find Bella . . . or maybe even Ruth or some other woman I've not yet heard of?'

He slammed a foot against the ground, halting the seat abruptly. 'Just stop there, Nora. Why do you do this?'

'Me? You're the one who started arguing the toss.'

He stood, picking up her plate. 'I'm not continuing the conversation. In case you misheard, I invited you for a *row*, not a *row*. If you want a fight, find someone else. I'm going to make coffee.'

He had stacked the dishwasher and was pouring coffee when she came into the kitchen, stood next to him, squeezed his arm and then steepled her hands together as if in prayer.

'Pax?' she asked. 'I didn't mean to upset you. I shouldn't let the week's junk spill into time with you. You know me and my fierce big mouth. A *row* in a boat would be amazing.'

Her grey-green eyes were tired and soft looking. He could never stay cross with her for long. 'Pax. Let's drink this and get ready. I'll check the tides and weather.'

* * *

Ashleigh Grafton's house had no doorbell, but a knocker in the shape of a leaping hare. Swift stepped into the narrow porch, rapped on it and saw the blue window blinds stir. It was a sizeable detached house on a small estate with a sweep of immaculate grass and neat flowerbeds to one side of the drive. The gravel border below the windows was decorated with shells, pebbles and pieces of carefully arranged driftwood. Two carriage lamps illuminated a sign in ornate gold lettering on grey slate. It told him the house was called The Old Post Office. It wasn't old and clearly had never been used to sell stamps or sort mail. It was 6 p.m. and car headlights swept the road. Commuters were returning home with a click of car doors and the hum of opening garages. 'Come around six. My husband will want to be with me,' Ashleigh had said when he'd phoned.

A well-built man in his late fifties with a military looking moustache opened the door. He was extremely tall — at least six feet six, Swift reckoned. He was over six foot himself and rarely had to look up at anyone. He introduced himself and the man nodded.

'I'm Barry Grafton. Come through. We're having tea in the gazebo, as it's such a mild evening. Extraordinary for November but the forecast says we'll suffer for it soon.'

A decorative white and navy blue lifebuoy hung on the wall inside the front door: *Welcome Aboard!* Swift followed Grafton down a wide, warm hallway. He glanced into the living room and saw that it was immaculate and clinical looking. Nothing out of place. They passed through a handsome kitchen that smelled of chicken and garlic. There were wall signs saying *To the Beach* and framed prints of sunny seaside scenes, rock pools and starfish. Patio doors led on to an AstroTurf lawn brightly lit by bevelled glass lanterns. More lights came on as they exited the doors, picking out glazed pottery tubs of miniature roses. Swift brushed his hand against a petal to check that they were real. The garden wasn't large and the octagonal wooden gazebo dwarfed the space. There was a gaily painted, blue and yellow wooden boat hanging over the door, bearing the refrain: *Oh, we do like to be beside the seaside!*

Ashleigh Grafton was sitting at a round marble table inside the gazebo with her feet up on a padded stool. A huge bunch of mixed flowers stood in a ceramic jardinière beside her. Swift's first impression was of someone posed, shiny and expensive, as if she was featuring in a colour supplement. She was exceptionally pretty with delicate features, long glossy black hair and lustrous skin and eyes. Her lipstick was a pearly pink, matching her false nails. She wore a woollen lemon dress with lace insets in the arms and bits of white ribbon on the seams and skirt. A cream cardigan was draped around her shoulders. She was as well-groomed as the garden. She was also heavily pregnant, one hand resting on the mound of her stomach.

'Have a seat,' she said. 'Do you want tea?'

'Please. Thanks for seeing me.'

She didn't reply and poured tea from a china pot, adding a slice of lemon. The nautical theme had been continued in the gazebo, with blue and white cushions and curtains patterned with anchors, a fishing net draped across the ceiling, a wooden plank on the wall saying *Sandy Toes & Salty Kisses,* a collage of crab shells, lighthouse shaped candle holders on shelves and a mobile of china seagulls turning gently behind Ashleigh's head. The Old Post Office meets the seaside, Swift thought. The pyramid-shaped heater standing near him threw out a steady warmth and made the gazebo a snug space in the winter evening.

Ashleigh handed him his tea. 'It's Earl Grey,' she said. 'I hope you like it.' Her tone indicated that she didn't care either way.

Her husband pulled a chair close beside her and placed his arm around her back. She looked at him and wrinkled her nose.

'Let's get down to it,' Grafton said. 'We like our evenings together and we'd rather relax and enjoy it. Ashleigh says that Pat Roscoe has got you asking questions about Greg.' He was as carefully presented as his wife, in sleek grey chinos and a blue linen shirt teamed with a grey cashmere sweater. He smiled frequently as he talked but there was no pleasure behind the smile.

Swift nodded. 'That's right. She wants to know what happened to her son.'

'Bit late for that, isn't it?' Grafton said. 'I mean, if the police had no luck, how likely is it that you can find out who did it?'

'I suppose for family, it's never too late. I can try — see if there's anything the police missed. Do you know of anyone who wanted to harm Greg?'

'Yes, *I* did,' Ashleigh said, tartly. 'I used to dream about murdering him. I didn't, though. I wouldn't have deprived Havana of her dad.'

He hadn't expected her to be so direct. Most people close to a victim put up some pretence of sadness where murder was concerned. Her husband patted her hand but seemed unsurprised by her comment.

'Were you angry with him because he had affairs?'

'Of course I was. What woman wants an unfaithful husband?'

Swift nodded. 'These affairs . . . did you know any of the women he was seeing? I'm thinking of shortly before he died.'

She took another slice of lemon and slid it into her cup. Despite the relaxed setting, there was a tension in the way she held herself and her movements looked awkward. 'No. I didn't want to know. I knew about Holly Armstrong because someone kindly slipped a note through my door, telling me about her. People love to share bad news. I was eighteen, naive and pregnant with Havana when I married Greg. I believed him when he told me I was *special*.' She made a moue of distaste as she said the word. 'I soon found out I wasn't. He was carrying on with some airline sales rep before Havana was even born. He came back from a long-haul trip to Tasmania and he'd brought free in-flight chocolate for me and Givenchy perfume for her. I looked in his flight bag and found a little card from *Laura*, thanking him for it and saying she'd wear it next time they met up. It had smiley faces drawn on it.' Ashleigh raised her shoulders and dropped them. 'What you need to understand about Greg is that he was a performer. He had to put on an act wherever he went and he liked an appreciative audience. Preferably female.'

That sounded accurate, from the other things he'd been told. 'You made him give up international flying to try and stop the affairs?'

'I was sick of picking up the phone and the other person ringing off. Sick of seeing him out of the corner of my eye, checking his emails and texts. Sick of finding little love notes with the smiley faces and kisses, smelling other women on him, wondering why he was delayed hundreds of miles away yet again.' She shook her head. 'Look, this is stuff I don't want to remember.'

'Yes, what's the point of going over this?' Grafton took her hand, linking her fingers through his. 'It's distressing and the police already have the information. My wife is almost eight months pregnant and needs peace and quiet. I don't appreciate you raking over the past.'

Swift adopted his mildest tone. 'I haven't come to cause any upset. I need to get to know Greg and I can only do that by talking to people who were close to him.'

Ashleigh looked at her husband and sighed deeply. He returned her look adoringly, the crow's feet crinkling around his eyes. Swift reckoned there had to be more than twenty-five years between them. He drank some tea. It tasted soapy and he remembered that he disliked Earl Grey.

The gate at the end of the garden was flung open and he turned as a tiny woman in high heels tottered through, calling, 'Hi Ash, Baz! Lovely evening for the time of year!' and crossed to the gazebo. Grafton stood courteously as she approached, but Swift thought he looked less than pleased to see her.

'Hi Jude! Come and sit beside me!' Ashleigh beamed at her friend and plumped the cushion on the chair next to her. 'Mr Swift, this is Jude Chamberlain, my bestie.'

Jude enveloped Ashleigh in a hug and then folded herself down in a quick movement and smiled at Swift. She wore a vivid red skirt and fluffy white sweater. Her streaked hazel and honey hair was pulled back in a chignon and her face was coated in heavy makeup. Her bright round eyes reminded him of a seal's. 'Lovely to meet you,' she said in a high-pitched voice, showing tiny white teeth, 'but I hope you're not grilling my friend about that awful man she was married to.'

'I don't think so,' Swift answered. 'I always think light poaching is better than grilling.'

Jude looked at him blankly, then shrugged, turning her mouth down.

'Want some tea, sweetie or would you prefer something bubbly?' Ashleigh asked, winking.

Jude laughed. 'Bubbly, of course. You know me!'

Ashleigh turned to her husband. 'Could you fetch a bottle, darling?'

'Of course.' Grafton's knee clicked loudly as he stood and headed to the kitchen.

Jude took Ashleigh's hand and rubbed it. 'You okay today? No dizziness?'

'I've been fine, just taking it easy.'

'Good. I got you some magazines, but I was in such a rush I left them at work. I'll pop them over tomorrow.'

'You're a darling. How was work?'

'Really busy. Don was off sick so I had double trouble and a man found that his new prescription wasn't right so, you know . . . drama and apologies. That locum optician is useless. I've literally lost count of the number of times he's got things wrong.'

'Jude is a technician at the opticians where I used to work,' Ashleigh explained to Swift.

'You've known each other a long time then?'

'We go way back. We literally lived next door to each other when we were little,' Jude said. 'Now our gardens back on to each other. We've been besties since we were toddlers. Pretty much see each other every day.'

There was a fuss as Grafton came back with a bottle of Prosecco and a champagne flute on a tray. He opened the bottle with a flourish, pouring the frothing drink into the glass and placing it in front of Jude.

'There we are, Madame,' he said.

'Ooh, Baz, how lovely! You know how to treat a girl. Can't wait for you to be able to join me again, Ash. Bottle of bubbly, feet up, all the goss.'

Ashleigh looked wistfully at the Prosecco as Grafton cleared his throat.

'Ashleigh will be concentrating on the baby for a while, I'm sure. Won't you darling? It's not a good idea to have alcohol while you're breast feeding.'

Ashleigh nodded in agreement.

Jude shot him a look and sipped her drink. 'You bottle fed Havana, didn't you, Ash?'

'Yes. It was too painful trying to feed her myself and I panicked. And of course, Greg was no help. In fact, he said he'd rather I didn't feed Havana myself in case it made my breasts droop.'

'He was always undermining you,' Jude sniffed.

'I know. Well, I'm going to do it right this time, give baby the best of starts. We can still have the goss without the bubbly.' Ashleigh puckered a kiss at her friend who blew one back.

Swift decided it was time to interrupt the love in. 'I understand that you married again soon after Greg's death,' he said neutrally.

'What's that got to do with anything?' Grafton asked, sitting up straight.

'I don't know. It's just an observation.'

'I'm a lucky woman,' Ashleigh said. 'I met Barry through my work soon after Greg died. It was love at first sight. We deserved to be happy so we married. Now we have our little miracle on the way. Our little boy. A Christmas baby. Barry's always wanted a son, haven't you darling? And he's going to be here for his child, a devoted father. Not like Greg who just dumped all the responsibility onto me.'

Her husband kissed the top of her head. 'I'm glad I needed to have my eyes tested and came into the optician that day,' he said fondly. 'I'm with you every step of the way.'

Ashleigh stretched and smiled complacently at Swift as if to say, *now I've got a man who really loves me.* She brushed the seagull mobile with her fingertips, setting it dancing and the clinking distracted him.

'Were you in the navy?' Swift asked Grafton. That could explain all the marine references so far inland.

Jude tittered and refilled her glass. She shifted onto the edge of her chair, so that she was nearer Ashleigh and straightened one of the ribbons on her friend's dress.

Grafton's eyebrows shot up. 'I run a landscape gardening business. What's with that question?'

'Ignore me.' Swift smiled at Ashleigh. 'Did your husband seem troubled about anything before he died?'

'My *first* husband. I have a husband. He's here beside me.'

'Of course. That's what I meant.'

'No. Greg didn't say anything about being worried. He'd been complaining about Paul Cairns causing problems so I thought they'd got the right person when they pulled him in.'

'It must worry you that whoever attacked Greg is still free and unpunished.'

She stared at him, a long cold look. 'I don't think about it. There's nothing I can do. It's not my fault if the police were incompetent.'

'It was such a savage attack. The card left pinned to Greg's penis and the salt water on his eyes. What could he have done to anyone to invite that cruelty?'

'Don't ask me. I've no idea.'

'Maybe cruelty was being repaid with cruelty,' Jude suggested, draining her glass again.

Swift considered her. 'You mean like an eye for an eye?'

'I suppose. Just a thought. He'd certainly got someone very angry. It was awful having to listen to those details at the inquest.'

Ashleigh topped up her friend's glass. 'Jude stayed with me all through that dreadful time. The endless police questions and then the coroner.'

Jude was getting quite tipsy by now. She slurred, 'that's what besties are for. Literally always there to hold your hand.'

'Presumably Havana didn't attend the inquest?'

'No, of course not. She's far too young,' Ashleigh said, impatiently.

'Does she know those nasty details about her father's death?'

'Yes. Some idiot put them on WhatsApp. That's when she stopped eating — when she found out about that.' Ashleigh shook her hair. 'I try not to think about it. I want to focus on new life and the future.' She placed both hands on her stomach.

'Your brother-in-law didn't mention that you were pregnant.'

'That's because he doesn't know.'

'Mrs Roscoe — Greg's mother — doesn't know either?'

'That woman! I want nothing to do with her. It's none of her business. This baby's no blood relation of hers, thank goodness. She sat back and condoned Greg's behaviour. She was the worst kind of mother, the sort who believes that her boy can do no wrong. And as for her prejudice towards me . . . I used to hear her refer to me as Greg's *oriental* wife. We all know what that meant. She didn't like the fact that my grandmother was Singapore Malaysian.'

'I couldn't stand her and the way she went on about Greg, as if he was some kind of saint,' Jude added.

Ashleigh waved a hand. 'I've cut them out of my life. I don't need reminders of Greg and what he put me through. I want to concentrate on being happy at last.' She took a sip of tea.

'Is there anything else?' Grafton sounded snappy. He adjusted the cushion behind his wife's back.

'Can you tell me what your *first* husband was doing during the day before he died?'

'I didn't see much of him, as per usual. He went out in the morning in the car. Just said he was off out for bits and pieces. He was giving flying lessons in the afternoon. He came home about five, had a bite to eat and a shower and said he had a meeting at the airfield. Next thing I knew, the police were at the door early the next morning.'

'You didn't notice that he hadn't come home?'

She glared at him. 'No. Sometimes if it was very late he slept in the spare room. He liked to drink brandy at the flying club and I couldn't stand the fumes. So I was woken up by the police making an awful noise. Havana went into hysterics. I had to call the emergency doctor.' She made it sound as if the whole business had been a terrible nuisance.

Swift wondered what Havana's role was in this new family. Presumably, she was a constant reminder of her father. There had been no sound from the house, no sign of the mess caused by a teenager and no mention of her. 'I would like to speak to your daughter.'

Ashleigh stiffened. 'Why?'

'I understand that she was close to her father. She might recall something.'

'She's not here,' Grafton said curtly.

'I could come back.'

Ashleigh put a hand to her head and rubbed her left temple. 'Havana's staying at a friend's at the moment. She's made my life a complete misery. In fact, she's been a bitch to me since Greg died. And she's been so horrible to Barry. She actually told me that she hoped my brat died. My own daughter said that to me! It felt like she was cursing me. You'd think she'd be excited about having a little brother and help me out but no . . . too much to expect.'

'Now, now, darling,' Grafton murmured, 'don't think about that. Havana didn't mean it. Teenagers can be awful monsters and say these random, hurtful things.' He didn't sound convinced.

Jude muttered something under her breath. Grafton dropped a kiss on the inside of his wife's wrist.

'That's sweet of you Barry but sometimes I wonder, and I think she did mean all of the rotten things she said. It's been . . . she's been so difficult . . . it's so awful . . . I've been at my wits end . . .' Ashleigh started sobbing. She slumped forwards, burying her face in her hands.

Jude immediately threw her arms around her friend, making shushing noises and stroking her hair.

Grafton exhaled heavily and stood, glaring at Jude's bent head. 'That's it, Mr Swift. You have to go now. I'm not having this.' He bent down and rubbed Ashleigh's neck, although it was difficult for him to reach her through Jude's embrace. 'Are you okay, darling? Come on, don't get upset. It's not good for you and the baby. We don't want your blood pressure going up. Practice your breathing. Remember what the midwife advised.'

'Yes,' Jude urged, 'just breathe, Ash. You'll be okay. Jude's here. Jude's always here.'

Ashleigh nodded and ran her fingers under her eyes. She snatched a cushion from a chair and held it to her face. The movement set the seagulls spinning again.

Grafton marched Swift to the front door and stood with folded arms.

'Could you let me know where Havana is staying?' Swift asked.

'Maybe. I don't know. That girl has caused us such trouble. I wouldn't have believed a child from a good home could be so badly behaved. I'll talk to my wife but I don't want her being distressed. She's had hypertension and she has to be careful with her health. I don't want you coming here again.'

Swift sat in his car, feeling dissatisfied. He thought he hadn't handled the meeting well or got much from it. He should have tried to see Ashleigh on her own. She'd turned the tears on readily and he wasn't sure he believed them. He reckoned there was a lot more that she could tell him. He reckoned too that Grafton must sometimes feel that his marriage was a bit crowded with the petite bestie, Jude, in the picture.

When he got home, he fetched cheese, biscuits and a glass of red wine and opened his laptop. Time for study.

He and Ruth were taking online courses in British Sign Language, ensuring that they completed the same levels simultaneously so that they could reinforce Branna's learning. There was an assessment at the end of each lesson, which involved watching a video and answering questions. He liked the way this kept track of his progress and helped him to revise or focus on areas he needed to work on. Tonight's lesson was on months and seasons. The sign for *Christmas* was first, which was crucial, given that the festivities weren't far off. He practised resting his primary hand — his right, on top of his left and then lifting it up while closing it into a fist. He spread some Camembert on a sesame seed cracker and moved on to the signs for the months of the year and *snow*, *windy*, *ice* and *stormy*. He finished with the sign of the day, the mime for taking a photo. Then he completed his assessment and received a certificate that he had passed, although he might care to revisit signing for *February*, *June* and *summer*. He emailed Ruth, telling her that he'd completed the level.

He took his wine to the window and stood watching the streetlights glowing through needles of rain. He wondered what the sign was for *bestie*.

Chapter 5

Swift was on the train to Blackheath when he saw he had an email from Oliver Sheridan. *Here we go*, he thought, opening it.

Just in case you were thinking that I've decided to let things slide, I wanted you to know I've taken action. I reckon you've been hoping I'd accepted my beating at the hands of you and your pals. No way! I've been talking to someone who's very interested in what I had to say about you and the way you muscled in on my dad. Someone who's on the side of the underdog and can create quite a bit of trouble for you. You might find you don't get so many people wanting your detective services once you're in the spotlight and it all goes public. Still, you've got my dad's money to keep you going so I won't feel too sorry for you.

Swift had no idea what Oliver was getting at. He assumed he'd find out in good time. It was possibly just a nasty, pointless communication to try to needle him and prolong the agony. He put his phone away and prepared to meet a grieving mother.

Pat Roscoe was a small, frail woman with a heavily seamed face and long white hair that straggled down her back. She was dressed in black trousers and jumper with a long grey cardigan. They drained all colour from her. The annexe that her eldest son had built for her was light and airy and smelled faintly of camphor. It was also very cold. The living room walls were lined with framed photos of Greg Roscoe, two young children, the Queen, Winston Churchill and of course the large colour photo of a smiling Jane Fonda with Greg beaming beside her like a cat who's been at the cream. Jeanie Roscoe had made coffee. She brought it to them on a tray with a plate of assorted biscuits before disappearing.

'Give me a shout if you need anything, Mum, and don't forget your tablets,' she said. She bent and felt the radiator. 'Have you turned the thermostat down again?'

'Leave it be,' Mrs Roscoe said tetchily. 'It's not that cold a day. I'll turn it on when I want it.' When Jeanie had gone, she looked at Swift and muttered under her breath, 'I can't get used to this central heating. It gets far too warm. I always had a gas fire.'

'It can be hard to get used to new things,' Swift said neutrally, deciding to keep his jacket zipped.

She nodded, his answer seeming to satisfy her. She sat in a recliner chair covered in a knobbly oatmeal fabric and twisted the beads of a jade necklace. It was the only bright thing about her.

'Greg gave me this for my seventieth,' she told Swift. 'It's Burmese, but he got it at a jewellery fair in Hong Kong.'

'It's very pretty.'

'He had an eye for quality. Pity that didn't extend to his wives.'

'You didn't get on with them?'

She frowned. 'He was a bloody fool with women. Too gullible and soft hearted. They were all after his money. Sam, the first one, was a flighty piece, just out of school. A beautician. She got Greg to pay for boob implants.' She made a motion with her hands, indicating large breasts. 'They cost him a fortune at some private clinic. Then after a year she told him she wanted a divorce and she walked away smiling with her new chest and a nice settlement. Yvette, the second wife, was a God-botherer, always clutching her rosary beads and going to church. She turned his son against him. Ashleigh's always been a stuck up cow with notions. She wore Greg into the ground, wanting new things for the house. Treated him as if he was one of those cash machines in a wall. Now she's sitting pretty with the house and his pension and a new husband. Greg was hardly cold in his coffin before she got married again. She did all right for herself and there's my poor son, dead in the ground and no one's paid for it.' Her hands moved constantly, fingers fidgeting with her trouser seams and necklace.

'I'm sorry about your son. That's why I'm here. To see if I can find out who caused his death.'

Tears filled her eyes. 'Please, please help me. No one else can. You look kind. I need to know who stabbed my Greg. Then I can go to my own grave with some peace of mind. I'll be happy to die if I know someone's paid a price for taking him away from me.' She leaned forward and grabbed his hand in light, bony fingers.

He nodded. 'I'll do my best.'

'See, on the cabinet there,' she said. 'Those are some of the things I treasure.'

It was a little monument to her dead son. A collection of objects placed in front of a large photo of him: his airline ID and airside pass, his passport, half a dozen airline lanyards and badges, a leather bound flight logbook, a flashlight and a checklist for a flight from Heathrow to Atlanta. Swift was reminded of the shrine to the Buddha at the airfield and thought that Mrs Roscoe probably conducted her own kind of daily meditation.

'I can see these mean a lot to you. You must have been very proud of Greg.'

'My boy . . . my lovely boy. I'm all alone in the world, you see,' she whispered. 'I have grandchildren but I never see them. I never thought it would come to this.'

'But you have Niall and Jeanie. This is a lovely home.' He could see, though, that she felt alone and that grief haunted her.

'Oh, they do what they can. But it's not the same any more. This isn't my home, no matter how much they say it is. I liked my old place. I knew where everything was there. I'd known the neighbours for more than fifty years. I don't see a soul in this street — they're all working. Jeanie's nice enough but she tries to boss me about.' She shook her head sadly. 'Greg was the only one who understood me. We had a special bond from when he was a baby. We shared our troubles.' She wept quietly, taking a hanky from her sleeve.

He waited a moment and looked at Jane Fonda's warm eyes. 'Have some coffee, Mrs Roscoe. It would help me if you could tell me about Greg. I can see how much he meant to you. You can describe what he was like, the troubles he had. Can you do that?'

He handed her a mug of coffee and she took it and drank. She dabbed her eyes and sniffed.

'I never used to be the crying kind. Never had time to cry — I was too busy working and making a home. There was one time I held down three different cleaning jobs to make sure my boys had a good life. Colin, my husband, died after an accident, you see. He fell from scaffolding at work. They were building an office block in Bromley.'

'Yes, Niall told me.'

'I didn't get any compensation. They said that the accident was Col's fault because he cut corners, jumped from one level of scaffolding to another instead of using the ladder. So I was the breadwinner. Well, you do what you have to and no way was I going on the social.'

He saw how lined her hands were and sensed a deep exhaustion in her. 'I think you've had to be a brave woman. Can you be brave now and talk to me?'

She gave a weak smile. 'I'll do my best. I owe it to Greg. When I'm feeling at my lowest I remind myself what Mr Churchill said.'

'I can see he's your hero. What did he say?'

'He was my dad's hero first. I grew up with his sayings. He said, "when you are going through hell, keep going." I said that to Greg when he was upset because he couldn't see Axel.'

'Good advice. I'll have to remember it.'

There was a silence while she finished her drink. She seemed lost in thought.

'What happened to Sam, Greg's first wife?' Swift prompted.

'She died in a car accident years ago. She always drove too fast. Fast and flighty, that was Sam.'

Two wives left, then. 'So why did Greg lose touch with his son?'

'That was Yvette's doing. Axel's mother. Pure nastiness and revenge. She rowed with Greg over the divorce settlement. She wanted the house but she took a wadge of money in the end. She told Axel awful lies about his father and turned him against him.'

'What kinds of lies?'

'Oh, dreadful things about Greg being cruel and unfaithful. All exaggeration. She was a horrible woman, always going on about how much she missed Sardinia, where she was from and that English people were cold and unwelcoming. She wanted to go back to Sardinia. That's what it was all about and she was determined that Greg's money would set her up there. Good riddance to *her* but of course she took my grandson with her. I loved little Axel. He was a mischief. All I've got now is his photo.' She gestured to a picture on the wall, of a dark haired boy with a huge grin.

'Is Havana the girl in the photo next to Axel?'

'That's right. Such different personalities, chalk and cheese.'

'Are Yvette and Axel in Sardinia now?'

'I suppose so, but I've no idea. She was from — I can't remember the place. Somewhere near the capital city.'

'It's Cagliari.'

'That's it. That's how Greg met her. She was working on a ticket desk at Cagliari airport and she caught his eye. Those kinds of women are always on the lookout for pilots. They see a meal ticket and she wasn't wrong, was she? I don't even get a Christmas card from Axel. At least Havana sends me one. I don't suppose her mother knows or she'd put a stop to it.' She took two pills from a bottle and swallowed them. 'I always hoped Greg would meet a nice, homely girl. Someone who'd support him and be there for him when he got back from his work.'

Hardly Greg's type, from what I've heard about him and his choice of wives, Swift thought. The chill of the room was creeping into him and his nose was getting cold. 'You mean someone like Jeanie?' he asked.

'I suppose, yes. She's a good wife to Niall, I have to hand it to her. Mind you, she only lets him have pudding twice a week, says he needs to watch his cholesterol. She makes him eat fruit. I don't hold with that. A man needs a bit of a treat after dinner. I always gave my boys a pudding.'

Swift decided not to go there. 'You said that you and Greg shared your troubles. What was troubling him?'

'Well . . . let me think . . . it's hard to remember some of the things. It was usually his marriage problems. Then he had a run in with some man at Cornford airfield.'

'Paul Cairns?'

'No, not him. He did talk about him being a nuisance but it was someone else. There was a lot of kerfuffle. Greg had high standards, you see. I think it was someone who worked there. And he had problems with a business he'd set up.'

'What was that?'

'I can't remember. It was a while back. He used to tell me these things when we went out to restaurants. He always took me to the best places, you know, top notch. I didn't always understand the menu. There was stuff I'd never heard of. The food was lovely, although you never got enough. Bits and pieces with drizzles of this and that on slabs of slate and wooden boards. And the prices! When I was young, foraging meant you were starving. It was often noisy and I couldn't always hear him properly.' She looked down at her necklace, running the beads between her fingers. 'I feel as if I've lost too many people. Greg and now my two grandchildren gone from my life. The days seem empty. There's nothing to live for, really.'

'I don't think Churchill would approve of you saying that,' he told her gently.

'No, I don't suppose he would.'

'And your grandchildren might be in touch again. You never know. Life changes. People change.'

She looked at him hopefully. 'You've got nice eyes. Honest looking. If you talk to Axel or Havana, can you ask them to ring me? Or to write. I worry about them both and I don't know what's happening to them.'

'If I see them, I'll tell them you'd like to hear from them.'

She brightened a little at that. He thought he'd have to tread carefully with this fragile woman because she would cling on to any hope offered.

'Let me show you Greg's lovely uniform,' she said. 'He looked so fine in it.'

She led the way into her small bedroom and opened the wardrobe, taking out the dark blue uniform and hanging it on the door. Swift admired it as she pointed out the stripes on the arms and the airline crest above the pocket.

'He missed wearing this,' she said. 'He was so talented and good at his job. Ashleigh made him take that poky job at Cornford because she was jealous of him going abroad all the time. He told me how she used to moan when he got back. He'd be tired out and she'd go on about how she was stuck there on her own with Havana. Well, if you have a baby you've got to expect to look after it and Greg had to earn the money. Mind, I always thought Ashleigh got pregnant on purpose, so Greg would have to marry her. She used to wear him down saying she was lonely but Greg reckoned she was hardly ever on her own because that friend of hers was always hanging around there — that Jude. Greg said she was like a limpet. She didn't like Greg and was always talking him down to Ashleigh. In the end, Greg gave in and stopped international flying. I know that broke his heart. He put on a good show and pretended he liked it but he was never happy at the airfield. His talents were wasted.'

He got a photo of her son from her and left her nursing her grievances at ex-wives and brushing imaginary specks from the uniform jacket. He found Jeanie sitting in her living room, knitting a jumper in purple wool. It was deliciously warm in there and he touched his chilly hands to a radiator.

'Did you get on okay?' she asked.

'Yes, thanks. Mrs Roscoe mentioned that Greg had problems with a business he ran some time ago. Did you know anything about that?'

She put her knitting on her lap. 'No. I think he did dabble in ways of making extra cash. He earned well but he had too much alimony to pay. And he liked playing Poker, but lost more than he won. He tried to get Niall to put money into some timeshare scheme in Menorca about eight years ago. He refused.'

'Did you know that Havana isn't living at home at the moment?'

She shook her head. 'No, but then I wouldn't expect to know as there's been no contact. Where is she? She's only fourteen. She should be at home.'

'I'm not sure. Staying with a friend. I didn't say anything to Mrs Roscoe. I didn't want to upset her. Ashleigh's pregnant, too. Eight months.'

'Really! Well, I suppose the new husband wanted a child. What's he like?'

'Older than Ashleigh. Very attentive to his wife.'

'Well . . . but that can't be easy for Havana.'

'No. Maybe that's why she's living elsewhere. Mrs Roscoe is upset that she's lost contact with both her grandchildren.'

'Best to go softly-softly with her. She's very up and down. We've done what we can to keep in touch with Havana but the door was closed on us.' Jeanie held up her knitting and examined the stitches. 'How can Ashleigh not want her daughter at home with her? Niall and I couldn't have children. People like Greg and Ashleigh have them easily but they don't seem to cherish them. If I had a child, I'd keep them by me.'

It was said in a matter-of-fact way but he felt the pain.

'Mrs Roscoe showed me Greg's Captain's uniform. That cheered her up.'

Jeanie cast her eyes upwards. 'Hmm. Sometimes I go in there and she's sitting in the chair hugging the jacket. There are times when I think me and Niall could be lying dead in here and she wouldn't notice. Or care that much.'

* * *

'I don't know what to think,' Ruth said. 'It's so complex. I might contact some of the parents in the support group — see how they came to a decision.'

They had attended the audiology clinic with Branna to examine cochlear implants in more detail. The audiologist had recommended simultaneous implants in both ears if they decided that Branna should have the surgery. She would need a general anaesthetic and the operation would take up to six hours. There would then be follow up appointments, when the implants would be switched on and monitored. The audiologist advised that they should make a decision about implants in the next six months, so that careful planning with the support team could take place.

Afterwards, they had dropped Branna off at her nursery. Now they were sitting in a café, worrying at the knots of their problem.

Swift wasn't so sure about the usefulness of discussing the issue with other parents of deaf children. 'Sometimes I find that talking to people just clouds my thoughts and confuses me more. I think I'd rather read as much as I can and discuss it with you.'

Ruth sipped a mint tea. 'You have to work on it the best way for you. I find it helpful to discuss it with parents who have the same difficulties.'

'Branna's doing so well with her signing and language as she is. It's tempting not to meddle with her progress.'

'But what if she can do even better? What if implants would open life up for her so much more?'

Swift nodded. 'I know, I know.'

'Well, let's both investigate further and then talk again. Now, I've . . . I've . . . erm . . . got a couple of bits of news for you.'

'Oh yes?' She'd seemed on edge all morning. He'd put it down to the stress of attending the clinic.

'I made an offer on a two-bedroomed flat in Gospel Oak and it's going ahead.'

'Emlyn agreed to release money to you?' Ruth's husband, Emlyn Taylor, still lived in their former marital home in Brighton and she had been hoping that he would buy her out so that she could get a bigger home.

'Yes, that's all sorted. The flat's lovely. Ground floor with a small garden.'

'Sounds ideal. I'm glad you'll be more settled.'

'Emlyn's agreed to a divorce as well. I'm relieved. He seems calmer these days and he's accepted that I'm never going back to him.'

'Good.' Swift didn't want to get into any discussion about Taylor, the man who had caused disruption and grief in his life. He and Ruth had been engaged when she left him and married Taylor. After a few years, Taylor had developed a severe and rapid form of MS and Ruth had turned to Swift for help. Branna had been conceived on the one occasion when they slept together. She had been born prematurely, and then hearing loss had been detected. Taylor's MS caused him to have unpredictable outbursts and rages. He discovered that Ruth had been seeing Swift and conducted a vicious campaign of harassment against him through a petty criminal who had murdered Kris Jelen, Swift's partner at the time. Taylor had been found guilty of assisting a crime. Ruth had stayed with her husband despite his behaviour, feeling that she should be loyal, but her own health had deteriorated and she had left him, unable to deal with the stress and unwilling to expose Branna to his volatility. She'd been renting a flat in London and successfully re-establishing her career as an educational psychologist.

She hesitated. 'The other bit of news is I've met someone. It's early days but I like him a lot.'

That explained the lift in her shoulders and the glow in her eyes. He could recall a time when that glow had been for him but he pushed the thought away. 'Well, that's good. I'm pleased for you.' He meant it. He wanted her to be happy.

'Thanks, Ty. I wanted to tell you because Branna's met him and she might mention him to you. His name's Marcel Vaudin.'

'He's French?'

'He lives in Guernsey. He manages a higher education college.'

'How did you meet?'

'At an education conference here in London a couple of months ago.' She was smiling now, relaxed that she'd got it off her chest. 'Obviously, we can't see each other that often because of the distance. He's been flying over for weekends. I'm going to Guernsey with Branna at the beginning of December to stay with him for a couple of days. He has a house overlooking Fermain Bay. I've googled it and it looks beautiful. Branna should have a lovely time on the sandy beach, although she'll have to be well wrapped up.'

'I'm sure she will.' He felt a tingle of unease. He'd rather have heard that Ruth had met someone who lived close by in London. 'And Marcel gets on okay with Branna?'

'Absolutely. He doesn't have children but he's a natural with her and he knows some sign language. Branna enjoys teaching him some more.'

'And his house . . . he knows that she's a toddler who's into everything and he needs to put harmful stuff, bleach and such out of reach before she arrives? And has he got a stair gate?'

Ruth glared at him. Her tone was scathing. 'Yes, Ty, Marcel's aware of Branna's needs. Put it this way, he'll make sure his home is safe and she's not likely to see a corpse in one of his wardrobes.'

Swift took a breath. Ruth was referring to Ben Ramsay, the young man who had been murdered in Swift's top floor flat. Ruth had Branna in her arms when she found his body. It had been a traumatic evening.

'That's a bit harsh.'

'Well, for goodness sake, Ty. Stop being such a fusspot. Marcel's sensible. And so am I, by the way.'

'Okay, okay. Over-concerned father.'

'Yes, quite. By the way, I've talked to Marcel about the implants. He thinks they'd be a good idea. He's had experience of providing extra support for students with hearing problems so, you know, he has useful knowledge.'

Great, Swift thought. Some man I've never met is giving his opinions and influencing my daughter's life. Since she left Taylor, returned to London and regained good health, he and Ruth had been working well together concerning Branna's welfare. Now he sensed that the dynamic between them was changing yet again. It was inevitable. It was likely that Ruth would meet someone.

There was no point in feeling grumpy but he couldn't help wishing that life could be simpler.

* * *

Silvio Horvat had emailed Swift to say that he would be in Croatia for at least another fortnight. They agreed a time to skype. Swift settled himself at the desk in his basement office. For years, it had been the scruffiest part of the house, with damp patches, peeling gloss and that slight hint of decay that permeated most basements. He'd spent too long mourning the loss of his relationship with Ruth, adrift in a melancholy fog and neglecting his life and home. He'd spurred himself into action after Cedric's death and had it decorated. He was still getting used to the bright, gleaming paintwork and newly varnished floorboards. He liked to think that when clients called in, it now presented a more professional looking business. He took little care with his own appearance. His shirt collars and cuffs were often frayed and he forgot to replace missing buttons. Mary had once described his look as shabby chic. A smart office seemed a good idea as compensation and reassurance for the customer.

His email pinged and he saw that he'd had a message from Fitz Blackmore.

Hi Ron, you're in the news! Have a look at Camilla Finley in the Cornford Mail. Dirt digging!

He'd added a link. Swift clicked it and was looking at a Finley's Finds column.

Murder : Private Eye in Town

Tyrone Swift is a London based private detective. He's looking into the shocking murder of Greg Roscoe at Cornford airfield a while ago. He'll probably meet with Paul Cairns. He's the man who almost died in police custody and made a successful compensation claim.

Readers will know that I've been helping Paul tell his story. I'm working with him on his book, One Man's Voice. It will be published next spring.

Mr Swift used to work for the Met and Interpol and has an impressive track record of solving cases. So far, so squeaky clean… but there may be more to him than meets the eye!

Recently, Mr Swift was involved in a court case of his own with Oliver Sheridan. Mr Sheridan contested his father Cedric's will. Cedric was a frail, vulnerable pensioner. He lived in Mr Swift's home as his tenant. After Cedric died, it turned out that he'd left most of his money to Swift and a few other friends. Oliver believes that Swift influenced his father concerning his will.

The judge in court didn't agree with Oliver, who was deeply upset by the outcome of the case. He told me, 'I loved my dad and did my best for him. But in the end, Swift was in the house with him day and night. The flat Dad lived in was pretty basic for the rent he was paying and Swift had it done up to a high standard after he died. Swift has never liked me and tried to come between us. He threw me out once when I was visiting and I could see Dad was really upset. So I got frozen out. I couldn't prove he influenced Dad but I saw and heard things. I think the judge was on Swift's side because he's been in the police. His cousin is an Assistant Commissioner in the Met. These people always club together. They're like the secret state, powerful but invisible. I'm just a struggling artist and a nobody to them. Now I'm going to have to use the small amount that my dad did leave me to pay costs. It's hard when it's the little person against the Establishment."

That's what Paul Cairns found too. He was the little man, facing up to life's challenges, trying to manage his dyslexia and his diabetes. All he wanted to do was enjoy his hobby of flying. He was abused by the powers that be, despite being innocent of any crime. Now he's too traumatised to work and lives off savings and his compensation.

Maybe Mr Swift would like to tell me his side of the Sheridan story. I'm sure he's got a point of view he'd like to share. I hope so, I'm easy to contact and I like to be fair!

Keep hoping, Swift muttered, closing his email. That explained Oliver's message. He'd found a clever way of retaliating. Innuendo and ambiguity were stealthy, nasty weapons. Swift was angry at the implication that Cedric had been living in reduced circumstances when his flat had been just the way he liked it, well maintained and equipped. He thought of how Cedric would have hated his name being bandied about and the insinuation that he'd been a doddery old man, incapable of looking out for himself. Oliver was a nasty piece of work who had always sought to excuse his actions and bleat about how unfair the world was. Swift recalled that time when he'd made Oliver leave, after he'd threatened and bruised his father. The problem was that Cedric had never gone to the police about his son's behaviour and had never told his friends, apart from Milo, his closest companion. He'd have been too embarrassed. So it was always Oliver's word against Swift's. Swift had no intention of engaging in a slanging match with Oliver through the media. He could only hope that if he blanked the journalist, she'd lose interest and move on to better pickings.

As if he'd summoned her, an email from Camilla Finley popped up with her own link to the Cornford Mail.

Hi Mr Swift. I've mentioned you in an article today. Do have a read and contact me. I'd love to have a chat as you seem an interesting character, in more ways than one. There's lots to talk about and I'm happy to put your point of view across. Look forward to hearing from you ASAP. Remember: all publicity is good publicity!

Happy to try and get a public spat going between Oliver and me, Swift thought. He deleted the email, taking great pleasure as it flew to the bin.

He checked the time and dialled Silvio Horvat, who answered immediately. He had a crisp manner, curling hair and long sideburns that reminded Swift of a 1970s pop star whose name escaped him. His English was fluent with only the slightest trace of an accent.

'I'm sorry, of course, for Greg's mother,' Horvat said in a silky voice. 'I understand why she wants to ask questions. I haven't any answers for you.' The implication was that he didn't want to have to deal with this difficult history.

'You might be able to help, even if you don't think you can. I visited the airfield and spoke to Holly Armstrong. She told me that Greg had a dispute of some kind with a colleague. His mother referred to it as well although she couldn't recall any details.'

'Hmm. Holly emailed me. I'm not sure about discussing the incident. I don't need any bad publicity. Greg's murder brought enough of that. When I took Greg on, I thought I'd made an excellent appointment but ultimately, he caused me headaches.'

'I can see that Greg was both good and bad for business. Apart from having sex on the airfield and being murdered on the premises, what kind of headaches?'

There was a ghost of a smile from Horvat. 'You've been finding out what kind of man Greg was.'

Swift nodded. 'When a case is stale, like this one, I have to get to know the person. I need to establish if Greg had fallen out with anyone. Someone ended his life and that person had a reason. His mother is still in a very bad way. Meeting her was painful. Her loneliness was tangible.'

If emotional blackmail was necessary, Swift could dole it out.

Horvat rubbed his chin and leaned forward so that half his head vanished. When he sat back, he was pulling on a king size cigarette. He blew smoke down his nostrils. 'I need your assurance that whatever I tell you will be non-attributable.'

'Okay, I can give you that. If I use what you tell me, I shan't divulge where I got the information.'

'Right. Well, you seem shrewd and steady and you have a difficult job. I liked Greg although he tested my patience sometimes and I thought he was immature. Greg had flaws, including his penchant for gambling, but he was a good pilot. His private morals were questionable but he was zealous about flying and scrupulous about maintaining excellent standards. About five months before he died he came to me and told me that another flying instructor in the school had falsified his CV to get the job. The guy concerned, David Boyd, didn't have the flying hours needed to be teaching at that level.'

This sounded promising: someone who would hold a grudge at being exposed as a fraud. 'How did Greg find out?'

'He got suspicious because Boyd seemed unsure at times. He avoided taking lessons if they involved night flying or using instruments. Greg checked Boyd's logbook and reckoned he'd been falsifying the hours he'd flown. Sadly, it's not unknown. It's called *parker* hours. As in Parker pens — massaging the records to make it look as if you've flown more hours than you have.'

'What happened?'

'I called Boyd in and spoke to him with Greg there. He was angry and he blustered, said he must have made some errors. But he had nowhere to hide because Greg was thorough in his examination of Boyd's records and cross-referencing with his flights. I sacked Boyd on the spot and reported him to the authorities. I don't know what happened after that. Worst case scenario is he could have had his licence revoked.'

'Presumably Boyd wasn't a happy man?'

'He was furious. I never saw him again and nobody contacted me for a reference.'

'Furious enough to attack the man who'd found him out?'

'I suppose . . .' He inhaled on the cigarette again, this time tilting his head back and blowing a smoke ring. 'I did tell the police when they were asking questions. I presume they followed up and didn't have Boyd as a suspect. Thinking about it now, he might have wanted to harm Greg. These issues are so difficult. A lot of pilots tinker with their hours because it gives them an advantage when it comes to job applications. Low-level stuff doesn't matter so much and it shouldn't impact on a pilot's ability. But Boyd's fraudulent records went way beyond that and made him potentially dangerous. He was young, immature and extremely arrogant. He'd been to Harrow and he thought that his rich parents and his posh accent would open doors in life. I think he'd never been challenged before or failed to get what he wanted and he didn't like it. He was the type who'd probably cheated at school exams.'

'I can see why you had to get rid of him.'

Horvat lifted an ashtray, stubbed his cigarette out and steepled his fingers. 'Indeed. Look, I had to sack Boyd but I gave him a very generous payoff to go quietly. I got him to sign something saying he wouldn't make a fuss in return for the money. I didn't want his deceit to get out because it might have reflected badly on the flying school and I didn't need unhappy students queuing at my door wanting their fees back. These things can linger like a taint. Publicly, we told people that Boyd had to leave because of family problems. He lived in London so there was no local connection in Cornford to complicate matters.'

'Did Greg ever mention Boyd again?'

'No. He seemed happy with my handling of the situation. Then, of course, we had all the aggravation with Paul Cairns, so Boyd was soon forgotten.'

'You must have thought at times that Greg was more trouble than he was worth.'

'What do you mean?'

'Well, his actions regarding Boyd were right but caused you major problems. Then he was behaving unprofessionally with Holly. His high standards meant that he fell out with Cairns and that brought even more difficulties to your door.'

Horvat took a breath. 'No flies on you, Swift. I'll be honest with you. Greg's contract would have been up for renewal not long after he died. I had doubts about keeping him on. He was a talented, skilful pilot with a terrific track record in flying and he worked well with many students. But he could also get on the wrong side of people if they didn't do exactly as he said and he provoked problems. A couple of female students had complained about his manner, saying he was too critical and snappy. One young woman told me that Greg advised her to use a better deodorant as she suffered with nerves. I had to give her two free lessons to calm that situation. Then some women who flew with him found him flirty in a way that made them uncomfortable. No one ever complained about that but I was aware of comments in the bar now and again. I was beginning to think that I needed a CFI who was more rounded, more diplomatic and predictable.'

'Have you found one in Holly?'

'Frankly, yes. She has a pleasant manner with people as well as good flying skills. Holly's quiet but she's ambitious and determined. She may not have had as exciting a career as Greg but I don't have to sort out complaints regularly and we think the same way about the development of the airfield. She keeps things ticking over well when I'm not around.'

'You've been very helpful. Do you know of any other women Greg was seeing?'

'No. As long as it wasn't Holly or any woman involved with the airfield, I didn't want to know.'

'I've heard about Greg's gambling and poker playing. Do you think he owed anyone money?'

'No idea. Card games are allowed in the flying club but not gambling. Who knows what debts he might have had in his personal life?'

'Do you know where David Boyd lives?'

'I don't think I'm willing to give you the address we had for him. It was in Knightsbridge. I'm sure you can find him. Please make sure not to mention my name.'

'Fair enough. Before you go, do you have any ideas about the meaning of the card that was left at the murder scene, or the salt water poured over Roscoe's eyes?'

'I don't have a clue. Some statement of revenge? A pin through the genitals is vicious, anyway. But then, so is knifing a man repeatedly.'

Swift ended the call, made a coffee and googled David Boyd. He found an address and phone number. He tried the number but got an answerphone and decided not to leave a message. He saw that he'd had an email from Paul Cairns and read it with interest.

I hear that you're looking into who really topped Greg Roscoe. About time somebody did. I might be able to help you. Everyone knows I'm innocent and the judges said I'd been treated shockingly but some people will always point the finger until the real murderer is behind bars. I know people talk behind my back. I knew a lot about Roscoe. More than he liked. That's why he had it in for me. I'm in the bar at the airfield most nights. You can buy me a pint.

Swift suspected that Camilla Finley had encouraged Cairns to contact him. She might be hoping to glean some useful information. Still, he'd have wanted to see Cairns anyway and a meeting had to be worth the price of a drink.

Despite Roscoe's international connections, Swift couldn't help thinking that his death was connected to the airfield. His attacker had chosen a plane for the murder when the stabbing could have been carried out anywhere. He replied, saying that he'd be in the bar the following evening — then sent an email to Fitz Blackmore.

Did you come across a David Boyd when you were asking questions after Roscoe's death?

He put his feet up on the desk and thought about Pat Roscoe's shrine to her son and her inability to see any bad in him. Roscoe had been a talented but disagreeable man. He might have made any number of enemies. Swift hadn't yet met a woman who had liked Roscoe, despite his much-married status. Maybe Havana would have good things to say about her father. His thoughts drifted to his own daughter and he started to read another article about cochlear implants.

Chapter 6

Barry Grafton had left Swift a brief voicemail, with an address and phone number.

Havana is staying with the Tansley family for now. Her friend is Sally and the mother is called Grace. This is what she wanted and we thought it would be for the best. Gives us all a bit of breathing space.

It seemed that neither her mother nor stepfather was concerned enough to be present when a man they barely knew wanted to interview their child.

Swift was sitting in the kitchen of a Victorian terrace, drinking coffee with Grace Tansley, who was vaping through a cylindrical grey tube. The house backed on to the River Lea, on the other side of town from where the Graftons lived. The street was narrow, with speed bumps. The terraced houses would have been two up, two down artisans' cottages originally but many had been extended with dormers and windows in the roof space. Grace's house was opposite a tiny pub called The Bird in Hand. It had a small cottage garden at the front, bedraggled after cold rain and in need of a good weeding. Bright yellow aconites, winter cherry and saxifrage were trying their best in the waterlogged soil. Through the glass of the back door, Swift could see a vegetable plot bordered by timber planks and a piece of rough, grassy ground with a henhouse and half a dozen roaming hens.

The untidy kitchen was narrow and painted dark purple. An ancient looking tumble dryer rumbled, grinding alarmingly now and again while the washing machine next to it shuddered on a spin cycle. The central heating gurgled and clanked as if the system was full of air. There was a dark green Aga against one wall, surrounded by ochre and green tiles. A line of well-used saucepans hung from hooks in the ceiling above a wide noticeboard festooned with notes, postcards, lists and cartoons. Scuffed shoes and trainers were scattered on the muddy tiles by the back door next to bags of chicken feed and there was a large burn mark on the worktop under the kettle. Used dishes were piled in the sink. A large loaf of bread surrounded by crumbs and an open pot of jam with a knife sticking from it was in the middle of the melamine table. It was messy but homely and a very different environment to the Grafton's staged, ordered house. Perhaps that was why Havana chose to be here.

Swift gestured at the three deep shelves behind Grace. They held a jumble of jars and bottles of different shapes and sizes. Some were vivid pinks, greens and blues. A tall, fluted amber jar with a stopper reflected the late afternoon sun.

'Those look medicinal,' he said.

She nodded and turned to look at them. 'Yes, they are. I collect and sell vintage apothecary containers. Mainly ceramic jars, although I haven't been able to resist the odd glass one. A bit of an obsession, actually. I rootle about at flea markets and house sales. Always trying to make a few quid, me. I keep a few for myself if I like them or can't find a buyer.' She spoke rapidly through the vapour she blew out and blinked frequently as she talked. She was a small, dishevelled woman, dressed in worn grey jeans. Her short brown hair was in a zigzag parting. A white dove flying through a rainbow featured on the front of her oversized sweatshirt. 'I thought we should have a brief talk before you see Havana,' she continued. 'She's upstairs with Sally, allegedly doing homework. More likely watching makeup tutorials on YouTube.'

Music was playing loudly above, the deep thump of a bass guitar vibrating in time with the washing machine. Now and again, there was a burst of singing or girls whooping.

'That would help,' Swift said. 'Also, as she's a minor, I'd like you to stay with her while we speak.'

Grace nodded. 'I take it that her mother didn't ask to be here?' Her phone buzzed and she glanced at it and swiped the screen.

'No, and it was Mr Grafton who told me where to find you. How long has Havana been here?'

'Almost five months.' She hesitated. 'What do you know about her background?'

'Very little. I know that she was close to her father and had anorexia after he died. I assume her mother's remarriage can't have been easy for her.'

'That's an understatement. I've known Havana for a good while now. She and Sally are both keen swimmers. Well, they *were* but then they lost interest. Sally still goes occasionally. I presume it's adolescence working its strange ways. They're in the same year at school but they got to know each other through swimming competitions and became great friends. I was really pleased for Sally. We moved back here after my divorce and it wasn't easy for her to settle, so the close friendship helped a lot.'

'Did you know Greg Roscoe?'

'Well . . . sort of. At a distance. He was away a lot when we first met Havana — before he started working at the airfield. Ashleigh usually drove Havana to swimming or collected her from here.' She paused, and then carried on in a rush of words. 'I'm trying to tread carefully now.

All families are odd but Ashleigh struck me as peculiar. She was always distant. I did ask her in but she'd never have a coffee or stop to chat. Havana always came here to hang out. She never asked Sally back to her house. She said her mum liked things just so and didn't want people messing the place up.'

'A baby will cause mess,' Swift said.

Grace smiled, clicking off her e-cigarette. 'Yes, that's true. Perhaps Ashleigh will have help — a nanny or an au pair. I didn't see Havana for a while after her father died. When I did, I was shocked at how much weight she'd lost. She looked skeletal in her swimming costume.' Grace rubbed the skin on the back of a hand. 'Havana refused to attend her mother's wedding to Barry Grafton. I have to admit, I was a bit shocked at how quickly she found someone new. Ashleigh wanted Havana to be her bridesmaid. Havana turned up here, pale as death on the morning of the wedding, saying she didn't want to go home. As you can imagine, I was in a very difficult position. I phoned Ashleigh and they had a blazing row. Havana was sobbing so, in the end, Ashleigh agreed that she could stay here for a couple of days.' She stopped, glanced towards the door and held a hand up in a theatrical gesture. She got up, looked through into the hallway, and then closed it firmly. 'More coffee?'

'No thanks. I'm fine. I don't envy your position.' Although there was something in her manner that made him think she drew satisfaction from it.

'It is odd but I get on well with Havana. I'm very fond of her and I feel for her. I think she's unwanted now — pushed out. She's told me things . . . that her mother always resented her and the bond she had with her father. And her mother has a close friend, Jude. She's always round there and she didn't get on with Havana.'

'I've met Jude. She and Ashleigh call each other "besties".'

Grace rolled her eyes. 'I've always thought Jude is jealous of Havana. She likes to monopolise Ashleigh's time. They worked together in Mylod's opticians in the high street for years and then Jude would be in the house in the evenings. Havana said she felt like a spare part sometimes. And then when Barry moved in, she reckoned she was always in the way. Anyway, after the marriage, Havana started staying here regularly. I'd come home from work and find her with Sally. I used to joke that I'd got a lodger. I didn't mind. Sally's an only child and the company is good for her. I checked with Ashleigh, of course, and she said it was fine with her. She seemed relieved at Havana's absence. The thing is, you see . . . Havana would barely eat at home but when she came here, she would. Not much but small amounts. I'd leave soup and sandwiches out and she'd have some with Sally.' She gave a little satisfied smile.

'So this was a healthier place for her to be.'

'It's complex, of course, but . . . yes, in the sense that she seemed happier and had some appetite. I'm a receptionist at the health centre that Havana attends. Her doctor hasn't discussed her openly with me — he can't do that of course — but he's indicated that staying here has improved her wellbeing. Certainly, she's gained weight. I know that she still takes laxatives sometimes when she's eaten but she's making slow progress. She was terribly upset when she found out about her mother's pregnancy. She'd been eating better but she was struggling again and she collapsed at school. She came here after that and asked me if she could move in. I didn't know what to say. I have a spare room but . . . I knew I had to tread carefully. Then there's the issue of her eating disorder and it's a big responsibility.'

'Her mother doesn't seem too involved in that. It almost seems as if she's abandoned her daughter.'

Grace wriggled on her chair. 'I don't know Ashleigh well but I do know an optician at Mylod's. My friend told me that Ashleigh and Jude were always on a diet or detoxing. Ashleigh was fixated on foods that should and shouldn't be eaten together. That must have impacted on Havana. I remember that when she first visited us, she'd never drink with a meal because her mother had told her not to. Something about it interfering with nutrition. It might be true for all I know but I'm not sure it helps to place odd rules around eating for children. So I think Havana already had a complicated relationship with food and her father's death made it worse. I'm no expert on these matters but I've read stuff at the surgery about it. I'm so glad that Sally's always had a good appetite.'

Swift recalled Ashleigh's emotional outburst when he asked about Havana. 'It sounds as if having Havana at home makes her mother uncomfortable.'

'I certainly think that she avoided dealing with Havana's anorexia.' Grace's phone buzzed again and she picked it up, hesitated and then put it back down.

'Do you need to answer that?'

'Hmm? Oh, no, it's fine. Just a bit of a schedule coming together. So . . . where was I?'

Grace struck him as a bit scatty. There was a saucepan bubbling and splashing on the Aga but she took no notice of it. The rattling saucepan lid, the dryer and the washing machine formed a distracting percussion. 'Havana had asked to come and live here?' he prompted.

'That's right. I mulled it over and thought I didn't mind giving it a go. I'll be honest with you . . . it wasn't just out of the goodness of my heart. If Ashleigh and Barry agreed to pay me something towards Havana's board and keep, that would help me out, too. Hope you don't think I sound grasping.'

'Not at all. Seems reasonable to me. I don't know many people who'd be willing to take someone else's child in.'

'Well . . . thanks. Life's expensive and there are months when the piggy bank's almost empty. Anyway, I went to see Ashleigh and Barry to tell them about what Havana had asked. I said I was willing to have her stay for a while and see how it worked. They jumped at the offer. Agreed immediately. I've never known anything like it. I mean, I thought they might at least want to think it over, but they were both falling over themselves. Ashleigh said straight away that they'd give me money for Havana's keep. She was talking about a standing order, asking me for my bank details and how she could pack some of Havana's things. She didn't even ask how long for or how we'd deal with Havana's health and medical appointments. She moved in that evening, after school.'

'Does she visit at home?'

'No, not to my knowledge. Ashleigh rings her. I don't know how often. She takes Havana to her doctor's appointments to have her weight monitored. I was clear I wasn't going to do that and I think she needs to maintain some responsibility. I'm not sure how this will work out. I suppose I assumed it was temporary, but sometimes I wonder if Havana will still be living here when she leaves school.' She gave a wry grin and ran her hands through her hair, pushing it back from her high forehead.

There were sudden thumps and bangs from upstairs, reverberating through the ceiling. Swift thought he saw some shards of plaster fall in the corner of the kitchen.

'The elephants are on their way,' Grace said. 'Be afraid, be very afraid!'

Footsteps thudded in the hall. The door opened and two girls entered. They were about the same height, both with long brown hair and skinny braids hanging over their ears. They wore heavy, smoky eye makeup, shimmering pale lipstick and bright blue nail varnish. One was sturdy and curvaceous, wearing a green and blue tunic over black leggings. She had a swimmer's well-developed shoulders and the bloom of youth in her cheeks. No guessing that the other thin, wan girl with dull-looking hair was Havana. If she'd put weight on, Swift didn't care to think what she'd looked like previously. She resembled one of those young, emaciated models that there was an occasional outcry about when they appeared on a catwalk. She wore a short denim skirt with a fraying hem that skimmed her bony hips and a tight blue T-shirt showing her ribs.

'This is Mr Swift,' Grace said. 'He just wants to have a chat.'

'Please, call me Ty. Hi, Havana, it's good to meet you.'

He smiled at her but she glanced away, looking at Grace, then at Sally.

'I want Sally to stay,' she said in a muted voice. She had misty, pale green eyes and a downy coating of hair on her arms.

'Of course,' Grace agreed. She rose and placed glasses, a carton of milk and a bag of scones on the table.

Sally poured milk for both of them, then cut a scone in half and buttered it. She raised her plate towards her and ate speedily. Havana cut a thin slice from a scone, crumbled a piece into her mouth and took small sips of milk. Her skin looked dry and chapped and she had a scab at the corner of her bottom lip. The washing machine juddered noisily on its final spin and the floor vibrated.

'Havana, I'm very sorry about your dad. Your grandmother, Mrs Roscoe has asked me to try and find out who killed him. I've spoken to your mother and she said it was okay for me to come and see you.'

There was silence. Finally, Havana nodded, looking down into her glass. She had a closed off, forbidding expression. She looked very like her father, with the same jawline and nose. Maybe that added to her mother's difficulties with her. A timer pinged on the Aga and the saucepan spat out hissing liquid that bubbled and steamed. Grace was looking at her phone, tapping keys.

'Do you need to turn the cooker off?' Swift asked.

'Hmm? Oh, yes.' Grace leaned over and hit a knob.

Sally licked her fingers and started on the other half of her scone.

Swift tried again. 'I know you were close to your dad. I wondered if there's anything you can remember about him just before he was attacked. Was anything troubling him or did he mention someone he might be meeting?'

Havana's gaze drifted across him and rested on Sally for a moment. She shrugged and murmured. 'He had lots of *meetings*. Mum said most of them were with skanks.'

He could barely hear her above the tumble drier. Yet she had been singing and laughing upstairs just minutes ago. 'This is difficult, Havana. I know you won't want to speak ill of your dad.'

She stared at him. 'Speak ill? You're having a laugh. He was a serial shagger. I reckon he'd poked most of the women in Cornford. I suppose that's why someone stuck a pin in his dick when they killed him. Poked him back.'

He stared back at her until she blinked and looked down. 'How did you know your dad saw other women? From your mum?'

'I suppose. She was always going on about him and how she couldn't trust him. And Jude. They went on and on and on. Bored me stiff.'

'Do you know of any woman in particular?'

She shrugged. 'Maybe. Can't remember now. Don't really want to.' Again, her glance strayed to Sally.

Sally smiled and hiccupped, banging her chest.

'How about you, Sally? Do you recall anything?'

'Me? No. Afraid not.'

'Oh? You and Havana have been close friends for a while. You share a lot of things.'

She didn't reply, just flicked a braid. As she moved, he was sure he caught a whiff of marijuana. Maybe the jollity upstairs stemmed from more than teenage high spirits. It might explain Havana's slightly hazy gaze although the heavy makeup could be causing that. He looked at Grace but she was sending a text.

Sally cleared her throat and assumed a solemn expression. She folded her arms under her breasts, leaned forwards and adopted a confiding, over the garden fence tone. 'Don't know if it helps . . . oh, crumbs, I don't know whether or not to say it . . . it sounds so awful.' She looked at Havana, whose mouth twitched.

'Go on,' he said flatly, suspecting he was being taken for a ride.

'Is it okay?' Sally asked her friend.

'Oh, go on then,' Havana said. 'I suppose it's best to be truthful.'

'It's just that Mr Roscoe — Greg — he did shag other women but the poor man had good reason.' She paused and smiled ruefully. 'See, he wasn't getting any at home.' She stuck her lips out in a Mick Jagger impression and sang, *'I can't get no . . . satisfaction . . .'*

The two girls snorted and high fived. Grace shook her head and rolled her eyes. Swift kept his face impassive. This double act had been prepared and they were good at it. He thought he'd try to interrupt the dynamic.

'Your Granny Pat misses you,' he said to Havana. 'She really appreciates your cards at Christmas. She's lonely. She'd love to hear from you. She doesn't know you're living here.'

The girl went still and picked at the sore on her lip. 'I can do what I like,' she said at last. '*They* always did.'

He focused on her, speaking gently. 'You do know a lot about the intimate details of your parents' lives. More than you should and I think that's a burden for you. Is there anything else you can tell me about your murdered father?'

She shot him a nasty look and took a drink of milk. She darted a glance at Sally, and then raised a bony hand to her mouth, speaking through her fingers. 'I can tell you that my mum was seeing creepy old Grafton before my dad died. I saw them at it in the living room. I'm amazed she wasn't worried about staining the sofa or him croaking on the job. Hashtag disgusting! So, one shagger blaming another. I reckon Mum was planning to bin Dad off. Maybe she killed him so she could marry the old fart.'

Sally dug her in the side and they both sniggered.

'Come on, girls . . . manners,' Grace said wearily.

'That's interesting. Is it true? Your mum told me she met Barry after your dad died.'

Havana made a gesture with a thumb and forefinger, as if she was extending her nose. 'She's a liar. They were both rotten liars, as bad as each other.' Her voice was firmer now. 'She was shagging the ancient bloke. Getting ready to make him a geriatric daddy. Yuk. *A little Christmas baby,*' she added, simpering.

'Maybe they'll call him Jesus!' Sally giggled.

A tiny frown crossed Havana's face but then she joined in saying, 'Baby Jesus, shut up! I can't have a brat brother called Jesus! No way!'

Could it be that simple? Ashleigh killed Roscoe because she hated him and wanted to be Mrs Grafton. She'd have got the house, a pension and presumably a life insurance payout. People had killed for less.

'Most murders are committed by someone known to the victim, aren't they?' Sally asked.

He nodded. 'That's true.'

'Well, then. Get Ashleigh arrested and banged up. She can decorate her cell in crappy beach tat like it's a ship's cabin and have her horrible sprog in jail.' She sang, *'Oh we do like to be in clink together. . .'* to the tune of *I Do Like to be Beside the Seaside.*

Havana threw her head back and let out a high-pitched cackle. Her glass rocked and fell over, spilling milk on the table. She continued grinning, almost a kind of leer but misery pooled in her eyes. Swift had met some wretched, messed up people in his time but this child was in a league of her own.

'Give it a break, girls, don't embarrass me,' Grace said, fetching a cloth from the sink.

Swift nodded to Havana. 'Do you ever hear from your brother, Axel?'

'*Half*-brother,' Havana said. 'Nope. I've never met him. Don't want to, either.'

'What about your dad, did he have any contact with him?'

She chewed on her bottom lip. 'I heard him on the phone one day. He was in the garage. That's where he sneaked off to when he wanted to make one of his cheat calls. Sounded like that's who he was talking to. Well, he was doing this false, cheerful voice, saying, "Hello there, young sir!" *Young sir*. Gross!'

'Do you remember when that was?'

'Not really. A while before it happened.'

Sally waved to a hen staring in through the back door and tapping the glass with its beak. 'Hello Meryl!' She went to the door and let the hen in on a gust of bitter air. It was quickly followed by three more. They strutted and clucked, picking their way around the shoes. 'We've named them after Hollywood actresses,' she told Swift. 'This is Oprah, that's Charlize and the reddish one is Nicole. They're such characters!' She picked Oprah up and cuddled her. The remaining hens had spotted the open door and ran in to the kitchen, milling around and ruffling their feathers.

'Do put her down, Sal, you know you shouldn't handle them,' her mother said, pulling clothes from the tumble dryer.

Sally ignored her and continued to pet the hen, which seemed to like it. The others roamed around her feet, sounding like a drunken chorus.

'I feel a bit tired and emotional now,' Havana said, getting up. She waved her fingers at Swift and put a hand mockingly over her heart. 'Let me know when mum's banged up. I'll make sure I visit her *every* week.'

'That's so *not* going to happen,' Sally laughed. She put the hen down and moved back to Havana, bumping a hip against hers.

They disappeared into the hall and tripped upstairs, giggling. A door slammed. One of the hens started pecking a pair of bootlaces.

'Oh, for goodness sake!' Grace stumbled over the shoes, shooed the darting hens out of the kitchen in a flurry of feathers and locked the door. 'That was easy. Sometimes I have to lay a trail of food back to the coop to get them out of the house. They like it in here and Sally's always letting them in when I'm at work.'

Swift wanted to ask if the girls often spoke so rudely about Havana's parents but Grace darted to the Aga, lifted the saucepan lid and started stirring furiously. A burnt smell lingered in the air and her phone buzzed, distracting her. He shook his head. None of his business. But he was going to make one comment.

'I think your daughter and Havana are smoking dope,' he said to Grace.

She put her phone down and stared at him. 'What on earth makes you say that?'

'I'm sure I could smell it. Once a cop . . . you get a nose for these things.'

She shook her head. 'No, I'm sure that's not the case. Sally's a sensible girl. She wouldn't do that. We've had the drugs chat.'

If only it was that simple. 'Okay. If you say so. But it might be worth looking in their rooms.'

'I'd never do that!' She looked at him in horror. 'We have trust in this house. We trust each other and we talk about everything. We don't have any no go areas.'

He thought that might be true of the hens but not of the inhabitants of the house. Havana had exchanged one strange home for another. 'Right. I always assume there are no go areas with teenagers. I was well camouflaged in my day.'

Grace made no reply, turning back to the saucepan.

'Has Havana had any counselling?' he asked.

Grace tasted the liquid on the wooden spoon and grimaced. 'I'll have to chuck this. Ah, yes, she went to a clinic for a couple of visits with her mother. That was over six months ago. She told me it was rubbish and she refused to go back. When I mentioned it to Ashleigh she said they'd seen some nosy do-gooder who was a waste of space.'

'That's a shame. I think it can take time for therapy to be helpful.' That's what Ruth had told him once. She reckoned that anyone needed at least half a dozen sessions for it to be meaningful.

'Do take some new laid eggs,' Grace said, as if he hadn't commented. 'I collected them just this morning. We have so many.' She reached into a cupboard and held out an egg box.

'If you're sure . . .'

'Absolutely. I'm always giving them away. We can only eat so many omelettes. They're delicious.'

He found himself standing outside, holding the eggs as an icy rain started. The next-door neighbour was by the kerb, washing her car.

'Typical, isn't it?' she said. 'Starts raining as soon as I step outside the door.'

'Your car will get a good rinse.'

She looked at him with interest and propped a hip against a door handle. 'Is Grace in?' she asked him, blowing her hair back.

'Yes.'

'Good. I want to complain about the noise last night and it's hard to get hold of her.'

'Are they noisy neighbours?'

She rolled her eyes. 'Those bloody girls are. Music, thumping around until all hours, screaming their heads off. It's got really bad since that Havana moved in. She's a right madam. Gave me a mouthful last time I knocked on the door. I thought they were going to come through the walls.'

'Doesn't Grace stop them if they get too noisy?'

The woman laughed. 'If she's there and not off being Anne Boleyn or whatever.'

'Sorry?'

'I know, daft, isn't it? She works with some outfit that provides themed evenings at restaurants and parties and such. Sometimes she's a Disney character, or a twenties flapper or a cowgirl.'

'I thought she worked at the health centre.'

'Yeah, part time. The dressing up is her other job. Evenings and weekends. She's always out and about, here and there. I do understand because she has to make ends meet and the ex-husband contributes the minimum he can for Sally. And I don't like to cause her any bother because she's so hard working and a nice woman. Well meaning. But those girls are left on their own too much. God knows what they get up to. It's a strange setup. And as for those hens, they make a dreadful noise. I don't need an alarm clock.' She locked her car. 'I'll go and knock now, in case Grace is off to be Alice in Wonderland for the night.'

Swift sat in his car, thinking. The rain was deafening, obscuring the windscreen and windows and creating a little haven. Havana was a mass of confusion and pain. Her attempts to shock him with her crude language had been pitiful. She had been exposed to details of her parents' sexual lives at a very young age, which must have disturbed her deeply. Her appearance was in stark contrast to her mother's glow of health and wealth. She had no one to trust except Sally and Grace and she was now living in a house which seemed benign enough but shambolic. He thought Sally was clever and possibly manipulative. Havana had looked to her constantly, but why? For reassurance or approval or because she was in awe of her friend? Again, he felt dissatisfied with an interview. He didn't think that Havana knew anything about her father's death but her odd living arrangements interested and worried him. She was observant and she must know more about her father's life and his activities before he died. Getting through to her would be difficult, as he couldn't risk seeing her alone.

Chapter 7

On impulse, Swift drove to Ashleigh Grafton's street and coasted past the house, peering through the downpour. It was just five o'clock and Grafton might not be back from work yet. There was no car on the drive so he decided to try his luck and see if Ashleigh was home alone. He pulled up his collar, ran through the rain and stood inside the porch.

'Hello, Daddy!' he heard Ashleigh trill as she opened the door. Her face fell when she saw him.

'I am a daddy, but not the one you were expecting,' he said.

'What do *you* want?'

She was in a golden skirt and cream jumper and her skin glowed with a light tan. It might have been the height of summer. She made him think of milk and honey but there was no sweetness in her expression. Her hair was twisted up on top of her head and tied with an ivory ribbon. She held her left hand outwards, the fingers divided by foam separators and the long nails glistening with a shimmering varnish. He wondered if she'd keep them like that once she had the baby, imagined the nails raking its delicate skin. He felt rain stinging the back of his head and trickling down his neck but he knew he wasn't going to be invited in.

'I have a question. Havana told me that you were seeing Barry before Greg died. Is that true? It might put a different slant on things.'

She frowned and her jaw jutted out. 'That's not true.'

'Havana's lying then?'

'Yes. Don't ask me why. She often has a problem with the truth, just like her father. Must be hereditary.'

Swift nodded. 'Did Greg leave you okay financially when he died? I suppose he had life insurance and he left you everything. Mrs Roscoe said you'd got a pension.'

A man had parked on next door's drive and was hurrying up his front path. He glanced across curiously. Ashleigh fluttered fingers at him, mouthing *hello* and smiling brightly. The smile vanished as soon as the neighbour was indoors.

Ashleigh folded her arms, her left hand placed carefully on her right forearm. The nails twinkled in the porch light. 'That's none of your business.'

'And speaking of business — do you know of any other businesses Greg was involved in, apart from his flying?'

She tapped a foot. 'Chasing skirt. That was his other business. A major investment with plenty of dividends.'

'So I gather. Well, going back for a minute to what Havana said, she gave me a pretty graphic description of seeing you and Barry being active in the living room before Greg died. I'll spare your blushes but she mentioned shagging and the sofa.'

Ashleigh gave a little gasp, her teeth catching on her lip. Then her right hand flashed out and she slapped him hard across his damp face. 'How dare you! Get off my doorstep or I'll call the police.'

He rubbed his stinging cheek. 'Okay. Seems as if the truth has annoyed you.'

A door slammed and Jude appeared in the hallway, her face encased in a pink clay mask and her hair arranged in huge rollers. She hurried up to her friend and put her hands on her shoulders. 'What's going on?' she asked. 'Are you okay, Ash?'

'No, I'm not. This man's being horribly offensive.'

Jude glared at Swift. 'I thought Baz told you not to come here again?' She spoke stiffly through the facemask, her high voice ending on a screech.

'From the look Barry gave you when I was last here, I wouldn't be surprised if he'd like to tell you the same,' he said.

'How dare you!' Jude's squeal went even higher.

If looks could kill, he'd be a dead man.

Ashleigh stepped back against Jude, shaking with anger. 'You can take your horrible stories and piss off. Havana's a lying little cow,' she spat. 'She hates Barry and she's been horrible about me marrying him. The drama she created on my wedding day! I suppose she thought she'd stop me or I'd postpone it. Well, she had another think coming! You'd expect her to be happy for me, after what I put up with from her father for all those years. But it's all about her! Always has been. Greg spoiled her rotten and left me with the little princess who had to have everything her way. That's what the food thing is all about. Just another way of making herself the centre of attention. If she's taken you in, you're not much of a detective. Now fuck off and don't come back here!'

'Yeah, fuck off!' Jude echoed.

The door banged. You're not much of a liar, Ashleigh, Swift thought as he got in the car. He looked in the mirror and saw a red mark on his cheek. She packed a punch. He was lucky that her dagger-like nails hadn't broken the skin. He shrugged off his wet jacket, turned the heating up full and wiped his face with the sleeve of his jumper. The rain turned to sleet as he drove back to London. A driver cut across lanes without signalling as Swift came off the motorway and he had to brake sharply. The box of eggs that Grace had given him fell on the floor. He heard a crunch and saw yellow yolk seep through the cardboard.

Sums up my afternoon, he thought.

* * *

The day was murky and squally with a whipping breeze that nipped the skin and set the teeth on edge. Swift fought his way back along the Thames to Hammersmith, using all his strength and skill to manoeuvre on the rushing tide. The surface of the water was dotted with frothy whitecaps. He'd been out on the river for two hours and had spotted two grey seals and a flock of oystercatchers, looking for mussel beds. The trip had been exhilarating and exhausting. He'd probably pay for it later with creeping fatigue but it was worth it for the buzz. He took deep breaths as he steadied his boat. The familiar Thames smell of drains, sludge, cabbage and diesel was like perfume. There had been a wonderful stretch past Putney where the wind at his back had been wild, driving him onwards. He had heard the bubbles beneath the boat as it flew effortlessly through the water. The oars, the river and his heartbeat came together in dynamic harmony and he had that out of time and body experience he craved. This was his medicine, his tonic in life. Rowing had carried him through sadness and grief, maintained his sanity.

He was panting hard as he drew onto the slipway at his club, Tamesas. He paused to wipe sweat and rain from his face and hair, draw breath and drink a bottle of water. Then he pulled his boat into the shed and cleaned it before jogging back to his house, which was ten minutes from the river. It was late afternoon and the sky was starting to clear, the heavy, bruised-looking clouds replaced by fluffier grey ones.

As he opened the front door, he heard *Blue Suede Shoes* playing upstairs. Chand was an Elvis fan and spent a lot of his leisure time going to concerts by an Elvis impersonator called Joe Derano. Swift was picking up his post as The King switched into *Suspicious Minds* and Chand appeared at the top of the stairs.

'Day off?' Swift asked.

Chand was light on his feet as he came down. 'Two days. I had a lovely lie in this morning. Bliss. You look windswept and knackered. Been rowing?'

'Couple of hours on the Thames. Great.'

'Bit like a drug, is it?' Chand disliked exercise and said he didn't see the point in working up a sweat. He had a relaxed, laid-back air. Swift reckoned it masked a quick brain.

'You're right, it is. There's an edge to it, a thrill that I crave. I get cranky and restless if I don't get my fix out on the river every couple of days. It's one of the reasons I love being my own boss.' He smiled at Chand's bewildered look. 'Think how you'd feel if you couldn't listen to Elvis regularly.'

'Gotcha. I used to watch the rowers when I was at college. They seemed like an exclusive cabal of fanatics. Very intent and dedicated. That's all they were interested in, all they talked about. I steered clear of them.' He put a hand up. 'I hasten to add that you're not much like them.'

Swift wiped a drip of rain from the back of his neck. 'I recognise the types you're talking about. I've never been a clubbable rower or competitive. I love it for the peace and solitude. The only competition is with myself. I just want to hear the boat sing and my blood flow.'

'Wow, sounds a bit Zen. Too deep for me.' Elvis swung into *Hound Dog* and Chand pointed a thumb up the stairs. 'Is the music okay? Not too loud?'

'It's fine.'

Chand looked relieved. 'It's great to be able to play it when I want. My parents always moaned if they heard it and listening through earphones isn't the same. They think it's Western rubbish.'

'They keep to their own traditions?'

'You bet. Punjabi music only — mainly bhangra. You wouldn't think they came here in 1980. Speaking of traditions . . . do you like spicy food?'

'Yes, love it.'

'Okay, good. See, I visited my parents at the weekend and my mum gave me enough food to bring home to feed a small country. Containers full of it and I've only a small freezer. She's convinced I'll starve, living on my own. Much as I love her cooking, I also like pizza, fish and chips and roasts. Would you like some? I can offer butter and tandoori chicken, vegetable saag, three kinds of dal and stuffed breads.'

'It all sounds wonderful. If you're sure. Nora loves spicy food, too, and homemade is an extra pleasure.'

Chand laughed. 'Believe me, if I give you half of what I have, there's still enough to last me weeks and mum will insist on giving me a load more next time I visit.'

'I've struck lucky. Cedric used to give me dishes he'd made and now I've got you to make sure I don't go hungry. I'd pass on thanks to your mum but that would only get you into trouble.'

Chand tapped the side of his nose and winked. 'It's our secret. Undercover meals.'

Swift put his key in his door. 'I'm cooling down now. I need to go and have a shower. Shall I come up and get the food in about half an hour?'

'I'll have it ready.'

Swift stood under a steaming shower, feeling his muscles unknot. He'd run out of shower gel and used some that Nora had left. It turned out to be a frothy mousse that smelled and looked like mashed avocado. He tasted a bit but it was just antiseptic and soapy, reminding him of Ashleigh Grafton's Earl Grey tea. He'd half expected Barry to ring, complaining about his unannounced visit, but he'd heard nothing. He wondered if Ashleigh had kept quiet about it, not wanting her husband to know that Havana had spilled the beans about her mother's adultery.

When he'd dressed in clean jeans and shirt, he knocked on Chand's door and collected half a dozen plastic food containers. They were all carefully labelled in a neat hand with warnings in brackets. He examined one: *Tandoori chicken wings. (Do not overheat! Ten minutes max once thawed or meat will be tough.)* He felt a pang of guilt at being the random recipient of this motherly love but didn't let it deter him from deciding on butter chicken and spinach dal. He kept an eye on the clock as he ate. He was due to meet Paul Cairns later. The food was delicious and warming after his hours on the river. As he forked it up, he read a reply from Fitz Blackmore to his query about David Boyd.

We talked to Boyd, as he'd been sacked because of Roscoe. He said he'd got a good payoff from the airfield and was already running a successful business. There was nothing to follow up and his dad said he'd been at home with him the night of the murder.

Swift finished his meal and made coffee. Chand had gone out so there was no more Elvis for the time being. Now Andy Fanning was playing his trumpet next door, a faint melody that might be Gershwin. Swift thought he was a lucky man with a private if muffled concert and Mrs Malla's clandestine cuisine.

* * *

The Check-In bar was busy with clusters of people drinking, chatting and eating meals. Someone was celebrating a birthday, with balloons, streamers and a huge iced cake with candles in the centre of a table. A large group was sitting on stools around the bar, wearing white silk scarves emblazoned with the Swiss flag. Swift recognised Paul Cairns from the newspaper photo. He was on his own at a small table just inside the veranda with his back angled to the room. He was a slight, nondescript figure with wisps of hair straggling over his scalp. He wore a chocolate-coloured, leather flying jacket with a sheepskin collar. It looked bulky and too big for him. He held a bottle of beer and a pair of binoculars hung around his neck. As Swift watched, he lifted them and stared out at the runways.

Swift ordered a glass of Shiraz. 'And a bottle of beer for Mr Cairns, whatever he's having,' he said.

The barman serving him glanced at Cairns and then back. 'You a friend of Paul's?' he asked guardedly.

'An acquaintance.'

'Not a reporter?'

'I'm not a reporter. Why do you ask?'

'He had that reporter Camilla Finley in here with him last week, going over what's happened in the past couple of years. She's writing a book with him. Seems like everyone wants to make money out of their troubles these days!'

'Or maybe Ms Finley will make the money,' Swift said, drily.

'Fair point. When Paul's been with the reporter, it makes him a bit loud and excitable. We can do without that.'

'Would you prefer it if he stayed away?'

The barman flipped the top from a bottle. 'No, it's not that. I feel sorry for the guy. He's always been a tad different and I mean he's been dealt a rotten hand. No one should suffer the way Paul has and he's dead nervy these days. I just don't think it does him any good when people get him worked up.'

'I've no intention of doing that,' Swift said.

'Well, glad to hear it. We've got our other customers to think about and we have visitors who've flown in from Geneva tonight. We want them to come back.'

'The reason I'm here is because I'm a private investigator. Greg Roscoe's mother has asked me to look into his death. Did you know him?'

'I knew Greg from way back, yeah? He came in here regularly, even before he worked here. Always had a friendly word. Liked to chew the fat.'

'Did he ever seem worried or had he fallen out with anyone?'

The barman was in his fifties but he had boyish looks, soft skin and a rounded face that belied his years. 'I wouldn't say worried. He was a bit preoccupied sometimes but then he had a very responsible job and he took it seriously. Very dedicated to the students. He fell out with another instructor. It was all kept a bit hush-hush, but I think there'd been some complaints and Greg took steps.'

'David Boyd?'

The barman pulled a face, nodding. 'Boyd. I was glad to see the back of him, swanking around as if he was lord of the manor. I didn't think he'd come back this way after he was given his marching orders but I reckon he had a girlfriend locally. I saw him in town the evening Greg died but I wouldn't have crossed the street to say hello.'

'Where did you see him? What time?'

'Walking along the High Street, looking at his phone. Must have been around six thirty.'

'Would anyone here know who his girlfriend was?'

'Don't think so. He never mixed socially with anyone, just came and went like he was doing us all a favour.'

'Did the police talk to you after Roscoe was murdered?'

'I missed that pleasure. I flew to Ottawa that night. Had a month there visiting my grandchildren. Okay, that's six pounds and thirty pence, please.'

Swift thought Boyd's dubious alibi might be a handy bit of information to confound Blackmore with some time. He'd noticed a familiar face in a glossy poster behind the bar, advertising an event. It was titled *Amazing Aviators*. He read the text as he paid.

A fascinating evening with some of the most famous flyers in history! Come along, hear their experiences from their own lips and ask them questions about their astonishing careers.

There were sepia tinted photos of men and women dressed as famous aviators in various types of flying gear, including one man with an Edwardian moustache. Their names were traced below them in a bold font: Amelia Earhart, Charles Lindbergh, Douglas Bader, Blanche Scott, and Louis Blériot. Grace Tansley was in the centre as Amy Johnson, wearing a close fitting helmet with goggles propped on top and a leather coat with a huge collar.

'I see you have entertainment.' Swift pointed to the poster as the barman placed his order on a tray.

'The Amazing Aviators? They're very popular, so if you want to come, best to book soon. We sold out last time. They're a great bunch who dress up as flyers who made history. People come and wine and dine while they mingle with the audience and tell their stories. Holly, the CFI found them a while ago. They've been here a couple of times and it's a terrific evening.'

'Okay, I'll think about it. I've not been to anything like it before. Sounds a bit like experiential theatre.'

'I don't know about that but, you know, it's the kind of stuff you have to do these days to get the punters in.' The barman rested on the till. 'People want something a bit different. Ring the changes and snag people's interest, that's how you keep a place like this busy.'

Silvio and Holly had certainly been getting the message across. Swift took the tray over to Cairns, who was still peering through his binoculars, and introduced himself.

'I bought you another beer.'

'Thank you, kind sir. That'll make my quota for the evening. I never have more than two. Got to keep my wits about me.' Cairns jerked his head to one side.

'Any particular reason?' Swift pulled out a chair and sat beside him.

Cairns put a narrow hand on the arm of his chair. 'Put it this way, I know a lot of people in this place have got it in for me.'

'You think? The barman seems to like you.' Close to, he saw that Cairns had greasy skin, with clusters of tiny pimples around his chin and neck. He gave off an intense heat and a strange odour. Something sharp and organic. Swift wondered if the flying jacket was treated with animal oils. It looked stiff and new and it dwarfed him, sitting proud of his slender shoulders.

'Craig's okay. We were at school together. But some of them here can't stand my guts.' He gave the little jerk of his head again.

'Why do you come here then?'

Cairns took a sip of beer. His shoulders went up. 'I love this airfield, always have. It's in my blood. My dad worked here as a mechanic and he used to bring me with him when I was little. I've every right to come here. My lawyer told me that. This lot treated me like shit, just like the cops did. Yeah, it's my right to come here and they can't stop me.'

Swift was reminded of Havana's assertion that she could do what she liked because her parents always had. Cairns sounded like a small boy in the playground.

'Well,' Swift said, lifting his wine, 'cheers!'

Cairns held his left hand out. It shook in the air. 'Look at that,' he said. 'See that tremor? My nerves are shot. I'm on tranquilisers as well as loads of other medication. I still can't work because of my anxieties.'

'What did you do before you were ill?'

'Worked at the information desk at the bus station. I couldn't go back there now and deal with the public. I can't stand noise and crowds. Too jumpy.'

'I suppose the compensation comes in handy then.'

Cairns bridled. 'What's that to do with you?'

'Nothing. I didn't mean to offend. I just wondered if it's been hard for you.'

'Right. I don't like nosy people. Everyone seems to think they know all about me, like my life's an open book. There are lots of bastards who want to get one over on me.'

Swift almost pointed out that letting a reporter splash you all over her newspaper column and write a book about you was an open invitation to the curious but the man was too much like a tightly stretched wire. His head jerked more violently and his face drained of colour as he grew emotional. He'd downed most of his second pint of beer and it was affecting his speech. Maybe he was one of those people who got drunk quickly or the alcohol was interacting with medication. Swift sat back from him and attempted to lighten the atmosphere.

'That's fine. Like I said, I didn't mean to cause any upset. My job does make me nosy. It goes with the territory. If I didn't ask lots of annoying questions I'd never solve a case.'

Cairns rubbed his brow and looked at him. He took a mouthful of beer. His jacket creaked as he moved. 'Okay, then. My mum died while I was sick. She left me her house and some money and I sold her shop. So what with that and my compensation, I'm okay. I just need to get back on my feet properly. Know what I'm going to do when I'm feeling better?'

'I've no idea.'

'I'll tell you, kind sir. I'm going to sign up at another airfield and take lessons again. Then I'll fly wherever I like. I'll bring my plane over here, buzz the control tower and give them a victory roll! Yes!' Cairns made a thumbs up and stroked his sheepskin collar. 'D'you like my jacket? It's brand new. I got it last week. It's the same as the ones the RAF boys wore during the war. It wasn't cheap. I'm going to wear it for my new lessons. Thought it could be my lucky jacket. Like a mascot.'

'It's very smart. Have you always been interested in flying?'

Another little jerk of the head. 'Since I was a nipper and my dad brought me here. I always dreamed of getting a pilot's licence.'

Time to introduce the enemy's name. 'So did Greg Roscoe, apparently. His brother told me he wanted to be a pilot from when he was very young.'

He was half expecting another angry outburst but Cairns' voice was mild.

'Yeah, Greg told me that when I first met him. He used to chat away about his pilot training. I loved listening to him. He had fascinating stories.'

'You fell out, though.'

'Too right. He was a bastard to me. He treated me like dirt. He shouldn't have died like that, though. We can't afford to lose excellent flyers. He was a real loss to the world of aviation.'

He spoke as if he himself was one of an elite band instead of a failed student. He was a sad figure, an impostor in his copycat RAF jacket but with no license to reach for the skies. He was as genuine as one of the Amazing Aviators. Swift watched him drink. He had the palest of eyebrows and lashes and his eyes were small and a watery grey. It would be hard to remember what he looked like.

'I'm surprised that you say that,' Swift said. 'I heard you threatened Greg.'

'I was bloody angry with him. He treated me badly and spoiled my life here as a student. I was just getting things off my chest when I said stuff. I'd never have actually harmed him.'

Swift thought someone had coached him in that response — his lawyer maybe, or Camilla Finley. 'So you didn't mean it when you ripped his photo?'

‘I was really riled at the time because Greg had messed me about. I was letting off steam. Spur of the moment.’

‘When you emailed me, you said that you knew things about Roscoe. I’m interested in your information. Did you know of any women he was seeing?’

‘Not *women*, no. That didn’t bother me.’ Cairns turned to him with an eager light in his washed out eyes. ‘If I help you find Greg’s killer, will I get credit?’

‘How do you mean?’

‘Well, will you and the police tell people I helped to track him down? There’s a reporter writing my story in a book with me and she said it would be a real angle. Her name’s Camilla Finley. She’s great, really boosts my confidence. I told her about the information I’ve got and she said I should contact you. She said that I’ve got to stop being a victim. I’ve got to take control and shape my own story, make it positive. If I’m named as the man who helped nail the killer, I’ll be a hero. She said the public love to read about the underdog making good.’

It sounded as if Camilla had been reading self-help books. Swift was getting some measure of Cairns: he was prickly and suspicious but susceptible to being flattered. ‘Ah, I see. Well, if you give me information that leads to the killer, I’m sure you’ll be acknowledged. I won’t have a problem with that. I can’t speak for the police. I read a piece that Camilla wrote about you in the Cornford Mail.’

‘That’s her. *Finley’s Finds*. She says I’m one of her best finds.’ He sounded proud, puffing his chest. ‘She’s been good to me. She got in touch when I was still in hospital. She said I’m a classic case of the little person against the system.’

Swift nodded, thinking that Cairns would be too dull and uninteresting to snag the attention of a national paper but a small town reporter could milk his story and make some money. ‘Well, if there’s anything you can tell me that helps, I’ll mention it.’

Cairns looked around and then pulled his chair closer. Swift felt that heat from him again and thought that you'd expect someone so thin and pallid to be chilly.

'Greg was in trouble with a bloke.'

Swift was disappointed, thinking that he already had Cairns' information. 'Do you mean David Boyd?'

'No, not him. Another bloke. They'd done some kind of business together. I think Greg owed him money.'

'How did you find this out?'

'Greg and me had been up doing circuits one day. We were walking back to the office to debrief and this bloke came from nowhere, marched up to him. He was tall, about your age and height, with blond, almost white hair. I'd never seen him before. He started shouting at Greg, calling him a bastard and a scumbag. Said he wanted his money and no more excuses. He was poking Greg in the chest. Greg looked scared but he told the bloke to calm down. "Okay, Stef, okay. . ." he kept saying. He asked me to wait for him in the office. I went to the office but I watched them out of the window. I thought I might need to call for help. This bloke was waving his arms and pointing a finger right in Greg's face. Greg was doing that holding his hands up thing, to try and calm him.' Cairns held his hands up, palms outwards to demonstrate. He was becoming energised and more agitated as he told the story. 'They were out there for a good ten minutes. Then the bloke walked off towards the car park. He still looked furious. Greg watched him and then came back in really slowly. I saw him stop to wipe his face with a hanky.'

'What did Greg say when he came in?'

'Not much. He tried to laugh it off and just said that he'd advise me never to do business with a friend. I could see he was rattled. Then he started talking about our flight. When we finished I asked him if he needed any help with this bloke but he got snappy with me and said it was nothing and to forget it happened. I'll tell you what, it didn't occur to me until I was in hospital and I had time to think. I used to go back over everything time and time again. It was after that day that Greg started criticising me and saying he doubted I could make it as a pilot. I reckon he didn't like the fact that I'd seen that argument and he wanted rid of me. I knew too much. What do you think?' There was a sheen of sweat on his brow and nose and a bubble of spittle on his lower lip.

Cairns could be right or his take on things could be rooted in his fondness for conspiracy. 'I don't know. It sounds as if Greg was in trouble of some kind. Did you get any sense of where this Stef was from?'

'He wasn't English. He had an accent, like Scandinavian or something. A bit sing-song.'

Swift finished his wine. 'When was this?'

'The March before Greg died. It was a bitterly cold day and Greg was shivering when he came in. I reckon the blond bloke was involved with flying.'

'Why's that?'

He has wearing one of those really expensive Parkas. You know, the ones filled with goose down. There was a badge on his chest, pilot's wings.'

'And you never saw him again?'

'No. Just that once.'

'Did you mention this to the police?'

Cairns laughed. 'You what? Course not! Why should I have told them anything, the way they treated me? The less I had to do with them the better and if I'd said anything they'd have been back around me and giving me grief. Let them do their own dirty work.'

'Did anyone else see this Stef?'

'Don't think so. It was late in the day and there were no other flights so the place was quiet as the grave.' Cairns glanced at his watch. 'There's a Cessna Citation due to land soon on runway one. It's a medium sized jet, built in Kansas.'

'Okay, sounds interesting. Can I just ask you about David Boyd? I know he and Greg didn't get on and he left here. Do you know if he had a girlfriend locally?'

'I didn't have anything to do with Boyd and he always looked at me as if I'd crawled out from under a stone. So no idea. I'd have thought he'd be going out with some posh totty in London.'

'I have one more question. Why did you run away when the police came to question you about Greg?'

Cairns gripped his jacket collar, digging his fingers into the soft sheepskin. 'I was shit scared. I've always been scared of the police and I knew they'd come for me because I'd fallen out with Greg and people had heard me badmouth him. I was worried they were going to force a confession from me. I mean, you hear about that, don't you? I know I'm not strong and tough blokes put the wind up me. I saw these big men coming towards me and I panicked. Hey, here's the Cessna arriving! Want to watch through my binoculars? They're top of the range with night vision.'

He asked so eagerly that Swift thought it best to humour him. 'Okay, thanks.' He took the binoculars and watched as the elegant plane approached the runway, lights winking in the dusk and came into land. It cruised slowly past the building, its engines whining.

'Nice one! Good control on that descent,' Cairns said knowledgeably.

'Do you spend a lot of time watching planes?' Swift handed back the binoculars.

'Fair bit. You can learn a lot, observing. I study takeoffs and landings on DVDs as well. And I've invested in some sophisticated desktop aviation programmes. I check meteorological charts every day and plot flight plans. Keeps my hand in until I'm back in the cockpit. I do online study for technical stuff and I'm going to have a go in a simulator next month. I did a special course for my dyslexia while I was getting over my heart attack. I'm a lot more confident now. It's all about managing the stress.'

He talked the talk but it sounded like hollow bravura. He seemed such an ineffectual, brittle man. Swift had a mental image of Cairns in a house crammed with expensive aviation resources, huddled in his RAF jacket as he watched other people describing planes or flying them. He looked at the man's fingers trembling around the binoculars and couldn't help pitying him.

On his way out, Swift bought two tickets for *Amazing Aviators*. Nora was always saying she wanted new experiences. She liked reading popular psychology magazines, the kind that Ruth looked down her nose at. Nora would occasionally quote articles she'd read, saying that couples needed to ring the changes, surprise each other or do something out of the ordinary. The *Amazing Aviators* should tick all of those boxes and it would be an opportunity to see the airfield regulars at play.

Yes, Swift thought, pocketing the tickets, let no one say I'm a man who can't multitask. As he drove away, he thought that he needed to consider David Boyd and the threatening Stef as main suspects in this case. If the barman was correct, Boyd and his father had lied to the police. And yet . . . he agreed with Blackmore and Nora that this killing seemed to have a woman's touch.

Chapter 8

Swift had had no success in tracing Axel Roscoe. Maybe he was living in Sardinia with his mother. Swift presumed that Yvette Roscoe must know his whereabouts so turned his attention to tracking her, hoping that she hadn't remarried or changed her surname. He wondered if she'd gone back to work at Cagliari airport. Luckily, the obvious route proved to be the right one. He rang the information desk at the airport and after a few minutes of trying to explain why he was calling, found an English speaker. Paola informed him that Yvette Roscoe worked at the airport as a customer service agent and gave him a business email address where he could contact her. He sent an email immediately.

Dear Ms Roscoe,
I am a private investigator based in London. Greg Roscoe's mother has employed me to find the person who killed him. I want to talk to all the people who were close to Greg and I would like to contact his son, Axel. Does Axel live with you or can you provide me with his phone number or email?
Kind Regards.

He microwaved some of Mrs Malla's butter chicken for lunch. As he waited for it to heat, he saw through the window that the forecast had been right. Snow was falling thickly from a metal coloured sky. The drifting flakes were feathering the ground and settling. A blackbird had made a dash for the bird feeder and was pecking at suet balls as the world whitened silently around it. A reply arrived from Yvette as he finished the chicken and poured coffee.

Sorry, I'm not interested. I don't want anything to do with this and I don't want Axel involved. I heard that someone had sued the police. We don't have any information about what happened to Greg and Axel had nothing to do with him after the divorce.
Regards.

Swift sighed. Yvette knew about Paul Cairns so she or Axel were keeping track of events. She wasn't as disinterested as she claimed and, if Havana had got it right, Greg had been in touch with his son at least once over the years. He took a sip of coffee. Time to roll out the emotional blackmail again.

I understand your reluctance, especially as there was no close relationship between Greg and Axel after your divorce. Greg's daughter Havana is terribly distressed about her father's death and in very poor health, as is his mother. Whatever your feelings towards Greg and the Roscoe family, you will understand how much a mother is mourning her son. I just want to check a few things with Axel. I am discreet. I really would appreciate your help.
Kind regards.

Come on, he thought: Axel is a grown man, surely he can make his own decisions about who he talks to. The reply was a little slower coming this time. Swift watched the snow blanket Cedric's tea rose. Cedric had hated snow and worried about falling on treacherous pavements. He preferred to stay indoors until it melted. Swift could still hear him. *It's all very fine and dandy on ski slopes, dear boy, and I wish it would stay there.* Cedric would recall the famously cold winter of 1962, when London had been blinded by blizzards and twelve inches of drifting snow. He'd had to dig his way out of his front door and most of the pipes in his street had frozen. There had been no cars or buses on the roads. Cedric said London had been still and silent, like an ice city, a place frozen in time. Swift was lost in memories of his friend's fund of stories when he heard the ping on his laptop.

Axel doesn't want to have anything to do with that family or with Havana. He's very bitter towards his father, who treated both of us appallingly. I don't want old miseries opened up for him.

He typed quickly, in case she closed down the contact.

I do understand, but someone has got away with a terrible crime. I'm not going to put pressure on Axel. Often, family members know things even if they believe they don't. I will be careful. You have my word that I won't give anyone else Axel's contact details. If he doesn't want to speak to me I won't pursue him.

He had finished his second coffee and had almost given up hope of a reply when it arrived.

I will ask Axel if he wants to discuss this with you. If he does, I'll let him have your email address. That's the best I can do. Please don't contact me again.

He wondered if she'd keep her word or if she was humouring him to get him to go away. Well, he'd given it his best shot. He put on his sturdy lace-up boots and scrunched through the deepening crust of snow in the garden where he refilled the bird feeders with sunflower seeds, suet and mixed nuts. The sky was now as bleached as the landscape and the air was icy in his throat. He dug out his padded jacket and a thick, checked wool scarf that his mother had bought him years ago and wound it around his neck. David Boyd had confirmed that he was living at his parents' house in Knightsbridge. *A couple of turnings past Harrods, on the left.* Swift didn't like travelling on the tube and usually avoided it if at all possible. But it wasn't a day for driving through choked traffic or taking a struggling bus. For once, he'd be glad of the overheated confines of the deep tunnels.

* * *

David Boyd lived on the top floor of an elegant, white stucco four-storey town house. The ground floor window ledges held luxuriant, beautifully tended boxes of purple and cream winter pansies. Someone had already cleared the snow from them. Not a dead leaf or browning flower in sight. There were balconies from the first floor upwards, all holding terracotta tubs of more abundant pansies and trailing ivy. The smart green van parked outside with the lettering *Garden Matters* on the side testified to professional care.

Boyd answered the intercom with a cut glass accent and told Swift to take the lift in the hallway to the top floor. Swift stamped snow from his boots and stepped into an enormous, thickly carpeted arched hallway filled with brightly painted abstract canvases. The lift was opposite him, a slim, minimalist grey glass box with a digital operating pad. It rose silently to the fourth floor, affording him glimpses of recesses illuminated by spotlights and filled with more abstract artworks and tall Greek urns. The lift opened straight into Boyd's spacious apartment and for a moment, Swift recalled James Bond entering the lair of Stromberg, the villain in *The Spy Who Loved Me*. He could only hope that Boyd didn't plan to feed him to sharks.

Boyd was standing by the ornate marble fireplace in the centre of the room, talking on his phone. A huge pair of red and black earphones hung around his neck. He gestured to Swift to take a seat on one of the three powder blue sofas. The room was painted grey and blue with white floorboards. It contained an expensive TV and sound system with winking lights, a bookshelf with magazines and a tall wine rack. At the far end was a complicated looking exercise bike. There was nothing to suggest an interest in flying. The view across the powdery white roofs of London from the front window was stunning. The snow had stopped falling and Swift could see the dome of the Royal Albert Hall and the wide spaces of Green Park.

A rectangular, Hollywood style mirror framed by LED lights hung above the fireplace. Boyd glanced in it as he talked, fingering the front of his dark floppy hair. His conversation was about someone's engagement party and the music list needed. He assured his listener that he was putting it together, saying he couldn't believe that India wanted Ed bloody Sheeran. He sounded peevish. Swift crossed his legs and waited, studying Boyd's reflection in the mirror. He had jug ears, a sharp jaw and a long, ridged nose that was too big for his face and seemed to overshadow his small mouth. He wore ripped jeans, a wrinkled white vest and a grey cotton scarf looped about his shoulders. Finally, he ended the call and flopped down on one of the other sofas.

'So, this is about what happened to that wazzock Roscoe?' he asked spitefully.

'That's right. His mother and daughter are still grieving for him.'

'I imagine they're the only people who are. I'm certainly not.'

'His ex-wife indicated she feels the same as you.'

'Really? I never met her. Doesn't she work in a shop? I heard that he played the field. He had a photo of his daughter on his desk. She was called one of those incredibly chavvy names like Savannah. He used to go soppy over her and say she was his "princess". Yuk —

pass the sick bucket or what?' He gave a malicious little smile.

'I'm interested in your view of him. Sounds like you didn't like him.'

Boyd looked down along his nose and smirked. 'He was like the worst sort of school prefect, spying on chaps and running to spill the beans to the head beak to get them jerks.'

'Jerks?'

Boyd stared at him as if he'd failed to understand English. 'You know -punishment.'

'I see. The headmaster in this case being Silvio Horvat?'

'Yah. He's another prick. You know he sacked me?'

Swift avoided answering. 'That must have been tricky for you.'

'Too right. Daddy gave me hell about it and said I should sue him. Wrongful dismissal or whatever, but I couldn't be arsed.'

More like you knew you didn't have a leg to stand on. 'So what was that all about? I've heard that Roscoe could be a bit over the top.'

Boyd nodded. 'A horrible little shit and a pompous arsehole. Always convinced he was in the right. He never liked me. He once told me I was a toffee-nosed git who didn't know what a hard day's work was. Used to joke that I wasn't wearing my straw boater. You get that, you know, just because you've had a private education. It's discrimination but you can't say it when you're down with the plebs. Roscoe had a chip on his shoulder the size of the Isle of Wight because he'd grown up on some grotty sink estate and I had a *privileged* childhood and went to Harrow. He found out that my grandpa had been an Air Marshal during the war and he hated that because he was a nobody, from nowhere.' His tone had grown more supercilious and whining. He thought he'd been hard done by which might mean he'd spill a lot of useful information.

Well, Swift thought, you did attend a school that has its own farm, swimming pool, fishing lake and squash courts. 'Sounds pretty awful,' he said sympathetically.

'Thanks. Yah, it was, you know. I mean, I'd worked as hard as Roscoe to train as a pilot. I knew he had it in for me. I should have been more careful. I made a couple of stupid errors in my flight log and he blew it out of all proportion and persuaded the dimster Croatian to fire me.'

'I was given to understand that you didn't have the flying experience you claimed and deliberately forged records. So it was serious, hence the sacking.'

Boyd flushed bright red and shook his head indignantly. 'That's crap, pure crap! Just petty, vindictive people getting things *so* badly wrong!'

He had a furtive, guarded look. Swift said nothing in response to the lie. He looked out at the view and the bare treetops moving in the breeze, scattering snowflakes.

Boyd rubbed his eyes and gave a huge yawn, rubbing his scarf to his cheek. 'I had a late night at work. Haven't even had brekker yet.'

'What do you do now?'

'I run a nightclub in Kensington with a couple of friends. *Myth.* Do you know it?'

'I've not been there.' Swift had read about it. It was the haunt of minor aristocrats and their hangers-on. The club's long-suffering neighbours occasionally kicked up about their late night antics.

'It's going well. Bloody hard work, though, and one of my friends doesn't always pull her weight. Honestly, I get exhausted, having to be nice to people.' He sounded full of self-pity as he yawned again.

'Have you given up flying?'

'Yah. Daddy was furious with me because he thought I was following in my grandpa's footsteps, going into aviation. I mean, the dadster wanted me to join the RAF but I'm not into that kind of stiff upper lip stuff and saluting. But I liked being airborne. There's a super thrill when you're in control of a plane. And the extra bonus is that being a pilot is a babe magnet.' He smiled to himself. 'But what could I do? It was me against Horvat and Roscoe and they backed each other up. The C.A.A. fell for Roscoe's lies and revoked my licence. That jumped up prick ruined my chances for good. I could have made a mint if I'd been able to get taken on by a big airline.' There was sudden, vicious fury in Boyd's voice. His eyes watered and he gripped his hands together.

'You seem to have a decent lifestyle, even so,' Swift observed wryly.

'Huh! The dadster lets me live here but he's all about standing on my own feet and making my own money. He lost a huge wadge of cash in the crash of 2008 so he says I needn't think I'm going to inherit loads. And the rate he spends it at, there'll be nothing left when he croaks anyway. He's yachting in Thailand this month.'

'So you must have really resented Roscoe for what he did to you.'

'Too bloody right I did. But my girlfriend told me I had to let go of the anger or Roscoe would always be in my head. I knew what she meant and then I got the chance to start up *Myth,* so life moved on.' He grinned and added nastily, 'and of course Roscoe did go away. For good!'

'Leaving two children fatherless.'

Boyd didn't blink. 'Oh, yah, there is that.' He waved a dismissive hand. 'They're probably better off without him. Not much of a role model.'

Swift felt disgust but bit back a retort. 'Did you have any contact with Roscoe after you were sacked?'

'Not bloody likely. We hardly mixed socially! So, what's going on? If that weirdo Cairns chap didn't kill him, who did?'

'That's what I'm hoping to find out. Did you know anyone else who disliked Roscoe or of any business deals he was involved with?'

'Afraid not. I really didn't take much interest in him or what he was doing.'

Swift pictured Boyd gliding through the airfield with minimal contact with the hoi polloi. 'There was a man called Stef who Roscoe seemed to have crossed. Did you know him at all?'

'Doesn't ring any bells.'

'Did you know of any women Roscoe was seeing?'

Boyd leered and made a rude gesture. 'Seeing to, you mean. Peacocking around wearing cheap aftershave, thinking he was some kind of cut rate Don Juan. I know he gave Holly a prodding. We were all laughing about it because they were seen in the bushes with their knickers down. She came into the bar one day and overheard us splitting our sides over it. One of the guys was saying she must have mistaken Roscoe for the Chief Fucking Instructor. She was white with anger, I can tell you. I saw her shaking. I felt a bit sorry for her because she was always decent to me, never made any cheap jibes about class. The sniggering went on for quite a while afterwards and of course everyone knew. I reckoned she might have decided to stick a knife in the Gregster because she lost a lot of face over it and she was very serious about her career. I mean, a woman always comes off worse in that kind of situation, doesn't she?'

Swift was surprised at the flash of insight. 'Where were you the night Roscoe died?'

'Not sure I can remember,' Boyd said haughtily. 'Why should I?'

'Most people can recall where they were the night someone they knew well was murdered. It tends to stick in the memory.'

'I have a busy life. Anyway, why should I tell you?'

'Well, just like the police, I like to eliminate people from my enquiries.'

Boyd drew himself up, giving Swift his best sneer. 'You're not the police and I don't have to account for myself to you.'

'True, but I can't think why you wouldn't want to help with an unsolved murder. It's just that I was told that you were in Cornford and that you possibly had a girlfriend there. Someone saw you on the High Street, early evening.'

The information made Boyd uncomfortable. He frowned and fingered his scarf. 'I suppose that's possible, then.'

'Yet you and your father told the police you were here that night.'

'Did we? Well, I probably was then. If that's what we said, that's how it was . . . I might have mixed that evening up with another.' He made a vague, dismissive gesture.

'I got the impression you didn't spend much time in Cornford, other than at the airfield and you hadn't worked there for a while at that point. So I wondered why you might have been there.'

'I suppose I *might* have been seeing my girlfriend *if* I'd been there, which I *wasn't* if the dadster said I was here. Got it?'

'Could I verify that with your girlfriend?'

'No, you couldn't. We split up.' He got up and strode to the lift, opening the door. 'I've had enough of talking about Roscoe and his unfortunate mishap. He's like a bad smell coming back when you think you've got rid of it. You'll have to go now. I've work to do and I haven't even had a tosh yet.'

Swift couldn't be bothered to query the slang. He went back down in the lift. The front door clicked open as he approached and closed noiselessly behind him. He walked towards Harrods, enjoying the crunch of snow underfoot and decided to stop at a small café. He took a seat just inside the window and ordered a coffee. He watched the world go by, allowing his thoughts to circle around this case. The people who might have wanted to murder Greg Roscoe were stacking up. Ashleigh might have wanted to get rid of a cheating husband, especially as she had fallen for Barry Grafton. Or Grafton might have decided to stab him. Holly might have resented him enough. Feelings of shame and slow-burning revenge could be potent and she knew the layout of the airfield. And she was ambitious and had stepped into his shoes as CFI. David Boyd had to be a possible candidate. Roscoe had ruined his chosen career and Swift had glimpsed a malicious streak behind the public school slang and talk of having moved on. His story about a girlfriend in Cornford had sounded glib and hollow. Or, given Roscoe's activities, there could be some other spurned lover or jealous husband he hadn't come across yet. And then he needed to trace Stef, who had visited the airfield to demand money. Perhaps he was part of the business deal that Roscoe was concerned about and had mentioned to his mother. There were so many possible paths to go down. His mind whirled.

He drank his coffee as people plodded past with shopping bags, kicking up sprays of slush and blinking in the hazy light. His phone buzzed and he saw that he had a couple of emails and a voicemail message from a no ID caller. He read the email from Axel Roscoe first, noting the phone number he gave.

My mum told me you want to talk to me. I don't mind. Ring me.

The second email was from Camilla Finley.

Hi again, Mr Swift. I know you've met Paul Cairns and he told you I'm writing his story with him: One Man's Voice. *I've been hoping you'd contact me after my last email. It would be good to have your view of what Oliver Sheridan said about you. He's holding quite a grudge and he's not going to let go. And of course, your investigation into Greg Roscoe's death is of great local interest. So you're a good subject for a reporter, in the nicest possible way! I'd love to write a piece about you and how you go about looking for a murderer, how you follow up clues and set up interviews etc. Do give me a call. I think you'd find it worthwhile. Look forward to working together.*

Working together? He didn't think so. She had a cheek, thinking he'd cooperate with her after her sly article. Swift admired some investigative journalists but distrusted most reporters. Last year, he'd been door stepped by tabloid hacks who'd taken photos of him and Bella, contributing to his rift with Nora. Camilla Finley had her teeth in Paul Cairns and Swift reckoned that she'd benefit most from the relationship. He didn't fancy her teeth in him. He scrolled to the anonymous voicemail and listened. It was muffled, as if the caller was covering their mouth. He thought it was probably a woman's voice but it was hard to tell.

'Greg Roscoe was a bastard, but what happened was awful. I don't know . . . I'm worried about something I said — the effect it might have had. Maybe someone wanted to right a wrong. I don't know but . . . oh, I just—'

The call ended abruptly. Well, that was something or nothing. At times like this, Swift missed being part of the Met. Being able to trace calls was a major help in investigations. He could only hope the caller would ring back. He might be able to persuade him or her to say more.

* * *

When Swift arrived home and opened his front door on Friday evening, he found Chand and Havana Roscoe standing in the hall. She was patting her face with a towel. Chand raised his eyebrows at him as if to signal concern and ran his hand through his hair. He stepped towards the stairs, ready to escape.

'Ahm, Havana arrived about ten minutes ago. She wants to talk to you.'

'Oh, right. Hello, Havana.'

'Yeah, hi,' she said. Her hair was hanging damply around her face and she wore a lot of make up again, with a thick layer of glistening silver on her eyelids. Her eyebrows seemed thicker and darker, accentuating her pallid complexion. She was wearing a thin black cotton jacket over a flimsy, pink floral dress and red leggings. Her high-heeled black ankle boots emphasised her stick thin legs. A small white patent leather bag dangled from her shoulder with the Prada logo. He assumed it was a fake and thought it reflected her look: a young girl playing at being a grown up.

'Have you come here on your own?' He was half expecting Sally to be around somewhere.

'Yeah. I left school early.'

'Does Grace know you're here?'

She shook her hair around her face. 'No. None of her business.'

'Right.' He wanted to find out why she was on his doorstep but he remembered her and Sally's behaviour, particularly their sexual precociousness. He needed to be careful and didn't want her in his flat alone with him. He glanced at his watch. He and Nora were taking his boat to the Wye Valley for the weekend. Luckily, the snow was bypassing the Welsh borders and she was picking him up in a couple of hours. He needed to pack a bag but he could do that quickly. 'Tell you what,' he said, 'there's a café around the corner. We can get a cup of tea there and chat. Okay?'

'I'll be off then,' Chand said. 'Finished with the towel?'

'Yeah, thanks,' Havana said.

As he headed upstairs, she called softly after him. 'Thanks ever so much, Chand. You're a hero.' Her cheeks were matching the pink of her dress as she spoke.

'No worries!' he called, disappearing through his door.

In the café looking onto the Thames, Swift ordered the diet coke she asked for, thinking she'd be better off having a hot chocolate, as he was. He glanced at her as he paid. She was sitting sideways on a bench, with her legs up, her knees pulled towards her. She crouched over her phone, staring at the screen, her face hidden in her curtain of hair.

'Before we talk, what time would Grace be expecting you at home?'

'Dunno. She won't be. She's going straight from work to one of her crazy theme evenings.'

'What about Sally?'

'She's at some club this evening.' She tossed her hair. 'We don't keep tabs on each other.'

He thought that she was less sure without Sally around but also less forbidding and perhaps a little more approachable. 'Can you text Grace then, just to say where you are and what time you'll be home.'

She looked mutinous. 'Why? It doesn't make any difference to her.'

'I doubt that, and it's important to me. You're fourteen and in Grace's care and I want you to. In this weather, trains might be delayed or cancelled.'

She stared at him stonily and he thought she was going to refuse. He wasn't sure what he'd do if she did because he wanted to know why she had come. But she sighed heavily, then took her phone from the table and sent a text. She wasn't wearing nail varnish today and he saw the small depressions on her fingernails, knowing they were signs of malnutrition.

'Thank you,' he said. 'Now, what did you want to speak to me about?'

'It's about my dad.' She stirred the ice in her glass of coke and took a sip. 'I . . . I followed him the evening he was stabbed. Well, I hid in the back of his car.' There was a glint in her eye like a taunt as she looked at Swift.

'Okay. Tell me more.'

'Did *your* dad cheat on *your* mum?'

He saw how she wanted to play it. Some people liked a bit of give and take before they offloaded what they wanted to tell you. The trade-off made them feel more comfortable. 'I don't think so. Or the other way around. They always seemed devoted. They're both dead now.'

She surprised him by putting her head to one side and saying, 'I'm sorry for your loss.'

'Thanks. That's kind of you. I still miss them.' He held up a finger. 'Let me guess . . . that night wasn't the first time you'd hidden in your dad's car, was it?'

'No. How did you know?'

'It's like shoplifting. The first time someone's caught isn't usually the first time they've done it. They've just not been caught before.'

'I've never shoplifted!' she said indignantly.

He'd forgotten how literal teenagers could be. 'No, I didn't mean that. It was just an analogy.'

'Oh, right.' She fished out an ice cube and cracked it between her teeth. The sound made him shiver. Then she licked her lips and started talking very fast. 'I hated my dad seeing other women. I was always worried he'd leave us and I didn't want to be at home on my own with my mum. We never really got on. She always made me feel like a burden. When Dad was away flying she was always short tempered and nagging. And Jude was always there like mum's shadow, criticising Dad and me. She can't stand me. She has a key to the house and I always hated the way she could just let herself in. She lives round the back of ours. Dad used to say if she got any nearer, she'd have moved in. She was around all the time.' She yawned and rubbed her eyes. 'I thought Dad couldn't really love me, the way he carried on with all those women. I mean, he said he did and he gave me big hugs but he can't have, can he? Or he would have stayed at home at night instead of slapping on aftershave and getting in his car. And he was so pathetic, the way he lied about going out to meetings or to plan a flight or whatever. I mean, it was dead obvious, but he seemed to think Mum believed him. I used to hear them rowing in their bedroom and she'd be going on and on about him being a cheat and a liar. Once, she said she wished she'd never got pregnant and had to marry him — that it was the biggest mistake of her life and she was paying for it all the time. So, you know, that meant she wished she'd never had me. I knew that anyway. I knew it. She really wants the new little bastard, though, especially as it's a boy. She was showing the baby scan to anyone who'd look at it and pointing out his prick. "Look at his tiny willy!" Gross!' She made a hand into a fist and stopped. Her thin chest was rising and falling quickly under her gauzy dress.

'Take a drink, Havana' he said. 'It's okay, take things slowly.' Although he was conscious of the time and that Nora would arrive in about half an hour.

She slumped back and drank, the glass chinking softly against her teeth. He felt an overwhelming sadness for this girl who was adrift in the world and who had been neglected and emotionally confused for years. It said a lot about her self-absorbed, warring parents that she had been out of the house at night with neither of them aware of her absence. She tucked her hands into the sleeves of her jacket as if she was cold, despite the snug warmth of the small café.

'Can you love someone and hate them too?' she asked.

'Yes. I think that happens quite a lot in life. People are complicated.'

'That's how I felt about Dad. It messed with my head. I just hate Mum so it's simpler.'

'I'm sorry. It's hard for you.'

'Yeah. Tough shit. I don't need either of them now. Got my own life.' She pulled herself up and her expression became steely again. 'So anyway, some evenings when Dad went out I hid in the back of his car if I got the chance, to see where he was going. I was keeping a list of dates and times and I was going to challenge him with it. It was always somewhere local. He pissed on his own turf. Then I left the car when he wasn't looking and walked home or got a cab. I'd nicked his spare keys so I was always able to open it.'

'How many times did you do this?'

'I didn't get that many chances. That evening, the night he was stabbed, was the fourth. The first time he did actually just go to the airfield. To the bar there. The second, he was meeting that bitch Holly Armstrong at her house and the third he went into a wine bar in the market square.'

'Which one?'

'It's called Jewel. Up itself kind of place, all cocktails and olives. I had a look through the window but he was sitting on his own, looking fed up. I reckon he was stood up that night. Served him right. The night he was attacked, I knew he was up to something because he spent ages in the bathroom and I heard him shaving. He and Mum had had a blazing row a couple of days before and were hardly speaking. There was a horrible atmosphere. I was so pissed off with them both.'

'Do you know what the row was about?'

'Not exactly. I heard them shouting and slagging each other off when I came home and she'd been crying. The usual, I expect. *I should never have married you . . . Yeah, I couldn't agree more but you did so you'd better watch your mouth . . . You're a cheating bastard . . . Oh, hum a different tune, I'm tired of hearing that . . . You're the one who's a broken record, always stuck in the same old groove . . .*' Havana rolled her eyes. 'Yadayadayada. So *boring.* Anyway, I knew he'd had to finish with Holly and I wanted to catch him with this new shag interest. I hid just before he got in the car. He had a carrier bag and it clinked in the foot well beside him like it had booze in. He drove to a lay-by at the river, just near the marina. I knew he was on a date because he always hummed under his breath when he was on the pull. Either that or he played Madonna. There was a woman sitting on a bench on the path and he went and sat beside her. I was going to take a photo on my phone but someone else parked behind the car and opened his bonnet and I thought Dad might turn round and spot me.'

'Can you describe this woman?'

'I only saw her sideways on and from a distance. She was young — natch — and she had dark brown hair down to her shoulders, flicked up at the ends. She had a lacy blouse on and a white jacket. Quite smart for a date by the river. I didn't see her face properly. I watched for about ten minutes. They were talking and he got wine and plastic cups out of the carrier bag. He was being very attentive, leaning towards her. I could see she was laughing. I suppose he was telling her what a brilliant pilot he was and how pretty she was, blah blah. Whatever it took to get into her knickers. I got bored then and I started to get cramp so I headed home. That was the last time I saw him. Playing away. Playing with our lives.'

She drank the last of her coke and pulled her dress down over her knees, fingering the hem.

Swift felt his phone buzz in his pocket. That would be Nora, wanting to know where he was. 'Do you think this woman got to the river by car — was there another one parked nearby?'

She frowned. 'I didn't think about that. I don't remember any other cars there; except for the one that arrived just after us and that was a bloke who was tinkering with his engine.'

'You didn't mention any of this to your mum or to the police at the time?'

'Nah. Didn't see the point. They said that weirdo Cairns had stabbed Dad so I thought it must have happened after his date finished.' She looked up and past him, as if she was going back to that evening by the river. 'I didn't want to tell anyone about him and that woman. I haven't even told Sally. Dad was a shit but he was dead and I couldn't stand the thought of Mum badmouthing him all over again. She even slagged him off to the undertaker when he came round to talk about the funeral. God, she's so embarrassing. I would have said something if he hadn't been murdered. If he'd lived. Anything to try and stop him pissing about.'

It was helpful to see and hear the real Havana, the girl who didn't have to grandstand for her friend. Swift leaned towards her slightly. '*You* wrote that note that your mother received about Holly Armstrong?'

She hunched her shoulders and nodded. 'I did it at school and printed it off. I thought it might make Dad stop. As if! My mum's always been right about one thing. She said he thought with his prick. I need the loo.'

She rose abruptly and hurried to the Ladies, banging the door. Swift texted Nora to say that he was delayed with a client and would be there ASAP. He saw that he had a voicemail. He hoped it might be his anonymous caller again but it was from Camilla Finley, the Cornford reporter. A confident, arrogant voice.

Hi, Mr Swift. Camilla Finley here, Cornford Mail. I was disappointed that you didn't reply to my emails. Never ignore a friendly approach! Just to say, I've spoken to Oliver Sheridan again about your recent court case. He was more than happy to talk at length and gave me loads of interesting information about you. And maybe we could have a chat about your Roscoe investigation, see if you're getting anywhere. As you know, I'm very much on Paul Cairns's side. So call me!

He listened to the message again thinking *no, I bloody well won't call you.* Camilla Finley could mind her own business. He had more pressing matters to think about right now. For one, why had this woman who had met Roscoe by the river not contacted the police after his murder? Because she was the perpetrator or had an accomplice or perhaps was too embarrassed or scared to make herself known? Whatever had happened, she hadn't had sex with Roscoe. If she hadn't driven to the river, she had to be local — not that that told him a great deal. Holly had said that she'd met Roscoe at the river, too, so it seemed to be one of his preferred places for seduction.

He spooned up the thick, sweet sludge of chocolate from his mug. He wanted to walk Havana to the tube and make sure she had a return ticket. There was something wired about her that worried him. One minute she seemed softer and communicative, the next she was tense and curt again. It was hard to know if it was part of her anorexia and emotional turmoil or if she was jittery because of what she was telling him and the memories it stirred. He rang Grace Tansley and left her a message, explaining that Havana had come to visit him and that he was seeing her to the train.

Havana was gone for almost ten minutes. He recalled what Grace had said about her taking laxatives and wondered how long she might be. He wondered too about the long-term damage she might be doing to her developing body and the effect it could have on her adult life. He'd read that anorexia could result in impairment to the heart, bones and vision. He couldn't help thinking of Branna, hoping that his own daughter would never want to self-harm in that way. Just imagining it made him feel helpless.

When Havana came back, she stood looking down at him. She'd reapplied glossy cherry lipstick and brushed her hair.

'Do you think that woman stabbed my dad?'

'I have no idea. But I'll do what I can with the information. I'm glad you've told me.'

'There's one more thing,' she said, running her fingers up and down the strap of her bag. 'A couple of months before he died, Dad was pacing round the garden, muttering to himself. He looked really worried. I asked him what was wrong and he ruffled my hair and said something about the past catching up with him. He said, "Nothing for you to worry about, princess, nothing I can't handle." Then he said we should go to the supermarket and buy stuff to make ice cream floats because we deserved it. He was like that. Suddenly, he'd drop everything, grab his car keys and we'd go and get things for a barbecue or he'd make southern deep fried chicken or sticky ribs or big stacks of pancakes with bananas or bacon and maple syrup. He had all these amazing recipes from his travels. We often did that together when Mum and Jude were having one of their girls' nights out. Those were the best times.'

She looked miserable, her eyes reddening. Now the refusal of food made even more sense. Swift rose and moved towards the door.

'I think you should go home now. I'll go to the tube with you.'

She turned and shook her head. 'You don't need to. I'll remember the way.'

'I want to see you safely on your way home, make sure you're on the train.'

She started to scowl but then she nodded, blinking rapidly. 'That's the kind of thing my dad would have said.'

'Well then, you see, he did love you. He had his faults but he wanted to protect you. That's what dads do.'

'Yeah. Whatever.'

They walked to the tube in silence. There was a knife sharp breeze blowing from the river and she shivered now and again. He thought she should be wearing thicker, warmer clothes and felt a flash of anger because no one was making sure she did. Her thin fashion boots slipped on the pavement, the toes damp. He saw that she had a ticket through to Cornford. At the barrier, she flicked her hair and looked oddly coy.

'Chand's a nice bloke. Dead handsome. Is he an investigator, like you?'

'No. He's a proper detective, in the Met.'

'Is that why he's so fit?'

'Probably,' he said repressively, 'and he's thirty.'

'So? Sally reckons older men are better lovers. My mum seems to think so, from all the hot panting I've heard when she's shagging Barry.'

'You know,' he said quietly, 'you're carrying a lot of troubles for someone so young. You must want to put them down sometimes.'

She shrugged and looked away, then tossed her hair. 'Sally thought you were okay for a guy of your age although your hair and your clothes are weird.'

'I'm flattered. Havana, listen to me. You're fourteen. You don't have lovers at your age. It would be damaging as well as illegal.'

'It would be *illegal*,' she mimicked. Now she was the brittle, sharp-tongued girl she'd been with Sally. Then her mood shifted again. 'You'll find who murdered my dad, won't you?'

'I'll do my best.'

'Please. Please find who did it. I want to know they're rotting in prison. Once I know that, I'll be able to breathe again. I might even eat again.'

She reminded him of her grandmother. Their wishes were different but both were looking for peace: Pat Roscoe to die and Havana to resume her life. He looked down at her. Tears shone in her eyes.

'Go on home,' he said. 'I'm going to ring you at eight o'clock to make sure you've got back safe.'

The anger flashed back. 'Fuck off, you're not my dad.'

'No, but I'm an adult who thinks that a grieving fourteen-year-old girl should have someone knowing her whereabouts and looking out for her.'

She gave him a strange, puzzled look. 'Wow, you're *really* weird! Okay. But tell hunky Chand he can call me *anytime*.'

He watched her walk to the elevator, gossamer light as she moved, tripping slightly in her spiky boots. Then he shook his head and sighed, glancing at his watch. Nora would be waiting and tapping her foot, her arms folded.

Chapter 9

Fitz Blackmore rang Swift as he was standing in his dressing gown, scrambling eggs and toasting muffins for breakfast and listening to a weather forecast promising more snow followed by freezing rain.

'Yo, Ron. Four inches of snow and bloody chaos on the roads here,' Blackmore said. He sounded relaxed about it, cheerful even.

'I had a colleague in the Met who said that statistics showed a correlation between very cold weather and a slowdown in crime. Is that your experience?'

Blackmore laughed. 'Apparently, criminals aren't as tough as they used to be, frightened of catching a chill these days. Still, I'm not complaining. Let's just say I'm not usually sitting with a coffee and reading the local rag at this time of the morning. Speaking of which, I thought I'd give you a heads up again about the *Cornford Mail.* I don't suppose it's a newspaper that's usually on your radar.'

'You're right. I'd never heard of it until I read about Paul Cairns. Then you pointed me to Camilla Finley having me in her sights. When I saw Cairns, he confirmed that she's helping him write a book about what's happened to him. She's been trying to contact me, emailing and leaving messages. Seems to want to write about how I conduct an investigation. I've ignored her.'

'Camilla Finley and her bloody self-publicity.' Blackmore adopted a falsetto tone. '"Did I mention I'm writing a book called *One Man's Voice*?" Yeah, she's been all over Cairns. There'll be a heart-warming story about the skinny, dyslexic kid who was never understood but won his fight against the state. David and Goliath. Always goes down well. She's a right shit stirrer but her column's popular in town and she's carved quite a niche for herself. She's always giving us grief, or trying to. Thinks she's a red-hot investigator. Just what Cornford needs. She's a real looker, mind, but killer instincts. She came on to me once and I was tempted but I thought no, I'd always be expecting a knife in my back after pillow talk. I didn't fancy ending up as one of Finley's Finds. Camilla reminds me of what the French president said about Maggie Thatcher having the eyes of Caligula and the mouth of Marilyn Monroe. Anyway, mate, she's mentioned you again in an article today. There's a photo of you too. I think she must be annoyed that you've rejected her advances.'

Swift's heart sank. 'Maybe I should have spoken to her but it felt like I'd be giving in to a kind of blackmail.'

'It's a difficult one to play. It's probably best not to get into any extended dialogue with her. She'd twist anything you said to suit her. Although, word to the wise, it might be a good idea to throw her something, just a diplomatic token to fend her off. Well mate, I thought you'd like to know in case it's mentioned when you're in town. How's the investigation going?'

'Slow, steady. Someone might have been after Roscoe for money, maybe another pilot. I've no other details as yet.' He wasn't going to mention what Havana had told him for now. The police had missed more than one trick when they were looking into her father's murder and he didn't want Blackmore hassling her. He was a full-on, abrasive personality and he might feel he had a reputation to salvage.

'Not making much headway then. Speaking of which, any good rowing recently?'

'I had a break in the Wye Valley with Nora last weekend. Bloody freezing but a great time. Listen, I've got eggs cooking so I'd better go.'

He saved his eggs from burning, added black pepper and spooned them onto the golden muffins. The weekend had been lovely and Swift had felt fitter than he had for a long time. He and Nora had enjoyed strenuous trips on the river followed by delicious meals and beer at a comfortable hotel with a deep, warm four-poster bed. She'd been in sparkling humour and time had flown. His news about Ruth's new partner seemed to make her particularly happy. She'd made a flippant remark about Ruth maybe moving to Guernsey, not aware that he'd already considered that as an outcome and she was touching an exposed nerve. He was trying not to think ahead and anticipate loss. After all, Ruth and Marcel might be a temporary item. But the possibility of them setting up home together and Branna living hundreds of miles away alarmed him. He knew he was feeling sensitive about it and wished Nora wouldn't tap into and magnify his gloomy imaginings.

They'd come home weather-beaten, tired and happy. Yet he had found his thoughts straying to Havana Roscoe throughout the weekend and in the early hours, when late night revellers on the street woke him. He'd checked that she'd reached home safely on the Friday night but she'd been curt and hostile when he rang her, telling him to piss off. He'd heard Sally in the background, asking if it was Sherlock calling and thought that Havana was playing up to her audience.

He read the *Cornford Mail* online as he ate his eggs. The article about him with Camilla Finley's strapline, Finley's Finds, was on Page 5. The photo showed him looking startled and he reckoned it was one taken by the reporters who'd door stepped him with Bella the previous year.

The Elusive Tyrone Swift

He's the private investigator who's in town, looking into the murder of Greg Roscoe. He's so private he won't return my emails and calls! Has he got something to hide? Now you know what he looks like so if you see him, tell him Camilla's waiting for a chat.

The hard-to-track Mr Swift has been seen talking to people at Cornford flying club, including Paul Cairns. Paul told me Mr Swift bought him a drink so I suppose he can't be all bad! The book I'm writing with Paul, One Man's Voice is coming along nicely. The more I talk to him, the more I admire Paul's courage and determination.

Mr Swift has also spoken to Havana Roscoe, the dead man's grieving daughter. Let's hope that all these questions are getting him somewhere, although a little bird told me that one of the people he talked to smacked him in the face. Oops! Maybe his interview technique needs a bit of polishing! He certainly seems to rub people up the wrong way. You'll remember I mentioned Oliver Sheridan, who lost a court case against Mr Swift. He's certainly a man with a grievance!

Talking about people not liking Mr Swift, I can report that last year, a young man, Ben Ramsay was murdered in his house. Mr Swift's baby daughter was present when the corpse was found. The killer turned out to be involved in Swift's investigation. I spoke to Mrs Ramsay, Ben's mother. She holds Mr Swift responsible for her son's death. She told me, "Ben was immature. He had a learning difficulty and was easily influenced. He hero-worshipped Swift. That man encouraged him and let him help on a case. He got Ben to do his dirty work for him and Ben ended up dead. I hope Swift doesn't sleep at night. I know I don't."

Hey, Mr Swift, it's good to talk and there seems to be plenty to chew over! Go on, pick up the phone!

Swift was furious. The woman was digging around in his life and breathing down his neck. She was certainly taking a keen interest in his investigation. He had a feeling that Jude must have told her about the slap in the face. Well, he wasn't going to contact the reporter to justify himself, no matter how much she set out to annoy him.

* * *

When Swift rang Axel Roscoe, he could hear loud background echoes and the noise of a Tannoy. Axel's voice was faint.

'In about an hour is convenient. You can come and see me then.'

'Okay. Where?'

'St Pancras International. I'll be playing the piano on the main concourse.'

Swift had never conducted an interview in a train station before but there was a first time for everything. He walked through the grand, bustling concourse, narrowly avoiding having his ankle ripped by a man with a rigid, wheeled suitcase like a tank and his nose glued to his phone. The Tannoy pinged and a woman with a breathy voice announced in English and then French that the 14.30 from Brussels had arrived. There were a further three musical pings as a severe sounding man delivered a security announcement and advised that CCTV was in operation. Then another ping and a younger, cheerful, cockney voice that reminded Swift of Niall Roscoe appealed for everyone to be alert and report anything suspicious: '*See it, Say it, Sorted*'.

Swift heard the piano as he approached, a pacy rendition of *Keep the Home Fires Burning* that segued into *Pack up Your Troubles*. A small audience laden with bags and suitcases clustered around the piano player. Many of them were taking photos of him and of the life size Perspex silhouette of a WW1 soldier holding a rifle and standing at the side of the piano. The silhouettes had appeared all over London in commemoration of the centenary of the Great War. They were called *There But Not There Tommy*. Swift thought they were effective and poignant, their transparency lending them an eerie, sad dignity as they mingled unexpectedly and silently with the public.

Swift waited to one side while Axel leaned into the keyboard and finished *It's a Long Way to Tipperary* with flying fingers. There were quite a few discordant or missed notes but what he lacked in skill he made up for with enthusiasm. He was a slim figure in a bottle green duffel coat with close shaved, hay coloured hair to an inch or so above his ears. Then thick, long dreadlocks took over, swept upwards into a kind of fan secured by a band of dark ribbon. Swift moved across and bent down to speak in his ear.

'Axel Roscoe? I'm Tyrone Swift.'

Axel executed a final ripple of chords, and then stood, taking a little bow to the applause. He had a pale, heart-shaped face, dark, hazel flecked eyes and the most facial piercings that Swift had ever seen: five silver studs arching across each eyebrow; two studs at the top of his nose; two more in each nostril and three hoops through his bottom lip. When he said hello he revealed another stud in his tongue.

'Is this a regular spot for you?' Swift asked.

'I come whenever I can in my lunch break. It's good to see exhausted travellers enjoying the music. And I have to sit around a lot for my work so I get to let off a bit of steam.'

The Tannoy boomed again with a deafening announcement about departures for Paris.

'Can we talk somewhere a bit quieter?' Swift asked.

'I have to go back to the stall. We can talk there.'

Axel spoke softly and precisely and headed off without checking if Swift was following him. He attracted some looks as he passed, his fan of hair swaying like a peacock's tail but he gave no indication of being aware of the glances. Swift caught him up and took a close look at his dreadlocks. They appeared to be woven from fabric. They walked back along the station concourse, through the arched entrance to a paved square where the snow had turned to a thick grey, icy slush. There was an outdoor market of about thirty stalls. It was just five weeks to Christmas and the place was busy with shoppers buying from selections of jewellery, charcuterie, scented candles, handmade crafts, ceramics, chocolates, toys, cards, cakes and liqueurs. Scents of mulled wine and frankfurters drifted in the air. A woman was playing *The Holly and the Ivy* on a glockenspiel.

Axel nodded thanks to a young man who was sitting on a stool behind a stall called *Art of Dying*. The man handed over a bunch of keys and moved off to the stall next door, which sold delicious looking crusty pies. Axel pulled out a second stool and gestured for Swift to sit down. The blue canvas awning over the stall snapped in the sharp breeze. It was decorated with puffy white cloud shapes, soaring golden angels and plump cherubs.

'This is where you work?' Swift asked.

Axel crossed his legs, pulled up the collar of his red polo neck jumper and tucked his hands into his deep coat pockets. He resembled a garden gnome in his hooded duffel, albeit a thin, alternative kind of gnome. 'Yep. I run the stall with Zeena, my girlfriend. She makes most of the mementoes and I manage the business side.'

Swift had to strain to hear him over the buzz of the market and traffic noises. He glanced at the array of goods set out in wooden trays on the stall. 'So you make things to do with dying?' He wondered how that sat amongst the festive cheer.

'For funerals mainly, yes. Zeena's mum's a vicar and she gave us the idea. Lots of people want friendlier, laid back funerals these days. You know . . . more colourful and involving. So we make funeral favours for mourners.'

Swift recalled wedding favours at Simone and Mary's marriage. It was the first time he'd heard of such things. Simone had made them, fussing for weeks over the cream and gold pyramid shaped boxes decorated with doves and containing miniature framed photos of the happy couple and a tiny personalised shot glass for each guest. Swift had dropped and smashed his glass some weeks later and hoped it didn't bode ill for the marriage.

'That's a new concept to me,' he told Axel. 'Do you make a good living at it?'

'We started last year and it's going fairly well. We do stuff online, too of course.' He must have noticed Swift's sceptical glance because he leaned forward. He had an earnest manner. 'Mourning jewellery and tokens are as old as humanity, you know. They can help people cope with a loss and feel that the person they loved is still with them, connected to them. Ancient people used to carry keepsakes, little reminders made from woven hair, teeth, skin, blood and fingernails of the dead. Victorians often had a family photo taken around the open coffin with the deceased. We're carrying on a long tradition. Have you had a recent bereavement?'

'Not that recent, no.' Although it seemed like just yesterday when he had sat by Cedric's hospital bed, watching him laugh and play dominoes and plan his return home, unaware that death would come for him in the early hours.

'Well, if you had and you consulted us we could offer you a range of options.' Axel's tone grew more solemn and measured as he went into salesman mode, switching up a gear. 'For the day of the funeral, we can provide small memorial stones, pocket charms or angel coins. We can personalise them with the name of the person who has passed or phrases such as *Always remembered*, *In our hearts* etc. Some people like to distribute our memorial tree seedlings or wild seed cards. Instead of wasting flowers, we can offer lovely paper flower wreaths for mourners to take home and keep forever. After the funeral, we can enclose the deceased's ashes or hair in earrings, pendants, rings, charms, bracelets, glass spheres, cufflinks, candle holders, wind chimes or sun catchers for the family or for more general distribution. One woman asked Zeena to incorporate some of her husband's ashes in a painting of his allotment.'

Swift found the array of possibilities baffling. He took an angel coin from a tray in front of him. It featured a plump angel with wide wings and a halo, floating up through clouds. *In Memory of a Special Mum* was engraved above the halo. Swift thought it was tacky and he'd have run a mile from all of the stuff on the stall when planning Cedric's funeral. He certainly didn't want anyone distributing bits of him around when he died, maybe gluing some of his ashes into the hull of a boat. It seemed to contradict the idea of *Rest in Peace.*

'Good luck with it all,' he said. 'Was there anything like this at your dad's funeral?'

'I've no idea. I didn't go,' Axel said dismissively.

'Right. You didn't want to?'

'No. I didn't have any tears to shed for him so I wasn't going to pretend grief. Unlike him, I'm not a hypocrite.'

'I suppose your mum wouldn't have wanted you to attend.'

'That's right. He cheated on her all the time and then replaced her with that awful Ashleigh woman. But I made my own decision. He treated us badly.' Axel drew a pair of woollen gloves from his pockets and put them on, pressing down between his finger joints.

'Did you see much of your dad after the divorce?'

‘Why are you asking?’ The new voice came from behind Swift. He smelled a dense, musky scent as he turned on his stool. She was stunningly beautiful and dressed in a velvet coat with a fur collar, cinched in at the waist and flowing to her ankles. Its inky blue colour caught and reflected the wintry light. A furry hand-warmer in the same material hung from her neck. Her dreadlocks were shiny and real, woven into an intricate grid pattern that rippled down the right side of her head.

‘This is Zeena,’ Axel said, reaching out to catch her hand.

‘Hi,’ Swift said. ‘I was asking because I’ve come to talk to Axel about his dad’s life and death.’

‘I know. Life and death . . . the stuff of our work.’ She sat on Axel’s lap, almost hiding him with her long, slender body and fixed an assessing, unsmiling gaze on Swift. She had her own facial piercings in the form of three jade coloured stars at the corner of each eye and three across the bridge of her nose. She wore no makeup and needed none. ‘Well, ask away then.’ She draped an arm around Axel’s shoulder and stroked his neck with long fingers. He closed his eyes briefly, a smile crossing his face.

‘I talked to Havana. She said your dad phoned you.’

Axel sighed. ‘Hmm. Look, my mum took me back to Cagliari to live when they divorced. It was bitter. She was bitter. I heard nothing from Dad for years. My mum didn’t want any contact. I came back to London when I was nineteen. I love my mum’s family but they’re very religious and claustrophobic. Plus there were few job opportunities and I feel English. I never really fitted in back in Cagliari. Dad found out somehow that I was here — he always had ways of getting information through the pilot mafia.’ He tightened his arms around Zeena.

‘So your dad contacted you?’

Axel looked up at Zeena as she held his face between her hands and touched her nose to his. She turned to

Swift. She had been staring hard at him with her dark, almond shaped eyes while Axel was talking.

'Stirring up memories for people can be dangerous. It can take them to bad, dark places they don't want to revisit.'

'I understand that. I'm only asking because someone killed Axel's father and mutilated him. Whatever wrong he did to his son, he didn't deserve to die in that way.'

She raised her eyebrows, unconvinced, but said, 'You have to promise not to tell Yvette any information that Axel gives you. He loves his mum. He doesn't want her hurt any more. She suffered.'

'Okay. I don't want to cause any suffering.' Although sometimes that was exactly what his work caused.

Zeena nodded to Axel, resting back against him. He rubbed his chin on the soft sleeve of her coat and took a breath.

'I met my dad just the once, here in London. It didn't go well. He was trying to justify his actions and started saying unpleasant things about my mum when I challenged him. I walked out. After that, he phoned me now and again. He kept going on about being given another chance. One time, he waxed sentimental and said he wished he'd stayed with my mum, as Ashleigh was hard work. I laughed at that. I knew what his agenda really was.'

'And what was it?' Swift asked.

'He knew my mum had inherited money and property when her dad died. Someone he knew who worked with her at the airport told him. The wealth was certainly as attractive as my mum.'

Zeena shook her head. 'What a complete bastard!' she said.

'Yeah, and some,' Axel agreed. 'Dad forgot that I saw my mum in pieces when he told her he didn't want her any more. I sat on the stairs and heard her pleading with him. I heard her say, "But what about our son?" and him replying, "What about him?" I heard her crying for months, sobbing her heart out. He'd persuaded her to leave her family and friends in Cagliari, give up her job and live in England. Then as soon as he married her, he started seeing other women. She used to be so lonely in Cornford, where she didn't know anyone. She found English people standoffish and she missed her work and her family. I didn't forget any of that.' Axel frowned, his mouth twisting.

'Men like him are careless with other people's lives. Someone got careless with his. Sad, but . . .' Zeena shrugged.

'When did you last speak to your dad?'

'A week or so before he died. He called a couple of times that month. He was trying to get me to meet again. He said I should get to know my sister. Mend things. Pretending he was family minded. I said no thanks. I could tell he was having an attack of conscience.'

'He got like that after his wife made him give up his stellar career,' Zeena said spitefully. 'He had more time to think once he was stuck in Cornford with his wings clipped. I reckoned he was bored and that's why he was looking for ways to meddle in Axel's life. I thought Axel should change his phone number.'

'His dad might have had some genuine regrets,' Swift said, playing devil's advocate.

Zeena snorted. 'I doubt it.'

'Did you know him?'

She tucked her hands into her furry warmer and gave him a blank look. 'Only by reputation. Axel told me all about him. I wouldn't have wanted to know him, thanks very much.'

They were a solemn, intense kind of couple, Swift thought. Perhaps dealing with the dead and bereaved made them that way. A light sleet started to fall and the sky was darkening. The market's customers had dwindled and now there were hardly any left.

Axel sat forward slightly. 'The last time I spoke to him, he said he had an important meeting coming up. Said it might change his life around and he'd tell me more later. But then there wasn't any later.'

'He didn't give you any details about when or who he was meeting?'

'No. He liked to drop hints. He sounded a bit excited about it. Knowing him, it was probably something to do with making money.'

'Speaking of which, I've been told that your dad might have had some tricky business dealings or owed someone money. Does that ring any bells?'

Axel shook his head. 'My mum always said that he was slippery where money was concerned. He liked to make it and spend it. She had to fight hard to get a decent settlement from him but she did. He underestimated her where that was concerned. A couple of years ago, she mentioned that she'd heard he was into some business deals with flight crew but I don't know any details. She said something about him being up to his usual tricks. There's a Sardinian saying: *you might as well try to hold an eel by the tail.* She often used that about my dad.'

'How did she know about that if they had no contact?'

'Aviation is massive but it's also a small world in some ways. The same crew turn up working for different airlines. I think Mum was chatting to a flight attendant who had come off a flight to Cagliari and who'd been working with my dad.'

The sleet suddenly turned icier and the wind was kicking up rubbish. Some stallholders were starting to pack away. Zeena stood abruptly, her hands linked in her warmer.

'None of this must get back to Yvette!' she said aggressively. 'You get it? Yvette and Axel don't need any more grief over that dead bastard.'

Swift stood too. He didn't like her tone or her attitude. He addressed himself to Axel.

'I will email your mum to ask her about the person who mentioned your dad's business dealings. I won't say anything about your having met him or spoken to him in England. Oh, and your nan said she'd love to hear from you. I said I'd pass the message on if I saw you.'

'No way that's going to happen,' Axel said flatly. 'She'll just want to go on about how Dad was a good bloke, really, and much misunderstood. And Nan was unkind to my mother when she was feeling down, criticised her religion and told her a moaning woman is unattractive. I don't need to hear that kind of stuff, thanks.'

'Up to you. I'm just passing on the message. Final question . . . where were you the night your dad died?'

Zeena answered. 'With me and my family in Hackney, celebrating my mum's sixtieth birthday.'

He left them and glanced back as he exited the market. No one had visited their stall while he was there, yet all the others had been hives of activity. Perhaps their goods didn't fit with the cheer of the season. But death visited at any time, ignoring the calendar. Axel and Zeena were standing in a close embrace, his head buried in her shoulder, her arms clasping him tight.

He walked for a while through the chill darkness, enjoying the rush hour bustle and clamour of the streets. The air was growing colder, iron hard in his nose. Both of Roscoe's children had commented on their father's concerns. Havana had said that he had been worried about the past catching up with him and Axel had recalled that Roscoe was due to have an important, possibly life changing meeting. Were these two things connected and, if so, was the meeting connected to his death?

* * *

Swift arrived in Cornford a couple of hours before the night's entertainment with the *Amazing Aviators*. He'd arranged to pick Nora up at the station at six thirty. He wanted to take a look at Jewel, the wine bar where Havana had once seen her father. He had to have met his mystery woman somewhere and Jewel had to be a possibility. Then Swift planned to visit the marina and the place where Havana said her father had met his latest date on his last evening.

He drew a blank in Jewel, a small bar with low lemon and green lighting, specialising in craft gins. The manager didn't need to look at Roscoe's photo. She confirmed that Roscoe had occasionally called in there but was always alone. He'd expressed interest in dealing in craft gin soon after it became popular and had picked her brains about the new and expanding market. But he cooled off when she'd told him they had a long-term contract with an east London distillery. She added that he hadn't been in for a while before he died.

He drove to the lay-by where Roscoe had left his car, parked his own there and walked across a patch of scrubby grass to the bench on the path. There was just the one wooden bench and a rubbish bin beside it. The river stretched away to the right, rippling darkly. To the left, the path led to the marina in the distance. The area was set apart, the kind of place you might choose if you didn't want to be interrupted.

He walked towards the marina in the dusk. It was quiet, a little bleak in the failing December light. Swift could imagine it in the warm summer months, bustling and attractive. He passed an area with boats for sale and a chandlery selling boat parts and accessories. The door was open and he caught wonderfully mingled aromas of oil, linseed and wax. There was a hard-standing area where boat owners could work. Two women were painting a small, panelled vessel with a cabin at the front in white and black. They were calling it a day, wiping brushes and discussing what they would have for dinner. About a dozen boats of different types and sizes were moored at the marina. A pub called The Ferry Inn stood at the further end, facing the river. It was half-timbered, the name in gothic script above the low door and gleaming windows. Swift called in there and asked the same questions about Roscoe but drew another blank. The bar staff didn't know him and none of them recognised his photo or remembered seeing him in there before he died. He walked back to the lay-by, thinking that Roscoe and his friend might have driven to the airfield in his car but had she knifed him or had it been someone else entirely?

Chapter 10

The Check-in bar at the airfield was busy when Swift and Nora arrived. He spotted Fitz Blackmore lounging at a table near the door with two empty chairs beside him. Blackmore waved them over, grinning.

'Hi, Ron! You can park here. No one wants to sit with a cop.'

Swift made introductions. Blackmore stood, offering his hand to Nora and directing a full beam smile at her. He looked raffishly stylish in a beautifully cut dark suit, with the top buttons of his white shirt undone and his tie unknotted.

'You look casually formal,' Swift said.

'I came straight from a divisional meeting with the brass, no time to change. I'm not sure this is my kind of thing but Cornford doesn't offer a lot of choice in terms of entertainment and they have decent wine here.' He leaned towards Swift. 'Hey mate, see that woman on the other side of the room, next to Paul Cairns? That's Camilla Finley.'

Swift glanced across and saw a blonde woman with long curling hair and carmine lipstick, holding a pint of beer. She was scanning the room and their eyes met briefly. She gave a little smile and tipped her glass towards him.

'Is she reporting on the evening?' Swift asked.

'Probably. But who really knows why Camilla is here? Occasionally she indulges her am-dram streak and appears as one of these strolling players. She played Nell Gwynne at the Cornford town hall Restoration themed evening a few months back. I reckon she's here tonight as Cairns's minder. Can I get you both a drink?'

As soon as he left the table, Nora tapped Swift's arm.

'*Ron*?'

'Don't ask. Blackmore's idea of fun and playing head honcho.'

'Nah, I reckon he fancies you and it's a term of endearment.' Nora made a silent kiss with her lips.

Swift shook his head at her. He hoped that Blackmore wouldn't indulge in any of his non-PC views during the evening. Nora would tear him limb from limb.

While Blackmore fetched wine, Swift looked again at Cairns. He was wearing his flying jacket, teamed with a neck scarf. His binoculars were around his neck. He said something to Camilla Finley and she patted his arm. Swift spotted Jude Chamberlain at the bar, standing on tiptoe and chatting to Blackmore. She wore a clinging, bright yellow dress and her hair was loose and styled in bouncy waves. As he said something to her, bending low, she twirled a strand of hair girlishly between her fingers and threw her head back, laughing.

'That's the scumbag reporter over there, is it?' Nora asked.

'Apparently. I'll avoid her if I can.'

'I bet she tries to nail you, as she seems to have recognised you. This is a novelty . . . middle England at play. Looks like most people have dressed from the same catalogue. We look a bit like the poor relations.'

Swift knew what she meant. The men were all in versions of chinos and check shirts with v necked sweaters, the women in dresses or black trousers with blouses. He was wearing jeans and a slightly frayed grey sweatshirt and Nora was also in jeans and a green hoodie. Her short hair looked as it usually did, as if she had just run her fingers through it. She was scrutinising the room, keen eyed, missing nothing. Her ability to assess and sum up a situation was one of the things he loved about her.

Holly Armstrong came in, still in her flying instructor uniform and nodded as she headed to a group at a table at the back of the room. Swift reflected that a number of the people associated with Greg Roscoe were present tonight. Cornford was a reasonably big town but paths seemed to interweave easily.

The pre-ordered food arrived as Blackmore returned with their drinks and the show started as soon as everyone was eating. The costumed Aviators came in one by one, introducing themselves and passing among the tables, causing laughter by stopping to steal chips or bread from the diners. The drama was cleverly constructed with their stories told through conversations and occasional arguments between them. Grace Tansley / Amy Johnson winked at Swift as she selected an olive from his plate and described landing in a sand storm in the Iraq desert during her solo flight from England to Australia. At the end, the Aviators sat on stools at the bar, facing the audience, and answered questions. There was deafening applause when the show finished.

Swift headed to the toilet and saw Jude Chamberlain tripping towards him on her high black stilettos as she came from the Ladies. She was rubbing a flowery smelling moisturiser into her hands. He could tell she was going to ignore him from the way she turned her eyes away so he spoke.

'No Ashleigh with you tonight?'

She glowered at him. 'Ashleigh's at home, taking care of herself and the baby. She hasn't been feeling well since you door stepped her and she hasn't long to go now. She's literally huge and a bit self-conscious. I'll call round there on my way home, make sure she's okay.'

'Hasn't she got a husband for that?'

'A girl always needs her bestie,' Jude said airily. 'Especially when she's feeling a bit poorly.'

Swift looked into her bright, liquid eyes. 'I think your friend is made of sterner stuff than you make out.' He moved closer. 'I bet you know the truth about Ashleigh and Barry. *Was* she seeing him before Greg died?'

Jude made a little moue of mischief with her mouth and stroked the back of her hair. 'Wouldn't you like to know? That's the kind of thing only your best friend knows about you.'

'Or maybe your neglected daughter who has eyes and ears.'

She tutted, gave him two fingers and walked away. When he exited from the Gents into the corridor, he almost tripped over Camilla Finley who was leaning against the wall.

'I was hoping to catch you, Mr Swift,' she said brightly. 'I'm Camilla Finley. I think the handsome but useless DI Blackmore pointed me out to you.'

'Do you often loiter around the Gents toilets?'

'When I need to. You'd be surprised where a reporter loiters to get a story. You haven't replied to my emails or my call.'

'That's right.'

'Not very friendly. I'm a tad disappointed.'

She was curvaceous and solidly built in a way that reminded him of female stars of the 1940s, her hair sweeping from a side parting low over her left eye. She wore dark red leather trousers and a plum coloured silky top. Her smile was lively but meaningless. He went to move past her but she stepped sideways, blocking him.

'Don't you want some publicity?' she cajoled. 'There's loads of interest in crime, especially a local murder that's unsolved. Have your questions got you anywhere? You must have talked to quite a few people by now, got loads of info.'

'That's not public information.'

'Oh, come on. Don't be so uptight. I'm sure you can share something. A little teaser or two. Throw a hard working reporter a morsel. It's not as if you've signed the official secrets act.'

'I suppose the clue's in the word *private* detective. If you were the one paying me, I'm sure you'd want to be the first to know what I'd found out.'

She tapped her nose. 'Ah, confidentiality. I get it. But you could just give me a hint if you have any suspects, for example. You could wink at me now.'

He gave her a blank stare. 'No comment.'

'You're so tiresome! And don't you want to put your point of view about Oliver Sheridan? I would if I was in your shoes.'

'No, I don't. I'd have thought my lack of communication must have told you that. You're the tiresome one, sending me unwanted messages.'

She pursed her lips. 'Mr Sheridan is going to try and cause further trouble for you, you know. He's a man on a mission to undermine your reputation.'

'And you seem to be giving him plenty of help.'

She shrugged. 'Just doing my job, putting stuff out there in the public domain. I could give you some positive PR, you know.'

'I'm not sure you could, not that I need PR. I don't want to discuss Sheridan or anything else with you. You'll just have to wait for the outcome of my investigation.'

'You're not very friendly. I guess you're just not getting very far and you don't want to admit it. Your reputation would suffer. As for your personal life, maybe you've got too much you don't want revealed. As you know, I've been doing plenty of digging about you. You lead an eventful life, what with murders and stuff happening all around you.'

'If you say so.'

'Oh, very cryptic. Well, how about Paul Cairns? Is he a safer topic? Did his information help you at all?'

'Early days. Maybe, maybe not.'

'Have you—'

Swift took advantage of a couple of women heading past them to duck to the side and go back to the bar. He saw Nora and Blackmore deep in conversation over cups of coffee.

'Shop talk.' Nora smiled at him as he sat down. 'Fitz was telling me about a major drugs bust they had recently. Did Camilla Finley track you? We saw her heading to the corridor.'

'She pounced on me and tried an interrogation. Said she wants to help me with my PR. I turned her down.'

Blackmore snorted into his coffee. 'God help us. Watch out for her, though, Ron. She's like a dog with a bone.'

'People have said that about me — at work, that is,' Nora said.

'Ah well, there are good dogs and bad dogs. I'd say you're a pedigree.'

Nora raised her eyebrows at him, looking displeased and he shrugged apologetically, mouthing *sorry* until she laughed. Swift left them to talk shop again, saying he wanted to catch Holly Armstrong. She was on the veranda, talking on her phone and he waited out of earshot until she'd finished the call.

'Hi,' he said. 'I tracked David Boyd down and spoke to him.'

She nodded. 'Silvio said he'd talked to you. I suppose Boyd was saying we stitched him up.'

'More or less. He was damning about Greg Roscoe and Silvio but nicer about you.'

'Really? Can't think why. I didn't have any time for the man. Couldn't stand him and his arrogant attitude.'

'He said you were okay to him. Also, he seemed to have some sympathy for you.'

She was standing with her back to the veranda rail in half shadow, just out of the light but he sensed her stiffening.

'Sympathy? I wouldn't have associated Boyd with sympathy. Egotism and elitism, yes.'

Swift moved to stand beside her, glancing down at her shaded face. 'He said that some people made fun of you when they heard about you and Roscoe. People were laughing in the bar one day and you came in. That must have been tough on you.'

She folded her arms and looked away to the side, so that he could glimpse only the curve of her cheek. 'Boyd's a real tell-tale tit. He was always exaggerating. I wouldn't pay any attention to his gossip. I've never cared about what other people say. When you're a woman in aviation you have to develop a tough hide.'

He could hear the strain in her voice and decided to leave it for now. 'Do you know if David Boyd had a girlfriend in Cornford?'

'No idea. He didn't talk about his personal life or mix socially here. Seems unlikely. He never expressed any interest in the town and just seemed to drive here from London for work. Why do you ask?'

'Just a remark someone made. When I spoke to Paul Cairns, he said that someone called Stef came here one day a couple of months before Roscoe died. This man Stef was threatening Roscoe, saying he was owed money. Cairns reckoned he was a pilot, or certainly connected with flying. Do you know who this guy Stef is or anything about the incident?'

She took a breath and shook her head. 'Doesn't mean anything to me. Cairns is another man who exaggerates, you know. Another attention seeker. I've got to go, that was a friend on the phone who needs a lift.'

He watched her walk speedily away, threading through the crowded bar. She was lying about something but he wasn't sure what and he didn't think she was as tough as she pretended to be.

He rejoined Blackmore and Nora. They talked for a while longer about rowing and the merits of different rivers until Nora called it a night, saying she had an early start the next day. She was going back to her flat, to work into the early hours on a report.

* * *

Swift had dropped Nora off and was driving home when Chand Malla rang him. He sounded terse.

'Are you in London?'

'Yes, not far from Hammersmith now.'

'Can you get here ASAP? We have an emergency. Havana's here again, very emotional. Something about a row with her mum. I've brought her up to my flat because she's in such a state. Call an ambulance.'

Swift accelerated, wondering what the medical emergency could be. He made the call for an ambulance as he drove. He was at his house within ten minutes. He ran up the stairs to Chand's flat. The door was open. He could hear Chand talking, quietly and calmly.

'It's okay, Havana. We can help you. You're not alone.'

'Stop saying that!' she sobbed, as Swift walked in to the living room, noting that the air was icy.

She was sitting in the wide open window, her legs dangling out, just one hand against the frame. Her cotton jacket was on a chair and she was dressed in leggings and a thin T-shirt, her white Prada bag slung around her chest. Her shoulder blades stuck out like sharp knives. Two full mugs of coffee were standing on a low table. Swift said her name and she turned her face. Her eyes were raw and bruised looking, black eyeliner streaking down her cheeks.

Chand was standing to the right of the window, not near enough to reach her.

'Don't come near me,' she said, without emotion. 'If you come any nearer — or if he does — I will jump.'

'Okay, I won't come any nearer. Can we help you, Havana?'

'Doubt it.' She shivered as a gust of bitter wind rattled naked tree branches outside. A full moon hung in the clear wintry sky.

Swift was trying to remember training he'd had on dealing with attempted suicide many years back. *Be supportive and keep the person talking* was the main mantra he recalled. He hoped Chand would be thinking the same. 'I'm sorry you're so upset. Chand said you rowed with your mum.'

'What's new there?' She was looking down.

'You could tell us about it. You came here for a reason.'

'Her and her fucking Baby Jesus. She said she doesn't understand why I'm so *ungrateful* and seeing me was too worrying and bad for the baby. Went on about her blood pressure. Told me I was always looking for attention and to pull myself together. She asked me not to contact her until after the sprog's been born.'

'That's very hurtful. I can tell how hard that must have been.'

'Can you? Funny, it wasn't really. I'm used to it.'

Chand had inched towards her as Swift was talking but she sensed it and whipped her head round. 'Don't! I'll jump!'

He put his hands up. 'Okay. Please, don't do that. I don't want you to do that.'

'Why not? You don't care about me. You're not interested. You didn't want to let me in here tonight. You brought me in out of pity. A pity party with Havana. You think I'm ugly. I could see it in your eyes. The same look my mum gives me. Well, I am ugly. An ugly stick insect.

Getting uglier by the day. Crap skin, crap hair, crap everything.'

'That's not true,' Chand said gently. 'You tried to kiss me and I stopped you. Not because you're ugly but because it wouldn't be right. Havana, I'm an adult and you're a child. I didn't mean to hurt your feelings. I think you know, deep down that it wouldn't be right because I reckon you're a decent person. I didn't want to give you any wrong messages, that's all.'

She sniffed and let out a deep sob. 'My whole fucking life's a wrong message!'

Chand threw a frightened look at Swift and shook his head, as if to indicate he'd better not say any more. From what he'd just heard, Swift realised that Havana had attempted to follow up on her crush on Chand and had felt rebuffed. He mouthed *ambulance* at Chand and indicated with his head that he should go downstairs. The last thing they needed was hammering at the door that would frighten Havana more.

Chand nodded and said, 'I'm just going to the bathroom, Havana. Okay? I'm moving away from you, not nearer. Okay?'

She looked around and watched him leave the room. 'Creep. Jerk. Bastard shit,' she said dully. 'Can't think why I thought I liked him. I get everything wrong.'

'Let me help you, please,' Swift said. 'I'm glad we had that talk before. It helped me understand some things. That café around the corner stays open late. We could go there.'

There was a long silence. She'd turned her back again and was leaning forward, peering down. He hoped she was considering his offer but then she just muttered, 'no point.'

'I've just come back from Cornford,' he offered as a distraction, trying to control his shallow breathing and keep anxiety from his voice. 'I saw Grace playing Amy Johnson at the airfield. It was a good evening.'

'Bully for you.'

'Have you seen Grace do her act?'

'Not likely. Adults at play. Well sad.'

'Havana, you must be getting cold. Can I get you your coat or a scarf to put on?'

'I like being cold and numb. It stops all the stuff. Stops my brain whizzing. Maybe I'll freeze to death and break away, like an icicle. Snip snap! That would make my mum happy. Get rid of the problem for good. Stay away from me, you. Stay away and shut your mouth. Nothing you say helps. Just shut the fuck up.'

Chand had managed to get down the stairs quietly but they were old and creaky. There was a faint sound of footsteps coming up. The sixth step tended to emit the occasional loud crack and it did so now. Havana tensed and edged further forward suddenly. As she did so, her hand slipped and she screamed, clawing at the window. Swift threw himself across the room, knocking over the table and mugs of coffee and grabbed at her as she fell. He thought he'd missed, imagined he'd heard the awful thud as she hit the ground but the Prada bag saved her. The strap held as he grasped it and a handful of her hair. He pulled hard as she screamed in pain and fear. His ears were ringing and his heart thumping but he had dragged her shoulders back through the window as Chand ran in with two paramedics. They helped him manoeuvre Havana into the room.

Swift stood back as the paramedics laid her on the floor. Chand slammed the window shut and locked it, then leaned against the wall for a moment. Havana was still screaming and sobbing. She lashed out at the ambulance staff, her nails aiming for their faces. The male paramedic told her his name was Jared and his colleague was Kitty. He took hold of her hands and held them gently while Kitty knelt at her other side and talked quietly, stroking Havana's hair.

'It's all right, Havana. Shh. It's all right. You're okay. You're okay. You've had a hard time. Take some breaths for me, Havana, come on. Look at me, into my eyes. That's it. Look, I'll take the breaths with you. Five deep ones, come on.'

She inhaled and exhaled slowly and talked on low and soothingly until Havana quietened and she could check her over.

'What happened here?' Jared asked, sharp voiced.

'This is my house,' Swift said. 'Chand's my tenant and he lives in this flat. Havana arrived here tonight from Hertfordshire in a bad way, after a row with her mother.'

Chand nodded. He'd sat down, looking dazed, rubbing his face. 'I allowed her in because she looked so upset and frozen. I didn't know what else to do and Ty was out. I went to the kitchen to make us coffee and, when I came back in, Havana had opened the window and was sitting on the ledge. I called Ty for help and he rang you.'

Jared looked sceptical. He moved into the hallway and called the hospital. He secured an agreement that Havana should be admitted for the night. 'She'll need to be examined, we don't know what's happened to her exactly but she was either trying to escape or she's a suicidal child. Looks anorexic, too.' Both paramedics were giving Swift and Chand hooded glances as they worked, clearly wondering what had been going on between two men and this young girl in the flat.

'I'm an ex-Met detective and a private investigator and Chand Malla is in the Met,' Swift added, knowing that wouldn't necessarily reassure them. 'I know Havana through an investigation I'm involved in. I'm about to call the police now about this incident. I'll ring Havana's mother as well.'

'You do that,' Jared said abruptly. 'I'll be ringing the police myself. Can you give me your full names?'

'I'll come in the ambulance, if that's okay with Havana,' Chand said. 'I can give you whatever information you need.'

Havana was sitting up on the floor, rubbing the back of her head. She looked tiny and frail.

'It's okay, you've just lost a bit of hair and you'll have a very sore head for a few days,' Kitty said. 'It'll grow back. Your back might ache too. Is it okay with you if Chand comes with us in the ambulance?'

She nodded. 'Whatever. It's not his fault. They didn't do anything to me. They were trying to help. It's all my crap.'

'We'll see,' Kitty said grimly. 'Up you come, then. You okay to walk down with us?'

'Suppose. I don't want the police involved. I don't want that.'

'We have to report this,' Jared said. 'It's what we have to do. Come on now, we'll get you sorted and comfy. Everything else can wait.'

Swift phoned the police as they got Havana to her feet and let her sit for a few minutes. She stared straight ahead, glass-eyed and gnawing at her bottom lip. Kitty gave her her jacket, saying that it wasn't much of a coat to keep the chill out on a freezing night. She put it on slowly, wincing as she moved her shoulders. She threw Swift a strange, beseeching glance as she moved towards the door but he couldn't read the meaning. The four of them went down the stairs in a slow procession. He was ringing Ashleigh's number when he heard shouts from outside. He ran down the stairs, his phone still to his ear. He saw Kitty sprawled on the frosty ground, Jared bent over her, his breath misting the air and Chand racing towards the end of the street.

Kitty pulled herself up on an elbow, groaning and looked at Swift. 'She's done a runner. Stronger than she looks.'

Jared stared at him. 'I don't know what's been going on here but you've got some explaining to do.'

In his ear, Ashleigh was saying, 'Hello! Hello! Who is this?'

* * *

'Still no news of Havana?' Chand asked Swift. He'd knocked on the door when he came in from a late shift, a thin dusting of powdery snow on his hair and shoulders. His black hair glowed in the light.

'Nothing. I spoke to Grace Tansley and the police again today. No sightings, no contact. Sally Tansley keeps hoping to hear from her. According to her mother, she's ill with worry.'

Chand shook his head. 'What about Havana's mother? Has she spoken to you again?'

'No, but I wouldn't expect her to. She's taken a great dislike to me. I rang her and left a message but no response. I've just made coffee. Come in and have one.'

It was a week since Havana had taken off into the night in her thin clothing and she had vanished. No one had heard from her. Swift and Chand had given statements to local police about the evening when she had threatened suicide. Swift had had to explain the reason for Havana's first visit to him and divulge what she had told him about her father on that evening in the café. Havana couldn't be questioned to check their version of events, so they both knew the horrible episode was left hanging and unresolved. True, she had told the paramedics that they'd been helping her but both of them knew that victims of abuse often blamed themselves and that the police would be thinking the same. It was worse for Chand because he was in the force. He'd had an uncomfortable interview with his senior officer. Blackmore had been informed and phoned Swift, his tone as abrasive as sandpaper, asking what he knew about this mystery woman that Roscoe was supposed to have been meeting the night before he died. He didn't sound convinced when Swift said he had no idea who she was.

Swift had contacted Niall Roscoe and explained what had happened. It had been a difficult call and Roscoe had been taciturn. He hadn't known whether or not to tell his mum about Havana, he'd said, sighing. He'd been worried that any more bad news would kill her but he'd had to inform her because the police wanted to call round.

'You can imagine what it's done to her. She hasn't got out of bed for days. It feels sometimes like someone's cursed us. You should have told us when Havana came to see you before. What was she telling you?'

'She said that she hid in her father's car sometimes, because she suspected he was seeing other women when he went out. She hid the night before he died and saw him meet a woman by the river.'

'You sure about that? She wasn't telling tall tales? Havana could be one for making up stories. Vivid imagination.'

'I'd no reason to think so.'

'So why didn't she tell the police?'

'Because she didn't think it was important at the time. They were talking to Cairns. And she felt protective towards her father, despite his behaviour. It was all very confusing for her.'

'You're telling me!'

'Look, I know this is very hard. Would it help if I visited and talked to your mother?'

'Nah, best leave it for now,' Roscoe had said abruptly. 'Are you getting anywhere with this investigation? If Greg met a woman, who was she?'

'I don't know yet. I believe I'm making progress but it's slow work. There are a number of things to do with Greg's life that I'm looking into.'

'Right . . . well, I don't know, this is all a right old bugger's muddle.'

Yes, Swift had thought, that did sum it up.

Chand came in and stood in Swift's kitchen, looking morose. 'Maybe Havana's in the river, or raped or dead in an empty building or she's fallen in with some gang. A kid like her . . . out on the street. She doesn't stand a chance. I wish I'd never let her in now. I should have just sent her back home that night.'

Swift shook his head and handed him a coffee. 'You did the right thing. You couldn't have turned her away in the state she was in.'

'I hate cries for help. People in emotional turmoil — especially kids. I'm no good at it. I prefer straightforward crime. Give me burglary, shooting or a major scam. Best of all, a bit of juicy surveillance.'

'I get it. I left Interpol mainly because I was working in sex trafficking and I couldn't stand seeing abused women and kids any longer.'

Chand sighed, nodding and rubbing the ball of one shoe against the floor.

'Have you eaten? I've still got some of your mum's food in the freezer.'

'Nah, it's okay. I ate earlier.' He pointed at the heaped fruit bowl. 'Those tangerines look good, though.'

They sat in the living room and Swift placed the fruit bowl on the coffee table. He had lit the fire and the orange flames crackled comfortingly. Chand peeled a tangerine, carefully removing the pith and putting it on the side of his plate. The delicate scent filled the air.

'That's always the smell of Christmas for me,' Swift said. 'Do you celebrate it?'

'Not really. Well, not with presents. We have a big meal.'

Swift selected a speckled pear and bit into the soft creamy flesh. He hadn't had much appetite for a few days. Havana's screams still rang in his ears. The nutty sweetness of the fruit was refreshing. Christmas was only weeks away. Nora was going to Dublin to see her family and Swift's stepmother, Joyce, had asked him to keep her company on Christmas day. He'd managed to avoid her invitations for the last three Christmases and felt that he had better fulfil his obligations this year. His spirits sank at the thought of the groaning table she would provide.

There would be other guests: Gilbert and Sullivan fans, members of her golf club or the people with whom she went on cruises. Still, at least he had his daughter for the day on Christmas Eve. He thought he might take her for a festive row, conditions permitting. They could look at the lights of the London Eye from the river.

Chand took another tangerine and rolled it between his hands, stroking the waxy skin. He looked melancholy. 'You know, it was just my luck that the only female who's attempted to kiss me in living memory was a fourteen year old suicidal girl.'

'You have problems meeting women?'

'I suppose. It didn't help of course, living at home with an interfering mum. But I haven't exactly been falling over women since I moved here. I'm a bit clunky — never know what to say. So then I get nervous and rabbit on too much about Elvis. I see their eyes glaze over and know I've blown it.'

'Aren't there any Elvis-loving single women at the impersonator gigs?'

'I haven't met any. Always seems to be couples. I'd like to meet someone. I'd like a family. All my mates seem to be getting engaged or married.' He put the tangerine back and sipped his coffee, gazing into the fire.

Swift sat silently, watching the wood hiss and spit. He'd sat here around this time last year with Bella, drinking hot rum in front of the fire. He looked over at Chand: he was a pleasant looking and kindly man, if a little immature. He had an idea. Worth a try, surely. He'd sleep on it.

When Chand had gone, Swift washed up the cups, put the guard in front of the fire and checked his emails. Yvette had finally responded to a message he had sent after he'd spoken to Axel.

This is the last time I communicate with you. I'm only writing because Axel said you seemed reasonable. He must have been remembering the time I spoke to a pilot called Stefan Makinen. He worked then for Scandi Air and he was living in London. This was about two years ago. He said he and Greg were involved in a business selling a herbal supplement. The sort of stuff they could buy cheap in the Far East. He said they'd had some problems. That's all I know.

At least he now had some chance of trying to trace the man who had threatened Roscoe. The second email was from Ruth.

Hi Ty,
Hope all is well. Branna really enjoyed her trip to the museum with you. She's still talking about the stuffed animals!

I wanted to say that Marcel is going to spend Christmas with us. I'd like you to meet him. Maybe you could have a drink with us after you bring Branna back on Christmas Eve. I do hope you will. It would be good for her to see us together, help her make sense of things. R x

He sighed. Branna had mentioned Marcel just once, glancing carefully at her father as she did. She'd talked about his house at the beach and the steps that led down from the back garden to the sand. Swift was aware that she had a life now that was divided between three different homes. He must do what he could to ease any strain she might feel.

He emailed back, accepting the invitation to have a drink. Well, life was full of having to do things you'd rather not.

Chapter 11

Scandi Air operated out of Heathrow. As Swift expected, a call to the airline there resulted in a polite but firm refusal to comment on whether they employed a pilot called Stefan Makinen. He turned to Google instead and, after a lengthy search, found a person of that name living in Turnham Green — a handy address for commuting to Heathrow. There was no phone number. A cold call, then. And no time like the present.

It was a bright, brisk morning, the air laced now and again with stinging needles of rain. He hoped that Havana wasn't out in it, shivering in her thin clothes — if she was still alive to be feeling anything. The shops were all in festive mode. Swift passed windows dressed with sparkling lights, sleighs, reindeer, snow scenes, a gaudy workshop with busy elves, brightly wrapped gifts and baubles, a selection of snowmen in a group of fir trees and an ice rink with penguins wearing red scarves and woolly hats. A cacophony of carols and Christmas classics blared onto the streets, Bing Crosby and Band Aid battling with *We Three Kings*. Outside a department store, a hefty Santa with a

Welsh accent rang a bell and announced that he would be in his grotto at two o'clock.

Swift hadn't bought Branna's present yet. He was still looking for inspiration. Her main interest at present was cutting shapes out of paper with her special scissors. She played imaginary games mostly and had two invisible friends called Spell and Hum. She signed with them regularly and they were frequently around at meal times. They were usually blamed for any mishaps such as spilled drinks or crayon marks on walls. He'd wondered if she had invented them because her deafness made her lonely but when he discussed it with Ruth, she'd explained that invisible friends were a common feature of childhood and were often invented by only children. She'd sent him an article, which he'd found reassuring:

There is a common misconception that children who invent imaginary friends might be lonely or socially isolated. Research does not support such assumptions. In fact, when compared to children who do not create them, those with imaginary friends tend to be less shy, engage in more humour and smiling with their peers and are better at trying to imagine how others might think.

After reading that, he'd been contented to watch and listen when Spell and Hum turned up. He'd even had a brief signed conversation about milk and biscuits with Hum one bedtime, thinking that being a parent involved a certain ability to accept and play along with the absurd.

He skirted a Salvation Army brass band playing *Winter Wonderland* and found the street he wanted. The address was in a boxy, modern block of flats with timber cladding. He rang the bell for Number 4, expecting the intercom to buzz but a woman opened the door after his second ring. She was wearing fleecy blue pyjamas patterned with puckered red lips, thick slipper socks and she was holding a tea towel. She frowned at him and he thought she seemed familiar but couldn't think why.

'Yes?'

'I'm looking for Stefan Makinen.'

'He's not here.'

'Any idea when he might be home?'

'No. I mean, he doesn't live here any more.' She blew a wisp of dark hair out of her eye and shoved the tea towel under her arm.

'Are you a relative?'

She rolled her eyes. 'No. My name's Heidi. Heidi Parr.'

'Hello, Heidi. Can you tell me where I can contact Stefan?'

'No idea. Who are you?'

He explained about the investigation into Greg Roscoe's death, showing her his ID. She examined it carefully, tapped it against her hand, and then said he could come in. He followed her up a flight of stairs and into a small, one-bedroomed flat. It wasn't so much that the kitchen-cum-living-room was a mess as that there was just too much stuff in it: a racing bike hung from a bracket on one wall; boxes were stacked on top of the fridge; free standing metal shelves were jammed with more boxes and folders; electrical wires snaked randomly around the skirting boards; clothes in dry cleaning bags hung from the window pole and a ping pong table was wedged behind the sofa, which was littered with magazines and female underwear. A long, mournful looking African mask carved from wood was attached to the back of the living room door. It was decorated with glazed pottery for eyes and the face was embellished with strips of cocoa brown leather and raffia. Swift found it disturbing.

'Excuse the terrible mess. I only got home in the early hours and my cleaner has done a bunk. Mind you, he was useless anyway,' Heidi said, sweeping knickers and bras from the sofa. She glanced around and threw them on the

Ping-Pong table. A frilly bra drifted to the floor but she didn't notice. She was in her late twenties, slim. She looked exhausted, as if she'd been partying hard. Her hair was caught up in a slithery bun that was coming undone and trailing onto her long, elegant neck, where she had a tiny purple birthmark. 'There, sit down. I've just made tea. I'll pour you one.'

He sat on the sofa, feeling a jab in his ribs and found two TV remotes wedged under a dusty cushion. Grace Tansley's home was messy but was cared about and homely. Heidi's flat seemed neglected with no hint of a life being enjoyed there. Even if it was tidied, it would look scratchy and make-do. She fetched mugs of tea and sat down in a canvas director's chair, bringing one heel up to the edge. Swift sipped the tea, which was delicious, with an unusual flavour like chestnuts.

'This is different, in a good way,' he said.

She nodded. 'It's Himalayan. I always drink it after long haul. It revives me.'

'Are you a pilot?'

'Flight attendant.' She yawned. 'Sorry, still time warped.'

'Is that how you know Stefan?'

'Hmm, not exactly. My cousin introduced me to him. He sort of got me my first job in Scandi Air.' She sighed wearily, as if the mention of his name exhausted her.

'Did you know Greg Roscoe?'

'Unfortunately, yes. He gave my cousin the run around, just like Stefan did to me. She was pretty sick about it.'

'Greg knew your cousin? What's her name?'

'Holly Armstrong. *She's* a pilot. Brainier than me.'

Swift saw now that Heidi had the same high forehead and fine hair. He had been right about Holly lying to him. He liked it when he found connections, although he wasn't sure if this one might be important. It had to be, or why had Holly denied any knowledge of Stef?

'So how did Holly know Stefan?'

Heidi stretched the leg she had folded and brought the other one up to her chair. Her slipper socks were purple and decorated with glittery pink stars. 'They met at flying training. They went way back. She brought me along to Stef's twenty-eighth birthday party and we clicked. He was the reason we fell out.' She pulled a face.

'Was he her boyfriend at the time?'

'Sort of. They were on-off. She reckoned he was the one but I'm not sure he ever saw it like that. She thought I pinched him from her, anyway. We haven't spoken since. I mean, I've tried contacting her but she doesn't reply.'

Swift thought through the links. 'Is that how Greg knew Stefan — through Holly?'

She nodded. 'Stef belonged to a pilots' club near Marble Arch. It's called Take Wing. Greg was a member too but their paths had never crossed. Holly used to meet Stef there sometimes. She introduced them after she got to know Greg and they became good friends.'

He turned over this close weave of relationships. 'So if you and Holly haven't been in touch, how did you know that Greg Roscoe had messed her about?'

'Stef told me. I can picture it . . . he and Greg propping up a bar, old mates discussing their latest conquests. Although I don't think Stef liked some of the things Greg said he got up to. Anyway, he knew that Greg and Holly had got into trouble over screwing around at the airfield.'

'It sounds as if the friends fell out. I've been informed that Stefan visited Greg at Cornford airfield and threatened him. Do you know what that was about?'

She gave a little frown and scratched her head. He thought she was going to say no but she leaped up and gestured dramatically at the stacked boxes. '*That's* what it was about. Look at this junk!' She lifted a box and turned it upside down, shaking hard. Dozens of pale blue plastic pouches tumbled all over the floor. She seized one and thrust it at him. 'This crap was supposed to make our fortune! I was going to be able to pack in trudging up and down plane aisles with trolleys and sick bags. *Allegedly*.'

Swift examined the pouch. It was a product called Pure and Strong. According to the label, it contained four detoxifying patches and sachets of a herbal drink. It also bore spelling errors: *Our carefully blennded herbs and minerals will clear impuritties, reebalance your body and create wonderful energies.* There was tiny print, almost too small to read in another language on the back of the pouch.

'What's this language?' Swift asked.

'Taiwanese.'

'So I'd guess that this was a dodgy kind of business venture?'

She sat down and stared at the mess on the floor. 'I can't believe I was stupid enough to let Stef get involved. Greg came up with the idea. He flew to Taiwan regularly and got to know some bloke who said he could produce this stuff for pennies. Greg met us at Take Wing and sold the idea to Stef. I wasn't keen but I liked the idea of all this money flooding in and Stef persuaded me. Greg said it had to be a winner. You know, buying into the trend for clean eating and detoxifying. He said his wife was always into this kind of stuff and the money she threw away in health food shops made him realise there was a big market for tapping into what he called "first world angst". Greg was persuasive, I'll give him that. Stef was all made up about it and stumped up money to get things off the ground. I got dazzled by pound signs. We thought we were onto a sure thing and had a rosy future. We were talking about buying a place together. Things were really good between us then.'

She looked wistful and got up, put one hand on the back of her chair and pulled her right leg up and backwards, groaning lightly. It was the calf stretching exercise he did before rowing.

'I don't want to get varicose veins, the curse of flight attendants,' she explained.

'So, the business didn't go too well,' he prompted.

'Yeah, that's an understatement. Greg sourced the product from this Taiwanese guy and got him to set up a website. He and Stef sold it on the internet as well as to anyone they could flog it to in person. It started well and they made a bit of money. Stef was optimistic. But then they started to get complaints. Some people got allergic reactions to the patches or said the herbal stuff made them sick or gave them joint pains. Greg said not to worry, there were always people who thought they'd been short-changed and he got some positive reviews put on the website. But sales dropped off and Greg had ordered so much stock, there was a warehouse full of it in Taiwan and they owed the supplier money. We couldn't even shift these supplies that we'd been selling direct to friends and airside staff. People heard of some of the bad reviews and got wary. Greg had been managing the profits and he told Stef there was nothing left to pay out. Stef looked into the orders and reckoned Greg had creamed off extra profits for himself. We were both pissed off with him.'

She was sounding righteous for a scammer. 'You don't sound too concerned about the people who got ill.'

'Well, it was only herbs and stuff. I don't think it did anyone that much harm,' she said defensively.

'Would you take it?'

'Me? No but then I never take stuff like that. Don't need to.'

Swift examined the pouch again. 'I'd say you're lucky that no one tried to sue you.'

She gaped. 'Really? It's just natural ingredients. How could anyone sue?'

She was either stupid or naïve or maybe just too greedy to have thought it through.

'This stuff's illegal. If it was legal, there'd be a green logo on it, showing it was an above board and registered product in Europe. I'd say you only got away with it because a lot of people don't know their rights when it comes to alternative type supplements — especially ones they buy online.'

'Oh, right. Well, I don't know about any of that. I thought you could sell whatever you like if it comes off the internet. Greg told us it was all legit. Anyway, talk about a bloody mess . . . Stef was livid because he was still flying to Taiwan sometimes and some heavy threatened him at the hotel he was staying at. Greg wouldn't admit to any underhand dealings and they had slanging matches on the phone. Stef became unbearable, always moaning about Greg and Greg kept ringing me, asking me to get Stef off his back. In the end, I'd had enough of both of them. I was worried about some Taiwanese guy turning up here looking for money. They've got those triads there, you know. Big criminal gangs. I had a huge row with Stef. I told him to pack his bags and get out.'

'This is your flat?'

'Yep. So Stef buggered off, leaving me with that bloody racing bike cluttering up the wall, that foul mask on the door and half my space covered in boxes of crap products.' She was reaching up with her arms, her spine clicking audibly.

'When did Stef leave?'

'The April just before Greg died. He's got some other woman in tow now, I hear.'

He wondered why she was still keeping Stef's possessions and the useless products in her home. Maybe deep down she regretted throwing him out and was hoping he'd come back. 'The bike's an expensive model,' he observed. 'You could sell it and make quite a bit.'

She glanced at it. 'Yeah, I know. I never seem to have time. I'm always meaning to sort this place out but work or something else gets in the way.'

'Is the website for Pure and Strong still live?'

'No. Greg got it closed down when things got sticky.'

'How much money was owed to this supplier in Taiwan?'

'I don't know. I wasn't involved in the details. I didn't want to be.'

'You must have some idea of where Stef is, surely? I understand the airline world is a small community in many ways.'

'That's true, but he joined a big Australian airline — Gold Coast, and I just do Europe. I heard a rumour that he's living in Brisbane.' She looked at him, understanding dawning. 'You don't think he might have killed Greg!'

'I don't know. He had a motive, from what you've told me. Do you think he could have?' She had a motive too, he thought, although she seemed too incompetent to plan a stabbing.

She sat back down, kicking one of the pouches out of the way. Her bun had almost collapsed and she burrowed for a hairgrip and coiled it back into place. 'I don't know . . . I suppose . . . But Stef wasn't an aggressive guy, not in that way. I mean, he got angry with Greg because of the money but I don't think he'd have taken a knife to him.'

Swift thought there was no more he could get from her. If Stef was now based in Australia, it was hard to see where he could go with checking him out. Unless she had another win on her Premium Bonds, he didn't think Pat Roscoe's budget would stretch to a trip to Brisbane. He recalled Fitz Blackmore's theory that Roscoe's death might be connected to his days of global travel and gambling and that his murderer might be impossible to track. It was hard to imagine that Taiwanese criminals would travel all the way to England to kill Roscoe.

'Can I take one of these Pure and Strong pouches with me?'

'Take the lot, for all I care. You'd be doing me a favour.'

At the door, he said, 'So does Holly know about this failed business and that you and Stef have parted?'

'I don't think she knew anything about the business. I'd have been too embarrassed to tell her, even if we were speaking. And Greg wouldn't have spread it around — especially not at the airfield. He wouldn't have wanted his wife to get wind of it. He was always saying that the less she knew, the less grief she could give him. I got the impression he always kept his cards close to his chest. I did email Holly to say I'd split with Stef. Thought it might mend some bridges. As if!'

'She still won't talk to you?'

She shook her head. 'That's Holly for you. Unforgiving. Rigid. Always has been. Once you've crossed her, she's done with you. I can't get that fussed about things. Life's too short.'

He didn't think she meant it, any more than she meant she didn't have time to get rid of Stef's bike or his mask or the remnants of the failed business. She was clinging on to the wreckage. She'd cast an interesting light on Holly, though: an unforgiving woman who kept secrets and didn't like being crossed. Worth mulling over.

Heidi rubbed half-heartedly at a dirty mark on the door with her sleeve. 'You don't happen to know a decent cleaner, by any chance? Someone who actually cleans rather than napping in the chair and making cups of tea?'

'Sorry,' he said. 'I do my own cleaning.'

'Oh. Very organised. Well, see you!'

He walked back to the bus stop, calling in en route to a toyshop. He bought a pack of colourful cut-out animal shapes for Branna. It was a start. As he paid, he was wondering what else Holly Armstrong might be concealing and why.

As he reached home, he saw that his anonymous caller had left another indistinct message. *'I don't know what to do. I want to help you but . . . I might be worrying about nothing and then I'll just have caused trouble. I should have kept my big mouth shut in the first place. It's a nightmare. This has been on my mind for so long, I just—'* There was a high, distant sound in the background like another voice, and the call ended. He listened to it several times, thinking that he could identify something in the background noise, but was unable to work it out.

Frustrated, he rang Fitz Blackmore to check if there had been any news of Havana. Blackmore was out, but a colleague told him the answer was negative. The frail and fragile young girl was on his mind, as was her grandmother. He pictured Pat Roscoe lying in her bed, grieving for another loss. He rang Grace Tansley but she sounded low and distracted, saying that neither she nor Sally had had any contact. She sounded guarded with him too, which he could understand. There was still a whiff of suspicion hanging around him and Chand about the circumstances that night when Havana ran away. It had occurred to him that Camilla Finley might well get hold of the information and make good mileage out of it.

Heavy snow was falling again and the roads to Hertfordshire would be slow going. He rang Holly Armstrong and got her voicemail, so tried the airfield. The receptionist told him that Holly was in Dusseldorf collecting a new aircraft and would be back in two days. He felt achy, yet irritable and restless. The unpredictable nausea he sometimes experienced had returned in the last couple of days. He couldn't face cooked meals and was living on bananas, muesli and prepared salads. He'd always been fit and healthy and hated feeling this way. He wondered how much longer it could last. He wanted to take his boat out but the weather didn't allow. He walked up and down the living room, noting that he was becoming like Fitz Blackmore pacing his office. There were so many elusive leads and possibilities in this case. He felt as if it could slip away from him and wondered if he was thinking like this because of his physical fatigue. His brain seemed blunted, less agile, and self-doubt was creeping in. Yet, at this stage in the investigation, there was nothing on which to get a grip.

He rubbed his hands through his tangled curls, which badly needed a trim and told himself to focus. What he did need to get a grip on was Christmas. There were only four days to go and he'd bought just that one present. When in a daze, make a list and do one thing on it. He picked up his phone, made notes and set out into the frosty streets.

* * *

Christmas Eve started badly and the day went downhill from there. Alerted again by Fitz Blackmore, Swift read the latest article by Camilla Finley that morning. His heart sank as he skimmed through it.

The Unfortunate Detective

I've told you about Tyrone Swift before. He's a London based private investigator with an interesting background. He's looking into the murder of Greg Roscoe at Cornford airfield, although as far as I can tell, he's made no progress after weeks on the case.

I believe that Paul Cairns has given Mr Swift some useful information. Hopefully, Mr Swift will give Paul credit for that. Paul could do with a boost after his awful experience at the hands of Cornford cops. The book I'm writing with Paul is called One Man's Voice and it will be out next spring.

You might recall that Mr Swift had an unpleasant meeting in court a while back. It was about a contested will. There were allegations that Mr Swift had influenced a frail, elderly pensioner friend to leave him money. The court ruled in Mr Swift's favour. He does have important contacts. His cousin, Mary Adair, is an Assistant Commissioner in the Metropolitan police.

Trouble does seem to follow Mr Swift. I've been digging around and I found out that one of Swift's girlfriends, Kris Jelen, was murdered a couple of years ago. She was Polish, far away from home and on her own in London and she got very unlucky. Her killer had been hired to torment Swift but the vulnerable young woman got it in the neck instead. I spoke to her mother through an interpreter on the phone. She said, "We are still mourning our lovely daughter. She had so much to live for. She had started her own business and loved being in London. She was happy that she had met Mr Swift. She died so far away from us. We cry every day."

And now Havana Roscoe, Greg Roscoe's fourteen-year-old daughter, has gone missing. She was last seen at Mr Swift's home in London, where she threatened suicide. Apparently, it wasn't the first time she'd visited him. Havana has been ill since her dad's murder. She's out there somewhere, hopefully still alive but lost to her family when she should be at home for Christmas. Her mother is about to give birth and was too distressed to talk to me.

It seems as if being friendly with Mr Swift can be dangerous. He doesn't mention that on his website. Well, it wouldn't make good reading. You only get to know about his successes but you might want to lock up your daughters. Mr Swift always seems to come out smelling of roses. He won't speak to me. You can read what you like into his silence.

Season's Greetings to all! I'll be back in the New Year with more Finley's Finds.

He shoved his chair back angrily. This was only a local paper but nasty stuff like this could travel and cause damage. Maybe Fitz Blackmore had been right and he should have offered the reporter some information to keep her sweet. It went against the grain, though.

His phone rang. Blackmore calling. He sounded amused.

'Ron, my man! Have you read it? Can I smell roses from here?'

'Yes. Just finished.'

'Hmm. Camilla's got it in for you. It . . . erm . . . it doesn't read too well.'

'I'm aware of that. Perhaps I should have given her something.'

'Hmm . . . the "when-they-go-low-you-go-high" mantra is all very well but sometimes you have to go down and dirty or at least trade in the same currency. Let's just say I'll be keeping an eye open in case Camilla breaks the speed limit, has a drink too many before driving or fails to recycle her rubbish correctly.'

Swift laughed. 'Thanks so much.'

'All part of the service. So, mate, what's this useful information that Cairns gave you?'

'No idea, all part of Camilla's fictions,' he lied.

'Okay. Because after not sharing Havana's info, I know you wouldn't keep anything to yourself that you should tell the police. Especially as this policeman is watching your back.'

'At the moment, there's nothing that I'm sure enough about to tell you.' That was honest, at least. If only there was something about the case that he was certain of.

'I see.' Blackmore sounded unconvinced. 'Sad about the Polish woman who died. Certainly tugs at the heartstrings. Who hired her killer?'

'My ex's husband. He was unhappy that we'd slept together and she was pregnant as a result.' Even as he said it, Swift realised it was the subject of a dream tabloid headline and that Camilla Finley could cause him a lot more difficulty if she dug deeper into his personal life and blew it into a lurid drama. He pictured her in Brighton, tracking down Emlyn Taylor, Ruth's husband and interviewing him. He had a sharp axe to grind and might give her juicy titbits.

Blackmore gave a little whistle. 'Crumbs. I'm not sure I want to hang around you, mate. Hope Nora watches her back for random killers.'

'Thanks *mate*.'

'Yeah, well, it's crap. And Camilla's clever in the way she delivers. What can I say? And how's it going with the wider investigation?'

He said it casually but Swift had known he would loop back to the question, could picture the sharp, intent eyes. 'Ongoing enquiries.'

'That old chestnut — if you'll forgive the seasonal pun! Why do I have the feeling you're still not telling me things? So, what are you doing tomorrow? Spending it with Nora?'

'No, she's off to her family in Ireland. I'm at my stepmother's. You?'

'At a friend's tomorrow, then flying out on Boxing Day for skiing in Chamonix with a lady of wondrous parts that I know. We recycle each other now and again when we've no other interests.' He dropped his voice. 'Frankly, Ron, I'm keener on the après ski than the skiing.'

Swift smiled. Blackmore's naughty boy act was sometimes amusing. 'I don't suppose there's any news of Havana?'

'Nothing, mate. We've got a Family Liaison Officer checking in with Ashleigh regularly. She's about to pod at any minute. The crocodile tears flow whenever the daughter is mentioned and Barry's had posters stuck up all around town - you know, the *Help find Havana* variety. They seem to want her now, despite the fact they were happy to farm her out. I don't reckon Havana came back here. God knows where she is, poor kid, but I'd place a bet on London. Unlikely to be tucking into turkey tomorrow. Well, mate, great as it is to chat, I've got to go. Festive greetings and maybe you'll find a crucial clue in a cracker!'

Swift threw the phone down. He knew that Blackmore was secretly pleased at his discomfort and suspected that was part of his agenda for staying in touch. And of course Blackmore took satisfaction from the fact that he hadn't yet come anywhere near finding Roscoe's killer. The man was bloody irritating, like a splinter below the skin, yet he couldn't help liking him.

Time to try and put it all out of his mind, have a coffee with Nora before she left for Dublin and then pick up Branna.

* * *

Branna was out of sorts and tired when he arrived. She clung monkey-like to her mother, arms wrapped about her neck, rubbing her forehead against Ruth's shoulder. Ruth said she'd had a heavy cold and was still getting over it. They had to cajole her into going out, with Swift dangling the prospect of a present to open. He decided against taking her on the river and instead they went back to his house. She fell asleep immediately in the car, snuffling loudly. He felt guilty, understanding that she'd wanted to stay at home when she was poorly. As he drove, he thought of all the other children of separated and divorced parents all over the country, spending hither and thither, back and forth Christmases with varying degrees of willingness.

He'd thought Branna would like to help him decorate the small tree he'd bought but she shook her head, yawning and saying she'd already done Mummy's. When he suggested building a snowman in the back garden, she said no. She watched as he lit the fire and then curled up on the sofa, stuck her thumb in her mouth and asked to watch TV. He sat with her, looking at cartoons. She gazed at the screen listlessly for a while, and then fell asleep again with her feet in his lap while he watched *The Three Bears*. His thoughts wandered to Cedric. They'd had a custom, of many years standing, of watching *It's a Wonderful Life* together on Christmas Eve. Up in Cedric's living room, they'd eat ripe Stilton cheese with his homemade pumpkin seed bread, drink spiced cider and turn to each other to say the line: *you look a little older without your clothes on*. Swift smiled, stroking Branna's hot feet.

When she woke, she was grumpy. He gave her pink medicine, fetched her milk and some fruit, made himself coffee and then read a story. She seemed to regain energy after a while and joined in with the story, pointing at the illustrations.

He gave her one of her presents to open, the paper cut-outs. She sat on the floor and became absorbed with scissors, guiding them deftly around the shapes. Swift turned the radio to a station playing traditional carols. It was cosy and peaceful by the fire, in the lamplight, just the two of them. Swift could hear heavy rain slamming down outside, turning the streets into rivers of slush. When he drew the curtains, he saw a pale moon reeling through fast moving black clouds. He was reluctant to go back out from the snug room into the wild night but at five o'clock, he said it was time to go home and suggested they clear up.

Branna assumed her mutinous look and signed *no,* then said 'stay here.' She held the scissors tightly as he went to take them.

'We have to go,' he said. 'We're having a special tea with Mummy and Marcel. For Christmas Eve. We don't want to be late and miss the goodies.'

'Stay *here*,' she said again, not looking at him.

'Branna, we do need to go. Mummy's expecting us. I think she's got raspberry ice cream, your favourite.'

His daughter shifted away from him on her bottom, sidling around the sofa, still cutting paper. 'I stay you!' she yelled.

He took a breath, and then crouched down near her. 'We can't stay here.'

'Why?'

'Because you're spending Christmas with Mummy.'

'No, with *you*.'

'You can spend another Christmas with me.' He knew this was getting too complicated and sensed a storm brewing as his daughter's eyes darkened.

She looked at him then and posed the killer question. He knew she was very upset because she made no attempt to speak, just signed it. *You don't want me Christmas?*

He blinked. 'Of course I do, you silly billy.' He switched to signing. *We're spending Christmas Eve together, aren't we? What other girl would I want to be with for Christmas?* He stroked her leg. At least she didn't pull it away.

She stared at him, and then smiled, signing. *Spell and Hum want to stay Christmas. They like here.*

He'd wondered if they might show up and signed back. *Well, I'll pour them both a glass of milk and then they can come in the car with us. Okay? I'll tuck them up with you for the night.*

She curled her shoulders in. 'No. Stay here you.'

'Branna, we really do have to go. We'll take your other presents so you can open them in the morning.' He attempted to take the scissors but she moved away. He made his voice sterner. 'Branna, give me the scissors and we need to get ready. I know this is hard, moving around between mummy and me. I know you feel poorly. But I need a bit of cooperation here.'

He reached for the scissors and paper but she whipped them behind her back and then threw them over his head. In one moment, she changed from a delightful little girl into a fierce creature. Her face crumpled, she drummed her heels on the floor, clenched her hands into fists and started crying loudly, yelling through a muddle of signs and sobs, 'Stay here! Stay! Stay!'

He watched, feeling helpless. This had happened a couple of times before when he needed to take her back. He understood the tension she felt when the frontier between her homes had to be crossed yet again. He just wasn't much good at handling her when she was like this. His own eyes were moist. He rang Ruth, hoping that between them, they could sort this out. He put the phone on speaker while Ruth talked, and he signed her words. Gradually, Branna calmed down. Swift thought it was exhaustion as much as her mother's influence. He managed to wipe tears and snot from her face and even got a watery smile when he said he couldn't take her home looking like an elf who'd been in the wars.

They were an hour late. As soon as they reached Ruth's, Branna was suddenly full of high spirits and started to run around the living room, stopping to ring the bells on the tree. Ruth introduced Marcel Vaudin as he came through from the kitchen with a tray of drinks, looking very much at home. There was an awkward handshake. Swift gave him the chocolates he'd brought and Ruth fetched Swift's gift of red wine. Branna cannoned into Vaudin and he lifted her into the air, saying she was a demon, making her burst into giggles. Swift looked on, drinking mulled wine and eating the smoked salmon rolls, Welsh rarebits and mince pies Ruth had prepared. He glanced at his watch, wondering how quickly he could make an exit.

Vaudin was neat and sleek looking with a trim beard and deep-set treacle-coloured eyes. His dark framed glasses sat high on the bony bridge of his nose. He seemed friendly, intelligent and entirely at ease, dispensing drinks and offering coffee. He and Ruth sat together on the sofa and Vaudin crossed his legs and stretched an arm out proprietorially behind her. She looked relaxed and happy, leaning back a little into his embrace. Branna sat on the floor between them, humming to herself and clicking colourful cubes of wood together. There was small talk about Vaudin's work and the beauties of Guernsey. The room was warm and comfortable, the fir tree pretty with bells and white lights, the mantelpiece decorated with cards and holly. The air was scented with citrus, nutmeg and cloves from a bowl of potpourri. Swift looked at the contented family tableau and felt like the spare relative who has to be indulged for a visit because of the season.

'Ruth's been discussing the possibility of cochlear implants,' Vaudin said. 'I think they would be beneficial to our little one. I've known a couple of students with them and they've made a big difference to their social interactions.'

'That's interesting to know,' Swift said coolly, ignoring Ruth's anxious glance. 'I'll bear it in mind. Ruth and I haven't come to a decision yet.'

'I hope you don't mind me offering my opinion. It's an area I have some experience in and I only have Branna's interests at heart,' Vaudin said.

'Not at all,' Swift lied. Branna, hearing her name, was looking up at their faces. 'I'd rather not discuss it now, in front of my daughter. We might cause anxiety and that's the last thing I want.'

'Of course, best to leave it,' Vaudin said.

'Sure,' Swift agreed. 'Best to leave it to her parents.'

'More mulled wine?' Ruth asked with a little laugh, jumping up.

Swift accepted another glass and helped Branna with her wooden construction. When Ruth served her ice cream, Vaudin lifted her on to his lap and she nestled there with her bowl. Swift had had enough. He said he had to get going. Branna blew him a cheery kiss and waved at him as he left. He felt his heart twist. He drove home slowly through sleeting snow, listening to Tom Petty. He had a sudden desire to get very drunk.

At home, the fire had faded to a flicker and his flat was chilly, the house empty. Chand was staying with his parents for a couple of nights. He switched the central heating up and topped up the fire, then opened the bottle of Tempranillo Ruth had given him and saw that he'd had an email from Niall Roscoe.

Dear Mr Swift,

Sorry to send this at Christmas but it's on my mind. A neighbour showed Mum some of the articles about you in the Cornford Mail. I'm not sure we'd have asked you to investigate if we'd known these things about you. I know mud sticks but I suppose some of it's true. Mum's pretty upset, what with reading those things and worrying about Havana. We still don't really understand what she was doing at your house that night. And that reporter Camilla Finley rang me, asking if you were getting anywhere with finding out who killed Greg. She asked if we'd talk to her but I told her to go away and put the phone down on her. The last thing Mum needs is the press at the door. You seem to be making things worse instead of better. We're going to have a think about whether or not to carry on with you over Christmas. Maybe raking all this up isn't such a good idea. I'll let you know. On the plus side, Mum had a Christmas card today from Havana. It made her day. It just says that she's okay, no contact details. We told the police and of course I phoned Ashleigh to let her know. I spoke to Barry Grafton. He'd just come from the hospital. Ashleigh had the baby, a boy.

Bad news and good news and another half-brother for Havana. Swift wondered if she'd ever meet this one. He was relieved that she'd surfaced at last and wondered if anyone had told Grace Tansley; she wasn't a relative and the police might not think about contacting her until after Christmas. The Graftons had their own added distractions. He sent Grace an email, informing her and a similar one to Chand. Then he took the wine and a glass and sat drinking by the fire.

At one in the morning, he draped a lonely strand of silver tinsel over his bare tree and staggered to bed.

Chapter 12

When Swift woke on Boxing Day, his stomach was still tight with his stepmother's hearty meals. For Christmas dinner, she had provided richly stuffed goose and a ham with roast and mashed potatoes, parsnips, carrots, baby onions, creamed swede and turnip, Brussel sprouts with chestnuts, charred broccoli, bread sauce and a wine heavy gravy. This was followed by rock solid, brandy laced plum pudding, double Chantilly cream and dessert wine. The dining table, like the rest of the house, was ornately decorated with scattered plump robins, golden angels, flashing LED stars, holly wreaths and waxed fruit. Around the table were several of Joyce's friends who liked her to boss them about and organise their lives. Swift became lost in a fog of talk about productions of Gilbert and Sullivan. 'I definitely think we should do *The Gondoliers* in the spring, it's time for a bit of satire' — and sea voyages—' there's a terrific cruise we absolutely must do, stargazing off Norway with an astrophysicist, I can't wait to book.' He was happy to pass the dishes and nod while Joyce sat at the head of the table, a small, stout figure in an orange velour dress matched with a triple row pearl necklace.

In the evening, after the other guests had gone, Joyce had insisted on serving him substantial ham and salad sandwiches with pickles and chutney, Christmas cake and Irish coffee and quizzing him about his personal life. Her gardenia scent enveloped him as she bustled around with her surprisingly light tread, repositioning robins and chatting in her breathy voice. 'Such a shame Nora couldn't come but maybe next year . . . is there any hint of wedding bells . . . and you must be missing Branna, today of all days . . . I suppose it was inevitable that Ruth would meet someone but it must be hard for you . . . do eat up, Ty dear, have another slice of cake, you really have lost weight since that awful crypto thing and I know you don't look after yourself properly . . . I hope you checked out this young man you've rented the top flat to, especially since that terrible business last year . . .'

He'd given her an extra-large hug as he was leaving because he was so glad to escape.

His stomach was tender now but his head was clear and focused. As he opened his eyes, he thought of Niall Roscoe saying that his concerns had been on his mind. On his mind . . . he reached for his phone and listened to the last message from his anonymous caller again, playing it several times. He thought he knew who it was. If he was right, he might be about to get a break, or at least hang onto the case. He didn't fancy being sacked and it went against the grain to leave Roscoe's death unsolved. He propped himself up on pillows and checked his emails. He'd had one from Bella Reynolds.

Hi, Ty.
First date went well. Chand's a lovely guy. Bit shy but warmed up once we got chatting. I had to steer him away from the Elvis obsession! We're meeting again and I'm looking forward to it. So thanks for the intro. Hope you've been having a good Xmas x

He'd suggested that Bella and Chand meet up. They were both looking for a partner, both wanting to find someone to settle down with. Good. That lifted his spirits, as did the sky when he opened the curtains. It was clear, an icy blue. The wind was a fresh easterly. He'd have a long row, maybe as far as Kew, work off Joyce's massive meals and think about the patterns forming in this investigation and what it could be that his anonymous caller had said to someone.

* * *

Holly Armstrong was reluctant to see him again.

'I can't think why you need to talk,' she said on the phone. 'I've told you what I know.'

'Just a few follow up things,' Swift said. 'Shall I come to the airfield?'

'No, I've got a couple of days off until after New Year. I'll meet you at the pub down at the marina, The Ferry Inn.'

She was there when he arrived mid-afternoon, drinking orange juice and sitting on a cushioned window seat in the bay window that looked onto the River Lea. She looked quite different away from the airfield and less assured, with her hair loose and wearing a soft, pale blue jumper with jeans and eye makeup. A uniform was certainly a disguise. She nodded at him and refused the offer of another drink.

Swift went to the bar and ordered coffee. The pub was almost empty and looked forlorn despite the handsome beams, polished brasses, copper pans and mullioned glass. Some of the lights on the Christmas tree had died and a large tinsel bell was semidetached from a beam but the barman seemed cheerful.

'Sorry, we're low on staff so not at our best during this "twixtmas" period but the coffee's fresh,' he said. 'Got to get the cleaning sprays out and gear up now for New Year.'

Swift sat across from Holly. They both looked out at the river in silence for a while. The day was grey with low cinder clouds and a racing north wind. The Lea was flowing full and strong. Boats moored on the opposite bank rocked and swayed and a man who was sweeping a deck clutched at the rail. A couple of bedraggled ducks paddled just below the window before disappearing into the grassy bank.

'Good Christmas?' Swift asked.

'Nothing special. I don't like this time of year. I get lots of wordplay on my seasonal name. There was too much food and TV with my parents. You?'

'It was okay. Like you, too much food.'

She glanced at him. 'Is that why you wanted to see me, to ask if I'd had a good Christmas?'

'No.' He thought he'd start with the easy question. 'I met Greg Roscoe's son, Axel. He told me that his dad said he was having an important meeting before he died. Does that ring any bells?'

'No, nothing. Sorry. I hardly saw Greg just before it happened. I had a full schedule of lessons. We met now and again for quick briefings and updates.'

'Okay. I wanted to see you as well to ask you why you lied to me last time I saw you.'

She looked back out at the river. 'What makes you think I lied?'

He sipped his coffee. 'I met your cousin, Heidi.'

'Oh, I see.' She seemed to relax and he wondered if she'd been expecting a different challenge. 'I wouldn't believe anything Heidi tells you. She's a back stabber.'

'So are you telling me you don't know Stefan Makinen? I understand you do and that you introduced him to Greg Roscoe.'

She said nothing, still staring at the river, and then turned on her seat. 'Okay, I lied about Stef. Is it important?'

'I don't know. Depends on why you lied.'

She put both hands to her face and pressed against her cheeks. 'Embarrassment and hurt pride, I suppose. I'd already had to tell you about the fiasco with Greg. Stef dumped me for my cousin and moved in with her, as I'm sure she was pleased to tell you. What kind of loser does that make me? I try not to think about either of them. That's it.'

He thought she was telling the truth about that but her body language suggested that she was concealing something else. He was sure of it.

'Do you know where Stef is now?'

'No idea. Heidi sent me a plaintive email saying he'd left. She seemed very sorry for herself. Karma, I reckon. I ignored her.'

'I've learned that Greg and Stef had a business going, selling dodgy herbal goods. They got into trouble with it and Greg owed Stef money.' He watched her closely but she seemed genuinely surprised.

'I didn't know anything about that and I was being honest when I said I didn't know Stef had been at the airfield, arguing with Greg. I'm not always at work, you know. Greg knew Stef had taken up with Heidi and he was surprisingly thoughtful about it and never mentioned him to me after we split.' She laughed without humour. 'Mind you, I suppose it made him reckon I was an easy target and he was right. He bided his time before he made a move.' She finished the dregs of her juice. 'Look, Stef was always a difficult man to pin down, but I really thought he intended to be with me long term. We were good together. We visited his family in Helsinki and I was made very welcome. I'd taken him to meet my parents — he spent a Christmas with us. Then I had to tell them he'd moved on to Heidi. Pretty mortifying. I've put all that behind me. I stay away from my cousin because she betrayed me and I don't want to be reminded of all the crap.' She stood up, reaching for her coat. 'It's painful, talking about this. You must cause a lot of pain in your line of work, raking over people's lives.'

'I don't set out to cause pain. Inevitably, it's part of the job sometimes. I think there's something you're not telling me.'

She stared at him, her expression cold and closed. Then she shrugged, hugged her coat around her shoulders and walked away. Swift watched the Lea for a while. A boat coasted slowly into the marina and moored. A huge dog jumped from the deck and relieved itself against a tree. He shivered, recalling Rocco, the dog that had been set on him the previous year. He could still see the yellowed teeth in the powerful jaws and smell his sour, meaty breath.

Swift understood why Holly didn't like Christmas with its poignant memories but there was something that didn't ring true. He'd have to let it lie. Maybe, like debris in the river, it would rise to the surface at some point.

* * *

He'd arranged to see the Roscoes late afternoon but, instead of heading to their address, he loitered outside Health Crunch at three thirty, waiting for Jeanie. She came out at exactly half past in a heavy double-breasted coat with a wide belt and a chunky hat pulled down over her ears. She was pulling a wheeled shopping trolley patterned with daisies. When he stepped forward and greeted her, she looked puzzled.

'We're expecting you at ours about five o'clock,' she said.

'I know. I wanted to speak to you on your own.'

'Me? Why? If it's about that stuff in the paper, I have no time for it.'

'No, it's not about that, not for now anyway. Let me buy you a cup of tea and I'll tell you. There's a café by the station.'

'Well,' she said, 'I've got to get some groceries but I suppose it's on my way. This is all a bit mysterious.'

'Not really. Or it doesn't have to be.'

In the café, he got a pot of tea for them both. It was laid out like a New York diner, with booths and seats covered in red plastic and a red and black chequered floor. When they were tucked into a booth, he poured tea. The sugar was in a retro glass shaker and Jeanie added a stream to her cup.

'Niall said he emailed you about Havana's Christmas card,' she said. 'It came Christmas Eve afternoon. The post delivery's always late then.'

'Did the card she sent have a postmark?'

'We checked that and the police came and took the card and the envelope away. Pat was upset but they promised she could have it back eventually. The postmark was Westminster. That doesn't mean anything necessarily, does it? She could have got someone to post it or just been passing through central London.'

'It's hard to know. What did the card say?'

'Just *Happy Xmas, Nana Pat. Don't worry about me*. Three little kisses. We were all in tears over it, even Niall and he rarely cries. The police checked it was Havana's writing. Pat had kept her old cards, so they could compare them. She never throws anything away.' She sighed. 'Well, at least she's alive, the poor girl. There's some hope to hang onto. But fourteen and all alone! And I understand Ashleigh has her new baby. One unwanted child replaced by another wanted one. I don't know how that woman sleeps at night, especially if what Havana told you that evening at your house was true.'

'I think it was. She was genuinely upset because her mother had rejected her again. I think it finally broke her.' He sat back, his steady grey eyes resting on her face. 'I think you're a sincere and honest person, Jeanie. You certainly come across that way.'

She looked startled. 'I hope so. What makes you say that?'

'I've been thinking about you. Thinking about how you're frank and up front. So you must be feeling uncomfortable at leaving me anonymous messages.'

She touched a finger to her lips. 'Messages? No, I haven't.'

'Jeanie, I know it's you. I didn't at first but when you left the last one I heard a sound in the background and I realised that it was Pat calling you.'

Her colour rose. 'No, you're imagining things.'

He looked at her unflinchingly but not unkindly. 'I bet that if I asked to look at your phone now, I'd find my number in the call history.'

She lifted her cup and blew on the tea. 'That's rubbish. You'd have seen the number if I'd rung you.'

'Not if you dialled 141 before my number. That conceals the caller. Come on, Jeanie, you might as well tell me. You know something about Greg and you need to share. You'll feel better if you do and you must want to. It's against your nature to hide things. That's why you've called me. You told someone something and it's been on your mind.'

She took her hat off. Her hair fell over her brow and she pushed it back. Her hair smelled of a spray from his childhood, something with lilac or lavender in it. He pictured her as a solemn little girl, one of those children who seemed born middle-aged. Her shoulders sagged. 'I should have known you'd work it out. You weren't born yesterday.'

'It took me a while.'

'Yes, okay, I did ring you. But I don't really know if it's relevant. It could just be me being a worry wart.'

'Maybe I can work that out.'

'Look . . . if I tell you, you absolutely can't mention it to Niall or Pat. It would be awful for them.'

'More awful than Greg's murder?'

She nodded. 'In a way. At least they have good memories of him.' She drank her tea and poured herself another cup, adding more sugar. It had cooled in the pot and the surface looked oily. Then she hunched across the table, her voice hushed. 'After Yvette and Greg split up, I met her one day for a coffee. It was just before she went back to Sardinia. We were never great friends but we got on well enough. She rang me and she was so upset, I agreed to see her. She was in bits when Greg ended the marriage. She told me that day that Greg . . . well, that he raped her sometimes. You know, when she didn't want to have sex. She was bitter about it and very emotional. Yvette was from a very conventional Catholic family in a rural part of Sardinia. She'd had a sheltered life in many ways before she met Greg. She told me she was a virgin when she married him so . . . well, you know . . .'

'She thought Greg's behaviour was just how marriage was?'

'Something like that. I remember she said she thought that was why Greg married teenagers — because they were less mature, more vulnerable.'

'How old was Yvette when they married?'

'Just seventeen and he was in his twenties. Sam, his first wife was seventeen when he married her and Ashleigh was eighteen.'

'He did like them young.' Swift recalled Fitz Blackmore commenting that Ashleigh had said that Greg liked fresh young meat.

Jeanie linked her fingers, pressing them together. 'I didn't know what to say to her, to be honest. I felt embarrassed. I've never been good with other people's private stuff, especially bedroom details. I never told anyone about it, not for a long time. I never meant to. I didn't want Niall or Pat to get wind of it.'

'But then you did?'

She gulped tea. 'Hmm. It was at Greg and Ashleigh's wedding. There she was, so young, just a child herself really and pregnant. You could see she thought she'd made a good catch, marrying the suave captain. He was flirting openly with other women. I don't drink much usually but I'd had a few glasses that day and alcohol always makes me emotional and gabby. I got angry about what I knew Greg had done. I suppose I wondered if he'd forced himself on Ashleigh. I was talking to Jude, that friend of hers. She was a bridesmaid and she was gushing on about how Ashleigh was her bestie and they did everything together. Real schoolgirl stuff. Then she started muttering that she didn't like Greg, he was flashy and arrogant. She thought Ashleigh had made a mistake, being taken in by him. You know the sort of thing. I could see that she was the jealous type. The kind of woman who hasn't got a man and resents her best friend getting married. As far as I can make out, Jude has no life of her own and feeds off Ashleigh's. She was always fluttering around Ashleigh like a moth to a candle. Anyway, I blurted out what Yvette had told me. I regretted it straight away and I asked her not to mention it to anyone.'

'How did she react?'

'She didn't say much. In fact, she went very quiet, thoughtful even. But she promised she'd never say anything to Greg's mum. She said there was no reason why another woman should suffer because of Greg's behaviour. I've not seen her since. But a while after Greg died I remembered telling her and it worried me.'

If Jude had decided to take revenge, she'd waited a long time. Unless Ashleigh had reported to her bestie that Greg had raped *her*. That was likely. Men who raped usually started the behaviour early in their lives and continued it. Jude would have remembered that other wife and her story. Resentment could burn slowly and Jude certainly struck him as a complex combination of needy and tricky. Or maybe she'd told the story to someone else who had decided to act.

Jeanie caught his arm. 'You won't mention this to Niall or Pat, promise me?'

'I won't mention it for now. I can't promise they won't find out if it has any bearing on Greg's death.' He glanced at his watch. 'It's gone half four, I don't think you're going to have time for your shopping.'

'Oh well, it can wait 'til tomorrow. It was just bits and pieces.'

The meeting with the Roscoes was hard going to start with. They all sat in the main living room. Pat was tearful, Jeanie still anxious and Niall Roscoe looked worn. The air was hot and stale, thrumming with tension. Swift decided to start on the offensive.

'Some of the things you've read about me in the Cornford paper are based on truth. My girlfriend was killed and I will never stop feeling guilty about that. But that was a personal matter and nothing to do with my work. There was a murder in my house last year, linked to the case I was working on at the time. When you're an investigator, you get on the wrong side of some people. You make enemies, especially if you're nearing the truth of a matter. Camilla Finley puts her own spin on events, for her own reasons and her own gain. As for the court hearing about my friend's will, it was a malicious allegation and the case against me was dismissed. The fact is, I have a proven track record in solving crimes.'

Niall Roscoe scratched his head. 'Well, I suppose you've made some fair points. Maybe I over reacted a bit but we were in a right state here at Christmas, what with Mum getting Havana's card and everything.'

'Thanks. It's up to you if I carry on with this investigation. I believe I'm making progress. Slow, but it's progress and more than the police ever uncovered. Greg was involved in a business deal that went badly and there were several people who might have had reason to do him harm.'

'I think Mr Swift should continue,' Jeanie said quietly. 'It's not his fault that Ashleigh's been so awful to Havana. At least Havana trusted him enough to talk to him. And as for that reporter . . . she prints tripe to sell her paper and her book.'

Pat Roscoe had been staring at him and dabbing her rheumy eyes with a shredded tissue. Now she placed her hands on her knees. Her voice was choked with emotion but determined. 'You're right, Jeanie. No point in turning back now. I was upset when I read about you, Mr Swift, but it caught me at a bad time and I know some of those reporters play dirty. One of them tried to get me to talk when my Col had his accident. I told him to get lost. I'm glad that Niall gave that Finley woman short shrift when she rang him. I want to know about Havana. Tell me about her. You're the last person I know who saw her. I need to know what was happening. Why wasn't she living at home?'

He took them through his three meetings with Havana, treading carefully, selecting his information. He didn't want to badmouth Greg or Ashleigh, yet he needed to make clear that Havana had felt unwanted at home. He told them that she had hidden in her father's car and had seen him with a woman on the evening he died.

'Finally, I'll tell you exactly what I told the police,' he finished. 'Havana had a crush on Chand Malla, my tenant. She was feeling lonely and upset, that's why she came to my house. Chand behaved properly, I have no doubt about that. She threatened suicide partly because she tried to kiss him and he told her it was wrong. She saw it as rejection and just another confirmation that she was ugly and unwanted.'

Pat Roscoe burst into tears again. 'She should have come to me!' she said. 'Little Havana should have come to me! Why was she living with strangers? I don't understand any of this, I really don't. It's shocking what's been going on and I've been kept in the dark. Greg must be turning in his grave.'

Jeanie put an arm around her but she shoved her away. Jeanie sighed and placed a box of tissues in her lap.

Niall Roscoe cast his eyes upwards and crossed his arms tightly over his chest. Swift thought that his Christmas must have been a walk in the park compared to theirs.

'I'm sorry to cause you this sadness,' Swift said. Although, looking at the sobbing woman, he couldn't help feeling annoyed at her self-pity. Now that he knew more about the family, his initial sympathy for her had ebbed. He thought that she was the author of own grief in many ways. She seemed to expect other people's loyalty and love even though she exhibited little herself - except to her dead son. He was the only one to whom she was truly loyal and yet he'd seen her infrequently and left her care to others. If she had been less indulgent of Greg, more tolerant of his wives and more careful with her opinions and her words, she'd have kept contact with her grandchildren. Instead, she'd allowed herself the luxury of speaking her mind and thereby severing ties. Maybe if she hadn't been so judgemental and partial, she'd have been able to help Havana and Axel through their troubles. Havana in particular could have done with a reliable grandmother to lean on. Just as well Pat Roscoe didn't know what Axel had said about her.

'I'll carry on with the investigation then,' he said, getting up. 'No need to see me out. Let me know if Havana gets in touch again.' He thought it unlikely, at least until the following Christmas.

* * *

Swift decided it would be best to try to speak to Jude Chamberlain at Mylod's opticians, where she worked. He was unlikely to get through her front door. The shop was in the centre of Cornford, opposite the old cattle market, which was now a courtyard of galleries and restaurants. It was New Year's Eve and there were already quite a few drunken revellers out and about in the bright, crisp afternoon.

A young bearded man called Assim greeted him eagerly in Mylod's. The shop was empty and his eyes lit up at the prospect of a customer but when Swift said he'd called by to say hi and Happy New Year to Jude, he seemed content to settle for some company.

'Jude's just with a customer, doing some tests. She won't be long,' he said, leaning on the counter and pulling at the point of his beard. He wore huge purple and red plastic frames that swamped his face.

'I just called by on the off-chance. I know her friend Ashleigh better, to be honest.'

Assim clapped his hands. 'Isn't it exciting about Ashleigh's baby! And Logan, such a lovely name! We had a collection and bought a gorgeous Babygro and little bootees.'

'Lovely. I can't wait to see the baby. Did you work with Ashleigh when she was here?'

'Oh yes. We were a great team — her, Jude, and me. I'm sad she left but, then again, I'm glad she met the right man at last. She deserved some happiness after what went on in her first marriage. The times I saw her cry!'

Swift nodded. 'I know. Greg was awful to her. Such a cheat. All her friends were happy that she met Barry.'

Assim pushed his glasses up his nose. 'To be honest, when I first saw Baz I thought, yuk, Grandad alert! And Jude thought he was a bit long in the tooth — but then she's *so* protective of Ash, it's sweet! But then I saw that Baz was good for Ash and why should love have age barriers?'

'Why indeed?' Swift leaned in. 'Mind you, I'm glad that Greg didn't find out that she was seeing Barry behind his back and I don't blame her for pretending that they met after Greg died. People can be so judgemental and she was right to grab some happiness.'

'Oh, that's just what I said to her,' Assim breathed, moulding his beard again. 'This is a small town and you get terrible gossips. We kept it to ourselves in here, in our little family. So, how do you know Ash and Jude?'

Swift was saved from having to think of a lie as a door opened and a woman came out, followed by Jude holding a clipboard. Her brow creased into deep furrows when she saw Swift.

'I just dropped by about something I need to ask you,' he said quickly, before she could erupt.

She flicked a glance at her customer and ignored him, asking the woman to sit at a desk near reception and handing the clipboard to Assim.

'Could you talk Ms Costello through her lens options?' she asked. 'I won't be a minute.'

She stalked back to the room she had come from and motioned Swift in with a quick jerk of her head, closing the door behind him. The room was small and windowless, containing a large white machine, two chairs and a wall chart explaining eye pressure and vision field tests. Jude stood with her back to a wall, glaring at him. She was in a neat navy blue shirt and skirt, her hair swept up in a ponytail.

'What are you doing here? Whatever you want, make it quick.'

Swift leaned back against the wall chart. 'I have a question. I was talking to Jeanie Roscoe and she said she once told you something and she regretted it.'

Jude frowned. 'Jeanie Roscoe? Oh yeah.'

'She met you at Ashleigh and Greg's wedding.'

Jude pulled at an earlobe, fiddling with a small pink earring and adjusting the stud at the back. 'Dull looking Jeanie with awful hair and a frumpy dress. Looked like the poor relation. I wanted to give her some tips about a makeover.'

'Jeanie said she'd had one too many at the reception and she told you something about Greg and his second wife, Yvette.'

'So?' she said truculently. 'What the hell's that got to do with you?'

'I am investigating Greg's murder. Do you remember what Jeanie told you? The sooner you tell me, the sooner I'll be out of your hair.'

'Good, because I literally can't stand the sight of you. Okay, mousy Jeanie in a dress like a sack told me that Greg had forced himself on Yvette. Raped her. It was ever so shocking, I can tell you. I mean to say, hearing that about the groom on his wedding day!' There was a gleam in her eye that told him she had been enjoyably shocked.

'Did you tell Ashleigh about that?'

She shook her head too quickly. 'No way.'

'I don't believe you. You'd hardly keep that from the woman who's your best friend and married to a man you dislike. You always look after her and protect her, don't you? Surely you'd have been worried that Greg would rape Ashleigh if that was his style?'

She looked at him and ran a hand over the edge of a chair back. 'Okay, look, I didn't tell her at first. I mean, she was pregnant and over the moon at getting married. I couldn't spoil her happiness.'

No, Swift thought, but I bet you savoured knowing what you knew, storing it to use at the right time. 'So you did tell Ashleigh eventually?'

'It was when Havana was about four. Ash looked upset one day. She told me that Greg had . . . well, literally insisted on sex even though she didn't want it. She said he'd bruised her. And I could tell it wasn't the first time. So then I told her about Yvette.'

'What was Ashleigh's reaction?'

'Well, she was ever so upset. Literally sobbing. I said she should go to the police but she said she couldn't. She said they might not believe her and she'd feel too ashamed. A while later she told me she was going to deal with it herself. She'd worked out a way to put a stop to Greg. And she did. Ash is a strong woman in her own way, you know. She's got guts.'

'How did she deal with it?'

Jude smiled slyly. 'She had a trump card, didn't she? She told Greg that if her ever did that to her again, she'd leave and take Havana.'

'And that worked?'

'Absolutely. He was terrified she'd do it. He worshipped the ground Havana trod on. Ash told me they hardly ever had sex after that. She did it sometimes, just to keep things ticking over.' Jude stopped abruptly, annoyed that she'd said too much. 'Look, what's this all about? I've told you what I know and I've got work to do.'

'I suppose I'm wondering if what you've said is true or if maybe Greg raped Ashleigh again. You know . . . once a rapist . . . maybe he found out about Barry and got angry. I know they had a big row a couple of days before he was murdered. Maybe you and Ashleigh decided that he should pay for what he'd done and free her up to remarry. After all, someone did stick a safety pin through his penis. Someone wanted him to suffer and cry. That sounds as if it could have been a woman he'd raped or a friend who took revenge on her behalf. A woman who wanted to inflict similar physical and emotional damage.'

Jude's eyes widened in anger but he thought he saw a flicker of anxiety too. She stuttered slightly as she spoke. 'You're having a laugh. How dare you come here and suggest I've literally murdered someone! You've got no right. And from what I've read about you lately, you should sort out your own life before you go around making accusations about other people.'

'Did you ever tell Barry about the rapes?'

'Baz? No way. Ash would have hated it if I'd done that. Now you can get out.'

She headed to the front of the shop, throwing the front door open. As Swift exited, she hissed, 'And don't you dare go near Ash, upsetting her with this crap! She's just had a baby and she needs peace and quiet! If you go anywhere near her I swear, I'll—'

'You'll what?' Swift stopped and looked at her. He could see Assim in the background, staring, a pair of frames raised in his hands. 'Stab me in the head and neck and maybe somewhere else too? Happy New Year!'

He walked back to his car. The sky was clear, the air ice cold and still. He stopped at an Italian delicatessen. A big ceramic pink and brown pig stood sentinel at the door. It wore a gold paper crown from a cracker. Swift browsed the counters and bought a selection of thinly sliced cooked ham, Taleggio cheese, artichoke and olive salads, bread and a lemon tart. Nora was coming to his place to celebrate New Year and she'd pleaded by email, *no steaming plates of food, just light salad stuff.* As he watched the pots being filled with salads, he thought that Ashleigh and Jude could have killed Roscoe. There was a strange light in Jude's eyes sometimes, as if she could blow a fuse. The two besties had been close since childhood and it was clear that Jude clung to her friend like an adoring, dependent leech. They could have decided to wreak revenge and humiliate the rapist. But why would Roscoe have met either of them at the airfield?

And it didn't explain the mystery woman he'd met by the river.

Chapter 13

Later, Swift opened his front door to both Nora and Bella Reynolds on the doorstep, standing well apart.

'We met outside the tube. I was just explaining that I've come to see Chand for the evening,' Bella said hurriedly.

'I hear you've been playing match maker.' Nora smiled but her tone was less than warm. The last time she'd seen Bella, she'd snarled at her.

'I gave it a shot,' Swift said, standing back to let them in.

Chand came running down the stairs. He kissed Bella on the cheek, took her hand and turned to Swift.

'Maybe we could all have a drink later? Want to come up to mine?' He smiled eagerly. 'I've some great lime and chilli rice from my mum.'

There was an awkward pause. Swift had said nothing to Chand about his previous history with Bella or Nora's dislike of her. He thought it was her prerogative to share what she wanted.

'Thanks, Chand, but I'm fierce shattered tonight, just want to chill out,' Nora said tightly. 'Another time?'

'Sure,' he agreed, looking rebuffed.

Bella blinked rapidly and glanced up the stairs, wanting to escape. 'Well, Happy New Year then,' she said.

'Yes and let's hope Havana is found soon,' Swift said to Chand, giving him a reassuring touch on the shoulder.

He nodded. 'I'm keeping an eye on the system. I'll let you know if there's any new Intel.'

In the flat, Nora warmed her hands by the fire while Swift poured wine.

'I wasn't sure I liked this wallpaper when I first came here but it's grown on me,' she said. 'What's the pattern called again?'

'Strawberry Thief. My great aunt Lily put it up herself, years ago. Mary says it's a bit scruffy now, like me.'

'Not at all. Lily did a good job. No tears or gaps.' She wrinkled her nose at him. 'You do look a bit frayed around the edges at times but I like you that way.'

'I've missed you,' he said. 'Life's seemed very quiet.'

'Me, too. Although life has been anything but quiet over the last week, with the extended Morrow family!'

They compared their Christmases and she laughed as he described Joyce's groaning table. She told him she'd had enough of her family and squabbling children after a couple of days and had taken off on her own, walking in the Wicklow Mountains. He listened to her light, musical voice and watched her wiry shape as she straightened cushions and looked through his scatter of Christmas cards. He thought that she'd been rude to Chand but he wasn't going to mention it. He wanted a pleasant, relaxing evening. Yet he knew Nora well enough to realise that she wouldn't be able to resist making some comment about Bella. As he was crouching before the fire, stacking it with logs she kicked her shoes off and collapsed on the sofa.

'You didn't say anything about introducing Bella to Chand,' she said.

'It didn't occur to me. It was just an idea I had because they'd both like to find someone. It might not have taken off.'

'But it has?'

'I think so. Looks like it, anyway.'

'So, how did you bring it about?'

'Sorry?' He turned to her, his face warm from the fire.

She leaned forward. 'Well, did you contact Chand or Bella to suggest it?'

'I spoke to Chand and then I emailed Bella. They both liked the idea so I gave them each other's emails and left it to them.'

'So you've been in touch with Bella about it?'

'Well, obviously, but only by email, as I said. It would be difficult to link up two people without contacting both of them.'

'There's no need to sound as if you're explaining to a child. And now Bella's back in your house.' Nora's tone was combative and she was pointing her glass at him.

He got up slowly and took his wine from the mantelpiece. 'This is starting to feel a bit like a formal interview. Could you put work mode aside for tonight?' He spoke lightly, not wanting confrontation. Some hope.

'But Bella is back in your house.'

'Yes. She's in Chand's flat. Nora, what's your point?'

'Well, it just seems to me that you've organised that she's back near you. I wonder why.'

Swift sat in a chair at an angle to the sofa. 'I'm hoping that Bella and Chand make a go of it. Is there something wrong with that?'

Nora took a deep draught of wine. 'Maybe you have mixed motives.'

He shook his head. 'You're over-thinking. Let it go. I've no romantic interest in Bella. I'd like to see her happy in a relationship, that's all. I've known her a long time and I'm glad we met up again. You want good things for your friends, don't you?'

'I'm just wondering why you didn't mention it to me. It's the kind of thing you'd discuss with your partner. You know . . . throw the idea around, ask my opinion. But then, you didn't think to talk to me about offering Ruth the flat upstairs last year.'

He sighed. 'Do we have to go over all of this again? It's New Year. It would be good to start as we mean to go on. With trust.'

Nora hunched in to herself. 'I just feel that you keep things from me and I wonder why. You don't include me in your thinking. Sometimes, it seems like you park me in a compartment, tucked away. And first you wanted Ruth upstairs, now you've managed to get Bella up there. Some people might see a pattern here.'

'Some people? You mean you, Nora. There is no *pattern* except in your suspicious mind. Bella hasn't moved in and I suppose Chand could just as easily have been at her place tonight.'

'You've always got an explanation ready. Have you noticed that?'

He took a breath and watched the fire for a moment. He knew that Nora still had scars from the time her partner had dumped her and taken a job in New York. 'Look, I'll admit that I'm not always very good at sharing my thoughts and talking things through. Partly habit, partly just my nature. But you're so quick to doubt me and think I have ulterior motives. I wouldn't go behind your back or betray you. If you really distrust me so much, I'm not sure why you want to be here with me, why you even want my company.' He had entered dangerous territory now; he could sense it. Knowing how quickly she could flare up, he wondered if she would walk out.

She narrowed her eyes at him. 'Ruth chucked you for another man and treated you terribly but you still hankered after her for ages and saw her when she allowed. You went behind her husband's back.'

'That's true. But it's not something I make a habit of and I'm not proud of it. I knew deep down that Ruth no longer loved me. I was damaging myself. And I shouldn't have spent so long staying tied to her. Older and wiser, that's me. But, then again, if I hadn't carried on seeing Ruth I wouldn't have Branna now so . . . swings and roundabouts.'

Nora nodded. Her shoulders relaxed. 'Well . . . I don't mean to sound jealous and suspicious. Sorry. I know I can get chippy. I just think you need to share more.'

'Okay, you have a point and I'll try. And I think you should be more careful about being rude to people. You hurt Chand's feelings.'

'Really? I didn't mean to. He's a good bloke. I'll apologise when I see him.'

There was a silence. Then she leaned over, kissed him on the cheek and ruffled his hair, stretching his curls out through her fingers. 'You're starting to look like Jimi Hendrix.'

'I know. Needs a cut.'

'Have you heard from your boyfriend over Christmas?'

They had a running joke now about Fitz Blackmore, deciding that his macho stance was a bluff and that his friendliness and use of the nickname Ron was a sign of attraction.

'He's away skiing with a lady friend.'

'Just a cover, he'll be back and pursuing you and a bromance, you'll see,' Nora said, making him smile.

He suggested they eat and they had a picnic in front of the fire. There were sounds of a party from next door and at midnight the trumpet playing *Auld Lang Syne*. Fireworks rushed and exploded nearby. They toasted the year to come and kissed, folding against each other on the sofa. He held Nora tight as she tucked her head under his chin. He was happy to be here with her, inhaling the familiar scent of her hair.

He was happy and yet the embrace felt somehow like an uneasy truce.

* * *

On January 3 it started snowing heavily again, settling inches deep on London. Swift woke to a hushed, bleached world and abandoned plans for an early row. He'd also woken with tired limbs so settled for some gentle stretches. He ate porridge laced with cinnamon as he took his next signing course online, focusing on words associated with nursery and school. He and Ruth had another appointment with an audiologist in the coming months and he thought that he'd better make up his mind about cochlear implants.

He knelt on the dark red rug to clear ashes from the fire, swept the hearth and brought more logs and kindling in from the store outside the back door. He laid a fire ready for the evening and was ambushed by a sudden, warm rush of memory: himself, Cedric and his great aunt Lily toasting bread at the glowing coals when he was a child. He could recall the crunch of the charred edges and the taste of melting butter as if it was yesterday. Good times. This house had been such a refuge for him when his mother died and he was confused by grief and adolescent turmoil. He rested his head against the cool tiles of the fireplace for a moment and then found his shovel and scraped snow from the steps at the front of the house. It was still soft and powdery. He was watching a couple of children across the road having a snowball fight when his phone rang.

'It's Heidi here. Heidi Parr. I thought I'd ring you because I've heard something about Stef.'

'Okay, thanks. What have you got?'

'I'm just off a flight in Madrid at the moment and I was talking to the pilot over coffee. She told me Stef's back flying in Europe. He's a captain now and in and out of Heathrow a fair bit. This pilot had seen him recently in that club I told you about.'

'Take Wing?'

'That's right. They have accommodation and he was staying over. So, you know, you might catch him there.'

'Thanks for that. I'll ring the club.'

'Right. If you see Stef, tell him I made a New Year resolution to clear him out of my life and I took his bike and his revolting tribal mask to the tip.'

'I doubt I'll mention it but I think that was a good move.'

'Yep. And tell him not to think of getting in touch.'

As she ended the call, Swift wondered if her insistence was genuine or if she was protesting too much. People's motives were often layered and most of the time they barely understood them themselves. Maybe Heidi hoped that he would pass on her messages and that Stef would take them as a challenge to contact her.

He looked up the number for Take Wing and rang the club. A cheery woman told him that she couldn't comment if Mr Makinen was staying there *at this present time* but was happy to take a message for him. Swift dictated a message: *I'm a private investigator. I need to speak to you urgently about Greg Roscoe.* He gave his number and email and rang off with little expectation of hearing from Makinen. He was surprised when his phone rang just an hour later and Makinen was on the line.

'How did you know where to find me?' He had a quiet, nasal voice.

'I've been speaking to Holly and Heidi.'

'Ah, I see.'

Swift explained his involvement with the Roscoes. Makinen didn't comment but said he was about to have a sauna and a sleep. They could meet at the club later that afternoon. He told Swift to ring the bell at Number 54, Sheldon Close.

Take Wing was ten minutes' walk from Marble Arch, in a street of elegant Regency houses. Number 54 looked like an ordinary four storey townhouse, with a dark grey door and cream windows. Members clearly paid for discretion as well as facilities as there was nothing outside to tell the public that it housed a club. Swift rang the bell and announced himself. He was asked to come to the first floor. He climbed narrow, bare oak stairs with a curving wrought iron balustrade to a reception area where he signed in and handed over his coat to hang in the cloakroom. The attendant glanced at an IPad, told him that Mr Makinen was at the swimming pool located in the wellness area in the basement, and gave him directions.

Swift went back down the stairs and through a door to the wellness area. The same grey and cream décor continued throughout. The building was warm, hushed and gleaming, the hallways and corridors simply appointed with mirrors and lush green plants in cream urns. There was a faint scent of sandalwood. In the basement, he stepped into a wide hall with small wooden signs on the doors leading from it: *Sauna, Fitness Studios, Yoga Centre, Swim and Massage.* It was a world away from the odiferous confines and plastic furnishings of Health Crunch in Blackheath.

He pushed the door to the swimming area. There were two pools: a larger one for swimming and a smaller, Jacuzzi type. The first thing that struck him was that there was no smell of chlorine. The second was that the only occupant of the large pool was a man slicing efficiently through the clear blue water. Huge mirrors at either end of the room reflected his progress. As Swift watched, admiring his economic, sleek crawl, huge chrome taps switched on at the side of the Jacuzzi, pouring out jets of steaming water. The man saw him as he turned his head to breathe and headed for the steps at the pool corner. He removed goggles, earplugs and a nose clip and took a white towelling robe from a rail. He wrapped it around himself, and then padded over to Swift.

'Mr Swift? Sorry about the damp handshake.'

'No problem.'

Makinen was tanned with pale blond hair darkened by the water and he looked in glowing health, apart from the slight purplish puffiness below his eyes. Jetlag, Swift presumed.

'I like to exercise when I can,' Makinen said, reaching for a towel and rubbing his hair. 'Flying takes its toll on the body.'

'That's what Heidi said when I saw her. She was doing leg stretches to ward off varicose veins.'

'The curse of flight attendants . . . being on their feet too much. My problem is the opposite. Sitting too much. Haemorrhoids are the pilots' nightmare. Shall we sit now?' He gestured at cushioned wooden chairs by the pool. His manner was friendly enough but Swift sensed that he was guarded and alert. 'I'm going to order some snacks. I deserve a treat after forty lengths. Will you join me?'

'Why not?'

Makinen nodded and pressed an intercom on the wall, ordering from a menu beside it. Swift was starting to sweat in the warm, humid atmosphere. He took off his jumper and rolled up his shirtsleeves. A button that had been hanging by a thread fell off a cuff and he pocketed it. He could feel his hair clinging to his neck and thought he must get it trimmed. Makinen sat down, propping his shapely feet on a small stool.

'So,' he said, pinching the bridge of his nose and sniffing. 'I suppose Holly and Heidi have been giving me a bad press.'

'That's true.'

Makinen grimaced. 'Well . . . in the end, if you're not with the right person, it's best to walk. Life's too short to be miserable.'

'Heidi said she asked you to go.'

'True, but I was about to leave anyway. Why do you want to see me?'

He surely had to have an idea, so Swift started with a question Makinen wasn't expecting. 'Have you any thoughts about why Greg Roscoe's killer stuck a safety pin through his penis with a mocking card?'

Makinen's eyebrows shot up. The surprise seemed genuine. 'Wow, no! I thought he was just stabbed. Did someone do that as well?'

'Yes. I suppose it was a humiliation.'

'Right. Well . . . vicious, eh?'

'Exactly.'

'Such a mess.'

A young man dressed in black T-shirt and jeans came in wheeling a trolley and set a tiered china stand of sandwiches, teacakes and scones on the table. There was also an oval plate of granola laced with honey and assorted berries, a beautifully arranged assortment of sliced apples, pineapple and guava and a large jug of tomato juice, accompanied by a silver teapot and milk jug.

'Tuck in,' Makinen said. 'I've not eaten today.'

Swift took a smoked salmon sandwich. The brown bread was crustless and light. Makinen scooped granola into a bowl and then piled half a dozen sandwiches on a plate. He proceeded to extract the contents of salmon, ham, chicken, slices of tomato and asparagus spears with his fingers, discarding the bread. He ate quickly, pouring tea for Swift and tomato juice for himself.

'Tell me about Pure and Strong,' Swift said.

Makinen closed his eyes briefly, and then reached for the plate of fruit. 'Ah. Heidi's been talking.'

'Not just Heidi.'

'Oh?' He paused with a ring of pineapple on the way to his lips. 'Who else?'

'A man called Paul Cairns. He saw you at Cornford airfield, arguing with Greg.'

The name didn't seem to mean anything to him. 'Hmm. Well, Greg owed me money and he was avoiding me. I went there one day to try to pin him down. He talked me into that stupid business scheme involving a petty crook in Taiwan. He was a very persuasive character, Greg. As you probably know, it didn't go well and some people had reactions to the ingredients in the products. I'm not surprised. On reflection, God knows who made them or what they used. Some little back street sweatshop grinding all sorts into powders. I'd parted with quite a bit of money to help get the business up and running and I was left badly stung. Hence my argument with Greg. He wasn't returning my calls so I cornered him at work. Not that it did me much good.'

'You didn't get your money back?'

'No. Someone killed Greg first.' He dabbed fruit juice from his chin with his towel.

'I pointed out to Heidi that you were trading illegally and someone who fell ill from using the product could have sued. You could have been much more out of pocket if that had happened. That kind of selling can attract heavy fines.'

'Well, no one did. If people were dense enough to use something without checking it out properly that was their lookout. And lots of people get side effects from things they take. Even mainstream medication comes with all sorts of warnings.'

Greg Roscoe had certainly chosen business colleagues who shared his lack of scruples. Swift helped himself to a cream cheese sandwich with olives. 'Heidi said someone in Taiwan threatened you.'

'It wasn't that serious. The guy we dealt with was small fry. Heidi got overexcited about it. She was convinced the Taiwanese equivalent of the Mafia was after me. But I did change jobs so I didn't fly there any more. No point in making yourself a target.'

'Do you have any idea who might have wanted to kill Greg?'

'I've given it some thought but no. Maybe one of his exes. Someone else he owed money to.' He stirred his juice with a long spoon and said casually, 'Maybe it was Yvette.'

'Why Yvette?'

'Greg was meeting her the day he died. He said he'd been in touch with her and he was trying to mend fences. Have you met Yvette?'

'No. I've emailed her.'

'Neither have I but she sounds bitter. Unforgiving. Maybe being with Greg made her like that. Anyway, he was trying to schmooze her because he wanted to see more of his son but also because she'd inherited money and he liked the idea of sharing it. I think he was indulging some fantasy about getting back together with her, particularly as he thought that Ashleigh had turned out to be hard work. I was hoping he'd be able to work some charm so that he could pay me back. His campaign seems to have had some success because she'd agreed to see him.'

'In Cornford?'

'That's what he said.'

'Did you get the impression that Yvette was receptive to the idea of a possible reunion?'

'No idea. I was surprised that she'd agreed to meet him but then, as I've said, Greg could be very persuasive and charming. Maybe Yvette still had feelings for him despite the fall out and animosity. It was all very hush-hush but he told me to keep me sweet, I suppose. He said he needed to work on her and he'd be able to repay me. I didn't necessarily believe him but it seemed the only hope I had of getting some of my money back. Next thing I heard he was dead. I didn't know for a week or so. I was away on a long haul to Mexico.'

Swift watched Makinen deconstruct another sandwich, rolling a slice of ham into a bite size chunk. He was reminded of Havana fiddling with scraps of food and wondered why the man hadn't just ordered a salad. Perhaps the business with the bread was a habit or a ritual. Axel had reported that his father was going to an important meeting before he died, one that he thought might turn his life around. Unless Axel was an expert liar, Swift was sure that he hadn't known that the meeting was with his mother.

'Did you like Greg?' he asked.

'Interesting question. Not that much, to be honest. He drew me in with his personality. He was fun to be around. The kind of person who makes things happen — a real party guy. So I used to hook up with him when I was in London — mainly in here. But then when I wasn't around him, I used to think he was shallow and a bit unpleasant. He really duped me about that business, I know it. He helped himself to profits and lied.'

'That could be a motive for murder.'

Makinen hooked a shred of pineapple from his teeth with his little fingernail. 'Own goal, surely? No chance then of getting my money back.' He smiled then, making an open-handed gesture. 'Plus I was in the cockpit of a 747 when it happened, high in the clouds over the Atlantic. It would have been difficult to have been murdering Greg and sticking pins in him. Have a teacake, they're excellent.'

* * *

Swift was tucked into his favourite corner in his local pub, the Silver Mermaid. He'd had lunch with his friend Milo, a contemporary of Cedric's who'd been to school with him. Milo had seemed frailer, bent more over his walking sticks, although he said it was just the cold getting into his bones. He was wearing a tie that had belonged to Cedric, yellow with lime green stripes. He had a key to Swift's house these days, so that he could sit in the garden as often as he liked to keep Cedric company. Sometimes Swift came home and found a flute of champagne, a handmade chocolate or a tiny pot of caviar by Cedric's spot under the tea rose.

'Have you seen anything of Oliver?' Milo had asked.

'No, but I've heard from him, indirectly.' Swift had explained about Camilla Finley.

Milo had tutted. 'How cowardly of him. How typical. Don't let it get you down. It will blow over. I didn't see much of Oliver when he was a child but what I did see was uninspiring. He was always a mean-spirited moaner. Cedric used to beat himself up about the way Oliver turned out but I think he was born that way.'

Milo had insisted on paying for lunch and now he'd departed in a taxi. Swift decided to stay in the warmth of the busy pub for a while. Sometimes, he liked to watch the world going about its business and let his thoughts roam and circle. He sipped his beer slowly, going back over the interviews he had conducted on the Roscoe case. Then he checked his emails. He'd sent one to Yvette earlier on:

I know that you met Greg the morning before he died. He'd told Stefan Makinen about it. I need to speak to you urgently.

She rang him as he was walking home. He leaned on a parapet by the river, resting his elbows on the icy rime of snow. He could feel the chill of the pavement through his boots.

'Why can't you just leave me alone?' she asked bitterly.

'Because a man was murdered. Because it's my job to find out who did it. Was it you?'

'Of course not!'

'Really? You're lining up nicely as a suspect. People who omit to mention important information in a murder enquiry usually are. Tell me why you met Greg. I was surprised that you agreed to. I thought you had no time for him.'

‘I didn’t. I couldn’t stand the sight of him. But I was doing it for other people, too. It wasn’t just me meeting him, you see.’

‘You’ll have to explain.’

‘This is difficult, you know.’

He hardened his voice. ‘I’m sure. But if you had nothing to do with Greg’s death there’s no reason not to explain. If you won’t tell me, I won’t go away. I’ll keep asking and I’ll probably have to discuss it with Axel. He knew that his father was having a meeting before he died but I’m sure he didn’t know it was with you. That would upset him terribly, I think.’

‘Don’t! Please don’t do that!’

‘Well then, Yvette. Speak to me.’

There was a long pause. Swift watched a navy blue dredger barging down the river in the dull light, its warning lights winking.

‘That morning, before Greg died, I met him with Jude Chamberlain. It was in a café at the services just outside Cornford.’ She cleared her throat. ‘Jude had contacted me about a month before. I didn’t know who she was but she traced me and phoned me. She explained that she was Ashleigh’s best friend and she told me that Greg had forced Ashleigh to have sex a number of times. He stopped after she said she’d leave him and take Havana, but then he did it again a while after she made him take the job at Cornford. He didn’t like being outmanoeuvred. It made him angry. He said he’d fight Ashleigh for the house and custody if she did leave, get Havana to say that her mother had ill-treated her when he was away from home. He talked about emotional and psychological abuse. He’d thought it through. Ashleigh was terrified.’ She coughed again. ‘Can you wait a moment, please? I’ve had flu. I need a throat lozenge.’

Swift waited. Havana had been her father’s ‘princess’. She’d probably have colluded with him against her mother if he’d wanted her to. He thought back to the unpleasant comments that Roscoe had written about his wife on the *Come Fly* website, referring to her as a *sullen sulky dame*.

'Okay that's better,' Yvette resumed. 'Jude Chamberlain. She said she knew that Greg had raped me because Jeanie told her. She asked for my help. She wanted me to warn Greg that I'd go to the police and report the rapes if he didn't stop tormenting Ashleigh. To be honest, I found her a bit peculiar and overwhelming. She was very insistent and it alarmed me. I said I couldn't possibly help and I ended the call. And then not long after, Greg contacted me after years of silence, asking me to meet and discuss Axel.' She laughed throatily. 'He was so obvious, talking nostalgically about old times as if I had rosy memories of being with him. I knew he'd found out that I'd had an inheritance. Hearing his voice brought it all back to me . . . all that shame and his betrayals, all I put up with in that marriage. His awful arrogance and the way he always thought he'd get away with things. Well, he always had. I thought about him, Ashleigh and Jude as well for days. I prayed to Our Lady for guidance and I talked to my parish priest who is a compassionate man. I decided that it was time that Greg was stopped from behaving like that. It struck me that Jude was brave, deciding to challenge him. I rang her back and agreed to help her. Oh, it all seems so strange now but at the time, when I thought it over, it felt like the right thing to do. And Jude - well, she seemed a very odd woman but I had to admire her courage and the way she wanted to protect her closest friend. I agreed that I'd tell Greg I'd go to the police about the rapes if he didn't leave Ashleigh alone.'

Swift thought about this. 'But I thought you had no time for Ashleigh. Why would you have wanted to help her?'

'Yes, that's the question I asked myself. But, you see, I knew what she must have gone through with Greg, and also . . . I've always felt terrible guilt about another girl he raped.' Her voice faltered. She stopped and for a moment, he thought she'd hung up but then she continued. 'The girl told me about what Greg had done and I did nothing. I didn't want to know and I buried my head. And I know now that Greg must have raped other girls. It's how men like him behave. They can't stop, can they? Especially if they get away with it?'

'I'm sorry, Yvette. I know this is hard for you. Who was the girl Greg raped?'

She was almost whispering now. 'I don't know her second name. She was called Melanie. I'd never seen her before. I'd been married a couple of months when she came to my door. She'd been up in a small plane at the flying school. The flight was a present, her fifteenth birthday treat. She told me that she'd met Greg afterwards in the bar. He used to drink there when he was at home. He took her to see planes in the hangar and then he raped her in the bushes somewhere nearby. She was in such a bad way when she was telling me. She said she couldn't tell her parents, she was too ashamed. She was begging me to help her. I kept her standing in the hallway and I told her to leave me alone. I refused to believe her and I said that no one else would. I didn't give her a glass of water or a word of comfort. Some Christian that makes me! All I wanted was to protect my comfortable home and myself. That makes me almost as much of a monster as Greg was.'

'Did you say anything about it to him?'

'No! He'd only have denied it and I'd have had to go through one of his cold silences. I wanted to forget what Melanie had told me. I didn't want to believe that he could have done such a thing but then when he raped me a number of times, I thought back to what she'd said. I've always felt guilty about that girl and how I wouldn't listen to her. So when I thought about what Jude had told me, I felt I had to do something at last. You see, Jude was doing what I should have done back when Melanie came to me. She deserved my support. It was the least I could do after my cowardice years ago.'

'So this girl, Melanie . .. this would have been how long ago?'

'More than twenty years, twenty-five almost.'

'Okay. And you never saw her again?'

'No. I've no idea where she lived or anything else about her.'

'What happened when you met Greg that morning before he died?'

'Oh, believe me, that was a mixture of pleasure and pain. Jude walked in five minutes after he arrived. His face was a picture when he saw her. He'd dressed so smartly, thinking that I was going to be romanced and persuaded. Instead, he was being accused about the awful things he'd done. I feel sick now, thinking about it. You can listen to it. I recorded it on my phone without him knowing. Then I told him at the end that I had the recording and I'd go to the police with it if he ever raped anyone again or threatened Ashleigh in any way.' She took a ragged breath. 'I can't talk about this any more. It's all so horrible. Please, don't mention any of it to Axel. He's happy in his life now.'

'I can't see that I'd need to but, you know, it might have to come out eventually. Will you send me the recording?'

'Yes, all right. If it helps you.'

'It might. Send it as soon as you can. Don't be too hard on yourself about Melanie. From what I understand, you were only a girl yourself at the time.'

'I was, and I was naïve and young for my age. But she's always been on my conscience. I've prayed for forgiveness for my unkindness to her. I'll send you the recording now. I didn't kill Greg, Mr Swift. He was my son's father, even if he was a rotten one.'

Maybe not, Swift thought, but he wondered if Jude had decided to finish off some business later on. He walked home, lit the fire and made coffee. Both Ashleigh and Yvette had described themselves as naïve when they married Roscoe. He had preyed on young women and the pin through his penis made sense if he was being punished for being a rapist. Silvio Horvat had commented that he'd made some female students uncomfortable with his flirting. Holly had told him that Greg liked having sex in the grounds of the airfield. Maybe there had been other rapes in the bushes there.

Chapter 14

The recording arrived from Yvette ten minutes later. Swift propped his feet on the coffee table and listened. The first few minutes were mainly of Greg Roscoe speaking. He sounded silky and warm, telling Yvette she looked great, her hair suited her that way, where did the years go, it had been too long etc. He had an energetic, vibrant voice. Then the voice changed abruptly.

Roscoe: *What the fuck! What's she doing here?*

Jude: *Hi, Greg. Surprise, eh? Good to meet you, Yvette.*

Roscoe: *What's going on? Yvette?*

Yvette: *Hello Jude.*

Roscoe: *You knew she was coming?*

Yvette: *Of course. You can cut out the fake compliments now. They don't impress me the way they used to. You need to stop talking and listen, Greg.*

Roscoe: *I don't want this woman here. Fucking freeloader! Fucking parasite pain in the arse! Hang on, how do you even know her?*

Jude: *If you shut up, you'll find out.*

Roscoe: *If you don't mind, I'm here to speak to Yvette about private family matters.*

Jude: *'Family matters?' That's rich!*

Yvette: *Jude and I have spoken on the phone. We both wanted to meet with you. So here we are.*

Roscoe: *Look, this is ridiculous . . .*

Yvette: *No, it isn't. You do need to listen. I know it doesn't come easy to you but you need to try. Because if you don't, you'll regret it.*

Roscoe: *I don't get it.*

Jude: *No, you never do.*

Yvette: *Let's get this over with. I don't like being here.*

Jude. *Really? I've been looking forward to it.*

Yvette: *I haven't. It just needs to be done. Greg, I think I know why you wanted to meet me. I have a different reason. You raped me during our marriage and I know that you've raped Ashleigh. I know that you raped a girl called Melanie a long time ago.*

Roscoe: *What are you ranting on about? Melanie? I don't know a Melanie. Never have.*

Jude: *I don't suppose you asked her name. Anyway, why would you remember her? She was literally just a piece of meat to you.*

Roscoe: *Shut up, you interfering cow. I've always thought you're a closet lesbian, hanging around my wife and making eyes at her.*

Jude: *You're so predictable and corny.*

Roscoe: *Yvette, I don't know why you're doing this. What's Jude been saying to you?*

Yvette: *You did those things, Greg. You've raped three women to my knowledge. Probably more. I want you to admit it.*

Roscoe: *Oh, come on. You are joking. You two are unbelievable.*

Jude: *You'd better believe it. Tough when the tables are turned, isn't it?*

Roscoe: *I don't have to stay and listen to this crap.*

Yvette: *True, but if you walk, I'll go the police and talk to them about what you did to me, and to Ashleigh. I'll tell them about a girl called Melanie who came to our house and sobbed because of what you'd done to her at the airfield. She was only fifteen. I'm sure the police would be able to trace her. How many other underage girls have there been?*

Jude: *Yeah, I wonder that too and in how many countries? The police are very good at cross checking all that stuff these days.*

Roscoe: *Listen, this is ridiculous. I don't know why you're doing this. The police aren't going to listen to some cock and bull story from you about stuff you say happened years ago. It's your word against mine.*

Yvette: *It's not just my word. I told someone else years ago and I think she'll back me up.*

Jude: *I'm a witness, too. And Ashleigh will probably make a statement if Yvette goes to the police. She'll know she's got support.*

Roscoe: *Ashleigh? Does she know you're here? Is she in on this?*

Jude: *Ashleigh doesn't know. I contacted Yvette. It was time someone did something about your crimes and your threats.*

Roscoe: *I've always known you were a mad, interfering bitch. You've been trying to break up my marriage for years. You need medication.*

Jude: *I don't think you need any help with breaking up your marriage. I've just sat back and literally watched you do it for yourself.*

Yvette: *Please, can we leave the arguing? Greg, if you don't admit that you've been a rapist and promise never to lay a finger on Ashleigh or any other woman again, I'll go to the police. Not only that, I'll tell Axel.*

Roscoe: *You wouldn't do that. You wouldn't tell Axel.*

Yvette: *I would. He'd find out anyway if the police prosecute you. Just think . . . reputation and probably your job gone, possibly a prison sentence and your son and daughter knowing what kind of man you are. And your mother. She'd probably refuse to believe it about you but even so . . . I don't want to break up your marriage. It's up to Ashleigh if she stays with you. But I don't want your wife to suffer any more.*

Jude: *There's nowhere to hide, Greg. Best to fess up.*

Roscoe: *Look . . . come on, cut me some slack here. I admit I might have been a bit out of order now and again in the past. I'm a red-blooded male. I worked hard and played hard. But you know I'm not some kind of criminal. And I honestly have no idea about a Melanie. How do you know she wasn't some teenage fantasist with a crush on me? Pilots get a lot of that. Maybe she met me or saw me at the airfield and got a bit imaginative. You read about stuff like that all the time — especially with adolescent girls. Poor blokes being accused and then it's all a pack of lies.*

Yvette: *You're such a liar and a snake, Greg. It's hard to believe I loved you once. Look at yourself! Sitting there trying to pretend and expecting me to feel sorry for you. You know what you've done. I know. I'm not the impressionable girl you married. Just say it, Greg. Just say it and promise it won't happen again and you can walk out of here. Of course, if I ever hear that you've raped again, I'll be back here in a flash.*

Jude: *You don't deserve the get out of jail card. I'd love to go to the police about you right now. But I know what it would do to Ash and Havana. If I were you, I'd take the offer on the table while it's there.*

Roscoe: *Okay, okay. I might have been a bit out of order. Didn't behave like a perfect gentleman sometimes.*

Yvette: *Not good enough. You have to say the word. Hurry up! I have a flight back to catch.*

Long Pause

Roscoe: *Okay, I suppose I did pretty much rape you. If we're being technical and nit picking.*

Yvette: *And Ashleigh.*

Roscoe: *Yeah, okay and Ashleigh. Whatever. I don't remember any Melanie.*

Yvette: *But that's possible.*

Roscoe: *I suppose. I just don't know. Whatever I say now, you won't believe me. How do you expect me to remember a fumble years ago? I don't know what's happened to you, Yvette. You're so hard and unreasonable. A right harpy. You used to be such a nice, sweet girl.*

Jude: *Yeah, 'til she met you.*

Roscoe: *That's enough. I'm going now. I don't want to see either of you bitches ever again. Don't show your face at my house again, Jude. Not while I'm there, anyway.*

Yvette: *I've recorded this conversation on my phone, Greg. Just remember that if you think about rape again, or pretend this meeting never happened. I have the evidence.*

Roscoe: *Oh, fuck off back to Sardineland!*

A chair screeched and the recording ended. Swift listened through again, and then phoned Holly Armstrong, catching her as she arrived home.

'All flying cancelled today because of the weather,' she said despondently. 'More snow forecast too. What do you want now?'

'When you told me you'd had a fling with Greg Roscoe, you said that the first time you slept with him, you were drunk. He took you home and you grappled on the sofa. You couldn't remember much about it the next day.'

'That's right.'

'I just wondered if you meant that he might have raped you.'

'Wow! Where's that coming from?' She sounded surprised but he heard something else, a note of caution in her voice.

'I've been hearing things about Greg. I thought that you might have felt the sex wasn't exactly consensual, at least to start with. It's the way you described it.'

'Well . . . like I said, I was pissed after my birthday. It was all a bit fuzzy and wham bam, you know? It happens.'

'You sound unsure.'

'Well, I am in a way . . .' She clicked her tongue, her tone growing hostile. 'Oh hang on a minute! I get it! You're trying to get me to say he raped me so then you can allege that I got my revenge and stuck a pin through his cock with a sarky note.'

'No, Holly. I'm just trying to find out—'

'Yeah, I know what you're trying to do! You're as bad as him, manipulating people. Leave me alone!'

Swift put his phone down. He was annoying a lot of women these days. Something was eating Holly and he wished he could work out what it was. He looked at the weather forecast. More snow and freezing conditions were forecast for London and Hertfordshire, but there were loose ends he wanted to check. He needed to get to Cornford as soon as possible.

* * *

Swift had been on the road for ten minutes, the car headlamps illuminating snow flurries, when Fitz Blackmore rang.

'Ron, hi. Grace Tansley's dead,' he said abruptly. 'Sally found her when she came home from school.'

'Dead how?'

'Strangled. The place ransacked. When did you last see her?'

'That night at the airfield — when she was with the Amazing Aviators. I spoke to her on the phone about Havana going missing but I haven't heard from her since. I emailed her saying that Havana had sent the Christmas card but she didn't reply.' He felt a twist in his stomach. He'd liked the scatty, warm-hearted woman and her marauding hens.

'You haven't found out anything that might throw light on why someone would want to kill her?'

'Afraid not. She didn't seem to be the kind of person who'd attract animosity. Could it have been a robbery and she got in the way?'

'Possible. But it struck me more as if someone was having a thorough search rather than just after money or valuables.'

'When did Grace die?'

'Not sure yet, but the next-door neighbour saw her around ten this morning. Sally got home at half five. I'm just outside the house, waiting for more forensics.'

'I'm on my way to Cornford now. What will Sally do?'

'Her father works in Dubai, so it'll take him a couple of days to get back. The neighbour's offered to have her stay for the time being. She's retired, so she can keep an eye open. What are you doing in town?'

'Asking Jude Chamberlain some questions.'

'What about? Oh . . . forensics here — got to go!' Blackmore hung up suddenly.

Swift drove on slowly, the snow thickening. It was unlikely that Grace's death was a random killing, especially as any self-respecting burglar would have realised from looking at the house that there was nothing worth stealing. Yet he'd discovered nothing to suggest that she was linked to Roscoe's murder. Havana was her main connection to the family and, for now, that bond had been severed.

He parked outside Jude's house just after 8 p.m., glad to see that the lights were on. He'd hoped that the new baby might mean she wasn't at her bestie's every evening nowadays. Somehow, he couldn't see Jude cooing over an infant. She might have loathed Greg Roscoe but, like him, she enjoyed being the centre of attention.

She was in a silky kimono and ballet slippers with a transparent plastic cap on her head. Her face was free of makeup and pallid.

'I don't remember inviting you here,' she said. 'Fuck off.'

He was tired of this woman's rudeness. 'I won't, thanks. I know you've been concealing things from me. You met Greg Roscoe with Yvette the morning before he died. I've talked to Yvette and I listened to the recording. The police would find it interesting.'

She blinked up at him, calculating how to respond and then stood back, letting him in. There was a strong chemical smell as he followed her into the living room and he guessed she was dyeing her hair. The room was a riot of pink fabrics and vases of tall paper sunflowers. A foot spa stood beside a chintzy sofa and the low coffee table was stacked with glossy magazines. A glance informed him that they were about clean eating and spa treatments.

'I didn't murder Greg,' she said immediately, flinging herself onto a chair.

'You sound as if you'd have liked to on the recording.'

She shook her head. 'I'd got what I wanted. We'd literally shamed him and he was going to back off Ash. I wanted him alive and pinned down.'

'You really believed that Greg Roscoe was the kind of man who'd feel ashamed?'

'You didn't see his face or the way he was squirming. Especially when Yvette said she'd tell Axel. God, that felt good after all the insults he'd aimed at me. Greg thought the sun shone out of his own arse but even he realised he was facing some kind of reckoning. He was in a corner, all right. Nowhere to run.'

She had a point. 'You might have thought about it more, decided to make absolutely sure he couldn't rape again.'

She adjusted the plastic cap and leaned forward. 'Why would Greg have agreed to meet me at the airfield? He'd have literally spat in my face rather than see me again. No, that meeting was absolutely satisfying. Job done.' She sniffed with satisfaction.

'And Yvette? Do you think she felt the same way?'

'For what it's worth, yeah. She couldn't wait to get away from him and fly home. Are you going to tell the police?'

'I don't know.' He thought he had to, now that Grace had died. But no harm in keeping Jude on tenterhooks.

'Well, I've got nothing to hide. But if it all comes out, Greg's family will be ripped apart even more.'

'You don't sound too bothered.'

'Why should I be? They're nothing to do with me. Anyway, that Jeanie shouldn't have told me about Greg being a rapist in the first place if she didn't want it to get out. I care about Ash, that's all.'

'Did you tell Ashleigh that you'd cornered Greg?'

'I probably would have eventually. But then he was murdered so, you know, the problem had literally gone away. No need to bring all of that up again, especially as Ash could be happy with Baz. I've got to rinse my hair now. Anything else?'

'Have you ever come across a woman called Melanie around Cornford?'

She stood, curling her toes inside her slippers. 'You mean that poor girl he raped back in the day? Nope. Name means nothing to me other than what I learned from Yvette.'

'Where were you today?'

'What's with that question? At work, where I usually am. Go away and stop bugging me, will you!'

Outside, the car was covered in snow, which was still falling thickly. It was inches deep on the road, covering impacted ice left from the previous falls. Swift scraped the windscreen and let the car warm up. Jude seemed sure of herself and her story. There'd been no sign of anxiety beneath the spikiness. He drove carefully to the end of her street. Ahead of him, a car was sliding on the glassy surface. He wasn't looking forward to driving back to London and was thinking of finding a B&B or hotel when Blackmore rang again.

'Just having a break. You're not driving in this, are you mate?'

'I was thinking of heading back to London but I reckon it's not a good idea.'

'Don't want to get stuck on the motorway all night. Want to stay at mine? I've a spare room. Up to you. Better than a rip-off hotel.'

'Thanks, if you're sure.'

Blackmore gave him the address and the code to the key safe, saying he'd had to have one installed as he was always losing his keys and had paid a small fortune to locksmiths. He was still at the Tansley house and would be back as and when.

'Make yourself at home. Your room is at the top, linen in wardrobe. Don't drink all the booze. There's some delicious Calvados I got in Chamonix.'

Swift was a tad suspicious of this hospitality. Blackmore would be digging for information. Still, any port in a storm and he was interested to know more about Grace's death.

Blackmore lived in a town house just behind The Ferry Inn, a modern development of a dozen houses in a crescent shaped courtyard. Inside, it was simply and handsomely furnished with blonde ash furniture and pale rugs on the parquet floors. When Swift slipped off his shoes, he was impressed that there was under-floor heating. As he walked around the open-plan ground floor, he saw that it was all hi-tech, with a smart ecosystem, security cameras and light sensors. He found an open bottle of wine in the French door fridge. He suspected it was the type that informed you when you were running low on items. He poured himself a glass, sipping it while he examined the books in the living room. They were mainly about canoeing and natural history but there was also a collection of twentieth century novels, including Steinbeck, Lessing and Greene. There were no photos, but then Blackmore didn't seem the sentimental type. Framed black and white pictures of rivers and lakes covered the dark grey walls. Swift admitted to himself that Blackmore's home surprised him. His take me or leave me macho style didn't fit with this stylish space with indications of cultured tastes. He had hidden depths. Maybe it suited him to act the hard man for his public.

Swift took his wine to the top floor and found a double bed with ensuite bathroom. He made the bed, and then stood looking out at the river. Snow was piled deep on the banks and a couple of houseboats rocked at their moorings. The lights of The Ferry Inn glowed welcomingly and his stomach was growling. He ate beer battered fish and salty chips there and was back in the living room and reading one of Blackmore's canoeing books when he came hurtling in a few minutes after 11 p.m. He was carrying a carton of Thai takeaway and a pack of cold beer.

'Snow to rival Chamonix out there, mate.' Blackmore opened beers for them both. He chucked his jacket over a chair and rolled up his sleeves, rubbing the bristle on his chin. 'God, I need a shave. Didn't have time this morning. Didn't wake up in my own bed.' He smiled at the memory, then sat and attacked the spicy noodles, saying he hadn't eaten all day. When he'd taken the edge off his hunger, he slumped back with his beer. 'No sign of a break-in — so Grace was taken by surprise or knew the killer or both. Whoever was there went through every room and every drawer as well as making a mess of her. A different method of murder but that doesn't mean it wasn't the same killer as Roscoe's. Have to keep an open mind on that for now. Those bloody hens were making a right racket.' He eyed Swift. 'What did you get from Jude, the bestie?'

Swift had decided it was time to share. He told Blackmore about Jeanie Roscoe's indiscreet comments to Jude, Yvette's information about Roscoe's previous rape of a young girl and then how Yvette and Jude had met Roscoe and challenged him about his history as a rapist.

'Jude denies having anything to do with Roscoe's death.'

'The rape stuff fits with Roscoe's penchant for young girls,' Blackmore said, finishing off his food and dropping a chunk of mushroom into his mouth. 'Do you fancy Yvette or Jude for his murder?'

'No. I can't see it. I think they got what they wanted from the meeting. Especially Jude. I did wonder about her because she's complex and clings on to Ashleigh like a limpet. But she'd have enjoyed knowing Roscoe was humiliated and that she'd effectively edged him that bit more from her best friend's life. I think that power play was enough for her and she'd have relished it ongoing. She's that type. I don't think Yvette would have killed her son's father. I haven't met her, but she's religious and has principles. You could check back on both their movements for the night Roscoe died — and for today.'

'Too right I will. So, do you fancy anyone for Roscoe?'

'Not yet.' But he was wondering more about Boyd and his dodgy alibi.

'How about Ashleigh? He'd been raping her. She might have flipped.'

'Possibly. I don't think it's her, though. Don't feel it in my bones.'

'You sound like an old woman. Not a quick solve then,' Blackmore mocked.

'I never claimed it would be.'

'Whatever. Pass me another beer. How's the lovely Nora?'

'She's fine. I spoke to her after I got here and she said to say hello.' She'd actually said, *There you are! I told you he's gay and now he's invited you round. Enjoy your bromance, Ron!*

'I've got a mate in the Met who knows her. Says she's rated. Takes no prisoners and has a real temper on her. Hope she doesn't take it out on you, mate!'

'Nora has her moments. We've had some ups and downs.'

'Hmm, I bet. Can't be doing with temperamental women myself. When you've had a hard day you want a bit of soothing, not grief in your ear.'

'You mean a woman wearing a pinny with your pipe, slippers and glass of wine ready?' Swift teased.

'God, no! But you know there's a happy medium! I went out with this woman last year and I really liked her but she was always checking up on me. She didn't like me going off on canoe trips on my own. Seemed to take it as a personal insult that I didn't want to spend all my spare time with her. It got to be a drag. Had to show her the door.'

Swift thought she sounded like Simone. 'Well, some of my differences with Nora have been down to me. I'm not always careful enough to let her know what I'm thinking about and planning.'

'Hey, Ron, listen to yourself! That's how it starts, they get you apologising for living your own life.'

Swift shook his head. 'It's not like that. But Nora does tend to get suspicious at times, thinking I'm seeing other women and I find it hard going.'

'And *are* you seeing other women?' Blackmore gave a wolfish grin.

'No. Generally, not my style.'

Blackmore was on his third beer and mellowing. He wagged a finger at Swift. 'You're one of those thoughtful, quiet types that women like because they think there's a mystery to solve. You pick your words carefully so the women reckon you're deep. You probably are — compared to me. Me, I'm an open book. I just say what I'm thinking. It gets me into trouble.'

'You can sound a bit clichéd. The bloke who thinks all women are out to tie a man down.'

'Yeah, I know. Sometimes I just like to get a ruck going. Keeps things interesting. I've got a low boredom threshold.'

'You're kind of refreshing in some ways, as well as corny. I don't think I'm deep, just confused sometimes and too used to living on my own.'

'See, there you are . . . thinking too much again. Have another beer, mate. You die if you worry and you die if you don't.'

They talked and drank for another hour before they turned in. Swift slept lightly and restlessly, waking up every couple of hours. He'd had too much beer and was used to the draughts in his Victorian house. This modern home seemed hermetically sealed. At 3 a.m., he opened the window wide and sucked in the cold, fresh air blowing in from the river. He wished now that he hadn't discussed Nora with Blackmore, his tongue loosened by alcohol. He wouldn't want anything he'd said to get back to her and he knew how gossip travelled in the police force.

An owl hooted, three long calls, each one seeming further away. He wondered if Sally Tansley was sleeping. He hoped so. Her close friend vanished and now her mother murdered. He wondered too if she knew something about her mother's life that might point to her killer. As he drifted back to sleep he hoped that someone was looking after the hens.

* * *

Blackmore was gone by the time Swift came downstairs the following morning. He'd left an almost illegible post-it note on the fridge door: Help yrself but don't nick anything cos ur on camera. Swift drank coffee and looked out at the swathes of snow and deep footprints outside houses. Several people were out clearing paths and a gritter lorry whined its way along the road. He'd woken thinking again of Sally, and decided that he should try to talk to her. If the police were with her, he'd probably be turned away, but it was worth a try.

The woman he'd met outside during his last visit opened the door next to the Tansley's. She looked bewildered. She stared at him, head to one side.

'Yes? I know you, don't I?'

'We met on the pavement a while back. You were washing your car. I'd visited Grace Tansley.'

'Oh yes. I remember now. Look, this isn't a very good time—'

'Yes, I know.' He explained who he was and showed her his ID. 'I wondered if I could have a word with Sally. Only if she feels up to it but it might be very helpful.'

'I'm not sure. The police said they'd be back this afternoon. I don't think she slept much and she's still in bed.'

'Okay. If she's awake, would you ask her? Sorry, I don't know your name.'

'Thea. Thea Cohen.'

'Would you try for me?'

'This is so dreadful,' Thea said. 'I can't believe that Grace is dead. I waved to her yesterday morning. Next thing I knew, Sally was hammering on my door at teatime. She was screaming and shaking. I couldn't understand what she was saying. The poor girl.' She beckoned him in. 'Have a seat in there and I'll see if she's awake. She's . . . she's got one of her mother's T-shirts and she won't let go of it. Like a child with a comfort blanket.'

He sat in a snug, neat back room with an abundance of trailing houseplants and googled *Melanie Cornford* while he waited. There was a Melanie Harris who ran a florist with a photo on her website and a Melanie Oyinde with a link to Instagram. They were both too young, one a teenager, one in her twenties. Then he clicked a link to a death notice on a local undertaker's website with names of family members and a cremation. *No flowers by family request. Please donate to the charity Target Ovarian Cancer.* The details he read sent the familiar tingle up the back of his neck, the frisson that said: *at last, maybe you get a break*. He closed his eyes for a moment, concentrating, and then he heard footsteps and Thea shepherded Sally in.

'I'll just make some tea,' she said. 'I won't be long.'

Sally was huddled in a grubby white dressing gown bunched at the waist with a thick belt. Her eyes were hollow and red and she had an angry looking patch of eczema on her cheek. She looked so young without her war paint and attitude. She sat opposite him, clutching a creased yellow T-shirt.

'I'm so sorry about your mum,' Swift said. 'It must have been a terrible shock for you, finding her.'

'Hmm. I thought she'd fallen over at first, tripped or had an accident. Then I saw. The house . . . it was awful, like a tornado had gone through it. All our things all over the place.'

'Sounds as if someone was looking for something.'

She nodded and sniffed. 'Yeah, well, there was nothing worth nicking. Someone killed my mum for nothing. She always said Cornford was a safe place to live. Yeah.' She lapsed into silence, and then stared at him croaking, 'Have you come about Havana?'

He was surprised. 'Havana? No.'

'Oh. I thought maybe you'd heard from her.'

'No.'

She slumped back in her chair. 'I really miss her. I don't understand why she didn't tell me what she was doing. She never said she'd been to London to see you. I thought we were best mates and we told each other everything. I'd have come with her, helped her out.'

'When people are suffering they can do strange things. Out of character. Sometimes they can't even talk to their friends.'

'D'you think she's dead?'

'I don't know but it seems unlikely because she sent her Nan a Christmas card.'

'Yeah. That policeman told us. She might have sent me one as well. Mum said . . .' She squeezed her eyes and took a breath. 'Mum said to try not to judge or worry — that Havana would get in touch with me when she was ready to. She said stuff like you have . . . that Havana was too messed up to contact us. Mum went to London, you know, looking for her.'

'No, I didn't know.'

Sally nodded. 'Yeah, she went to all the train stations and some places where homeless people hang out. She said putting posters up in Cornford wasn't going to find her.' Sally's face crumpled with misery. 'She said . . . she said if I ever went missing she'd tear down buildings with her bare hands until she found me.'

Swift nodded, thinking that's how he'd react if Branna disappeared. 'Your mother was a good woman to do that. Havana was lucky to have her around.'

Thea inched the door open and came in with a tray of tea and a plate of biscuits. 'I've put milk and sugar out. A lot of people don't take either these days.' She glanced anxiously and a little warily at Sally. Swift recalled that she'd protested about disturbance and noise from Sally and Havana in the past. 'I'll stay if you want,' she said, her tone indicating that she'd prefer to escape.

Sally was staring down into her lap, stroking the T-shirt and running the fabric between her fingers. She looked worn out, but Swift suspected she'd still be capable of a flash of wiliness. He didn't need any more disapproval from anyone's family.

'If you wouldn't mind,' he said.

Thea looked resigned and sat in the corner, picking up a Sudoku puzzle book and a pen.

Swift took a mug of tea and placed one in front of Sally. 'Have a hot drink. It helps. I don't know why, but it does. Shall I put sugar in for you?'

Sally nodded, so he sugared the tea and gave it a brisk stir.

'Apart from Havana, did your mum seem worried about anything else recently?'

'Just the usual. Money. She was always trying to make ends meet.'

'She had two jobs, didn't she?'

'Yeah but, y'know, neither paid that much so we were still pretty hard up. Our rent had gone up too. So she was always looking for ways of making dosh.' She rubbed her eyes, pushing her fists in. 'She did one of those proofreading courses to be able to work from home but she wasn't much good at it.'

'Did she owe money to anyone?'

Sally took a sip of tea, pulled a face and replaced the mug. 'Don't think so. Mum was good at budgeting. Do you think she died quickly?'

'Only the police can tell you that,' he said gently. 'Ask them when you see them.'

'I hope she did. I hope she didn't really realise what was happening.' Sally crushed the T-shirt to her face. 'I nearly didn't go to school yesterday because I had stomach ache. I wish I hadn't now. I could have protected her.'

More likely, you'd be lying dead next to her, Swift thought, but nodded.

'She tried so hard to make life good for us,' Sally continued, staring into space. 'She'd turn her hand to anything. She was selling this herbal stuff at one point and she thought it would make a lot of money but it didn't work out.'

Swift stared. 'When was that?'

'I dunno. A while back.'

'What was it called?'

'Dunno. It was in a sort of pouch — a blue colour.'

'Pure and Strong? Was that it?'

'Yeah, that's right.'

'Do you know how your mum got into selling it?'

'I'm not sure. She said someone had told her about it and she was keen to give it a go. It was supposed to detox you or something. I made one of the powders into a drink. It looked like mud and it was bitter and disgusting — made me want to throw up. Mum took a sip and said that the worse things tasted, the more good they did you. But then after a while she just said it hadn't sold well and it had been a waste of time and energy.'

'Was this before Greg Roscoe died?'

'Dunno. I suppose.'

'Your mum told me she didn't know Greg well. Do you think maybe she did?'

'Dunno. How would I know? She knew Ashleigh.'

'Did your mum still have any of the Pure and Strong left in the house?'

'Maybe. I'm not sure. She did have stock she couldn't get rid of.' She shook her head. 'I'm tired. I can't do this any more.' She rose listlessly and trailed to the door, hugging the T-shirt. 'Find Havana. Please? I really miss her.'

Thea saw him out. 'Grace asked me if I wanted to buy some of that Pure and Strong,' she said. 'Tried to give me the hard sell, saying it could make you feel healthier and fitter but she wasn't very good at it. I could see she wasn't convinced. I said no. I wouldn't touch anything like that.'

'Did Grace say where she got it from?'

Thea frowned. 'I don't think so. I can only remember she said it was a business opportunity somebody had offered her. She was always clasping at straws where money was concerned.'

* * *

Swift drove to The Ferry Inn, where he ordered coffee and a sandwich. His brain was busy with ideas about Sally's revelation and what he'd read on Google. He didn't hear the barman at first.

'Sorry, what did you say?'

'Not with your girlfriend today?' the barman repeated.

'My girlfriend?'

'The lady you were with before, just after Christmas.'

'Oh, yes.' Holly, of course. 'She's not my girlfriend.'

'Just as well or she'd be two-timing you, mate!'

'How do you mean?'

'She's been in here a couple of times with another chap. Posh bloke.'

Swift had only met one man connected to Cornford who fitted that description. Now that this case seemed to be breaking, it was like dominoes falling. 'Guy with a long nose and big ears?'

'That's the one. Looked around as if he reckoned he was slumming it.'

'Have they been in recently?'

'Don't think so. She's not a regular.'

Swift ate his cheese and tomato sandwich, chewing thoughtfully. Boyd had offered Holly some sympathy when her affair with Roscoe was discovered. Sympathy could be attractive, even if the man wasn't, especially as Holly had been feeling exposed and upset. It could explain why Boyd had been in Cornford the night Roscoe was killed. Swift liked Holly and he hoped that her liaison with Boyd was the only reason she'd been evasive with him. He needed to strike her and Boyd off his list of suspects. When he rang her number, she picked up.

'Not you again.'

He was getting used to this greeting. 'Afraid so.'

'I've just heard about Grace Tansley. It's so awful.'

'Yes, it is. I'm not calling about that, though. Are you still seeing David Boyd?'

An intake of breath, then a resigned sigh. 'No, I'm not.'

'Did you meet him the night Greg died?'

'Yes. He came round to mine. We weren't out with a knife killing Greg, if that's why you're asking.'

'Why didn't you just tell me?' But he thought he knew and her reply confirmed it.

'I was embarrassed — all over again. Seems to be my permanent state where you're concerned. I'd already had to tell you about the unprofessional fiasco with Greg and Stef chucking me. David's a cheat and an idiot and I didn't want anyone to know I'd been involved with him. Another rotten choice by yours truly. I should think the only gentlemanly thing he's ever done is agree not to tell anyone. But then he was probably embarrassed about me as well. I'd say it was sympathy fucking for both of us. Two lame saddos propping each other up for a while.'

'When did it end?'

‘Couple of weeks after Greg died. I can’t stand you, Swift, nosing around with all your intrusive questions. You leave me no dignity. Are you going to tell people?’ She sounded as if she was crying and there was raw pain in her voice.

‘I don’t think I’ll need to tell anyone. I’m sorry, Holly, but Greg was left with even less dignity.’

‘Yep. I can’t ace a dead man. Will you leave me alone now?’

Swift finished his cooling coffee and ordered another while he spent half an hour on Google, looking up members of the Cornford community and linked newspaper articles. He found an interview that brought more threads together and turned again to the death notice he’d found earlier. All along, he’d thought that Roscoe’s death had to be connected to the airfield and now he reckoned he’d been right.

He thought back to when he’d first met Grace Tansley and she was trying to shoo the marauding hens from the kitchen. She’d said that sometimes she laid a trail of food to lure them back to their coop. He realised that her daughter had now unwittingly given him his own bait, enough to make him feel confident about the plan forming in his head.

He sent the undertaker’s link to Blackmore with a message asking him to ring as soon as he could then sat back with his fresh coffee. No hurry now, just a trap to set. When Blackmore called, Swift talked about Roscoe’s failed business venture with Pure and Strong, the information Sally had given him and Grace’s link to the product and Roscoe.

‘Grace Tansley’s an active investigation. Who said you could go round and talk to her daughter?’ Blackmore snapped.

‘Okay, a bit of a liberty, I grant you but it got me somewhere and I’ve shared it with you straightaway. There’s other stuff too.’

'What?'

Swift went through what he'd read online. Blackmore hissed softly as Swift joined up the facts to the names in the interview he'd seen and the death notice. He reminded Blackmore of the lack of forensic evidence at the scene of Roscoe's murder and the likelihood that Grace's death must somehow be connected to his. He pointed out that a confession would be useful and that he'd come up with a way to try and secure it. He proposed his plan. Blackmore sounded like a steaming kettle. There then followed a prolonged, heated argument with neither man prepared to back down. Finally, Swift waited for half an hour while Blackmore went away, consulted his boss and rang back. They reached a compromise that was grudging and tetchy on Blackmore's part.

He issued a final threat. 'I'm sticking my neck out here and there's a lot that could go wrong. This had better not go tits up, Ron. If it does, I'll be after you like a hound from hell!'

Chapter 15

Swift drove to the airfield that night and parked at the front. He saw no other car but that didn't mean there was no one else there. It was just after eleven and half an hour to the meeting time. There was a brilliant full moon, a wolf moon. He had explained to Branna that wolves howl when they're hungry in the deep of winter and Native Americans believed that they were howling at the full moon. She'd thrown back her head, emitting a piercing shriek.

He closed the car door softly and walked around the side of the veranda towards the hangars. A path had been cleared through the snow and his boots crunched the grit. The moon lit his way, glinting coldly. The icy air blasted his sinuses. There was a profound silence. No owls or foxes. It felt as if all living things were hunkered down, keeping warm. He imagined the panic that his email had caused. He'd sent it that afternoon after talking to Blackmore, laying his trail, offering a meeting. *I know you were involved in Greg Roscoe's death with someone but you could have been coerced into what you did. If you talk to me, I might be able to help you before I go to the police.*

He followed the path to the hangar where Roscoe had died. Blackmore had obtained a key for him and he undid the padlock. He slid the door slowly back and then used his pocket torch to sweep inside, checking each small plane. There was no one.

He closed the door, glancing at Niran's shrine. Gaudy blue and yellow Iris petals lay at the Buddha's feet. There was a faint scent of jasmine from joss sticks overlaid by aviation fuel. He opened the door to the plane where Roscoe had been attacked and sat sideways in the passenger seat, facing outwards towards the entrance. He switched his torch off, watching his breath puff in the bitter air and then pulled his scarf up around his face and waited. If this didn't work, he'd be a frozen fool and Blackmore would never stop mocking him. He sat in the silence, breathing into his scarf to create a pocket of warmth and teasing at the knot of why Grace had to die. He heard a tiny noise and the door slid open just wide enough to let a figure slip through. There was the sound of quiet, controlled breaths. Then a voice.

'You there, Swift?'

'I'm here.'

'Where?'

'In the plane where Roscoe died.'

A pause. 'On your own?'

'Yes. I'm going to switch my torch on. Stay where you are.'

The bright torch beam picked him out, standing by the shrine. Swift nodded.

'I thought you'd come. I was wondering if you'd tell her about my email. I'd have liked it if she'd walked through the door with you. But then, you've got more to lose because you carried out the killing. I thought maybe self-preservation would come before sharing my contact with your accomplice. I expect she was the bait and you used the knife on Roscoe.'

Barry Grafton wore a bulky padded coat that made him look even taller. He swayed and put the flat of his hand against the hangar wall to steady himself.

'What do you want?' he asked.

'The truth. Why you killed Roscoe and how you got him here that night.'

Grafton took a step forward. Swift danced the torch in his face.

'Stay where you are.'

He stopped, blinking in the light. 'What did you mean about you might be able to help me?'

'Until you talk to me, I can't tell you what I can do exactly. I know how the police work and I have contacts.'

Swift had thought that Grafton might ask why he was offering any help but the man was too anxious and distracted. He looked down at the ground, his face in shadow. When he spoke, it was in a wheedling voice.

'Logan . . . my baby son's not well. Some kind of chest thing. Maybe an infection. He has a temperature and he's on antibiotics. I can't stay long.'

Swift nodded. 'Then the sooner you explain things to me, the sooner you can get home to Logan,' he lied.

Grafton slipped off a glove, rubbed the back of his neck and shivered. He looked at the shrine and reached out to touch the feet of the Buddha before pulling the glove back on. 'I'm not sure about this, about what to say. After all, you're not the police. It all seems so risky.'

'Hmm. But you came. You must have thought it was worth it and I suppose you had to take the chance, given that I've found you out. You're not in a good place, whatever happens.'

There was a long silence.

'Look,' Swift said,' I know about a woman called Melanie who died not too long ago and I know who her daughter is. So I think I have some idea why the safety pin and card were used on Roscoe's body, but I don't know why you wanted him dead. Was it because he'd raped Ashleigh and was in your way?'

Grafton gave a sad little laugh. 'I suppose that in itself would be enough for some men. Roscoe was a despicable bully. What he did to Ashleigh was unforgivable and made me want to see him suffer. But no, that wasn't my only reason.'

'Go on.'

He swallowed. 'This . . . this other thing happened before I met Ashleigh. I have a daughter, Swift. An adult daughter, Meg. She's had thyroid problems since childhood and she's always struggled with her weight. She became terribly obese once she left school. It made her socially isolated and she's lived on her own since her mother died. She's been on all kinds of diets but none of them really help. She bought a bogus product that Roscoe was marketing, called Pure and Strong. It was supposed to promote detoxing and rebalancing of the body. Rubbish, of course but the kind of stuff that appeals to the gullible. In the way that anxious people do, she pinned her hopes on it helping her. It seemed to at first but then it made her very, very depressed. She's still not right. She gave up her job and now she's heavier than ever because she comfort eats. If I'd known she was buying it, I'd have tried to warn her off it. It was produced in Taiwan. You never know what's being used in a product made abroad, or what the controls are. When I saw the stuff, I was appalled. God knows what was in it.'

'I know about Pure and Strong,' Swift said. 'Greg Roscoe was into ways of making extra cash although that venture didn't go well.'

Grafton clenched his gloved hands. 'When Meg contacted Roscoe and spoke to him about this stuff, he was dismissive about it and said she couldn't prove anything. He actually told her that her depression was due to her greediness and advised her to try a boot camp. Such cruelty! When she finally told me about it, I saw red. I phoned him and explained that Meg had an illness and had experienced a bad reaction. He said that Meg must have used the product wrongly and it was up to her to read the small print and take medical advice. He was so indifferent. Spoke to me as if I was dirt.'

Ice cracked loudly on the roof of the hangar, sounding like an explosion. Grafton twitched and glanced up. His face in the torchlight was distraught and he looked exhausted. A sick baby would give you sleepless nights, wear you out, tear at your heart.

'I'm sorry about your daughter but that's hardly a reason to take someone's life.'

'Not on its own, no. I mean, I was furious on Meg's behalf and I did think of insisting on meeting that bastard or reporting him, maybe suing him if it was possible. But Meg begged me not to make a fuss because she felt such a fool at being conned into using the stuff and she didn't want anyone else to know about it.' He faltered, his shoulders slumping.

Swift thought of Melanie, Holly, Yvette, Ashleigh, Meg and countless other women who put up with rape or other exploitation and harm because of embarrassment and wanting to avoid shame. He might have been softer on Grafton if it hadn't been for his suspicions about Grace.

'I'm waiting,' he said.

Grafton took a deep breath. 'I met Ashleigh just after I found out about Meg. Then I discovered that Greg was her husband. I didn't say anything to her about what had happened to Meg. I was so happy at what we had together. My first marriage was miserable. I didn't expect that kind of second chance at my time of life. I didn't want to spoil things. When I discovered from her and . . . well, others that he was a rapist as well as a charlatan, the gloves were off. All he did was hurt people. He didn't deserve to live.'

'And he'd found out about you and Ashleigh?' Swift guessed.

'Yes. I don't know how. He told Ashleigh he'd make her life a misery before he'd agree to a divorce. They had a flaming row the week . . . the week he died and he raped her then too. She was in a terrible state but she begged me not to intervene. She thought it would only make him angrier.'

'Going back to Meg, did she buy the Pure and Strong direct from Roscoe?'

'I'm not sure,' Grafton mumbled. He fumbled at his sleeve and looked at his watch, agitated. 'I can't stay. Ashleigh's really worried about the baby. He had a vaccination and he might be having a reaction, we just don't know. I need to be there with them in case we need to call the doctor again.'

Swift let the lie about Meg's purchase go for now. He wanted to concentrate on Roscoe's death. Everything else could follow. He judged that Grafton would be answering for more than one killing, even if he didn't know all the reasons right now. 'You can get back to them soon. Did Ashleigh know about your plan to kill Roscoe?'

Grafton's head jerked up. 'My God, no! You have to believe me. She doesn't know anything. I kept it all from her! You don't think she's involved? That's not who—'

'I know. I know who. I told you, I know about Melanie and her family. But you . . . you did murder Roscoe. Your wife and son are waiting for you. Why don't you get on with telling me and we can work out what to do.' Swift could detect a shadow through the small gap in the hangar door. He felt a tiny hint of sympathy for this man who wasn't going to see his family any time soon. 'Did your friend, your accomplice, get Roscoe to come here that night? Did she set him up?'

'Yes.'

'Say her name.'

Grafton licked his lips and stared down at his feet. 'Camilla. Camilla Finley. But she didn't do it herself.

Someone helped her. Helped us. How did you discover the connection with Camilla?'

'Never mind. But I know that her mother Melanie's ashes are in Cornford cemetery. Then I saw that she'd featured you in an interview about your garden business. I reckoned that you might have shared confidences and discovered that you also shared a hatred of Roscoe.'

'Camilla's suffered too, finding out about her mother.'

'I'm sure. So she got Roscoe here and then you took over and stuck the knife in him.'

'This is . . . this is unbearable. I didn't know Camilla was going to do that business afterwards with the safety pin and the card. That was horrible. But she wouldn't listen to me when I told her to stop. I didn't know about the salty water either. You must believe me. She said she was going to leave Roscoe degraded, the way he'd done to her mother. I didn't want her to humiliate him like that.'

'Seems a moot point to me, considering that you'd ended his life. Funny how even murderers can have their odd sensitivities.'

Grafton looked startled by the sharp change in Swift's tone. 'You don't understand—'

'I don't have to understand. I do understand now why you were so keen to get rid of Havana and make sure she stayed away from home. It can't be easy being around a child when you've murdered her father. Watching her misery and the damage it did to her every day. Just say it, man. Say that you killed Roscoe. Otherwise I can't help you.'

'All right, yes!' Grafton screamed suddenly, the weight of suppressed guilt echoing in the hangar. 'He was a complete and utter bastard and I stabbed Roscoe. There, is that what you wanted?'

'Yes, that will do, Mr Grafton.' Blackmore slid the door back slowly, his own torch playing. 'Barry Grafton, you do not have to say anything . . . '

Grafton backed to the side of the shrine, shielding his eyes. 'You bastard, Swift! You utter bastard! You set me up!'

'But it may harm your defence . . .' Blackmore continued.

Grafton yelled in despair and lunged, seizing the Buddha. He swung around, cracking it against Blackmore's head. Blackmore grunted and fell to the ground, surrounded by petals and floating incense ash. Grafton dashed through the door, slipping and sliding as he ran into the night.

Swift jumped down from the plane and skirted Blackmore. He sped through the door, playing his torch into the darkness. Grafton was ploughing across the wide expanse of snow towards the perimeter fence, arms flailing. He floundered and fell, then picked himself up. Swift headed after him, plunging through the packed, unyielding snow and gaining on the older man. His breath was tearing in his lungs as he drew nearer. Grafton glanced behind him, then stopped and turned. Swift saw the glint of steel in the torch beam.

'Don't come any nearer, Swift. I'll hurt you. I will!' He was panting hard as he held the knife out, jabbing it in the air.

'You don't want to do that, Grafton. You've enough to answer for already.'

'Nothing to lose now. Nothing at all.'

'There's your baby son. Logan. He won't want to lose *you*.'

Grafton lunged and Swift felt a stinging pain across his cheek. He moved back in case Grafton came at him again but the man's face was a mask of misery.

'Oh Christ! This is such a mess!' He started to cry and dashed a glove against his eyes.

Swift took the chance and moved in fast, kicking Grafton in the groin. He dropped the knife as he gave an anguished yell, doubled over and fell in the snow. Swift heard shouts and saw several dark, uniformed shapes running and converging on them from the trees at the edge of the airfield. Snow was flying under their feet, dislodged flakes whirling through the air like a mini storm. He scrabbled for the knife, found it and handed it to one of the police officers who had surrounded Grafton and were handcuffing him. The man opened his mouth wide and screamed, a banshee wail that echoed through the night.

Swift ran back to the hangar, the air biting into the cut on his cheek. He found Blackmore trying to sit up and groaning. Swift bent down, shining his torch on Blackmore's head. He saw blood but the wound looked superficial. He found a couple of tissues in his pocket, handed one to Blackmore and dabbed at his own face.

'They got him. You okay?'

Blackmore leaned on an arm and sat, holding his head. 'You're the bastard who set him up but I'm the one who gets bashed. Where's the justice?'

'Hard to find. And the Buddha is supposed to be an instrument of peace! Although I didn't get away unharmed. I seem to be dripping blood.'

Blackmore looked to where he was pointing. 'I thought that was mine.' He glanced up. 'Looks like we both need a plaster. Was that Grafton screaming?'

'Yes.'

'Christ. Sounded like a stuck pig.'

'He's a man in torment.'

Blackmore grinned at him. 'I haven't started on him yet. Feel good that we've nailed Camilla?'

'Not really. Well, okay, a bit. But now I understand why she kept contacting me — why she wanted to try and keep close tabs on what I was finding out. She steered me towards Cairns so he'd distract me with his information about Stefan Makinen. The more I avoided her, the more annoyed she got and kept coming after me.'

'Yeah. Know your enemy. Get close to him. Smoke and mirrors and confusion. She's a player.'

'Not for much longer. Want a hand up?'

'Nah, mate.' Blackmore looked around him on the floor. 'Bloody hell, what are all these flowers and ash? Looks like someone's tried to cremate me!'

* * *

Branna, of course, was fascinated by the dressing on her father's cheek and wanted to prise it away to look underneath. Ruth cast her eyes upwards when she saw him and pressed her lips firmly together. Nora said the injury gave him an intriguing look.

Blackmore was back at work after an X-ray and Swift heard nothing for a couple of days. He phoned Niall Roscoe to tell him whom the police had arrested but said he needed to wait for fuller information. He warned him that he might be hearing some unpleasant things about his brother. Roscoe answered wearily, saying that he'd try and prepare the ground with his mother. When Swift phoned Thea Cohen to enquire about Sally Tansley, she told him that Sally was at a hotel with her father for the time being. Sally was insisting that she wanted to stay in the UK because Havana would get in touch when she could. He emailed Yvette and Axel to inform them of the arrests but gave no other information. He had no idea how Axel was going to deal with the details that were inevitably going to come out about his parents' meeting and his father's behaviour.

A sudden thaw had set in and the weather was sunny and mild. The world was full of dripping sounds and the gurgling of snow run-off. Swift took his boat out on the Thames for a day, rowing to Teddington under an intense blue sky. The river was surging on a high tide, demanding his full concentration as he navigated the locks. He felt the satisfying surge of blood, the pull of muscles, the damp of perspiration on his back and neck as the boat hummed on the dark waters. When he pulled in just below Kingston for water and a couple of bananas, his thoughts turned again to Greg Roscoe and all the people who'd been hurt through their contact with him. He wondered if a judge might tend to leniency in sentencing if Grafton and Camilla went to trial and were found guilty. He found it hard to have any sympathy for Camilla and not just because she'd harassed him and tried to undermine his reputation. Whatever her own pain and motives had been and however justified she'd felt, she'd adopted a cloak of concern to try and stop the truth emerging. And she'd exploited Roscoe's death and Paul Cairns's fragility to advance her career.

* * *

Swift was waiting for Nora and Chand in the Silver Mermaid when he had an email from Blackmore with the subject: *Sweat and Results*. He read it through. He'd worked out most of it, apart from new information about Camilla's sister and the details of Grace's death. He'd just ordered a bottle of wine and bread with olives when Nora and Chand arrived together.

'This is my shout by the way,' Nora announced. 'An apology for being a wet blanket at New Year.'

Chand looked surprised but said, 'Thanks, I never turn down an offer like that.'

'How's Bella?' Nora asked him, glancing at Swift as if to say, *See, I can play nice*.

'She's well. At auctions in Paris this week. I miss her. Can't wait for her to get back at the weekend.' Chand passed on wine and ordered a coke. 'Still nothing on Havana,' he told Swift. 'I checked again just before I left work.'

Swift nodded. 'I've heard from Cornford police. If Havana gets to read or hear anything about what's happened in the coming months, she might surface. If she can.'

Nora took a long drink of wine. 'What has Blackmore come up with?'

'Where to start? Grafton's been charged with the murders of Roscoe and Grace Tansley. Camilla Finley and her sister, Dawn, have been charged with being accomplices to Roscoe's murder.'

'Camilla has a sister?' Nora passed around mixed olives and thin strips of herby focaccia.

'A younger sister. Their mother was Melanie. Roscoe raped her in the hedges at the airfield when she was fifteen. She died of ovarian cancer about two years ago. Before she died, she told Camilla about the rape. It was the first time she'd told anyone, apart from Yvette. Roscoe was charming to her, offered to show her his plane, then invited her for a walk around the grounds and attacked her. He also gave her chlamydia and it was undetected for a long time. The trauma damaged her for life. She was never able to maintain a relationship, had two failed marriages and a couple of miscarriages. She told Camilla that she'd always felt like tainted, damaged goods.'

'Deathbed revelations,' Chand said. 'They pack a punch.'

Swift nodded and chewed a peppery olive. 'Camilla told Dawn about what had happened after their mum died. They read up about the long-term effects of rape and it explained why their mother had frequent nightmares and suffered with depression and chronic pelvic pain. Their childhood had been blighted by her numbness and illnesses. Their father had left because he couldn't cope and they'd lost contact with him. They became convinced that Melanie's cancer had been caused by the past trauma. The untreated chlamydia had possibly contributed to her miscarriages and ill health. Roscoe had ruined their mother's life and they decided he would suffer. They talked about it constantly, egged each other on. Became obsessed with what he'd done.' *You know how it plays,*

Blackmore had written. The old formula: Hurt+Grievance=Revenge.

'So how did Grafton get involved?'

'Happenstance. Camilla met Grafton because she interviewed him about his business. They hit it off and she mentioned that she was always on the lookout for good public interest stories. He mentioned Roscoe and told her how he'd treated Meg. He hoped she might do an exposé about Pure and Strong and shame Roscoe. When Camilla heard his story, she told him about her mum's rape. Then the floodgates opened and Grafton told her that Roscoe had raped Ashleigh and was threatening her when she wanted to get out of an awful marriage to be with him. Camilla went away and talked to Dawn about the further evidence of Roscoe's career as a rapist and general bastard. A print exposé about a dodgy business deal just didn't seem enough payback. They came up with the murder plan. They wanted him to die where he'd violated their mother. Camilla took the plan to Grafton. He was fired up enough to agree, especially as he saw months of grimness ahead for him and Ashleigh. Dawn lived in Berkshire, so there was little chance that Roscoe knew her. She pretended to be "Collette". That was Melanie's middle name. She seems to have shared her sister's acting skills and she lured Roscoe in at some bar and said she'd love to visit the airfield that night. She got him to show her to the plane in the hangar then Grafton and Camilla took over. Camilla had thought it all through. She'd got hair covers and gloves for her and Grafton and disposed of the knife in the river afterwards.'

The waitress arrived to take their orders. Swift poured more wine. Chand's eyes lit up as the voice of The King singing *It's Now or Never* sounded in the background.

'Recorded April 3rd, 1960, Nashville, and released July 5th,' he said. 'Elvis first heard this song when he was stationed in Germany with the US army and knew he wanted to record it.'

'You're a sad sap, Chand,' Nora told him. 'Your head's full of useless information about a fat guy who died on the bog. I hope you don't bore Bella with it all. She'll walk if you do.'

Chand shook his head. 'She says I'm allowed five minutes max of Elvis talk when we're together. Luckily, she's okay with his singing.'

'Rather her than me.' Nora winked at Swift. 'I want to know why Grafton killed Grace Tansley.'

'She became too much of a risk. She'd lied to me about not having met Roscoe. They'd hooked up and talked at the swimming pool. Roscoe heard she was hard pressed financially and persuaded her to sell Pure and Strong. Grace knew Meg Grafton as a patient at the surgery and sold her some of the stuff. When she had a bad reaction, Grace directed Meg to Roscoe and jacked in selling it. She got too frightened about fallout and the illegality. Now and again she'd have an attack of conscience about it and worry that people might still get hold of the product and harm themselves. She read an article in a magazine at the surgery about the dangers of buying herbal remedies from unregulated sources. So she was in some ways a ticking time bomb.'

'At least someone had a conscience about selling illegal crap, even if was all too little too late,' Nora said.

'Grace was a decent woman,' Swift agreed, 'just strapped for cash. A couple of weeks back, she saw Barry Grafton bringing Meg to a doctor's appointment. She realised he was Meg's dad and remembered Meg telling her that her father had been furious when the product made her ill. She got talking to him in the waiting room while Meg was with her GP and mentioned the problems with Pure and Strong. She asked him if he'd tackled Roscoe at the time. She told him she still had some of the stuff at home and didn't know what to do with it. She'd thought of going to the police but she was concerned that she might be prosecuted, even after the event. She asked

Grafton his opinion. Grafton lied and said he didn't remember anything about it but he could see that Grace didn't believe him. He went away and fretted. He reckoned she might start asking more questions, maybe involve Meg or go to the police and she still had the product. If she unpicked stuff, it might lead back to Roscoe's murder and Grafton didn't fancy the risk. He said he didn't plan to kill her. He went round to ask her to forget about the product and to offer to take away the stuff she had left. She didn't like his manner and said she thought he'd be more concerned, given what happened to Meg. They argued and he grabbed her by the neck. Next thing she was dead, he ransacked the place and took the Pure and Strong. The police found it in the safe in his office.'

'That bastard Roscoe,' Chand said. 'It's like he's still been hurting people from beyond the grave. Good for you for breaking the case open, Ty.' He raised his coke.

'Thanks. Fitz Blackmore didn't bother with any gratitude.' His email had ended: *Bit grim. On bright side, don't think you'll be subject of Finley's Finds any time soon. So you can upset as many husbands/swindle as many old gents/have as many people topped in your house as you like!!!*

Spoke to N. Roscoe and outlined as above but I'm sure you'll want to talk to them. Don't envy you that visit.

'Blackmore's not the grateful kind,' Nora said, taking his hand. 'Presumably Camilla did her bit with the pin, card and salty water as a salute to her mum?'

'And as a way of humiliating Roscoe. When Melanie was in pieces after the rape and sobbing, Roscoe grumbled about "so many tears" and told her she'd feel better after a good cry. Hence Camilla's extra touches for her dead mother.'

Nora nodded. 'I can see the satisfaction. What goes around comes around.'

'It's going to be hard for Havana if she reads about the trial,' Chand said, gloomily.

'Yes. Roscoe's "little princess" won't have any illusions left about her dad.'

* * *

Swift rarely received handwritten letters, but one dropped through the letterbox on the day he was due to visit the Roscoes. It was from Camilla Finley and written in blue biro on lined paper torn from a perforated pad. Her handwriting was cramped, with little curlicues on the bottom of the t's and y's.

Hey Swift,

I hope you're pleased with yourself. I'm sure you are. You're that smug type. You think you're so smart and untouchable. Yes, you've gone through a lot of dirty laundry and trampled on a lot of people but have you really achieved anything good? Whatever money the Roscoes pay you is tainted. A horrible man is dead. He didn't give a toss for anyone else. Now you've succeeded in trashing him to his family and if we get convicted, yet another child is without his father.

You've caused a shed load of pain and hurt. Hope you sleep at night. I don't. Not because I feel guilty but because of the racket in here.

Don't think I'm going to roll over. I'll find a way of finishing the book with Paul and I'll be keeping in touch with Oliver. I'm going to encourage him to appeal against the court ruling. I've plenty of friends who'll support me. And I wonder what did happen that night when Havana tried to throw herself out of your window? I feel there's a story in there that hasn't been told. So you haven't heard the last of me.

C.F.

Pot calling the kettle black as far as dirty laundry was concerned. Camilla would have to brood away in her cell. He tore the letter up and threw it in the recycling so that the paper could be put to better use and set off for Blackheath.

He rang the Roscoes' doorbell with a sinking feeling. Greg Roscoe had left a long legacy of damage. Not what you want to hear about your murdered son and brother. Niall opened the door and showed him into the hall. He needed a shave and his eyes were heavy. He looked dishevelled and greyish, as if he'd been on a gruelling overland journey with no chance to wash or change his clothes.

'Mum shouldn't be up really, but she insisted on talking to you. The doctor's told her to rest but she won't listen. Ashleigh's been on the phone, blaming her for what's happened by getting you to ask questions. They had a right shouting match, went on for ages. All ended in tears.'

No wonder Roscoe looked exhausted. 'Have you told your mother all the details the police passed on?'

'Yes, he has,' Jeanie Roscoe said firmly, coming through from the kitchen. She was holding a small vacuum cleaner, the nozzle pointing like a weapon. 'Niall didn't want to but I said he must. I know I sound hard but it's better that Pat hears it from us rather than a neighbour or a newspaper. It will all come out in the end, won't it? And of course she would go asking questions, stirring it all up so I reckon she should have all the answers.'

'Okay, Jeanie, okay . . .' Roscoe said, heavily.

'But it's not okay, Niall. We're going to have our lives picked over by Camilla Finley's mates in the press. The Roscoe name will be associated with rapes and conning people — harming them. Reporters will have a field day with the sleaze. It's like we're in a tin can and someone's got an opener.' Angry tears stood in her eyes but she swallowed and glared at her husband.

Roscoe just nodded and opened the door to his mother's living room. She sat hunched in her chair, holding her cheek in one hand, a walking stick propped beside her. The photo of Greg Roscoe in his captain's uniform was next to her on a small table. She looked at Swift but didn't acknowledge him. Niall pulled chairs up and tapped his mother's hand.

'Mr Swift's come, Mum. You wanted him to.'

She sighed and muttered something under her breath that sounded like *bastard*.

'The police have charged your son's killers,' Swift said. 'Unfortunately, that meant some difficult information came out about Greg and their reasons for what they did. It will be made public at their trial.'

Pat Roscoe muttered again, then glared at Swift. She had dwindled physically since his last visit but her eyes were ablaze, glowing in sunken sockets. 'Sounds to me as if people want to put my Greg on trial, rather than the filth who killed him. Where's the justice in that?'

'Camilla Finley and Barry Grafton have given a lot of background to the police and there are other people who will corroborate some of their statements as well as contributing their own evidence. It doesn't justify what happened to Greg but a trial has to present all the facts to the jury.'

'*Present all the facts*,' she mimicked. 'I paid you to find Greg's murderer, not drag his name through the mud! These lies they're all telling about him . . . it's just to try and get themselves off the hook. That's what it's about and you needn't try to tell me any different!'

No, there wasn't any point in trying to tell her. 'I'm sorry,' he said, the automatic response when someone is hurting and there are no words that can help.

'Sorry! I should think so! How did you get into all this stuff about my son anyway? I never asked you to listen to Yvette's tittle-tattle. Why did you contact her about her time with Greg, especially after I told you she was no good for him?'

Swift was aware of Jeanie's discomfort, saw her from the corner of his eye as she crossed her arms defensively.

'Mrs Roscoe, I think it's best to wait and see what information comes out. The police might decide not to use some evidence. It will depend on the case they have.'

'Listen to you, trying to dodge the question! You've done nothing but bad mouth my Greg since I first met you. These people will say anything to weasel away from the spotlight and you're helping them. Who's speaking up for Greg in all of this? Why aren't you telling the police that all those women used Greg and cheated him? His son was taken away and now they're saying he raped women and sold people stuff that poisoned them. Anything to blacken his name with him dead and not able to defend himself!' She'd pulled herself up in the chair, seized her walking stick and slammed it against the floor as she shouted.

Swift shook his head, tired of trying to ease the situation for her. 'I can only remind you that your son was involved in numerous rapes and selling an illegal product that made people ill. Hard to know how to speak up for him but I'm sure you'll try.'

'You bastard!'

'Mum, please . . .' Niall started.

'You can shut up as well! You've had nothing good to say about your own brother and that wife of yours always hated him. I know you always resented Greg because you couldn't match him. All you are is a glorified dogsbody with a badge! And that Jeanie's been pouring filth in your ears for years about Greg. Oh God, I wish I'd never let you persuade me to move in here! I wish I'd stayed where I was, where I knew what I was doing.'

'You're not the only one,' Niall whispered wearily.

She shook her stick at Swift. 'I'm going to sue you,' she threatened. 'I'll sue you for defamation or whatever it's called. Someone's got to defend Greg and if no one else will do it, then it'll have to be me. Yes, his lily-livered brother won't do it so I will. Mark my words, I won't die until I've stuck up for Greg's reputation and seen off all the naysayers!'

Swift could see through the shell of the frail old woman to the robust, determined Pat who had worked all hours to provide for her family. She was burning with sudden strength, energised by a new purpose and meaning in life. He felt sorry for Niall, but there was nothing he could do for him. This was a family mess that they had to resolve for themselves.

'I wouldn't waste your money trying to sue me, Mrs Roscoe, but that's your choice. You'd do better using it to try and trace your granddaughter. I think I should go.'

'Oh yes. That's the coward's way, all right.'

As he stood, she took her stick in both hands and swiped him across the legs, a surprisingly strong blow that took his breath away. He staggered sideways and managed to right himself by clutching a chair. She stood and struck him again, this time across his arm.

'Mum! For God's sake!' Niall wrestled the stick from his mother as she tried to shove him away. They looked for a moment like a comedy double act, cavorting for an audience. Niall pushed her back into her chair.

She crumpled and held her head in her hands yelling, 'Get out! Get out, all of you! Get out or I'll call the police and tell them you've been manhandling an old lady!'

Jeanie hovered anxiously as they left the room. Niall stood with his back to the door. He was pale and breathing hard.

'Leave her,' he said to Jeanie. His mother was howling now, loud, racking sobs.

'But she sounds . . .' Jeanie put a hand on his arm.

'Leave her a couple of minutes. Let her calm down. I'm going to call the doctor.'

Swift was rubbing his arm, although his left shin ached more.

'Are you okay?' Jeanie asked. 'Are you injured?'

'I think I'll have some bruises but otherwise all right.'

'I'm so sorry.' Niall rubbed his eyes. 'I don't understand it. Mum's never done anything like that before. She's so upset with all this stuff about Greg—'

'It's okay.' Swift just wanted to get away and turned to the front door.

Niall said he was going to ring the GP and apologised once again. Jeanie opened the door and saw Swift out. She stepped on to the path, glancing behind her before she spoke.

'It's not the first time Pat's done that,' she said. 'She's hit me twice with her stick in the last couple of months — once when I spilt her tea and another time when I knocked over Greg's photo. I had nasty bruises but I didn't like to say anything to Niall because he worries so much about her. Do you think I should?'

Oh God, he'd had enough of these people. 'It's up to you. Yes, you should and you should tell the doctor. Maybe she's ill.'

He walked away to get the train, his cheek smarting in the chilly air, his leg and arm aching. It was a dank afternoon, no hint of sun or comfort in the gloomy sky. He felt thin-skinned and weighed down by other people's turmoil. He recalled what Zeena had said over her memento mori. *Stirring up memories for people can be dangerous. It can take them to bad, dark places they don't want to revisit.*

There was a pub opposite the station. Its amber lights danced through inviting gold and green windows. He decided to have a restorative red wine and a breather. The woman behind the bar poured him a large Pinot Noir.

'You look a bit pale, love. You okay?'

He took a deep draught of the oaky wine, closed his eyes in appreciation and laughed. 'I've just been beaten up by an old lady.'

The woman looked startled, and then laughed with him. 'Good start to the New Year!'

'It's a first,' he agreed, 'but I've had worse.' He ordered a packet of crisps, took his drink and snack over to the wood burning stove and sat with his feet stretched to the glow. He saw that he'd had a text from Jude.

Who'd have thought creaky old Baz had it in him? Two murders! I literally gasped when I heard. You get right up my nose but I have to hand it to you, you did the job. Ash is in bits and crying all the time but at least she's got me to help her out. I've moved in for now, best to be on hand. She says I'm her tower of strength. I just told her I'm always there for her, by her side.

Typical of Jude to make it all about her. She'd come through it all unscathed and with a smile. The ground had been cleared of annoying husbands. Now she had her bestie to herself again and under the same roof. Once the baby was asleep, there'd be no one to interrupt glasses of Prosecco, home manicures and discussions of diets.

Chapter 16

Swift rang the doorbell for Flat 3 and waited. He was standing on the cracked concrete steps of a tall, shabby house in Greenwich. A buddleia had rooted in the guttering and weeds were growing up through the gravel outside the front window. A broken pipe dripped steadily by the side of the door. It reminded him of his first student flat when he was at Warwick university, a shambolic warren of grimy rooms, overflowing kitchen bins and the redolent smell of cheesy socks and Pot Noodles. One morning he'd stumbled from bed to put the kettle on and saw a rat on the draining board.

He pressed the bell again. He'd been looking forward to this visit, anticipating the pleasure. He heard a familiar heavy tread and Oliver Sheridan opened the door, wearing jeans and a black canvas apron covered in splashes of clay.

'Sorry to interrupt an artist at work,' Swift said, cheerily.

'What do you want?' Sheridan had gone back to shaving his head and growing thick sideburns. Not an attractive look on a squat man.

'Have you heard about your journalist friend?'

‘Camilla?’

‘That’s the one.’

‘No. Why?’

‘She won’t be much use to you any more.’

Sheridan rubbed his clay-daubed hands on his apron. ‘Oh Yeah? Why’s that?’

‘She’s going to be unavailable for work.’

‘What are you on about? Look, if you’ve come here to ask me to back off telling my side of things, you’re wasting your time. So don’t try wheedling or threatening. I’m due to ring Camilla on Friday. Believe me, I’ve got things up my sleeve you know nothing about. I’ve got sod all to say to you but I can understand why you’re anxious enough to ring my bell. Things are going to get a lot worse for you.’ He smiled unpleasantly.

‘Don’t think so. Don’t think Camilla will be answering the phone, unless it’s a call she’s allowed from her solicitor.’

Sheridan licked his lips and shivered as a chilly north wind snapped suddenly, whipping at his apron hem. ‘I suppose you’ve gone moaning to your friends in the cops. Maybe Cousin Mary has come riding to your rescue and tried to gag the press. You’ve always been such a golden boy, getting everyone to dance around you, including my poor old dad. Well, I can tell you that Camilla won’t stand for that. She’s got balls. You won’t stop her writing the truth.’

‘Hmm. Thing is, I don’t need to stop her.’

‘Look, say what you have to say and fuck off. I’m in the middle of a project.’

’Poor Oliver. You don’t read any news, obviously. I’m afraid Camilla has had to tell the truth, just not in a way she expected. She’s signed a statement for the police in Cornford.’

‘What? What are you on about?’ Sheridan stepped forward, tripping on the doormat.

Swift was tempted to prolong the agony but it was cold and he'd had enough satisfaction and enough of looking at Sheridan.

'Camilla Finley and her sister have confessed to being accomplices in the murder of Greg Roscoe, a pilot at Cornford airfield. They've been remanded in custody pending trial. The reporter has become the story.'

'Shut up! You're winding me up!'

Swift shook his head. 'It's the truth. Google her. Your friend's going to be banged up. Telling her your tale of woe has come to an end. I don't like the woman but I feel sorry for her in a way, because of what drove her to murder. It's a wretched business although you're so self-absorbed, I don't suppose you'll be interested. But it's kind of ironic that she's the one who told me I had things I didn't want revealed.'

He turned and skipped down the steps and then looked back. Sheridan was staring down at him and clutching at his apron. Swift tipped an imaginary hat and walked away, feeling a radiating glow of pleasure that warmed the cold air. The glow lasted until he was near the bus stop and thought he saw a familiar figure with her back to him. A young girl, skinny, with straggling hair, ripped jeans and a thin cotton jacket.

'Havana?' he said but he knew even before she turned around that it wasn't her. This girl had a healthy complexion and wore no makeup. 'Sorry, I thought you were someone I knew.'

THE END

Thank you for reading this book. If you enjoyed it please leave feedback on Amazon, and if there is anything we missed or you have a question about then please get in touch. The author and publishing team appreciate your feedback and time reading this book.

Our email is office@joffebooks.com

www.joffebooks.com

ALSO BY GRETTA MULROONEY

ARABY
MARBLE HEART
OUT OF THE BLUE
COMING OF AGE
LOST CHILD

TYRONE SWIFT BOOKS
THE LADY VANISHED
BLOOD SECRETS
TWO LOVERS, SIX DEATHS
WATCHING YOU
LOW LAKE
YOUR LAST LIE

Manufactured by Amazon.ca
Bolton, ON